PRAISE FOR
Blood & Beauty

"Impressively confident . . . colorful, sensual and characteristically atmospheric. . . . Dunant's biggest and best work to date, this intelligently readable account of formative events and monster players has Hilary Mantel–era quality bestseller stamped all over it." —*Kirkus Reviews* (starred review)

"A wonderful study of one legendary family's much-vaunted blood ties and vaulting ambition from a master of historical fiction. . . . An insightful, fresh take on the whole Borgia clan. . . . A comparison to *Wolf Hall* is not out of place here." —*The Times*

"The infamous Borgia family is the subject of *Blood & Beauty* by Sarah Dunant. Her epic breathes life into Renaissance Italy, challenging what we think we know about this corrupt dynasty." —*Good Housekeeping* (UK)

"The corridors of power are hotbeds of political intrigue, and few more so than those of the Vatican when the Borgias held sway. . . . A must read for anyone interested in the period, and for those who simply enjoy intelligent historical fiction." —*Daily Mail*

"Hilary Mantel fans and historical fiction readers in general looking for another meaty novel won't want to miss Dunant's latest." —*Library Journal*

"What a marvellous feast of vices and desires—absolutely convincing on every page. I was enthralled." —Paula McLain, author of *The Paris Wife*

"A masterpiece of biographical fiction, and likely her best novel yet. Never have religion, politics and power been so personal, so passionate. It's a work I'm not likely to ever forget."
—Sandra Gulland, author of *The Many Lives & Secret Sorrows of Josephine B.*

Blood & Beauty

Blood
&
Beauty

The Borgias
A Novel

Sarah Dunant

HarperCollins*Publishers*Ltd

Published by HarperCollins Publishers Ltd

Originally published in the United Kingdom by Virago Press,
an imprint of Little, Brown Book Group, London

First published in Canada by HarperCollins Publishers Ltd in a hardcover edition: 2013
This trade paperback edition: 2013

HarperCollins books may be purchased for educational, business, or
sales promotional use through our Special Markets Department.

HarperCollins Publishers Ltd
2 Bloor Street East, 20th Floor
Toronto, Ontario, Canada
M4W 1A8

www.harpercollins.ca

Library and Archives Canada Cataloguing in Publication
information is available upon request.

ISBN 978-1-44340-645-1

Book design by Donna Sinisgalli

Printed and bound in the United States
RRD 9 8 7 6 5 4 3 2 1

To Anthony,
who has made the present as rich as the past.

HISTORICAL NOTE

By the late fifteenth century, the map of Europe would show areas broadly recognizable to a modern eye. France, England, Scotland, Spain and Portugal were on their way to becoming geographical and political entities, run by inherited monarchies. In contrast, Italy was still a set of city-states, making the country vulnerable to invasion from outside. With the exception of the republic of Venice, most of these states were in the hands of family dynasties: in Milan the House of Sforza, in Florence the Medici, in Ferrara the Este and in Naples and the south the Spanish House of Aragon.

In the middle of all of this sat Rome, a bear pit of various established families jockeying for position, but also, more importantly, the seat of the papacy. While the Pope's earthly territories were modest—and often leased out to papal vicars—his influence was immense. As head of the Church, the man himself, usually Italian, controlled a vast web of patronage throughout Europe; and as God's representative on earth, he could and did wield spiritual power for strategic and political ends. With Catholicism reigning supreme and corruption in the Church endemic, it was not uncommon to find popes amassing wealth for themselves and favoring the careers and well-being of those in their families. In some cases, even their own illegitimate children.

Such was the situation in the summer of 1492, when the death of Innocent VIII left the papal throne in Rome empty, ready for its new incumbent.

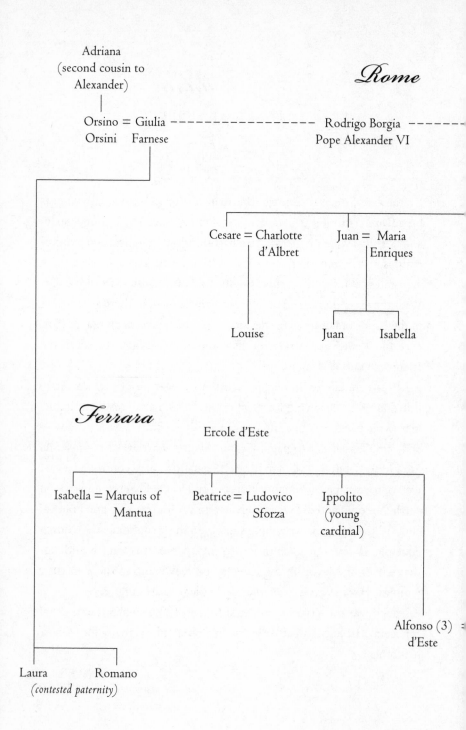

Adriana
(second cousin to
Alexander)

Orsino = Giulia ----------------- Rodrigo Borgia -------
Orsini   Farnese   Pope Alexander VI

Rome

Cesare = Charlotte   Juan = Maria
          d'Albret   Enriques

Louise   Juan   Isabella

Ferrara

Ercole d'Este

Isabella = Marquis of   Beatrice = Ludovico   Ippolito
            Mantua   Sforza   (young
                                                 cardinal)

Alfonso (3) =
d'Este

Laura   Romano
(contested paternity)

Milan

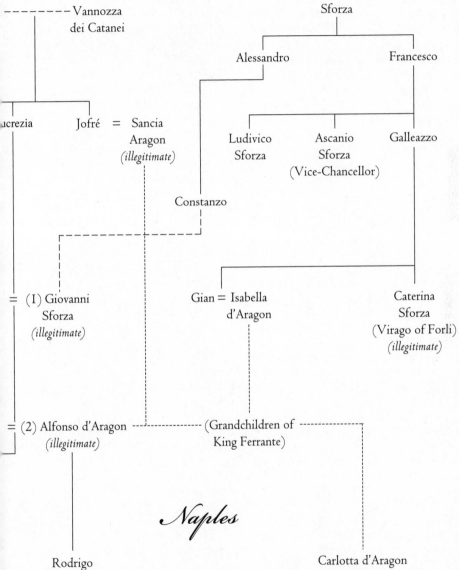

Sforza

Alessandro — Francesco

Vannozza
dei Catanei

Lucrezia — Jofré = Sancia
Aragon
(illegitimate)

Ludivico
Sforza

Ascanio
Sforza
(Vice-Chancellor)

Galleazzo

Constanzo

= (1) Giovanni
Sforza
(illegitimate)

Gian = Isabella
d'Aragon

Caterina
Sforza
(Virago of Forli)
(illegitimate)

= (2) Alfonso d'Aragon
(illegitimate)

(Grandchildren of
King Ferrante)

Naples

Rodrigo

Carlotta d'Aragon
(also daughter of King Federico)
(unsuccessfully wooed by Cesare)

REPUBLIC
OF VENICE

Milan •

Venice •

DUCHY
OF MILAN

Mantua •

• Ferrara

OTTOMAN
EMPIRE

Bologna •

• Imola

• Forlì

REP.
OF
FLORENCE

• Florence

• Cesena

• Pesaro

Spoleto •

PAPAL
STATES

REP.
OF
SIENA

• Perugia

Piombino •

CORSICA

• Nepi

Rome •

• Velletri

• Naples

KINGDOM
OF NAPLES

SARDINIA
(Spain)

SICILY

Italy
at turn of
15th Century

150 km
60 miles

PART I

We Have a Pope

He is the age when Aristotle says men are wisest: robust in body, vigorous in mind, perfectly equipped for his new position.

Sigismondo de Conti, Papal Secretary, 1492

Chapter I

August 11, 1492

DAWN IS A PALE BRUISE RISING IN THE NIGHT SKY WHEN, FROM IN-
side the palace, a window is flung open and a face appears, its features
distorted by the firelight thrown up from the torches beneath. In the
piazza below, the soldiers garrisoned to keep the peace have fallen
asleep. But they wake fast enough as the voice rings out:

"WE HAVE A POPE!"

Inside, the air is sour with the sweat of old flesh. Rome in August is
a city of swelter and death. For five days, twenty-three men have been
incarcerated within a great Vatican chapel that feels more like a bar-
racks. Each is a figure of status and wealth, accustomed to eating off a
silver plate with a dozen servants to answer his every call. Yet here
there are no scribes to write letters and no cooks to prepare banquets.
Here, with only a single manservant to dress them, these men eat frugal meals posted through a wooden hatch that snaps shut when the last
one is delivered. Daylight slides in from small windows high up in the
structure, while at night a host of candles flicker under the barrel-
vaulted ceiling of a painted sky and stars, as vast, it seems, as the firma-
ment. They live constantly in each other's company, allowed out only
for the formal business of voting or to relieve themselves, and even in
the latrines the work continues: negotiation and persuasion over the
trickle of aging men's urine. Finally, when they are too tired to talk, or
need to ask guidance from God, they are free to retire to their cells:
a set of makeshift compartments constructed around the edges of
the chapel and comprised of a chair, a table and a raised pallet for sleep-

ing; the austerity a reminder, no doubt, of the tribulations of aspiring saints.

Except these days saints are in short supply, particularly inside the Roman conclave of cardinals.

The doors had been bolted on the morning of August 6. Ten days earlier, after years of chronic infirmity, Pope Innocent VIII had finally given in to the exhaustion of trying to stay alive. Inside their rooms in the Vatican palace, his son and daughter had waited patiently to be called to his bedside, but his final moments had been reserved for spatting cardinals and doctors. His body was still warm when the stories started wafting like sewer smells through the streets. The wolf pack of ambassadors and diplomats took in great lungfuls, then dispatched their own versions of events in the saddlebags of fast horses across the land: stories of how His Holiness's corpse lay shriveled, despite an empty flagon of blood drained from the veins of Roman street boys on the orders of a Jewish doctor, who had vowed it would save his life; how those same bloodless boys were already feeding the fishes in the Tiber as the doctor fled the city. Meanwhile, across the papal bedclothes, the Pope's favorite, the choleric Cardinal della Rovere, was so busy trading insults with the Vice-Chancellor, Cardinal Rodrigo Borgia, that neither of them actually noticed that His Holiness had stopped breathing. Possibly Innocent had died to get away from the noise, for they had been arguing for years.

Of course, in such a web of gossip each man must choose what he wants to believe; and different rulers enjoy their news, like their meat, more or less well spiced. While few will question the cat claws of the cardinals, others might wonder about the blood, since it is well known around town that His Holiness's only sustenance for weeks had been milk from a wet-nurse installed in an antechamber and paid by the cup. Ah, what a way to go to heaven: drunk on the taste of mother's milk.

As for the conclave that follows, well, the only safe prediction is that prediction is impossible: that and the fact that God's next vicar on earth will be decided as much by bribery and influence as by any saintly qualifications for the job.

––––––––

At the end of the third day, as the exhausted cardinals retire to their cells, Rodrigo Borgia, Papal Vice-Chancellor and Spanish Cardinal of Valencia, is sitting appreciating the view. Above the richly painted drapery on the walls of the chapel (new cardinals have been known to try to draw the curtains) is a scene from the life of Moses: Jethro's daughters young and fresh, the swirl of their hair and the color of their robes singing out even in candlelight. The Sistine Chapel boasts sixteen such frescoes—scenes of the life of Christ and Moses—and those with enough influence may choose their cell by its place in the cycle. Lest anyone should mistake his ambition, Cardinal della Rovere is currently sitting under the image of Christ giving St. Peter the keys of the Church, while his main rival, Ascanio Sforza, has had to settle for Moses clutching the tablets of stone (though with a brother who runs the bully state of Milan, some would say that the Sforza cardinal has more on his side than just the Commandments).

Publicly, Rodrigo Borgia has always been more modest in his aspirations. He has held the post of vice-chancellor through the reign of five different pontiffs—a diplomatic feat in itself—and along with a string of benefices it has turned him into one of the richest and most influential churchmen in Rome. But there is one thing he has not been able to turn to his advantage: his Spanish blood. And so the papal throne itself has eluded him. Until now, perhaps; because after two public scrutinies there is deadlock between the main contenders, which makes his own modest handful of votes a good deal more potent.

He murmurs a short prayer to the Virgin Mother, reaches for his cardinal's hat, and pads his way down the marble corridor between the makeshift cells until he finds the one he is looking for.

Inside, somewhat drained by the temperature and the politicking, sits a young man with a small Bacchus stomach and a pasty face. At seventeen, Giovanni de' Medici is the youngest cardinal ever to be appointed to the Sacred College, and he has yet to decide where to put his loyalty.

"Vice-Chancellor!" The youth leaps up. The truth is one can only wrestle with Church matters for so long and his mind has wandered to the creamy breasts of a girl who shared his bed in Pisa when he was studying there. There had been something about her—her laugh, the smell of her skin?—so that when he feels in need of solace it is her body that he rubs himself against in his mind. "Forgive me, I did not hear you."

"On the contrary—it is I who should be forgiven. I disturb you at prayer!"

"No . . . Not exactly." He offers him the one chair, but the Borgia cardinal brushes it away with a wave of the hand, settling his broad rump on the pallet bed instead.

"This will do well enough for me," he says jovially, slapping his fist on the mattress.

The young Medici stares at him. While everyone else is wilting under the relentless heat, it is remarkable how this big man remains so sprightly. The candlelight picks out a broad forehead under a thatch of tonsured white hair, a large hooked nose and full lips over a thick neck. You would not, could not, call Rodrigo Borgia handsome; he is grown too old and stout for that. Yet once you have looked at him you do not easily look away, for there is an energy in those sharp dark eyes younger than his years.

"After living through the election of four popes I have grown almost fond of the—what shall we call it?—'challenges' of conclave life." The voice, like the body, is impressive, deep and full, the remnants of a Spanish accent in the guttural trim on certain words. "But I still remember my first time. I was not much older than you. It was August then too—alas, such a bad month for the health of our holy fathers. Our prison was not so splendid then, of course. The mosquitoes ate us alive and the bed made my bones ache. Still, I survived." He laughs, a big sound, with no sense of self-consciousness or artifice. "Though of course I did not have such a remarkable father to guide me. Lorenzo de' Medici would be proud to see you take your place in the conclave, Giovanni. I am sincerely sorry for his death. It was a loss not just for Florence but for all of Italy."

The young man bows his head. *Beware, my son. These days Rome is a den of iniquity, the very focus of all that is evil.* Under his robes he holds a letter from his father: advice on entering the snake pit of Church politics from a man who had the talent to skate on thin ice and make it look as if he was dancing. *Few men are to be trusted. Keep your own counsel until you are established.* Since his father's death only a few months before, the young cardinal has learned its contents by heart, though he sorely wishes now that the words were less general and more particular.

"So tell me, Giovanni"—Rodrigo Borgia drops his voice in an exaggerated manner, as if to anticipate the secrets they are about to share—"how are you holding up through this, this labyrinthine process?"

"I am praying to God to find the right man to lead us."

"Well said! I am sure your father railed against the venality of the Church and warned against false friends who would take you with them into corruption."

This current College of Cardinals is poor in men of worth and you would do well to be guarded and reserved with them. The young man lifts an involuntary hand to his chest, to check the letter is concealed. *Beware of seducers and bad counselors, evil men who will drag you down, counting upon your youth to make you easy prey.* Surely not even the Vice-Chancellor's hawk eyes are able to read secrets through two layers of cloth?

Outside, a shout pierces the air, followed by the shot of an arquebus: new weapons for new times. The young man darts his head up toward the high, darkened window.

"Don't fret. It's only common mayhem."

"Oh . . . no, I am not worried."

The stories are well known: how in the interregnum between popes Rome becomes instantly ungovernable, old scores settled by knife-thrusts in dark alleys, new ones hatched under cover of an exuberant general thuggery that careers between theft, brawling and murder. But the worst is reserved for the men who have been too favored, for they have the most to lose.

"You should have been here when the last della Rovere pope, Sixtus IV, died—though not even Lorenzo de' Medici could have made his son a cardinal at the age of nine, eh?" Rodrigo laughs. "His nephew was so hated that the mob stripped his house faster than a plague of locusts. By the time the conclave ended only the walls and the railings remained."

He shakes his head, unable to conceal his delight at the memory. "Still, you must feel at home sitting here under the work of your father's protégés." He lifts his eyes to the fresco on the back wall of the cell: a group of willowy figures so graceful that they seem to be still moving under the painter's brush. "This is by that Botticelli fellow, yes?"

"Sandro Botticelli, yes." The style is as familiar to the young Florentine as the Lord's Prayer.

"Such a talented man! It is wonderful how much . . . how much flesh he gets into the spirit. I have always thought that Pope Sixtus was exceedingly lucky to get him, considering that three years before he had launched a conspiracy to kill his patron, your own father, and wipe out the whole Medici family. Fortunately you are too young to remember the outrage."

But not so young that he could ever be allowed to forget. The only thing bloodier than the attack had been the retribution.

"Luckily, he survived and prospered. Despite the della Rovere family," Rodrigo adds, smiling.

"My father spoke highly of your keen mind, Vice-Chancellor. I know I shall learn a lot from you."

"Ah! You already have his wit and diplomacy, I see." And the smile dissolves into laughter. The candle on the table flutters in the wind of his breath and his generous features dance in the light. The younger man feels a bead of sweat moving down from his hair and wipes it away with his hand. His fingers come away grimy. In contrast, the Borgia cardinal remains splendidly unaffected by the heat.

"Well, you must forgive me if I show a certain fatherly affection. I too have a son of your age who needs counsel as he climbs the ladder of the Church. Ah—but of course, you know this. The two of you studied together in Pisa. Cesare spoke often of you as a good friend. And an outstanding student of rhetoric and law."

"As I would speak of him."

In public. Not in private. No. In private, the cocky young Borgia was too closeted by his Spanish entourage to be a friend to anyone. Which is just as well, since whatever money he put on his back (and there was always a sack of it; when he came to dine you could barely see the cloth for the jewels sewn onto it) a Borgia bastard could never be the social equal of a legitimate Medici. He was clever, though, so fast on his feet that in public disputation he could cut to the quick, pulling arguments like multicolored threads from his brain until black seemed to turn into white and wrong became just another shade of gray. Even the praise of his tutors seemed to bore him: he lived more in the taverns than the study halls. But then he was hardly alone in that fault.

The young Medici is glad of the shadows around them. He would not like such thoughts to be exposed to daylight. If the emblem on the Borgia crest is that of the bull, everyone knows it is the cunning of the fox that runs in the family.

"Well, I admire your dedication and pursuit of goodness, Cardinal." Rodrigo Borgia leans over and puts his hand gently on his knee. "It will loom large in God's grace." He pauses. "But not, I fear, in the annals of men. The sad truth is that the times in which we live are deeply corrupt, and without a pope who can withstand the appetites of the wolves prowling around him, neither he nor Italy will survive."

While the back of his hand lies thick as a slab of meat, his fingers are surprisingly elegant, tapered and well manicured, and for a second the younger man finds himself thinking of the woman who graces the Vice-Chancellor's bed these days. A flesh-and-blood Venus she is said to be: milk-skinned, golden-haired and young enough to be his granddaughter. The gossip is tinged with disgust that such sweetness should couple with such decay, but there is envy there too; how easily beauty snaps onto the magnet of power, whatever a man's looks.

"Vice-Chancellor." He takes a breath. "If you are here to canvass my vote . . ."

"Me? No, no, no. I am but a lamb in this powerful flock. Like you, I have no other wish but to serve God and our holy mother the Church." And now the older man's eyes sparkle. They say that while Giuliano della Rovere has a temper fit to roast flesh, it is the Borgia smile that is more to be feared. "No. If I put myself forward at all it is only because, having seen such things before, I fear that a deadlock could push us into hands less capable even than my own."

Giovanni stares at him, wondering at the power of a man who can lie so barefacedly and still give the impression that his heart is in his voice. Is this then his secret? In these last few days he has had occasion to watch him at work; to notice how tirelessly he weaves in and out of the knots of other men, how he is first to help the elder ones to their cells, or to find the need to relieve himself when negotiations stick and new incentives are called for. A few times the younger man has walked into the latrines and found the conversation fall silent at his entrance. And almost always the Vice-Chancellor will be there himself, nodding and beaming over his large stomach with his tool held loosely in his hand, as if it was the most natural pose on earth for God's cardinals to adopt in each other's presence.

Inside the cell, the air feels as thick as soup. "Sweet Mary and the saints. If we are not careful we will boil alive as slowly as Saint Cyrinus." Rodrigo fans his face theatrically and digs inside his robes, holding out a glass vial with an intricate silver top. "Can I offer you relief?"

"No, no thank you."

He digs a finger inside and anoints himself liberally. As the young man catches the tang of jasmine, he remembers how he has detected remnants of it—and a few other scents—around the public spaces over the last few days. Does each camp, like a pack of dogs, identify itself by its smell?

The cardinal is making a business of putting the bottle back in his robes while he stands up to take his leave. Then, suddenly, he seems to change his mind.

"Giovanni, it seems to me you are too much your father's son not to recognize what is happening here. So I shall tell you something I have not made public." And he bends his large frame to get closer to the young man's face. "Don't be alarmed. Take it as a tribute to your family that I share it: a lesson as to how influence moves when the air grows as thick as stinking cheese. Della Rovere cannot win this election, however it may look now."

"How do you know that?" the young man says quickly, the surprise—and perhaps the flattery—overcoming the reticence he had vowed to hold.

"I know it because, as well as being able to count, I have looked inside men's hearts here." He smiles, but there is less mirth in him now. "In the next public scrutiny the della Rovere camp will pick up more votes, which will put him ahead of Sforza, though not enough to secure victory outright. When that happens Ascanio Sforza, who would not make a bad pope, though he would favor Milan too much for Florence—and you—to ever stomach him, will start to panic. And he will be right to do so. Because a papacy controlled by della Rovere will be one that favors whoever pays it the most. And the money that he is using to buy his way there now is not even his own. You know where it comes from? France! Imagine. An Italian cardinal bought by France. You have heard the rumor, I am sure. Gross slander, you think, perhaps? Except that in this city slander is usually less foul than the truth." He gives an exaggerated sigh. "It would be disastrous of course: a foreign power sitting in the papal chamber. So, to sink his rival, Ascanio Sforza will turn to me."

He stops as if to let the words sink in.

"Because at that point I will be the only one who can stop the water from rushing downhill in that direction."

"Turn to you? But—" *I say it again, my son: until you become accustomed, you would do well to make use of your ears rather than your tongue.* "But I thought . . ." He trails off.

"You thought what? That a Borrjja pope would be a foreigner too," he says, resurrecting the hawking guttural of his name. "A man who would advance only his family and be more loyal to Spain than to Italy." For a moment there is a flash of undisguised anger in his eyes. "Tell me—would a Medici pope care less about the Holy Mother Church because he loves his family and comes from Florence?"

"Cardinal Borgia, it was not my intention—"

"To offend me? No! And neither did you. Powerful families must speak openly to one another. I would expect no less."

He smiles, only too aware that the comparison between the two could be read as offense the other way.

"Yes, I am a Borgia. When I embrace my children we speak in our native tongue. But I defy anyone to say I am less Italian than those who would now put their noses into the French coffers. If the papal crown is up for sale—and as God is my witness I did not start such a process—

then at least let us keep the sale inside this room." He sighs again and claps him on the shoulder. "Ah! I fear I have said too much. See! You have pulled the truth from me. Your father's blood runs deep in your veins. Such a politician he was! Always with one finger held up wet to the wind so that when he felt it changing he could move the sails to keep his ship of state on course."

The young Medici does not answer. He is too impressed by the show. The politics of charm. Having grown up with a father who could turn vinegar to honey when it suited him, he knows better than most how it works; but this mix of geniality, cunning and theatrics is new even to him.

"You are tired. Get some rest. Whatever happens it will not be settled until tomorrow at least. You know, I think my Cesare would look almost as fine as you inside scarlet robes." And the last smile is the brightest of all, possibly because there is no dissembling. "I can see you both standing together, tall and strong as cypress trees. Imagine what a fire such youth and energy would light under this deadwood of old men." And he lets out a gale of laughter. "Ah, the foolish pride of men who love their sons better than themselves."

After he has gone the young man sits examining all that he has heard, but while he should be considering the next public scrutiny, he cannot get the image of Cesare Borgia in scarlet out of his mind. He sees him inside a tight knot of men, striding through the streets of Pisa as if every closed door will open to him before he has to knock, and even then he might not choose to go in. God knows the government of the Church is full of men who have only a passing acquaintance with humility, but however contemptuous or lazy (and he is too much his father's son not to know his own failings), in public at least they make an effort to do what is expected of them. But never Cesare Borgia.

Well, whatever the Borgia arrogance, his father's ambitions will fail him. He might be laden with Church benefices, but he will rise so far and no further. Canon law, which they have wasted years of their lives studying, is marvelously clear on this: though there are riches to be had for those born on the other side of the blanket, no bastard—even a papal one—can enter the Sacred College of Cardinals.

Outside, people are gathering in readiness for supper. He hears Rodrigo Borgia's laughter ringing out from somewhere in the main body of the room where the more public canvassing takes place. If the della Rovere camp is to gain votes before losing, then someone must be canvassing for him now, in order to make victory seem secure.

From under his robes he pulls out his father's letter, the paper limp with a sweat that comes from more than the heat of the room. For the first time since he has set foot in the conclave, when he gets to his knees the prayers come from the heart.

Chapter 2

NEXT MORNING, THE THIRD SCRUTINY OF THE CONCLAVE TAKES place in the formal antechamber off the great chapel.

The count shows the della Rovere faction pulling ahead by a small but appreciable margin. Della Rovere sits stony-faced, too good a politician to give anything away, but Ascanio Sforza, who wears both pleasure and pain on his sleeve, registers his alarm immediately. He glances nervously in the direction of the Vice-Chancellor, but the Borgia cardinal keeps his eyes down as if in prayer.

Outside, the camps disperse in their different directions. Borgia takes his leave to visit the latrine. Sforza watches him go, moving nervously from one foot to another, as if his own bladder is about to burst. The doors have barely closed when he follows. When he comes out a few moments later he is ashen. His brother may rule over a swath of northern Italy, but it is a different kind of muscle needed here. He disappears into the throng. After a while a few of his most powerful supporters also feel the call of nature. Finally, Borgia himself emerges. For once he is not smiling. It is the countenance of a man who seems resigned to the process of defeat. Except of course such a pose would be exactly what was called for if the losers were turning the tables on the winners before they knew it was happening.

Despite the locked doors, by the time darkness falls the news has slipped like smoke out of the Vatican palace and is gossip at the city's richest dinner tables, so that all the great families, the Colonna, the Orsini and the Gaetani (each with their own interested cardinals in the fight), go to bed that night with the name of the della Rovere family rolling around their mouths, the winners dreaming of the spoils in their sleep.

Meanwhile, halfway between the Ponte Sant' Angelo and the Campo de' Fiori, darkness provides cover for another kind of business. The Borgia palace is known throughout Rome as a triumphant marriage of taste and money. It is not only the house of an immensely wealthy cardinal, but also the office of the vice-chancellorship, raising revenues for the papacy and a profitable accounting business in itself. Before the final scrutiny takes place, those who are paid to watch for such things claim they spot the stable doors at the side of the palace opening to let out a pack of animals. First comes a fast horse—a Turkish purebred, no less—carrying a cloaked rider. Following are six mules. The horse has already reached the northern city gate while the mules still plod their way up one of Rome's seven hills. But then silver makes a heavy load, even for beasts of burden. Eight bags of it, they say, each one packed long before, for so much money can never have been counted in one night. Its destination? The palace of Cardinal Ascanio Sforza. If defeat is bitter then there are ways to sweeten the taste it leaves behind.

Inside the conclave, the gold-painted stars in the Sistine Chapel ceiling look down on a night of high activity. Old and young, venal and saintly are all kept awake by the chatter of men. So much horse-trading is taking place that it is a wonder men do not come with abacuses under their robes, so they can work out the profit margins on the offered benefices faster. Once the tide starts to turn the trickle soon becomes a flood. Plates of food are left untouched. The wine is drained and there are calls for more to be passed through the hatch. Johannes Burchard, the German Master of Papal Ceremonies and a man of exquisite precision, notes each request and the time of it down in his book. What he himself thinks remains a secret between him and his diary.

It is the stillest, deadest time of night when the cardinals take their places in a formal circle in their great, carved wooden chairs under canopies, each one embroidered with the crests of their individual benefices. The air is a mix of stale body odor, dust and heavy perfumes. Most of them are ragged with tiredness, but there is no mistaking the underlying excitement in the room. To be part of history is a heady business, especially if you can make a profit from it yourself.

The vote is taken in silence.

Now as the result is announced the room erupts into a loud "AAAAH" in which it is not easy to distinguish fury from triumph. All eyes turn toward the Borgia cardinal.

Tradition calls for only a single word. *"Volo."* "I want." But instead this big man, fine-schooled in politics and subterfuge, leaps up from his seat, brandishing both his fists high in the air, a prizefighter with his greatest opponent at his feet.

"Yes! Yes. I am the Pope . . ." And he lets out a great guffaw of childish delight.

"I AM THE POPE."

"HABEMUS PAPAM!" "WE HAVE A POPE!"

At the palace window the figure pauses, gulping in the fresh night air. Now another figure joins him, arms outstretched with tightly closed fists, like a street magician about to deliver a trick. The hands unclench and a storm of paper scraps is released. They flutter down in the breaking light, a few catching on the dying embers of the torches and flaring up like drunken fireflies. Such a piece of theater has never been seen in the history of a conclave and the people below jump and fight each other to catch them before they land. Those who can read screw up their eyes to decipher the words scribbled there. Others hear it from the voice.

". . . Rodrigo Borgia, Cardinal of Valencia, is elected Pope Alexander VI."

"Bor-g-i-a! Bor-g-i-a!"

The crowd goes wild at the name, the square fuller by the second as the news brings people running from the warren of steamy streets on either side of the Ponte Sant' Angelo, the old stone bridge that crosses the Tiber. After such a wait, they would probably cheer the devil himself. Yet this is more than fickle love. The established families of Rome may moan about tainted foreign blood and a language that sounds like hacking up phlegm, but those with nothing to lose warm to a man who opens his purse and palace at the drop of a feast day. And Rodrigo Borgia has been spending his way into Roman hearts for a long time.

"BOR-G-I-A!"

Unlike many rich men, he always makes it clear how much he enjoys the giving. No discarded basement hangings or halfhearted generosity from this vice-chancellor. Oh no: when a foreign dignitary tours the city or the Church parades its latest relics, it's always the streets outside the Borgia palace that are strewn with the freshest flowers, always his windows that unfurl the biggest, brightest tapestries, his fountain that turns water into wine faster and longer, his entertainments that tickle the most jaded palates with firework displays that light the night sky into the dawn.

"BOR-G-I-A!"

It was barely six months ago when Rome celebrated the fall of Moorish Granada to the armies of Christendom. A triumph for his native Spain as well as for the Church, and he had opened his palace and turned his courtyard into a bullring, with such a frenzy of the sport that one of the bulls, goaded into madness, had run amok in the crowd, spearing half a dozen spectators on its horns. In swift retaliation it had been skewered by the young Cesare, his church garments discarded in favor of full matador finery. How he brought the raging bull to its knees and then severed its throat with a single knife-thrust was all anyone could talk about for days. That and the money paid out to the families of the two men who later died of their wounds. The purse of a wealthy old man and the athletic prowess of his strutting son. Generosity and virility entwined. What better advertisement could there be for the reign of a new pope?

The runners are already spreading into the city. At the Ponte Sant' Angelo moored boatmen slip their oars into the water and cut a rapid line toward the island and Ponte Sisto, broadcasting the news as they go. Others cross the river then span east into the thoroughfare of the bankers, the ground-floor trading houses still boarded up against random violence, or south into the busiest part of the city, where rich and poor live separated by alleyways or open sewers, all huddled inside the great protective curve of the Tiber.

"ALLESSANDEER."

In a second-story bedroom in a palace on Monte Giordano, a young woman wakes to the sound of men, wasted on gossip and booze, careering their way down the street. She flips over in the bed to where her companion lies sleeping, one shapely arm flung across the sheet, thick eyelashes laid on downy pale cheeks with lips like peach flesh, open and pouting.

"Giulia . . . ?"

"Hummm?"

They are not usual sleeping companions, these two young beauties, but with the nerves of the house all a-jangle, they have been allowed to keep each other company, listening for the shouts of the mob and teasing each other with stories of chivalry and violence. Two nights before, a man had been running through the streets howling, begging for his life, a gang at his heels. He had thrown himself against the great doors, hammering to be let in, but the bolts had remained in place as his screams turned to gargles of blood and the girls had had to put their heads under the pillows to shut out the death rattle. Come the dawn, Lucrezia had watched as a band of friars in black robes picked up the body from the gutter and placed it on a cart to be taken, along with the rest of the morning harvest of death, to the city morgue. In the convent she used to dream sometimes about the wonders of such work: seeing herself swathed in white, a young St. Clare aglow with poverty and humility, eyes to the ground, as the howling mob parted to greet her saintliness.

"G . . . IA . . . HABEMUS BORGIA."

"Giulia! Wake up. Can you hear them?"

She has never liked sleeping alone. Even as a small child, when her mother or the servant had left her and the darkness started to curdle her insides, she would steel herself to brave the black soup of the room as far as her brother's bed, creeping in beside him. And he, who when awake would rather fight than talk, would put his arms around her and stroke her hair until their warmness mingled and she fell asleep. In the convent she had asked to share the dormitory rather than the privilege of a single cell that was owed to her. By the time she came out, Cesare was long gone and her aunt impatient with what she called such nonsense.

"And what will you do when you are married and sent off to Spain? You cannot have your brother with you then."

No, but the handsome husband they had promised her would surely guard her instead, and when he was out at war or business she would keep a group of ladies around her, so they might all sleep together.

"AALESSANDER. VALEEEENCIA. BOOORGIA . . . YEAAAH."

"Wake up, Giulia!" She is upright in bed now, pulling off the anointed night gloves that she must wear to keep her hands white. "Can you hear what they are shouting? Listen."

"BORGIA, ALEXANDER."

"Aaaah." And now they are both shouting and scrambling, clambering over each other to get from the bed to the window, the nets slipping off their heads and fat ropes of hair escaping and tumbling down their backs. They can barely breathe with excitement. Lucrezia is pushing at the shutter locks, though it is strictly forbidden to open them. The great bolts jump free and the wooden boards snap apart, flooding the room with the light of a white dawn. They dart their heads quickly to look down on to the street, then pull back as one of the men below spots them and starts yelling. They slam the shutters again, convulsed with laughter and nerves.

"Lucrezia! Giulia!" The voice of Lucrezia's aunt has the reach of a hunting trumpet.

She is standing at the bottom of the great curved stone staircase, hands on stout hips, plump face flushed and small dark eyes shining under black eyebrows which grow thicker and closer together the more she plucks them: aunt, widow, mother, mother-in-law and cousin, Adriana da Mila, Spanish by birth, Roman by marriage but first, last and always a Borgia.

"Don't open the shutters. You will cause a riot."

Later, she will bore the world and its wife with the story of how she herself learned the news. How she had been woken in the dead of night, "so black I could not see my hand in front of my face," by what felt like the stabbing of a dozen needles in her mouth. Such a vicious tooth pain that it was all she could do to pull herself out of bed and make her way to the great stone staircase in search of the bottle of clove wine. She had been halfway down when her taper had gone out. "As suddenly as if someone had put a snuffer cap over it."

It was then that it had happened: something or someone had passed by her in a great wind. And though she should have been in terror for her life, for the city was full of burglars and brigands, instead she had felt warmth and wonder filling her whole being, and she had known, "*known*—as certainly as if they had stopped and whispered it in my ear," that her cousin, Vice-Chancellor and Cardinal of Valencia, was chosen as God's vicar on earth. The pain had disappeared as fast as it had come and she had fallen on her knees on the stone steps then and there to give thanks to God.

As the city stirred she had dispatched a hasty letter and woken the servants. Theirs would soon be one of the most important houses in Rome and they must be ready for a deluge of visitors and feasts. She had been about to rouse her charges when she heard the girls' voices and the crack of the shutter frame.

"If you are so awake, you had better come down here."

Her command is met by a tumble of laughter and voices, as the two young women throw themselves out of their room, across the landing and on to the stairs.

A stranger seeing them now might well think they are sisters, for though the elder is clearly the star—her adult beauty too arresting to brook comparison, while the younger is still closed in the bud—there is a camaraderie and intimacy between them which speaks more of family than friendship. "Borgia! Valencia! That's what they're calling. Is it true, Aunt?"

Lucrezia takes the last flight so fast that she can barely stop herself from colliding into her aunt at the bottom. As a child it was always her way to greet her father thus, launching herself into his arms from the steps, while he would pretend to stagger as he caught her. "It is him, yes? He has won?"

"Yes, by the grace of God, your father is elected Pope. Alexander VI. But that is no reason to parade around the house like a half-dressed courtesan with no manners. Where are your gloves? And what of your prayers? You should be on your knees thanking Our Lord Jesus Christ for the honor He brings upon the family."

But all this only meets with more laughter, and Adriana, who even in stately middle age still has something of the child in her, is won over. She hugs this young woman fiercely to her, then holds her at arm's length, pushing back the shock of chestnut hair, not so full nor so golden as Giulia's, but wonder enough in a city of raven-haired beauty.

"Oh, look at you. The daughter of a pope." And now there are tears in her laughter. Dear God, she thinks, how fast it has gone. Surely it cannot be so many years? The child had been not yet six when she had arrived to live with her. What bloody murder she had screamed at being taken from her mother. "Oh, enough now, Lucrezia." She had tried her best to soothe her. "You will see her still. But this is to be your home now. It is a noble palace and you will grow up here as a member of the great family to which you belong."

But the soothing had only made her sob louder. The only comfort she would take was from Cesare. How she worshipped her brother. For weeks she would not let him out of her sight, following him around, calling his name like a bleating lamb until he would have to stop to pick her up and carry her with him, though he was barely big enough himself to stand the weight. And when Juan mocked her for her weakness, he would punch and wrestle him until the younger one ran screaming to whoever would listen. And then the baby Jofré would join in, until the house was like a mad place and she had no idea how to calm them.

"Ah, we Borgias always cry as hard as we laugh." It did not help that Rodrigo always indulged them so, allowing everyone to yell and climb all over him the minute he walked in. "It is our nature to feel each slight and compliment more deeply than these insipid Romans," he would say, besotted by whatever incident or story of misbehavior had just been recounted. "They will settle soon enough. Meanwhile look at her, Adriana. Feast your eyes on that perfect nose, those cheeks plump as

orchard plums. Vannozza's beauty is there already. Her mother's looks
and her father's temperament. What a woman she will become."

And how nearly she is there, Adriana thinks as she stares at Lucrezia now. Fourteen next birthday and already her name is on a betrothal
contract to a Spanish nobleman with estates in Valencia. Her eyes will
shine as brightly as any of the gold in her dowry. But then they are all
handsome, these bastard children of Rodrigo Borgia. How merciful of
God to so readily forgive the carnal appetites of a servant he has singled
out for greatness. Had she been a more envious woman, Adriana might
feel some resentment; she who despite Borgia blood and an Orsini marriage had only managed to squeeze out one scrawny, cockeyed boy before her miserable, miserly husband died in apoplexy.

Life had been infinitely richer since his death. No widow's cell in a
convent for her. Instead, her beloved cardinal cousin Rodrigo had made
her guardian of his four children, and the status had brought her a pleasure as deep as the responsibility she felt on their behalf. Family. The
greatest loyalty after God in the world. For these eight years she has
given it everything: no lengths she has not gone to to elevate their
name, nothing she would not do for her handsome, manly cousin.
Nothing, indeed, that she has not done already.

"And good morning and congratulations to you, Daughter-in-Law."

She turns now to the oh-so-lovely creature who stands nest-ripe
and willowy on the top step, and for a second her beauty takes her
breath away. It had been the same three years before, when Giulia's
marriage to her son had been first suggested by the cardinal, a man
who could make even an act of procurement—for that was what it
was—an elegant proposal.

"Giulia Farnese is her name: a magnificent girl, sweet, unaffected.
Not a fabulously rich family, but you may trust me that that will change
soon enough. After their marriage, young Orsino will want for nothing. Not now, nor ever again. He will be a rich man with an estate in the
country to rival any of his father's family, and the freedom to do with it
as he wants. As his mother—and in many ways the mother of all our
family—he will, I know, listen to you. What do you say, Adriana?"

And he had sat back smiling, hands clasped over spreading stomach. What she had said had been easy. What she had felt, she had buried too deep to allow access. As for the feelings of the girl herself, well, they had not been discussed. Not then and never since that day. At the time of the wedding the girl had not been much older than Lucrezia is now, but with a more lovely—and perhaps more knowing—head on her shoulders. In a city of men sworn to celibacy, beauty such as hers is its own power broker, and with the promise of the papacy there is already talk of a cardinal's hat for one of her brothers. Family. The greatest loyalty after God.

"You slept well, Giulia?"

"Until the noise, well enough." The young woman's voice, sweet though it is, is nowhere near as melodious as her body. She pulls back the long strands of hair that have slipped around her face, while the rest falls down her back, a sheet of gold reaching almost to her knees. That hair, along with the scandalous smoke of her marriage, is the stuff of the latest Roman gossip: Mary Magdalene and Venus fusing into the same woman in a cardinal's boudoir. It is said that the Vice-Chancellor moves his intercessional painting of the Virgin into the hall on those nights, lest the blessed Mary should be offended by what she might see. "When should I be ready? When will I be called for?"

"Oh, I am sure His Holiness will be busy with great business for some days. We must not expect a visit soon. Use the time to be at your toilet, sweeten your breath and choose carefully from your wardrobe. I do not need to tell you, Giulia, the wondrous favor that is now bestowed upon us all. And perhaps most upon you. To be the mistress of a pope is to be in the eye of all the world."

And a flush of color rises in the girl's cheeks, as if she is indeed a little overwhelmed by the honor. "I know that. I am prepared. But I . . . should . . ." She hesitates. "I mean—what about Orsino?"

Rodrigo was right, as always. Sweetness, and a certain simplicity in her honesty. They were lucky. Beauty such as hers could easily breed malice or manipulation. Adriana gives the tight little smile with which they have all grown familiar. "You need not concern yourself with that.

I have written to my son already and the letter is dispatched. With God's grace he will receive it before the news becomes general knowledge."

"I . . . Even so, I should surely add some words of my own . . . He is my husband . . . I mean—things will be—"

"Things will be as they will be. Your husband is as much a Borgia as he is an Orsini and he will be proud for the honor of his family. As you should be for yours. There will be wonders in this for everyone. This house will become an embassy for suitors in search of favors. We will have to ask Rodrigo for a full-time secretary to deal with the weight of petitions."

Now Lucrezia intervenes, laughing, taking Giulia's hands. "You are not to worry, Liana. Orsino will be happy for you, I am sure." She holds her gaze, until she coaxes a smile out of her. "And we shall visit him sometimes in the country to cheer him up. But mostly we shall hold court together in the great salon. Aunt Adriana will bring in the visitors and break the seal on the letters, yes? And then you and I will read them and assess each one for its worth. And those we think are worthy we will present their suits to Papà when he comes and he will congratulate us on our judgment, as his domestic ambassadors."

And all three women are laughing, because the last few days their nerves have been pulled as tight as garroting wire and the thing that they have most desired, even if also a little feared, has happened.

"And we will not let Juan or Jofré into the room. For they will all have come to visit *us,* not brawling, spotty boys. Isn't that so, Aunt? Where are they? Do they know? They can't still be asleep?"

Oh yes they can, thinks Adriana, for after all these years she knows her charges well. Jofré will be curled up with his thumb in his mouth like the ten-year-baby he still is, while Juan too will be in bed, though most likely it will not be his own. Whoever she is this time, she will probably try to charge him more when she learns who he is now become. Or offer it for free . . . a set of silken handcuffs. Rome. The city of the Holy Mother Church, renowned for being home to as many courtesans as clerics. There have been moments when Adriana has wondered if God is too busy keeping the Turks at bay to notice the exuberance of sins elsewhere. Still, they must all be more careful now. She must get Rodrigo . . . no, Alexander—His Holiness—what must they call him now when he visits?—she must get him to talk to the children, especially Juan. Make clear the responsibilities of this new status. Sweet Jesus, how the wheel of fortune spins. While they have been sleeping it has taken all of them and flung their lives around in ways that none of them can yet imagine.

Chapter 3

As the streets of Rome grow raucous with the news, inside the Vatican palace a transformation worthy of Ovid is taking place: a paunchy sixty-one-year-old is turning himself into one of the most powerful men in Christendom.

Rodrigo Borgia has said his private prayers: a jubilant outpouring of thanks to the Virgin Mary, Mother of God, his guiding light, his constant emissary and the only woman for whom his devotion is matched by unquestioning fidelity. His cardinal's robes are now discarded on the floor and he stands naked, barrel chest and sagging abdomen over heavy legs, toweling the sweat off his flesh. In front of him, pressed and ready, sit three sets of papal raiments: three white undergarments, three flowing white silk robes and three caps, each set a different size to accommodate whatever shape of man should now find himself deserving of them. Over the course of his career Borgia has watched four men, at least one more dead than alive, emerge from this room transformed by the power of the robes. Each time he has had an image of himself in their place, while in between his body has grown as substantial as his desire.

He anoints himself with sweet musk oil: his forehead, under his arms and around his groin in an unconscious echo of the sign of the cross, and reaches for the largest undergarment.

From outside, he can hear the sound of the swelling crowd. He is humming to himself, lines from a motet by the Flemish musician whose compositions are becoming all the rage in the papal court. It has been inside him for days, this plaintive sweep of notes. Of course he will need to commission more music now, masses, special liturgies. A new era and a pope must make his mark on everything, from the allegiances of state to the melodies than run around men's heads. So be it. The Walloon, what is his name? De Pres? Yes, he will do for the music. Too eager to wait for the help that will come, he struggles with the main robe; a man doing battle inside a sea of silk, marveling at the softness, which is as great as the weight. Soon he will be putting on the velvet and ermine. He had a coat with the same fur when he was young and vain enough to wear court robes alongside his clerical gowns. Ah, how grand he had thought himself then; stepping off the ship onto Italian soil, an iron-chested young Hercules, puffed up with Spanish confidence and Spanish manners, come to serve his cardinal uncle, soon to become Calixtus III, the first and—until now—the only Spaniard to ever accede to the holy throne.

It had not taken long to register the acrimony: the way accusations of nepotism went hand in hand with the sneers of the established Roman families. He had heard the first sniggers as soon as he walked into the room, noting how the more effete Italian clerics brought up their pomades to their noses and closed their eyes in a theater of disgust, as if they might swoon at any moment. Though it would have given him more pleasure to punch their noses into the backs of their heads, instead he had done what was necessary, espousing the hygiene habits of his new country so effectively that for decades now he has been able to detect a newly arrived Spanish countryman from the smell that precedes him before he walks through the door. It makes up part of his first words of advice:

"This obsession with bathing is something that the Romans share with the Arab infidel, but the truth is, brother, if you want to get on in this city . . ."

And then he flicks open a small pillbox and offers a perfumed lozenge to help sweeten the delivery of the language they must now talk, filled with blowsy open vowels. After so much practice his manners are more Italian than Spanish these days, yet there are those who still call him a Marrano, a Dago Jew behind his back. Except from now on, before they do so, they will have to make sure the doors and windows are bolted and that the company around them is either blood or bought.

And finally the papal cap. It fits awkwardly over the broad baldness of his tonsure. He squints into the shine of the brass vase: his white hair sitting like a ruffle of piped cream around a cake, the great eagle nose jutting out beneath. So, the biggest hat is too small. Well, it will do until there is another made. He stands back, lifting his right arm and bringing it down in a solemn gesture of blessing, the wonder of it all flooding through him, and it is all he can do not to cry out in triumph again.

He notes a flicker in the surface of the brass and turns to see the Master of Ceremonies, Johannes Burchard, standing in the doorway, come, as tradition demands, to help him dress should he require it and to measure the new Pope's finger so that the goldsmith can start work straightaway on the papal ring. He has known a couple of cardinals who walk into conclave with their own ready-made fisherman's ring in their pocket, just in case. But over the years Rodrigo Borgia has grown to have too much respect for God—or perhaps it is that other deity, Fortuna—to take such chances.

If the bony-faced German is pleased or displeased at the Spaniard's elevation, he doesn't show it. His job is also his natural talent: to note everything and express nothing. They have things in common, these two men: they are both foreigners at the court of Rome, and both skilled at negotiating the right price for the right job. (Ten years ago, four hundred ducats had been an excellent bid for the post of Master of Ceremonies—it would cost him triple that now.) Yet in the fifteen years that they have known each other they have exchanged no more words than their roles demanded. Now they will be joined together for as long as they live. Before the new Pope can speak, the German falls to his knees and prostrates himself on the ground, judging perfectly the distance in order to kiss the other man's naked, and mercifully clean, feet. The Master of Ceremonies at work.

The Cardinal of Valencia—and it is the last time anyone will think of him thus—feels a deep glow of pleasure rising up inside him. He picks up his skirts and walks out toward the public balcony.

Sixty-one years old. How many years does he have in front of him? By his age four of the five popes he had served were already rotting in their tombs. But the Borgias have more staying power. His uncle, Calixtus III, had survived to almost eighty. Sixty-one. Three sons, a ripening daughter and a sublime young mistress, young enough to drop more fruit. Borgia blood. Thick with ambition and determination. How long does he need? Give him another . . . ten—no, fifteen—summers and he will have the bull crest emblazoned over half of Italy.

He strides out onto the balcony into the light of a new day. The crowd roars its greeting. But as Pope Alexander VI lifts his hands to offer the traditional blessing, silence falls. The clothes have become the man.

Bought from Mantua, where those who know say the Gonzaga dukes breed better Turkish stallions than the Turks themselves, the Borgia horse and its messenger are making excellent progress.

The journey from Rome to Siena is harder than its distance warrants. Once outside the great walls of the city the route becomes as treacherous for humans as for animals. Before the coming of Our Lord, when men knew no better than to worship an army of badly behaved gods, the countryside around Rome was legendary for its fertility, with well-kept roads filled with carts and produce pouring into the city's markets. But over centuries of the true faith, it has degenerated into wilderness and brigandry, divvied up between the families of the great Roman barons; men hidden inside castles and fortresses who would prefer to carry on slaughtering each other than to create stability together.

Still, to be robbed and murdered, the victim has to be caught first. And this rider, a young man born in the saddle with a passion to make his mark on the ground, stops for no one and nothing. The heat rises with the sun, but as long as he keeps moving the sweat on his clothes stays cool in the wind he creates. The more he sweats, the further he can ride without needing to empty his bladder. It is past ten o'clock when he reaches Viterbo, inside the borders of the northern papal state. The staging post is one that the Vice-Chancellor's postal system has used for years, and it has been on standby since the conclave convened. The stable master himself does the handover of horses. No point in trying to read the boy's face: there is nothing there but grime and exhaustion; when the sealed letter had been given to him, Pedro Calderón did not know and did not ask. It would not do for the cardinal's eldest son to remain in ignorance while others celebrated or commiserated on his behalf, and those who work for the Borgias learn fast what is to be gained from doing what you are told.

Back on the road, the new mount is skittish at first, but they come to understand each other's rhythm fast enough. He rides through the furnace of the day and by mid-afternoon he is soaked with sweat as he climbs the curling road up toward the city gates of Siena. From woodlands and scattered hamlets he is suddenly enveloped into a maze of dirt alleys, alive with other horses, some ridden, some being led. In August, Siena is a giant stable filled with snorting purebreds on their way to the exercise tracks. Carts and merchants, even the best-dressed of men, make way for them. The city is high on the perfume of horse sweat and excrement, the alleys ankle-thick in leftover dung. In less than a week, the best racehorses in Tuscany will be stampeding around the great piazza in a storm of dust and straw; a chariot race without the chariots, mowing down anyone or anybody who gets in their way. On street corners money changes hands under long sleeves. The frenzy of the Palio is everywhere. Cesare Borgia, who should by rights be finishing his studies in Pisa, is as mad for hunting and sport as the next rich young man, and has two horses with a good chance of taking the prize.

They are resting in the stables now, enjoying better treatment than most of the human population of Siena. They train each morning at dawn, which fits in perfectly with their owner's lifestyle, for recently the newly appointed young Bishop of Palomar has taken to entering the day when it is almost over, then working—and playing—through the night while others sleep. And since what is good for the master is also good for his men, the house is snoring when the rider arrives, the only people up and about a few servants and the old stable guard who acts as watchman.

"You'll have to come back. We don't take visitors till after six p.m."

In answer the great horse snorts in the man's face, steam rising off its flanks.

"I am ridden from Rome on urgent business."

Begrudgingly, the old man hauls open the doors to a silent inner courtyard.

"Where is your master?"

"Asleep."

"Then wake him."

"Hoa! I am sixty-five years old and want to reach sixty-six. You wake him. No. On second thoughts, even that would have me gutted and fried."

From the corner a door opens on a short, half-dressed figure, thick-chested and with a latticework of healed wounds on his upper torso and a face that looks as if it has been sliced into bits and rearranged carelessly.

"Miguel da Corella?" The boy's voice is hoarse with dust, or it might be trepidation for the man has a reputation more colorful than his scars. "I am ridden from Rome," he adds hurriedly in Catalán.

"When?"

"Just before dawn." He slides from the horse, a cloud of dirt rising around him. He thrusts out a gloved hand and they clasp each other by the wrist, once, twice. "With no one behind me."

"You can ride, boy. You're Pedro Calderón, yes? Romano's son."

Their language is rough and ready, a long way from home with the touch of gang talk. The boy nods, pleased beyond measure that he is known.

"Where is it then?"

From inside his jerkin, the young man pulls out a leather pouch, dark with sweat.

"I'll take it."

The rider shakes his head. "I . . . my instructions are to put it into his hands only, Michelotto." He risks the popular name, used by those who love him. And hate him.

"You already have." The man holds out his palms. "These belong to him, boy."

Still the rider doesn't move.

"Dawn, eh? All right." He gestures to a door on the floor above. "But you shout before you go in and keep your eyes down. He's not alone."

Halfway up the stairs the rider finds his legs buckling. He hauls himself up by the banister, biting back the cramp. Two years in the service of Vice-Chancellor Borgia, two years of cross-country deliveries and the odd piece of thuggery to get to this. Of course he has seen Cesare Borgia, but in company, never to meet directly. He knows something of the others, one Spanish family to another, but this inner circle is something else.

"My Lord Cesare!"

He lifts his hands to smash on the door, but it is already open in his face, the sword coming so close to his ear that he wonders if he'll ever hear again.

"Rome, my lord," he squeaks, flinging up his arms in surrender. "I bring news from Rome."

"God's wounds. You climb stairs like a bullock, man." The other arm grabs him and pulls him inside as Michelotto's laughter rises up from below.

Cesare takes the offered pouch and turns his back, the door left open for the light, the boy already forgotten. He breaks the seal and unfolds the paper. The room smells of sex, sweet and sour. Pedro stands transfixed. He cannot take his eyes off him: this man who can cleave through a bull's neck with a single blow and jump between galloping horses. Or so they say. They say he makes Michelotto ram his fist into his abdomen every morning to test the mettle in the muscles. They say . . . But then they say so many things.

In the golden light of the afternoon the body looks as tender as it is strong: the sheen of sweat along the muscles of the upper torso, the scattering of hair around the nipples, the taut stomach and the vulnerable hollow inside the hip as it dips toward the groin and the tucked sheet. With his head bent over the words it is possible to make out the shape of a small, ill-kept tonsure amid the mane of hair. Everyone knows, yet it still comes as a shock. When the angels look down on

him, are they equally perplexed to think of Cesare Borgia as a man of
the Church? While youth is blithely immune to the threat of age, the
thickening flesh, the dulling of the glow, young men judge each other's
bodies with clear enough eyes and they know when they are outclassed.
It is not only the athletic beauty; it is the very way he holds himself,
aware and unaware at the same time, as if the world exists only to wait
on him when he is ready. Power bought or power born? Pedro feels a
shiver of excitement even at the question.

Cesare's face is impassive as he reads. Not a twitch or a breath, even
the eyelids lizard-still. From somewhere in the gloom comes a cooing
noise; something willing and lovely is turning over, beginning to wake.
Too late Pedro remembers the order to keep his eyes down. He snaps
his head to the floor. The cooing subsides. He waits. And waits.

Then, without his hearing any footsteps, Cesare is in front of him
again.

"You will never deliver a sweeter letter in your life," he says, his
voice now loud enough to be heard far outside the room.

From the courtyard below Michelotto lets out a howling whoop.

"Oh, my lord. I knew . . . I mean . . . I hoped." Pedro falls to his
knees. It is a less painful position than staying on his feet.

"Oh no, soldier." Cesare laughs. "Not me. Not yet. Keep your devotion for your new holy father."

Pedro pulls himself up, covering his own embarrassment. "You
have a reply to go back?"

Cesare studies him through half-closed eyes. "When could you be
ready?"

"Now, sire. I am ready now."

"You, perhaps, but your horse will die under you."

"I . . . I can take another."

"Ha. You are keen to serve."

"With my life," he says, slapping his arm over his chest, the drama
of the gesture undermined by the explosion of dust that it raises. "With
my life."

"That will not be needed quite yet, I think." And there is amusement, though no smile.

The sweet pigeon coo comes again. In the corner of the room the gloom has lifted to show a bed, a tumble of covers and a glimpse of rising flesh. "My lord?" followed by a silvery laugh, like a small wave breaking onto a sandy beach.

Cesare glances behind him, then puts his arm on the young man's shoulder and walks both of them out of the room, closing the door behind them.

"Michelotto?"

In the courtyard below Michelotto is grinning ear to ear, his face made even uglier by joy. Other doors off the courtyard are opening, half-clothed men emerging, rubbing their eyes, half awake when they should be asleep.

"Tell Carlo he rides to Rome within the hour."

The servants, a few older men and younger women, hover in the shadows. The Spanish dialect is not so far from their Tuscan tongue that they cannot decipher insults from praise, but they have made it their business to understand neither until they are told directly. The management of Cesare Borgia's household is a subtle art.

"Do I tell him why?"

Cesare nods. And for the first time a smile breaks his lips.

Michelotto takes in a lungful of air. "Christendom has a new pope!" he yells in Italian, in a voice to carry halfway through the city. "Rodrigo Borgia, Vice-Chancellor and Cardinal of Valencia, is elected. And everyone in this house serves his best-loved son."

As Cesare walks down the stairs the men go crazy with joy. Many of them had their money as well as their ambitions on the outcome and they will be drinking the profits for weeks. At the bottom of the stairs, Cesare and Michelotto face each other without moving for a moment, then Cesare opens his arms and they embrace, a bear hug that takes the breath out of both of them. The Borgia is a head and a half taller than his swarthy henchman, his features as regular as the other's are crooked. Beauty and the beast, some of the men have been known to call them, though never to their faces.

"So?"

"We go to Spoleto."

There is a second of hesitation. "Not Rome?"

Cesare flicks his eyes to the ground. Whatever it is, this is not the time for it.

"And the Palio?"

"There will be others."

"What about the girl?"

"Send her back to Pisa with a full purse. Make it big enough so that the next time that sap Giovanni de' Medici comes knocking she will say she is spoken for. Come, I need food and pen and paper. See to the mount and the messenger. What's his name?"

"Pedro Calderón."

"Right," he says, calling more loudly as he moves across the court-yard. "And make sure you treat the rider as well as his horse."

Michelotto turns, expecting to find the boy somewhere on the stairs, drinking in the praise. No sign. He glances up to the floor above. Propped up against the wall next to Cesare's closed door, the young Pedro Calderón is asleep on his feet.

PART II

Love and Marriage

He is a carnal man and very loving of his flesh and blood.

Cardinal Sforza, 1492

Chapter 4

ROME: A CITY BORN FROM THE MILK OF A SUCKLING WOLF. ROME: the center of the strongest empire the world has ever known. Rome: birthplace of the Holy Mother Church. Rome: the very word paints pictures of splendor and wonders.

The reality, as any number of visiting pilgrims will testify, is a miserable disappointment: not so much a great city as small islands of wealth poking their heads up amid a sea of festering slums and wilderness. It is history that is to blame. History, which had made the city imperial, had gone on to rip out its innards and leave the remains for the jackals and the vultures to feed on. Centuries of war and neglect have eaten like deep frost into the very structure of living: with no fresh water, no sewage system and precious little employment except the burying of its dead, much of the population had fled or bled away, with such government as there was undermined by the tribal violence of a few great families.

When other Italian cities—Florence with her cloth and Venice with her ships—were fusing wealth and scholarship in the great rebirth of classical culture, Rome was still waking from the nightmare of the great papal schism. The return of the papacy from Avignon seventy years ago had brought with it the promise of a better future: cardinals, bishops, papal lawyers, secretaries, copiers, ambassadors, diplomats, all with households to be fed and watered.

By the time young Rodrigo Borgia arrived here at the age of twenty-five, there were already clear signs of progress: men and horses were moving through the streets with less fear of injury from gangs of thugs or falling masonry, and Church officials with patronage to dispense and appearances to keep up had spawned an industry of cloth merchants, tailors and jewelers. As the young Borgia climbed the rungs of Church power, so came further changes: a new bridge over the Tiber after the old one crushed a multitude of pilgrims, an edict cleaning away centuries of unauthorized building to create new thoroughfares and markets. And, most wonderful of all, the mending of a hundred subterranean water pipes, so that what was once the greatest fresh-water system in the known world could at least offer its citizens an occasional fountain to drink from or, at a cost, siphon water into the new palaces that the papal officials were eagerly building, each one bigger, richer and more fashionable than the last. Rodrigo had benefited like all the rest, but he had also been part of it, since as Vice-Chancellor it became his job, through the selling of offices and other imaginative taxation, to keep the money flowing: Church wealth and city growth rising entwined out of the fertile soil of corruption.

This then is Borgia Rome: a city where a traveler entering the gates must still cross acres of country before he reaches the center, where animals still outnumber citizens, goats and cattle grazing the imperial ruins, their insistent teeth pulling weeds—and mortar—from between the stones of history. A city still struggling with a chasm of hardship between rich and poor, still ripped apart by gross family violence. But also a place of growing magnificence and confidence where, for the first time in centuries, the future no longer looks bleaker than the past, and where the new Pope has chosen for himself a name designed to foster a belief in magnificence again.

Alexander the great . . . Alexander the warrior . . .

His first job as head of the Church is to dispatch a number of errant souls to eternal judgment. The mayhem following the old pope's death has delivered hundreds of corpses to the morgue and the city has grown accustomed to lawlessness. He increases the Papal Guard, makes it illegal to buy or sell arms without a papal license and speeds up the judging process. When caught, many of the wrongdoers are strung up from gallows built in the ashes of their own houses, smoke plumes of summary justice rising high into the air.

To show that he is fair as well as ruthless, he personally inspects the city jail, then throws open the great salon of the Vatican palace one day a week to take petitions from ordinary citizens. The people flock inside: it is a long time since they have had a pope able to sit upright on his throne, let alone one so glowing with health and energy. Clothed in lustrous velvet (and a cap that fits his large head perfectly), he listens, deliberates, fine-picks the arguments and delivers his summations: a Solomon as well as an Alexander, with a voice as resonant as a church bell. Even those who lose come out satisfied.

The heavier labor he leaves to others: mules, carts, servants bowed under the weight of tapestries, bedsteads, chests of gold plate and majolica and great coats of arms of the Borgia bull. As his old palace empties from one door, it fills up through another. Cardinal Ascanio Sforza is the new vice-chancellor and the office of the job will now become his home.

Those he cannot win with favors Alexander woos with good behavior. In the first weeks the Vatican sees no instant invasion of Spanish freeloaders as was feared. Most particularly, his adored children are noticeable by their public absence. Instead the talk is all of the integrity of the Holy See, the banishing of corruption and his intention to abide by the wishes of the College of Cardinals. Old enemies are wrong-footed, and those ambassadors and diplomats who barely two weeks before had been damning him as a crude and venal manipulator now risk falling into hyperbole to do justice to the wonders of this new reign.

His coronation helps. How could it not? It's the party the Borgias have been waiting to throw for thirty years. After ten days of intense preparation, the day begins soon after dawn inside the great barn of old St. Peter's Basilica, where all those with the money or the influence cram themselves in, craning their necks to watch as an army of peacock cardinals make public obeisance, prostrating themselves at the Pope's feet, kissing first his shoes, then his hand and then his mouth.

The Vatican square afterward is, in contrast, a battleground: squadrons of city troops, archers and Turkish horsemen jostling alongside the retinues of bishops, cardinals and city dignitaries, each one ablaze in their family colors, the flags of their coats of arms somersaulting through the air to the heartbeat of drums. Finally, when everyone is gathered and pointing in the same direction, the procession moves across the river over Ponte Sant' Angelo, led by the Papal Guard, the morning sun crashing off their polished shields, winding their way through the city and countryside toward the Cathedral of St. John Lateran at the southern gate.

The Borgia appetite for theater reaches new heights: along the route great arches garlanded with flowers have appeared, as if by sorcery, during the night. Free food and wine flow from different staging posts and to counter the scorching heat the dirt roads have been doused with water. Useless, of course. By mid-afternoon everyone is half blinded and choked by the dust and people are passing out under the hammer of the sun. Still, the crowd goes wild wherever he appears: a big man on an even bigger white horse. His smile never wavers: Alexander VI, Sovereign Pontiff, Vicar of Christ, Supreme Lord of Rome and the Papal States and guardian of all human souls, his face bright with sweat, showers blessings on each and all of them. Rome's new Pope is having the time of his life and wants everyone to join in.

Long after the wine runs out, people remain drunk on the memory.

"The city was awake all night, my lord. Even the stars in the sky were celebrating."

All this and more Cesare learns, not only from the letters which arrive regularly from his postal service, but also from the lips of the young man whose exclusive job it is now to bring them, and whose acceptance into the fold has encouraged him to try his hand at poetry in order to serve his master better.

"'Antony was not received with as much splendor by Cleopatra as Pope Alexander by the Romans.' I heard those very words said by a nobleman in the crowd as they passed. And leading it all, our Holy Father . . . Oh, his mount, my lord, it was the most beautiful of creatures, seventeen hands or more, white as new snow with a step like a dancer. The bridle, I swear, was solid gold and—"

"I daresay the people had no time to notice who was riding." Cesare, who might knock another down for taking liberties, has taken an unexpected liking to this eager young man.

"Oh, no, sire, the sovereign Pope, your father, rode like a conqueror. I heard one man liken him to the great lord of Revelation himself."

"'And I saw heaven open, and behold, a pale horse, and He who sat on it is called Faithful and True and in righteousness.'" Cesare watches the young man's jaw drop. "I am a man of the Church, Calderón. It is my business to know the scriptures. Tell me again about the moment when he swooned. How many people saw that?"

"Oh, it was nothing. He had come ten miles, maybe more, and half of Rome was fainting with the heat and the dust and the crush. If anything it made the people understand that he was human. He recovered soon enough. And when he did those around called out even louder for him. As if his very glance would bring them a blessing." He hesitates. "Or that is what I heard, for I could not be in all places at once."

"I don't see why not," Michelotto mutters. There is a second's silence, until Cesare laughs and relief breaks out like sweat on the boy's face.

In his enforced exile, this fast-footed young Borgia is restless for entertainment. He sits, draped over a chair in one of the staterooms of the castle of Spoleto, perched on the hill above the city, a merciful cross-breeze moving in through the windows to counter what, even in September, remains a suffocating heat. In front of him sits a chest, its elaborately carved lid cluttered with maps and papers.

Pedro Calderón has earned his spurs these last weeks, making no fewer than seven return journeys carrying news from both the Vatican and the house of Adriana de Mila. It is a longer ride than Siena, for Spoleto is deep in the hills of Umbria and by the time he urges the horse up through the winding cobbled streets toward the castle gate they are both in a lather of sweat. Still, it is worth it. Now when he arrives, he is shown straight into Cesare's private apartments, moving past a row of people outside clutching petitions. More often than not when he comes into his presence Michelotto is with him, for he acts as his master's bodyguard as well as his chief of men. In the kitchen, Pedro has heard, they have taken on new poison tasters. Already it is a palace of two tongues: one for the men and women who come from Spoleto itself and another for those who are intimate only in Catalán. What was once the language of secrecy is now the language of power.

"I . . . I fear I have not done it justice, sire. You should have been there yourself."

"Oh, I am sure the Orsini and Colonna families were all shouting for me. 'Where is the Pope's bastard, the new Archbishop of Valencia, so we can squeeze his balls to congratulate him on his rise?'"

They all laugh now and Pedro feels a glow that makes his aching thighs and thick throat seem a mere inconvenience.

"It is a great appointment, Your Excellency. No one can deny it."

"Careful there, Calderón," Michelotto growls sweetly. "You get your nose too brown and the smell of it will reach others. Then you will be of less use to us."

The boy's eyes stay bright, but the laughter stops in his throat. Michelotto finds that even funnier.

"What of the Florentine contingent?" Cesare is kinder. "Piero de' Medici was there with his cardinal brother, yes?"

"Yes. Yes. Though I . . . I heard talk that there was trouble in Florence."

"It is more than talk. His father's shoes sit like boats on him. Not that his sap brother Giovanni would manage any better! Meanwhile, I see you bring no letter from my own dear brother," he says, a thin layer of ice coating the endearment. "Perhaps Juan is too busy celebrating to find the time to write."

"I—I don't know, my lord."

"But he is not to be found at Adriana's palace?"

Calderón shakes his head. The Pope's women had been there though. They had been in the room just before him, of that he is sure: the air had been heady with perfume, roses and frangipani, and the rush of their rolling skirts as they left had caused the dust to dance in the sunlight. The first time he had gone to collect letters he had sat on a chair where a strand of long fair hair lay carelessly across the arm. A cloak of beaten gold, so the gossip has it. He had wound it around his finger when the aunt was not looking. Later he had tied it around the clutch of letters, to keep his journey safe, but it rubbed off in his pouch somewhere on the road.

"What about the word on the street?"

"On the street? About your brother?" He hesitates. "On the street they . . . they say that the Duke of Gandia cuts a fine dash and that the tailors and jewelers are flourishing under his patronage." They also say he is enjoying a juicy young bride while her half-baked husband is not looking. But it is hard to gauge what he is employed to find out and what to forget. "Certainly he is not much at home these days, my lord."

"Indeed." Cesare gives a mirthless laugh. There is nothing he could be told about Juan that he doesn't know anyway. With barely eighteen months between their births, they were in conflict before they had the language to express it. Perhaps if Juan had climbed off his father's lap sooner he might have found a way to stand up to his older brother. There are moments when Cesare wonders if he isn't still there; it would surely explain his father's indulgence toward a young man whose bad behavior makes enemies faster than left meat breeds maggots.

"You should know that the household will be moving soon, Calderón."

"What! You are called to Rome?"

"Not us. No, the household of Adriana de Mila." Cesare glances at Michelotto. The other man purses his lip, as if to show disquiet at the direction of the conversation. "They are to live in the Palazzo Santa Maria in Portico. You know it?"

Pedro nods. He would probably say he did even if he didn't, but in recent weeks he has made it his business to know all the buildings close to the center of power. It is one of the newer palazzi, full of sweeping lines fluent in a classical language he does not understand but knows to be all the rage among those rich enough to follow fashion. More important than its architecture is its situation: directly to the left of the Vatican palace, so close that it is rumored that a person does not need to step out of one to get into the other. "It is Cardinal Zeno's palace?"

"Yes. But soon he will kindly offer it to our family," he says, and the wording brings a guffaw from Michelotto.

"When will that happen, my lord?"

"When we tell you it has," cuts in Michelotto curtly. "This is not public information you are being given here, you understand, boy."

No. Though it is a piece of gossip worth more than he will ever be paid for galloping halfway across Italy.

"I know that, Signor Corella," he says, staring straight back at him. As someone who spends so much time in the saddle he is used to keeping his mouth shut. Too much dirt gets in otherwise. He turns to Cesare. "I trust you will be in Rome long before it happens, my lord."

"Indeed. And when we are I daresay we will need a rider as fast on his feet as he is in the saddle." His fingers move a little in his lap and Michelotto closes his mouth on whatever he might be about to say. "Perhaps you will know someone we might approach," he says lightly.

Cesare has good reason to feel benign. Though his natural state is of a man driven, with only his own will for company, the dispatches from Rome are heavy with promise. It had been discussed before the conclave anyway: how, if his father should be chosen, the first and greatest charge against them would be that of nepotism, the fear of a great flock of foreign birds swooping down into the orchard and picking the trees clean. The archbishopric of Valencia will do him well enough for now. Of course, some will squeal at the wealth that comes with it. But every pope is obliged to hand on the Church offices he held before his election, and if any benefice should stay in the family it is that of Valencia, for the Borgias were born out of its soil, and when it comes to spinning marriage webs to consolidate their power, one of them will surely be with Spanish blood. From his father's letters there are hints that it may not, after all, be Lucrezia. Barely six weeks in and it seems other suitors are starting to pick up on the scent. Cesare wonders how much Lucrezia herself knows of it all. No—if she knew, he would be the first she would tell.

"What?" He looks up to see Michelotto frowning at the floor. "Don't worry about it. Calderón knows it is a test as well as we do."

"We don't need him. We have enough riders. He's just young and hungry."

"I know those who started younger. And hungrier. Let him be for now. We have bigger matters to attend to."

His brother's whoring apart, his only concern—if you could call it that—is the Pope's continued weakness for this Farnese girl. What is the point in trying to conceal your family, when half of Rome knows that your teenage cousin by marriage is in your bed? For a man to be so dependent on a woman is a mystery to Cesare, who at eighteen spends his life plucking girls like ripe fruit, only to let them drop half eaten. It is not cruelty so much as a lack of interest; like the hunt, for which he has a similar passion, the chase can sometimes be as exhilarating than the kill.

His father, though, he knows, has always had a need for affection as well as flesh. As a cardinal he could have kept a dozen different courtesans, yet for years he had remained faithful to their mother, Vannozza. And she, for all her beauty, had been more a wife than a mistress. While there must have been jewels and favors, when he thinks of them together Cesare's most vivid memory is of his mother in plain house clothes, kneeling in front of a great bowl of hot water, his father sitting, his head thrown back and laughing as he plunges his feet into it. A woman to ease swollen feet as well as a swollen prick: it is an intimacy that makes him shudder.

Even when they had split up, when he had left her bed for good and taken all the children from her, she remained in his affections, well cared for with houses and estates and a cuckolded husband ready to slip into the place left between the sheets. When Cesare thinks back on it now he recalls no weeping or wailing or scenes of distress. It was clever in its way, since it would only have caused damage to everyone for her to shout her suffering from the rooftops. Instead, to this day, she remains gracious and good-humored, eager to see him when he visits, but equally willing to let him go, so that he, Cesare, who has never worn his heart on his sleeve (some would say because he doesn't have one), always feels relaxed in her company. No. For all its strangeness and whatever the venom that an army of sallow-faced moralists might spit out against it, for years theirs had been a private, happy family, loved and loving.

But this affair of the Farnese girl and his father is cut from different cloth. The news of her arrival in Rome even made it to the lecture halls of Pisa: la Bella Giulia, hot-housed to produce spectacular blossom, ravishing and ready to be ravished, with the family pack in the background, betting their variable future on the fortune between her legs. It was a smart wager, Cesare thinks. Her churchman brother will be made a cardinal soon enough: a good yes-man for the Borgia faction as well as a benefactor to his own tribe. Thus does a new dynasty begin the climb up the giddy ladder of power.

Across the room Michelotto sits, his arms wrapped clumsily around his stocky body, his right foot jiggling restlessly. He had never been the courtier type, even when his face was prettier: sweet talk sullied the clarity of his instinct.

"I swear you are more impatient than I am, Michelotto," Cesare says, aping his scowl, which now grows wider.

"I just think if we were in Rome—"

"If we were in Rome people would be watching every time we took a crap. This way they relax and we get to ruffle feathers outside the city." Though of course he is eager to be home, he has used his exile wisely, reading the undulations in the larger political landscape more clearly. He gestures to the clutch of letters on the table. "My father says he has already dispatched papal troops to Perugia. They'll be there by the end of the week."

"Ha! The Baglioni family won't like it. They'll know the information came from you."

"That's exactly what I want them to know."

They had all lived in and out of each other's pockets once: when Cesare had been young, studying in Perugia, and the Baglioni boys were around the same age. They had been a bunch of thugs even then, sons of the two ruling brothers dropping out of their varying mothers' wombs with metal wrapped around their fists, busting for a brawl as long as their opponent had one hand tied behind his back. The papal legate of the town could barely breathe for fear he would offend one or the other of them. Now, with so many of them grown and so little on offer, they are intent on dicing up the power even smaller. And with more violence.

"It's not their city. They have no business gorging off it as if it was their own fresh kill. It sends out a message to other papal states that they can do the same and get away with it."

Michelotto snorts.

"What are you laughing at?"

He lifts his hands in fake surrender. Despite the clear difference in status between them they enjoy taking nips out of each other, like dogs at play. "I'm just savoring the shift away from canon law. It was always dry as a witch's teat. I think—"

"I know what you think: that all this could be done better with a sword than with a tonsure."

Michelotto grins. "I haven't taken any vows."

"Something the Church is eternally grateful for, I am sure. Don't worry. When the time is right it won't take long for the hair to grow."

Chapter 5

Nᴏᴛ ғᴏʀ ᴀ ᴍᴀɴ, ᴘᴇʀʜᴀᴘs. Bᴜᴛ ғᴏʀ ᴀ ᴡᴏᴍᴀɴ, ᴛʜᴇ ɢʀᴏᴡɪɴɢ ᴏғ hair can be the work of a lifetime.

The first time Rodrigo Borgia had taken Giulia Farnese to his bed she had stood nervously in front of him clothed only in her hair, her breasts and pubic bush peeking out from the sweeping golden curtain. How could a man resist?

The Pope's mistress's hair: such a rich topic for gossip. And why not? When holy men lived on the top of columns to worship the Lord, the length of their hair was proof of their devotion. For Mary Magdalene it was both the cloak that covered her shame and the cloth she used to dry the tears in which she washed Our Savior's feet.

For Giulia Farnese, though, it had always been the key to glory.

At her birth the midwives had been astonished when, cleaning the blood slime from her head, a set of damp dark curls had sprung forth. By the age of one they had ripened into a yellow harvest, snaking around her ears. By three the locks were on her shoulders; by seven halfway down her back. When had they realized it was to be her fortune? Certainly the household was in thrall to its demands early: the washing, the lightening, the oiling, the rinsing, the drying and the brushing. The endless, endless brushing. While her brothers learned Latin and practiced jousting, she sat immobile, neck muscles braced against the force of the brush, unable to read, unable to sew, unable to do anything but study the weave of her dress in her lap. By the time she started to bleed, her hair, this seventh veil, this river in spate, this golden shroud was down to her knees, and the news of it and her beauty was no longer confined to the house.

Once she was in Rome it had taken no time at all. Everyone knew how much Cardinal Rodrigo Borgia loved women. They also knew that his second cousin Orsino Orsini was of marriageable age, and that despite his pedigree, a boy with eyes going both ways at once would not find himself targeted by the great beauties of the day. From there it was just a question of the right "chance" encounter in someone's house, orchestrated to the last detail, she and her hair sitting in the afternoon sunlight as others moved around her. He—not Orsino, of course; the pup was held on business by a friend of the Farnese—had made straight for her, charming, solicitous, his admiration beaming out of him, but kind: a man who listened as much as he expounded. As she had risen to leave, he asked—with such a twinkle in his eye that who could refuse?— if he might touch her hair. He had placed himself behind her, and lifted it up, as if weighing it for purchase, and she had felt his breath on her neck, and then his hands resting oh so lightly on her shoulders and telling her in a whisper how lovely she was and how he would so much like to see her again.

"You are not to be alarmed." That first night it had been brute winter and he had warmed his hands so that as he reached inside her his touch would not shock. "I promise I will do nothing to hurt you."

It was not a promise that anyone could make, least of all a man of his power. Still, she had been reassured that he had said it. There were many who would not have bothered.

Later, he had arranged her locks across the pillows and over the bed, like a giant sunburst pulsing out from her head, and later still he had coaxed her into riding on top of him and letting it fall and sweep over his chest and face. In all this he was a courteous and fulsome lover, delighting so much in his own delight that it had been impossible to be frightened of him.

Yet she had been afraid. Not just of her own power (because by now she had some understanding of that), but because this silky wonder that she carried with her would stay perfect only when left alone. Once the sweat and suck of skins took over, it began to snag and tangle. Then there were the moments when he would roll over onto it, and her head would be caught by his weight. Of course she did not cry out. For it was her and she was it, and together they were his mermaid and his Venus and his very own Mary.

After the first five or six encounters, the daytime house rang out with the sounds of her yelps. By now the matting and tangling had set fast and however gently the house slave pulled at it, however wide-toothed the comb used, Giulia could not stop herself from crying, so that after a while neither she nor they were sure it was her hair or her life that she was weeping over, for so much had changed in so short a time.

In the end, she had had to tell him. He had been surprisingly under-standing; her desire to please was so touching and, truth be told, he too had been finding it somewhat tiresome, negotiating this third lover in the bed. Together they agreed to its imprisonment. From then on when they made love it was held inside a heavy rope plait. Which in its way did as good a job, for when she stood naked it hung down over her but-tocks into the crack between her legs. Now as he entered her he scooped it up and looped it once, then twice, around her neck, as if it was a heavy gold necklace. Or a noose. And she, because she was a fast learner, threw back her head and groaned as if he was indeed strangling her and the experience was as exciting as it was fearful.

Three years on she has a husband who cannot see straight and a lover who is now raised from cardinal to Pope. And while Alexander's pas-sion has not abated (if anything it has grown), the constant drive for copulation has lessened somewhat, so that there are moments now when that weight of gathered hair is as much a pillow as a sex aid as he buries his head, or nuzzles—yes, nuzzles, no other word will do, even for such a great man—into it.

What deep comfort she brings him. Sometimes after they have mated he will put his head between her breasts and rest there, until his breathing moves into a heavy snore while she lies caressing his ox shoulders with their sprinkling of coarse black hair. Only when she is sure he is deeply asleep does she gently, but firmly, push him off, for she cannot breathe properly when his dead weight is upon her.

Later in the night he may stir and slip his hands between her legs or run his fingers down the curve of her perfect back, but as often as not it is a gesture of ownership rather than a call to lust. It is an onerous business running Christendom, and though he is famed as a man of wondrous stamina in the world at large, it is not always so when it comes to bed, and this too she has grown to understand.

He still strives to give her pleasure in the way he uses his fingers to play with her, parting her pubic hair and slipping and hooking deep into the back of her, which to her surprise she finds can make her breathless in a way she does not need to pretend. And how he smiles then, because for all his grandiose power Alexander is a man who likes as well as loves women, and it is important to him that they like him too.

Having moved her first into the family house through marriage, he has recently moved the family house next to his. And though he works all hours of the day and night at being Pope, it gives him a special joy when he picks up his skirts and strides through the secret passages from the Vatican to the palace of Zeno, knowing that the whole household will light up in welcome at his arrival.

It is most wonderful when he visits unexpectedly: Giulia's face never fails to glow with pleasure, the faithful Adriana overflows with twittering admiration, and the children—ah, the children . . . Lucrezia still flings herself at him whenever he walks in the door, Jofré still treats him like a climbing frame and Juan—well, on the rare occasions when Juan is there, he is cocky and proud as a young lion. Juan with his mane of red-brown hair and a nose as straight as his own is beaked. Juan, so fresh and smooth that there is almost a girl's prettiness to his face. But at nearly seventeen, there is nothing feminine in his behavior. Such boundless energy, such outrageous confidence. Where others see vanity, Alexander sees only promise. A young man roaring and chafing at the bit, ready to take on the world. And why not? When did life ever reward those who cowered in its corners?

Alexander had had a brother once, as wild and impatient as Juan.

Oh, how he had loved him. When their uncle Calixtus was Pope he had made him prefect of the city, earning him the scalding hatred of Rome's old families. His downfall and death had cut deep into Alexander's heart, hardening into a desire for revenge that has yet to be assuaged. But it also taught him what one should show and what one should hide. Cesare, with his strange, cold heart, had been born with the talent. It is something the ebullient Juan has yet to learn. Well, it will come . . .

What a family he has been blessed with. How much energy they give him, all these beautiful, powerful young people; he sucks in their vigor like great lungfuls of fresh air, so that he becomes stronger and more potent in their presence.

Slipping his arm from under Giulia's sleeping body, he pulls himself upright to address the numbness in his fingers. There is a knot of indigestion in his chest. He is impatient with such aches and pains, he who has always had the constitution of an ox. Or a bull. It will pass. These last months there has been too much rich food. A pope must wine and dine so many others, and a level of magnificence is expected. For all his wealth, he is a man who likes simple fare and country wine. How many times has he attended banquets where people bellow their status through an endless procession of roasted meats and thick sauces until all they can do is fall, gorged, onto their cushions, letting half-secrets drop from their slackened tongues? No one ever came away from the Borgia house nursing their gut, nor carrying gossip that they were not meant to have learned.

He studies her hollows and curves. The swell of her abdomen is obvious now. It must have happened before the conclave, an auspicious moment for a new Borgia child, even if it will take time for him (of course it will be a him) to be acknowledged as such. No matter. With Adriana's supervision and the right seamstresses the pregnancy can stay hidden for as long as necessary, after which Giulia will suffer a short illness which will empty the house of visitors until she is ready to receive again.

He slips his hand under her belly, as if weighing up the new life growing there. He finds the ripening of a woman's body an aphrodisiac

She shakes her head but in the dark it is hard to read her eyes. "There is nothing else, my lord."

They stay still for a moment. Then, gently, she takes his hand and guides it back to where it was before. And as his fingers connect with her moistness she gives a little sigh.

"You are all I want," she murmurs, shifting her hips to accommodate him better. "Before you go . . ."

And because he wants to believe her, he does.

It is a strange sound, harsh, high-pitched, like a fox or some other animal in pain. In the gardens and lands surrounding the castle at Subiaco where they stayed as children to get respite from the summer plagues, she would hear something like it in the night and it always made her think of death.

But it is not an animal and it is not dying. Lucrezia knows that well enough. It is the sound of her father in bed with Giulia. She turns her head further into the pillow to muffle it. It comes again. She waits to hear if Giulia's voice will join in; she makes a sweet warbling noise sometimes, a songbird rising out of a tree. It is love, not violence, she is hearing. She knows that too. She has seen the two of them together, felt the tenderness as well as the desire. But she also knows that what they are doing is forbidden. That Giulia is another man's wife. That by the rules of the Church this is a sin. Yet the man is her father. And her father is the Church. More than that: without this same sin she would not be here. Not her, nor Cesare, nor Juan, nor Jofré. For their mother had been married to someone else as well. Does that make all of them sinful too, they who are loved so much and treated so well? Or does that mean that sin itself changes, depending on who commits it?

Lucrezia thinks about these things more since the convent. Before, when she was a child, everything that happened around her was simply life; she barely remembers her mother—maybe the warmth of a body or a broad smile—but her father she has always adored, always known to be a great man who served God in ways that meant that sometimes he was with them, and at others not. All this was normal. When Cesare talked back with icy insolence to his tutors, or Juan walked around the house howling at anyone who disagreed with him, she thought it was the behavior of boys. In contrast, she learned early that sweetness would bring her everything she wanted. Which was not such a trial, since so much of what she might want she had anyway, and it was her natural disposition to smile rather than scowl.

"Come—let me see my burst of sunshine" was how her father would greet her when he arrived back weary from whatever tasks God had given to him. What else could she do but smile for him?

Cesare had once put it differently. It was before he was sent away to study and already there had been a fierce rivalry between him and Juan: Cesare provoking with quick clever words and Juan responding with fists, a fight that the younger would always lose. Adriana would deal with Juan, a mix of comfort and bribery, soothing his pride along with his bruised flesh. But Cesare, even in victory, held on to the anger for longer, as if it was a splinter festering in the skin. At such times she would go and sit with him, slipping her hand into his and waiting, like a dog at his side, until he was ready to notice her. Which he always did.

"I think there is some alchemy inside you, 'Crezia," he had said as she coaxed a smile from him. "Where others have poison, you have balm."

Except she seems less full of balm these days, more plagued by doubt. Recently she has started bleeding and with it have come storms of feeling over which she has no control: a sudden crossness, or impatience with the world, tears for no reason. Even her skin, once down-smooth, erupts at times, as if these small fountains of pus are the only way to let such things out. Adriana follows her around the house with ointments and special drinks, bitter to the taste. It will pass, she says. It will pass. I know that, thinks Lucrezia, even more angrily. Why does everybody still take me for a child? In the convent such things were happening all the time. There were days in the month when the smell of stale blood was everywhere, swirling through the cloisters, leaking out around them in the chapel at night.

It had not been compulsory for the boarders to attend the night service of Matins. The convent was their school rather than their life and they had privileges that the novices and nuns were denied. Lucrezia, however, had always had trouble sleeping. When Cesare left home, she had substituted God as her companion in the night, so she had found it comforting to be with others who were even more in love with Him. It was a venerable place, San Sisto, centuries old and close to the site where St. Paul himself had been martyred, the abbess recounted when she addressed them during those first days. If they emptied themselves in preparation for God's grace they might catch the echo of his last prayers. The convent was filled with the daughters of Rome's most powerful families, all of them rich, most of them waiting for husbands either promised or yet to be decided. They would exchange smuggled trinkets or sweetmeats, whispering and laughing in the night, tales of love and scandal. It was there, when the gossip turned cruel, as it must between young girls, that she was made aware of some scandal in her father's household; the hint of sin in her own birth. The nun in charge of the boarders had found her in tears, so inconsolable that she had taken her to the abbess.

"You are not to let such things muddy the love of God that I know you have, Lucrezia," she had said, with such kindness and passion that Lucrezia had been hard-pressed not to fall in love with her too. "He understands everything and His capacity for forgiveness is boundless."

It is only recently that she wonders how many other young boarders might have needed the abbess's same words of comfort.

The house has fallen silent. She is wide awake now. It is close to dawn: she can feel it in the air. She is struggling with other thoughts, and it would be good to be more directly in God's presence when she addresses Him. She slips from her bed and braves the darkness to make her way downstairs.

In the grainy light, Alexander, deep in thought, waddling his way back to the Vatican through the little house chapel, is confronted by what seems to be a floating ghostly figure at the altar. He, who has never in his life seen anything that is not flesh and blood, registers a rush in his gut, a sudden fear of the incorporeal; a visitation for a man who has been making passionate and unrepentant love to someone else's wife.

The figure turns.

"Lucrezia!"

"Papà! You startled me!"

"What are you doing here, child?"

"Ah—I . . . I am praying."

He gives a little laugh to recover himself. He should have known. For years Lucrezia has been the only one of his children who would spend time in church of her own volition. She rises from her seat and he comes to greet her. He takes her face in his hands, studying her in the half-light. Her skin is moist and there are small shadows under her eyes, a hint of the adult that she will soon become, though the cherub double chin remains, reminding him of the baby who had so torn at his heart-strings.

"It is barely light, *carissima*. Could you not sleep?"

"You forget, Papà. In the convent we were up well before dawn. I woke . . . well, I woke early today. And I . . . I needed to talk to some-one."

She glances toward the figure of Christ.

"Ah. Do you think your Pope would do instead?"

She smiles and he settles himself next to her. There is a faint sour smell about him, the remains of passion. There has been no time for him to wash. They are both aware of it. He pats her hand fondly. It is too late for it to be any different.

They sit for a moment contemplating the altar: the crucifix with its emaciated body, head hung low in deathly sorrow. Cardinal Zeno, who built the palace, prided himself in being a connoisseur of art and this muscular Christ, especially commissioned for the space, looks real enough to take into one's arms. To the side stands an older wooden statue of Mary, heavy folds of cloth falling to her feet and pinpricks of woodworm in the rosy glow of her cheeks. He must get someone to come in and look at it. It does not do to have Our Lady pockmarked.

"How is Giulia?"

"She is . . . she is well." The pregnancy is still a secret in the house. At least he believes it is so. "I was late with business, so I arrived when you were in bed."

She nods, as if to say she understands and that it does not need explaining.

"So, tell me what troubles you, you who must be one of the most fortunate young women in Christendom."

"Oh, I know that, Papà. I remember it every day in my prayers. But still . . ." She takes a breath. If God has brought them together in the chapel, then surely He means it to be talked about. "Well, I am thinking about my husband."

"Your husband! Ha! It seems everyone wants to talk about husbands tonight." He gives a little shake of the head. "And what is it in particular you are thinking?"

She glances at him to try and read his mood better.

He squeezes her arm. "Come, tell me. I am your father and I love you dearly."

"I am wondering if he will come from Milan or Naples."

"Milan or Naples? What gives you that idea?"

"Because I have heard . . . because I have heard that the Spanish marriage to Count d'Aversa will not take place now."

"From whom have you heard this?"

"Oh, Papà, people talk. I know that we, well . . . now that you are Pope things are different. We are now allied to the Sforzas in Milan, yes? Because they helped you in some way. And to keep an alliance in place you need a marriage. But Adriana says—well, not to me, but I heard her talking to others—that Milan and Naples are in disagreement with each other and so I thought that—that you must keep a balance between the two of them which means Naples needs an allegiance too . . ."

"My, my." Alexander squeezes her hand, laughing. "Clearly you are wasted in study and sewing, Donna Lucrezia. You should be in the Pope's Consistory. You understand more about things than most who sit there."

"That is not true," she says indignantly. "I think that many people understand more about this than me. Really! Two days ago Aunt Adriana turned away a messenger from Count d'Aversa. I could hardly not know, since he made a great fuss at being refused. She said it was on your orders."

"What else did your aunt say?" he says, trying to keep the amusement from his voice.

"Nothing. But we have many visitors."

And gossip springs out from between the stitches in their cloth. Sometimes he thinks it is the only real occupation of Rome, listening to whispers: that for all the banking tables and the tanners' yards, the economy is driven more by chatter than commerce. No wonder they do not grow as rich as Venice or Florence.

"People pay suit to us to get close to you. We had the Prince of Ferrara here a few weeks ago! Alfonso d'Este. His father wants a cardinal's hat for his younger son. Did you know that? We took his gifts but made no promises. We are most proper. Aunt Adriana sees to that. She is very good at it, Papà. Better than Giulia or I."

As befits a woman who has negotiated the cuckolding of her son for the pleasure of her cousin. Ah. It seems he is to be pursued by such thoughts tonight. Well, what is done is done. Orsino has not fared badly from it. The man wants for nothing. Except perhaps for his wife. He can almost hear Giulia's voice again in the darkness.

"I am surprised young Alfonso didn't ask for your hand in marriage while he was at it."

"Are you angry, Papà?"

"No, no, child. I was thinking of something else."

"I am sorry if this is difficult," she says with sudden intensity. "But it seems to me that if I am old enough to be married then I am old enough to know these things."

He takes her hand, white as a dove's feathers. In Spain, under the grill of a cruel sun, they treasure the beauty of pale hands over all else. She would have been so admired in Valencia. But he needs—and he wants—her here now.

"Very well," he says more seriously, making a decision to tell her the truth. "It is likely that you will not be married to Don Gaspar d'Aversa."

"But we are betrothed! What will he say when he finds out?"

"He will shout bloody murder. Most of Rome can hear him taking in the breath already. But he will settle for it."

"So will it be Milan or Naples?"

"I can't say for sure. We are still talking." He smiles. "Perhaps our Holy Mother can help us with the answer."

"I didn't have time to talk to her properly. Though . . . though I know another way to find out." She is eager. Since he has become everyone's father he has less time to be hers alone. And the pleasures of mutual adoration are—well . . . mutual.

"And what would that be?"

"You take a bowl of water, and you draw a circle around it in wax or with the black soot from candles." Her eyes are shining now. "And then you say some words and stir the surface with a wooden spoon and as it settles you look into it." She stops, for effect. "And there you will see the face of your husband."

He must not laugh. "I think it unwise for the daughter of a pope to conjure up the devil to see her own future."

"Oh, it is not the devil, Papà. Far from it. The words are all good words."

"Nevertheless, such superstitions are forbidden. Who taught you them?"

"I . . . er, no one," she says weakly. "I mean, it is only a game."

"Not a game that the abbess of San Sisto would approve of, I am sure."

"But the convent is where I learned it! The boarders do it all the time." Now it is her turn to squeeze his arm. "The abbess didn't know, of course. Ah, you have no idea how boring it can be sometimes with so much worship and so little fun."

Nuns conjuring up spirits to divine the future! If his life was not so busy pulling the fangs from poisonous snakes in every corner, he might fruitfully add the conduct of convents to the work of being the Pope. Well, it can wait. He looks back into her dancing eyes. Love games. The puppy fat is not just physical. At thirteen, she is still too coddled, too young for marriage. Whoever the man, there will be a clause on delayed consummation written into the contract.

But he will not come from Spain, that much is clear. Is she disappointed?

She considers the question. "I used to want to live there. You and Aunt Adriana told such stories of it: about Valencia, how the sea shone like diamonds under the sun and the breezes came through the town and there were so many churches and palaces and the people there were so . . . so fiery and friendly and fine. But I want to stay here now. We are one of the great families of Italy. Each of us has a part to play in our future and marriage is the strongest knot that can be tied," she says, as if someone had taught her the words along with her catechism.

"Bravo. Spoken like a Borgia. Don't worry yourself further. Once it is decided you will be told."

She rises. "Papà. One favor."

Anything, he thinks. Then remembers. "Perhaps I had better hear it first."

"I don't want a really old husband. Juan says they dribble and pass water in the bed."

"Does he indeed?" He stares at her.

"Oh, I don't think he means you."

"No."

"And one more thing . . ."

He sighs in an exaggerated manner, as if this is far too great a burden to be borne. They both smile.

"Bring Cesare home soon. He pines for Rome. I can feel it underneath the words."

"He will be here well in time for your wedding. That I promise you."

Chapter 6

THE CONCEALED ROUTE BETWEEN THE TWO PALACES BRINGS HIM out into the booming darkness of the Vatican chapel.

He moves by a guard, whose job is to make sure the lamp that burns constantly at the altar does not go out. Across the nave, another guard sits, watching the watchman lest he should fall asleep. They both look up, then down as their Pope passes. They know what they are supposed not to see.

With his own lamp Alexander crosses into the center of the chapel, feeling the rise of the marble under his slippered feet as it moves toward the transenna. Like many men who live inside power, he has grown used to its trappings. When his own palace was finished twenty years ago, for the first weeks he had wandered around it like a child entranced by the wonder of a new plaything. Yet his mind soon moved back to business. The assessing of petitions, the wording of agreements, the manipulation of men and money, these are the things that absorbed him, while the vaulted ceilings, tapestries and gold plate faded rapidly into the background. Wealth was necessary for status, for the respect and admiration it engendered in others. The infinite niceties of taste, however, he leaves to the more foppish of his fellow cardinals.

But not even he can walk through this newest grand chapel without appreciating its splendor and ambition. What a sly old fox Sixtus IV had been. While Rome was a city full of ancient buildings big enough to make men dizzy, Sixtus had understood that the shock of the new has its own power to impress. In the ten years since its completion, Alexander has watched the Sistine Chapel work its magic on everyone who enters: how their mouths fall open as they register the scale—the dimensions of the temple of Solomon is how it was planned—how the luminosity of the frescoes of Moses and Christ brings an involuntary smile to their lips, making them crane their necks upward, past the painted figures of the popes into the vast vaulted ceiling, the brilliant blue of a night sky peppered by stars.

He too now gazes up into the darkness. Oh, yes. It is a clever thing to make a man feel so small and humble against such majesty. Leave the wonder of a bird wing or the simplicity of the blade of grass to the saints and the hermits. Most men need to be overwhelmed in order to appreciate the divine. That is Rome's job. Every good pope leaves something hewn in stone and marble behind him. He had witnessed that as he stood in the wings waiting for his turn: how the fever of construction took hold of the most modest as well as the most arrogant of men. But of all of them, Sixtus had been the most surprising. Here was a man who began life as a Franciscan, espousing poverty and writing pious treatises. Yet barely had the papal crown been lowered onto his humble head than he was issuing instructions to architects and engineers, growing misty-eyed at the prospect of the great chapel that would bear his name. The mounting bills had had him, Rodrigo Borgia, Vice-Chancellor, turning somersaults and selling a thousand futures of pardons to find the money. Not satisfied with that, Sixtus had rebuilt churches, his own private altar in the crumbling St. Peter's. Also a new bridge over the Tiber to bear his name. Such was his building mania that it had been uncertain as to whether he would live long enough to see this, his major project, finished. The great opening mass of the Assumption had taken place less than a year before Sixtus died and he had already been more the shell than the man.

How well Alexander remembers that ceremony: the benches groaning with dignitaries from all over Christendom, the air thick with incense, the great papal choir pouring out jubilation from its gallery stalls, so that the voices seemed to descend from heaven itself. It had gone on for so long that most of the older ones fell asleep. But not him. No. He was too busy noting every detail. He had become fixated on the frescoes on the upper walls; not so much the beauty of Ghirlandaio and

Botticelli but the diplomatic daring on the part of Sixtus, who had managed to buy their services from Florence so soon after he had masterminded a conspiracy against the city. The intention had been to wipe out the Medici and replace them with, among others, his own nephew. Where was the pious Franciscan preacher then? Had it worked, he himself would not be standing here now. Instead he would have lived and died a wealthy vice-chancellor, blocked from higher office by the della Rovere family, which would have run the conclave as well as the state of Florence.

No, Sixtus, for all his pious prayers, had been in thrall to another kind of immortality: that of family. It is a passion that Alexander understands through every fiber of his being.

Now it is the Borgias' turn. For all the fancy bronze sculpture of Sixtus's tomb, the man himself is breeding worms like any other corpse, while he, Rodrigo Borgia, holds the reins of power. Yes, there will be artistic and religious works to mark his papacy. The ceiling of the great chapel remains a challenge, but for now he is too busy with the city fortress and his new apartments and their decoration. But in terms of the immediate future, his priorities are clear. For the Borgias to achieve the next rung of immortality the bricks and mortar must be human ones: sons and daughters, cousins, nieces and nephews, each one bringing another silken thread of loyalty and influence into the web of family, secure and powerful enough to run Rome and beyond.

His mind moves over the possibilities like fingers across the beads on a rosary.

His beloved Lucrezia will be the first. What a jewel her husband will be given. A minor Spanish nobleman might have been good enough for an illegitimate cardinal's daughter, but not the offspring of a pope. He gives a little growl of pleasure at the thought. Of course Count d'Aversa has got wind of it early, such is the well-oiled gossip machine of Rome. While the negotiations for an alliance with the house of Sforza continue, they still need Spain as a smoke screen. He will grant the man an audience and soothe his wounded pride. "No, no, my dear Count. The rumors are put about deliberately to throw others off the scent. Of course she is yours. Just give me time to make it secure."

What pleasure there is in the finessing of manipulation. Later, when the time is right, he will ditch the count, booting him out of town with a big enough purse to cover the bruise.

After that it will be Juan's turn. Juan who, with his easy swagger and chatter, had climbed his way early into his heart. Already carrying the title of Duke of Gandia in Spain, he will be the great prize in the marriage stakes since it is his seed that will carry the dynasty. His wife will be legitimate and royal. Alexander knows which family he wants for him, but not yet how to achieve it. Well, it will happen. Every state and ruler in Christendom has need of papal approval for something at some point in their life. That is the beauty and power of the office. The only question is what, when and how can it be used as barter.

Then there is Jofré. Jofré—the thought of his youngest son makes him frown. He is a sweet enough child: a clumsy plump body on the edge of puberty, big moon face and gap teeth. But the truth is, there are times when Alexander wonders if he is indeed the father of a boy whose features and markedly simple disposition have more than a hint of Vannozza's last husband, brought in to make her respectable while she was still entertaining a cardinal in her bed. It would never have been deliberate betrayal. Vannozza was too loyal for that. But who would not pass off a child between fathers, if the rewards for doing so were so great? Still, even if his suspicions are correct, he can make it work for them. It is a decision already taken: this gift horse will be a Borgia, whatever his parentage.

And finally there is Cesare.

Cesare.

Even the most doting father can see the strengths and faults within his own children. He knows his eldest son is powerful and clever. He has seen the speed of his mental swordwork and the charm he uses to salve the wounds he inflicts. But he has also felt the coldness in his soul, so different from his brother's transparency. In many ways he would have made a better soldier than a priest. But the decision was taken early and it is too late to change it now. No great dynasty in Rome can survive without a secure hold inside the Church. And the higher they climb, the greater the chance of cultivating another pope. Alexander's cousin Juan Borgia Lanzo is a good churchman, competent and loyal, but he will never get further than the College of Cardinals. No, Cesare alone has the steel and the drive to rise. He is certain of that. He already has a host of Church lawyers working on his illegitimacy. Bastard or no bastard, his son will become a cardinal.

"Your Holiness. This is not an easy problem to solve."

"Then solve it as a difficult one!"

It will be done before the end of the year. And it will not be unrewarding for Cesare, however he may balk at the idea. In a world where the politics of God can be as ruthless as the politics of man, his eldest son will surely grow to love the Church as much as he does.

"And one more thing, Papà . . ." He hears Lucrezia's voice, soft in his ear. "Bring Cesare home soon. He pines for Rome. I can feel it underneath the words."

Alexander turns and bows his head in the direction of the altar. Prayer and supplication. They come in many forms. As he moves out into the Vatican corridor, he calls for his bedchamber servant, who lies on a pallet dozing, waiting for his master's return.

"Come." He shakes the man. "We will breakfast and start work early today. Wake Burchard for me."

Chapter 7

"ALL I AM SAYING, FATHER, IS THAT WE COULD DO BETTER. THIS Sforza bridegroom is a puppet of Milan. The city of Pesaro is hardly worth the cannonballs we would use on its walls. Why waste a good marriage to get us in there?"

"I must say it is a pleasure to have you home, Cesare." Alexander leans his head back against the gilded wooden frame of the papal throne where he has settled himself, and where, after only a few days, he feels most comfortable when in the presence of his eldest son. "I don't know how the government of Christendom has managed to limp on without you. Since you excelled in logic as well as in rhetoric, perhaps you can answer the question yourself."

Cesare's new archbishop's robes sweep the flagstone floor as he paces the room. The echoing state chambers of the Vatican are new to him and, though he would never admit it, along with the thrill of the inner sanctum there is also a certain jangling of nerves. The sarcasm in his father's voice is not unnoticed. While Cesare has been waiting in Spoleto, he knows that Juan has been the intimate son and he needs to prove his worth quickly.

"Because we owe the Sforzas for your election and because we need them as allies to give us muscle against the Roman families. Yet we must also balance Milan against Naples. And if we appoint enough of our own cardinals to the Sacred College, surely we can control the families that way."

"Excellent! Your professors should have awarded you your *laude* even earlier." No trace of sarcasm now. "Certainly the College of Cardi-

nals will help, yes. Though not on its own. There is the question of timing. Too many of our own men elevated too soon and our enemies will
howl corruption. It's already started. 'Ten papacies would not satisfy
this horde of relatives.' Ah! What exaggeration!"

"Who dares to say that?"

"The ambassador of Ferrara, no less! In a private letter home to the
Duke d'Este."

Alexander beams. There is nothing he enjoys more than poking
around in other people's intelligence services. No man gets to where he
is today without having a better spy network than those who oppose
him. "Still, the man has a point. You should be in my receiving room
some mornings: Spaniards coming out like frogs in the rain, each and
every one claiming he is married to the daughter of a cousin of some
aunt I never knew. Valencia must be half empty by now." He chuckles
at the thought. "Well, we will nose out the best and let the others fall.
As for Ferrara—the duke will be licking our hands in gratitude as soon
as he gets a cardinal's hat for his son's head."

"We can buy half of them off the same way, Father. The rest were
always going to complain. But the fact is, it is done." Cesare waves his
hand around the room. "We are here and they can't take it away from
us. And when it comes to Lucrezia's marriage—"

"When it comes to Lucrezia's marriage no man would be good
enough for you, Cesare. And we will discuss this further when you are
seated somewhere. I am suffering old man's dizziness watching you
cavort around the chamber as if it was a dance floor."

"I thought it was forbidden to sit in the Pope's presence without
permission," he shoots back mischievously.

"So it is. But you have a way of seeming as tall as your Pope, even
when he is higher off the ground. So—sit," he says, making it sound like
a command to a dog.

Cesare throws himself into a wooden chair, its intricately carved
arms and slatted seat too delicate for this athletic young body. The Holy
Father's furniture, it seems, was designed with frailer clerics in mind.

"So. Tell me what you have against the Sforzas."

The questions are getting easier. "We have paid our dues to them already. Six chests of silver and a vice-chancellorship was a generous price, given that Ascanio Sforza could never have won the election anyway."

"True. But it is not Ascanio we are keeping sweet. It is his brother in Milan."

"He won't thank us for it. Ludovico Sforza is a thug, Father."

"Absolutely." The Pope laughs. "It is a compliment that has been paid to me many times. A thug, yes, but an impressive one. Any man willing to seize power from his own nephew is a dog with a rabid bite."

"All the more reason to keep him at arm's length." Cesare pauses, affecting a certain nonchalance. "Is it true what they say about France?"

"What do they say?" Alexander says sharply.

"That Ludovico Sforza will invite the French king to forward his claim on the throne of Naples?"

"Ah! Rancid gossip. He would be a fool to let it happen. A foreign army would unleash Milan's destruction alongside the rest of Italy's. Where do you hear that?"

And now it is Cesare's turn to smile. "You were the one who taught me how to lay a table, remember, Father?"

It is true enough. Like the best aspiring politicians, Cesare Borgia had learned many of his skills at his father's knee. They had always been the best of visits: those evenings when, after dinner, Rodrigo would dismiss the women and servants and call him and Juan to sit up around the table where he would then rearrange the chaos of the leftovers to set up a map of his beloved Italy across the great wooden surface. "See—this land is four times as long as it is wide. And each part has different textures." Fish skeletons for Venice at the top right, chicken and steak bones for Milan and Naples at either end, with a smattering of leftover soft fruits for Florence, Siena and the smaller states. And across the center a sprawling set of interlocking spoons to show the land that belonged to the papacy, with Rome itself marked by a knife. Juan always went for the knife and took out the soft fruit. But its edge was not so sharp that it could cut through the bones. Cesare, in contrast, spent as much time looking and thinking as acting. To this day, for him chess is a poor substitute for the power play of the dinner table and in his mind the great boot-shaped land that makes up Italy has tougher leather at the top and the bottom than the middle.

"I still think Ludovico Sforza might do it," he says carefully. "He is turned inside out with ambition."

"What are you saying, Cesare? That we should cultivate Naples and King Ferrante instead? A man who likes to hang his captives in cages around his court so he can watch them die slowly?"

"Oh, you don't care about such things, Father. You are just displeased with him because Naples supported the sale of Pope Innocent's castles."

"Yes, you could say I am 'displeased,'" Alexander growls, though his pleasure at his son's acuity is obvious. For months he has had advisers coming out of every fold of his papal garments, but few of them cut to the quick like Cesare. Well, he had sent him to Pisa to get his mind sharpened. He cannot complain if now he uses it to draw blood.

"Those castles were fiefdoms that belonged to the Church, not for selling for profit by his poxy son. And certainly not into the hands of the Orsini. The devil take them. It is a crime against the papacy. Look at the routes in and out of Rome that the Orsini family control now."

"The map is in my head, Father. You forget, I came in riding those very roads."

He had slipped out of Spoleto ten days before, incognito, with only Michelotto for company, the route back into the city chosen deliberately so that he could study the placing of the Orsini castles.

Once inside the main gates, he had gone first to Vannozza's house. Mother and son had not seen each other for almost two years and her delight at this fiercely handsome son of hers was infectious. She had plied him with her latest wines (after the children had been taken from her she had turned to nurturing vines) and fussed over him in a way he would allow no other woman ever to do. Even Michelotto had relaxed that night.

Next day, as they made their way to the Vatican, anonymity allowed him to see Rome through sharper eyes. The gaudy coronation arches—revealed now as painted wood—had long since flaked and cracked and the streets were as filthy as ever. On the way to the river they passed the remains of the Colosseum and the Forum, under gray winter skies, their appearance more ragged than he remembers. No doubt a few more ancient treasures had been dug out of the ground since he left; the fashion for new learning had sparked a rising market for old Rome, though Cesare himself has little time for such artistic snobbery.

At the western edge of the Forum gangs of men were hauling fallen masonry on to carts. What isn't worth saving is ripe for reuse. Except that, thanks to his father's new decree, every stone dug up and used for building will now yield a separate tithe to the Church: a pope who has been a vice-chancellor half his life still has a few new revenue tricks up his sleeve. No—there is not a lot going on in Rome that Cesare has missed in his months of exile. Except perhaps the chance to show his father how much he knows.

"But it wasn't only Naples who defied you over those castles, Father. You said in your letters that della Rovere negotiated the deal."

"Negotiated it and witnessed the signatures on the contracts in his own house, the Judas prick," Alexander snarls. "Still, since our enemy's aim is to make us angry"—he takes a long theatrical breath—"we will be sanguine instead. To hold the balance, we will bind Milan fast with the thread of Lucrezia's marriage and Naples a little looser with another alliance. I thank the Blessed Virgin that I have been gifted with not one but three fine children ready for wedlock."

"Take me out of the Church and you can have a fourth." The words spill out so fast that it seems Cesare might not have given them permission.

"This is an old conversation, my son," Alexander counters carefully. "You know it cannot be done. We need a Borgia in the Church."

Juan. The name hangs, unspoken, in the air. God damn it, the worse his brother behaves, it seems, the more his father's favorite he becomes. Well, there is no point in revisiting it now. "So let it be Jofré instead."

"Ah! Your brother still sleeps with his thumb in his mouth."

"Yet you say you are ready to marry him off."

The doubt slides in again, but Alexander pushes it away. "The betrothal will last for years. And the organ he needs for that job will mature faster than his mind. Enough now. You are like a dog that will not let go of the bone on this. It is already decided. Lucrezia will marry Giovanni Sforza who, while he may be a puppet, will become *our* puppet, and bring with him the city of Pesaro and, if we handle him right, an insight into whatever Milan does before she does it. And then, after we have clawed back some recompense for the castles, Jofré will take a wife from Naples."

"And Juan?"

"Ah! There are also talks in hand with Juan. I will discuss them with you both when he comes. First, I want you to see the new apartments."

"What talks? Is it Spain? Will he marry into Spain?"

"I said enough, Cesare!" And now his tone says it too. Cesare bows his obedience. He has pushed too hard too quickly and he knows it. He offers a hand to help his father down the steps from the great chair, but it is brushed away impatiently.

"I am not so old I need your help yet. Come. I have things to show you. I know painting is of little interest to you, but a modern pope must impress with art as well as politics or we will be damned as philistines as well as foreigners. You will use some charm in place of muscle now, please."

It is true that Cesare, like his father, is not much moved by art. For him the greatest excitement in Rome now is the work being done on Castel Sant' Angelo, the great fortress on the river with an imperial mausoleum deep in its bowels where the architect and engineer Giuliano da Sangallo is carving out new rooms, reinforcing the outer fortifications and repairing the upper-story walkway between the castle and the Vatican palace.

Cesare has a lot of time for men like da Sangallo. He identifies with the way they look at the world: seeing what could be, rather than what is. The way they build first in their minds, higher, stronger, greater, the power in the challenge as much as the achievement. Like the best generals, the vision is theirs alone. Yet they too need an army of muscle to make it happen. One of the things that he holds against Ludovico Sforza is how he squanders the talents of such warrior artists. Even now he has a man at court in Milan who claims to be able to build bridges indestructible to any army, yet what does Sforza have him doing, this da Vinci, but making clay models for a giant bronze horse commissioned to bolster the family's monstrous pride? The wasted energy of vanity. When he, Cesare Borgia, rides out of Rome at the head of an army (and he knows, as only a young man can, that it will happen), he will have such an engineer at his side, so that for every castle or fortress that confronts him, there will be a mind cleverer than his own working on its destruction.

Father and son make their way through the downstairs salon and along the corridors of the old Vatican palace. Alexander's considerable bulk does not prevent them from walking faster than most around them. Those they encounter stop and bow low as he passes, though their heads snap up fast enough to catch a glimpse of Cesare. His arrival has been long anticipated and he does not disappoint: this handsome young man in full ecclesiastical robes, hair still as thick and long as that of Our Lord—a reminder that though he has a clutch of benefices to his name he has yet to take final holy orders. When he gets to his new home in Trastevere, he will find a dozen invitations to dine at the houses of lovely if disreputable women. Why not? With his elevation to archbishop he is worth over sixteen thousand ducats a year, and as long as the Holy Mother Church demands celibacy, but does not impose chastity, the entrepreneurial spirit will always rise to fill the gap.

The apartments which Alexander has taken for himself are made up of a string of first- and second-floor chambers at the corner of the existing palace, alongside a blunt, workmanlike new tower, mostly built, save for its crenellated battlements. When finished, there will be both intimate and public spaces. Like much of the Borgia papacy, it is an accelerated process. For now the race is on to decorate the chambers in time for whatever wedding celebrations will be held there. The ceilings are already throbbing with embossed gold, picking out the Borgia crest, but the wall frescoes will take longer and Pinturicchio, the Pope's chosen artist, is working under strain. Not a state that brings out the best in him.

"One chamber will be dedicated to the saints." As Alexander and Cesare sweep in, the clutch of apprentices busy over the worktables in the middle bow clumsily, then scatter to the edges. The Pope beams at them, the slanting sunlight through the open windows catching the white-gold trim of his cap. When they are given leave to visit their families they will talk of how His Holiness brings his own halo with him. "The centerpiece will be the disputation of Santa Caterina at the court of Alexandria, with our own Lucrezia as Caterina herself. Such a sweet saint she will make—Pinturicchio has already done the sketches. Now you are back he'll want your likeness soon for someone or other, I am sure.

"Meanwhile, this will be the room of the mysteries! And I will be up there. See?" he says, his voice much louder now, as he points to covered scaffolding to the top of the generous lunette above the door, where the figure of Christ is already rising up against a bed of golden flame, cherub heads on sprouted wings dancing around him. Further down, the rest of the lunette is marked out in sinopia with the design of Christ's tomb and figures of sleeping soldiers nearby. "There. To the left. See? I will be kneeling in my papal robes, bearing personal witness to the divine resurrection."

"Not unless you take time to sit for your portrait, you won't." From behind the covered scaffolding a booming male voice calls out.

"Ah, Pinturicchio. I wondered where you were," he bellows back. "Come, come down here. I have brought another peerlessly handsome face for your walls."

The cloth bulges as a figure starts clambering down the ladder. They watch as he emerges: a singularly ugly, misshapen little man with a head too big for his body and a knot of bone high on his right shoulder that makes one wonder how he is able to look up to appreciate, or more importantly assess, the power of his creations.

"I had to pay a sack of money to get him. He left a della Rovere chapel half finished on the way," Alexander says in a theatrical whisper.

"That hunch comes from spending half his life down the sewers, excavating old Rome, studying the ancients' paintings. Smells like he's still there." Alexander wrinkles his nose and raises a finger to one ear. "Deaf as a post too. His wife screams at him. Though no one knows if that is a cause or a symptom."

He beams at the man now standing before them. "How is your wife, Pinturicchio?" he booms.

"She never sees me," the man grumbles amiably, rubbing his hands on a piece of cloth. It is impossible to age him. He could be forty, he could be sixty.

"My son, the Archbishop of Valencia."

"Pleasure, Your Excellency," he says, though there is no sign of him feeling any. He sniffs loudly, cocking his head to one side in search of Cesare's profile: fine nose; cheekbones sharp as slate; lips full, almost like a girl's; square, clean chin. It's the eyes that do it though: dark stones shining as if underwater, but opaque, no hint of what is behind. A fighter? Or a judge maybe? But with an edge of cruelty. If he had the time . . . Well, family portraits are the burden he must bear in order to people the worlds he seeks to create.

"You are still saying you need me to sit up there?" Alexander points to the platform constructed halfway up.

"If you want your image finished fast, yes. Your Holiness," he adds, the last two words something of an afterthought.

"Well, we shall speak to Burchard. He will find you a suitable time." He smiles at Cesare. "See how a pope must rise toward heaven even while he is here on earth."

There is a cough from the vicinity of the open doorway behind them.

"Johannes. How is it that whenever I speak of you, you are always there, as if you were outside listening?"

The Pope's Master of Ceremonies says nothing, simply slides softly across the floor. Cesare stares at him. Johannes Burchard. The only man in Rome whose face remains the same be it perfume or shit under his nose. Whose gossip was that? Cesare himself has a memory of him from years ago: a tall man like a thin bird, a heron or a cormorant, beady eyes, still, oh so still, until suddenly he starts pecking at the world around him. Now what he sees is more like a lizard, heavy-lidded and slow, the telltale folds of gizzard skin forming around his neck. Here is another one it is impossible to age correctly. Like the painter he seems shriveled, as if neither of them had ever been young. Some men are born dry, he thinks. While others—like his father—have too much juice.

"Your Holiness. Your Excellency, Archbishop." Burchard is bowing so low it seems a miracle he does not fall over. "I bring a message from the Spanish ambassador. He is delayed with urgent dispatches from home and craves your indulgence. And . . . the Duke of Gandia is arrived."

The Pope claps his hands like a delighted child. "Ah. Good. Show him in."

But the Duke of Gandia, otherwise known as Juan Borgia, is already showing himself in.

Cesare has not seen his brother since before the conclave, and while he has heard rumors of eccentricity via the loyal Pedro, he is not prepared for the sight that now greets his eye.

The young man striding into the chamber is in full oriental dress. His hair is caught up in a pale silk turban so fat and high that it looks like a tiered sugar sculpture upon his head, and necessitates him walking with an exaggerated swagger to make sure he does not dislodge it. The outer garment is purple, embroidered silk, down to his knees, with billowing green trousers underneath and two curling embossed-leather slippers peeking out from. At his belted waist hangs a shining curved scimitar.

Cesare throws a glance at his father, but Alexander seems to have overlooked the absurdity of his son's costume in the pleasure at having him again in his presence.

Pinturicchio, who has taken a step back to allow the family reunion, can feel his fingers itching for paper and chalk. In his mind, the court of Alexandria is filling up beautifully with the eccentric spectators.

"Cesare!" The young man shouts the name like a war cry and the two of them meet and embrace, Cesare careful to tuck his body around the curve of the sword. As they draw back the fearsome warrior is revealed as a smooth-cheeked boy with a straggle of hair on his upper lip striving for the status of a moustache.

Cesare's distaste registers as a sour pinch in his gut. He has forgotten quite how much he dislikes his younger brother. His smile, however, is fulsome. It is one of the many things he has learned from his father.

"Look at you! Your sense of style is common gossip in Spoleto, but we have yet to hear that you had left the Holy Mother Church for the infidel faith. What? Should I raise an army against you or shall it be hand-to-hand combat?"

Juan laughs, evidently pleased at the impact he has had.

"Combat, definitely." He gives a turn on the spot and pulls the scimitar from his waist in a well-practiced gesture. It slices through the air, the tip coming to rest not so lightly on Cesare's robes. "But be careful, brother. You are in the company of a master swordsman now."

The edge glints in the sun. Cesare moves the tip gently to one side. Johannes stands still as a lump of wood, but in the recesses of the chamber the apprentices' mouths are opening and shutting like hungry fish.

"Your brother has taken a fondness for the style of Prince Djem," says the Pope, his voice warm with pleasure at the high spirits on show.

Juan lifts the scimitar and then, twirling it in the air, brings it to land smoothly back in its sheath. It is not nothing, the skill in this display, and it speaks of time taken, if not wasted, in its perfecting. "Oh, yes indeed. He is a wild and fascinating man. You know, Cesare, he has fought in almost every country of the East and escaped death a thousand times."

"Only a thousand?"

"Ah . . . you are jealous. He is a man of history already. He has killed more people than you ever will."

"Yes. I have heard rumors how many died laughing."

The Pope himself laughs at this, for his bantering sons are so clever and handsome and vital. And now everyone finds it funny. Across the room the apprentices are giggling openly, Pinturicchio is grinning, even Burchard's face has cracked painfully into an obedient smile, and it is all suddenly a charming family scene. Cesare picks up his father's cue, hugging Juan again and slapping him on the shoulder. "It is good to see you again, brother."

"You too. We have missed your sour face at court, haven't we, Father?" Juan punches him on the chest. "Still, I think you would not mock Djem to his face. He is a tiger of a man. When I walk out with him in the city people get out of our way."

Cesare holds his smile as he glances again at his father. "You walk the streets like this?"

"Oh, your brother exaggerates as always. The two of them have been in procession during certain ceremonies. They cause quite a stir. But come. No more on infidels and tigers. If we don't let Pinturicchio get on with his work there will be nothing to dazzle your sister's wedding guests. And Burchard? Perhaps you would join us to discuss the protocol of all these celebrations. Without your expertise I fear we will make all manner of mistakes."

Over his brother's head, Cesare watches Burchard's face. The smile has gone as fast as it arrived. There is a rumor around the Vatican that he keeps a secret diary into which he writes every detail pertaining to matters of papal ceremony. The orchestration of the marriage of a pope's daughter, attended by his teenage mistress, three sons, a clutch of cardinals and half of Italy's great families, will be a challenge even for him. You should be grateful to us, he thinks. There have been none like us before. And there will be none afterward. Be careful what you write.

Chapter 8

"Papà says it's all harmless. That Juan and Prince Djem are like actors in theater and that Rome loves theater. But you know there are dreadful tales about that man. Once, apparently, when his servant dropped something he had his hand cut off!" Lucrezia shivers with shocked delight at the thought.

She is particularly joyful these days, since she has not only her father but also her big brother to care for her. Today it is her turn to visit Cesare in his home in Trastevere. While not as grand as Cardinal Zeno's palace, it is fine enough for a rich cleric, with a frieze of painted cherubs running below the receiving room ceiling and the terra-cotta floor laid in perfect herringbone, as smooth on the feet as it is warm on the eye.

"It may just be gossip, of course." She shrugs. "How would I know? I've never been allowed to meet him."

She sits, back straight, hands curled in her lap, aware of her grown-upness.

"You should keep it that way," Cesare says with mock sternness. "The man is a drunkard and a murderer."

Ah, how his little sister has changed in the time he has been away, the line from girl to young woman crossed in her wardrobe as well as her attitude. The dress she wears today is cream and gold brocade, delicate flower shapes picked out within the weave, gathered under a high waist and dissolving into a waterfall of the tiniest pleats, the wonder of fashion defying the weight of cloth. Above, her breasts are now encouraged upward, glimpsed over the top of the constructed fabric fortress that holds them in place. Her hair, brushed till it shines, is caught in a half-garland, from where it flows down her back. There is even something about her smell that is different, a certain ripening within the perfume. Cesare does not like to think that others might have become aware of it before him.

"You know his story, yes?"

"Of course. He is the brother of the sultan." She waves her hand airily, the young coquette courtier. Then sighs. "But that's all I know. Don't look at me like that, Cesare. I could go hoarse from asking about some things. Adriana tells me it is none of my business. Everyone treats me like a child. Which I am not anymore."

"No. You are not. And now I am home I will make sure they all know it."

"Oooh, I have missed you, brother."

It is true for him also. Though the feelings it brings are not entirely comfortable.

"So. When the last sultan died, there was a war of accession between Djem and his brother. Djem raised an army in Egypt and when he was defeated, he went to the Knights of Malta in Rhodes, asking them to back him in his revolt. But they betrayed him and he ended up their prisoner, paid for by his brother. Then he was transferred to Rome. It is a perfect piece of diplomacy. The new sultan remains in our debt and Djem languishes in silken imprisonment in the Vatican palace."

"His own brother *pays* us to keep him? Surely we should try and convert him. That would send out a message to the infidels."

"No. The man is too corrupt for that. Though you might manage it, perhaps. You still pray for me, I hope."

"Every day." She wrinkles her nose, and the child he grew up with, sweet and serious by degrees, is back again. "Sometimes twice, to make up for the times you forget."

He laughs. "Then I am safe indeed."

"For you do forget, yes?"

He pretends to think about it.

"Oh, Cesare. You may have all the wonders on earth, but without Him in your heart—"

"I will have to make do with my sister." He sits looking at her. God damn this. It will be like giving Venus to a blind man. "So—if you can bear to carry all those skirts around with you, I have something to show you."

She rises up with recently practiced grace, putting her hand on his offered arm. They take the stone staircase with its graceful low treads (he rides his horse up and down them for sport) into the back court-yard, where there is a newly planted grotto, with a few trees and a seat. Close by on a plinth a sculpted naked boy child lies sleeping, one plump arm thrown out in abandonment, his young flesh sinking into a pliant bed of stone.

"Oh, brother, what a sweet thing!"

"You know who he is? Look closer."

And as she does she sees the patterns of feathered wings spreading out like a pillow behind his back. "The god of love! Cupid. Oh, but he looks so real." She runs her fingers down his shoulder on to his creamy stone chest. "Where does he come from? Is he out of the ruins?"

"In a manner of speaking."

"You must have paid a lot for him. Aunt Adriana says men are mad for such statues these days. I didn't think you cared for such things!"

"I don't, usually. How old do you think he is?"

"As ancient as Rome, at least."

"Wrong. He is younger than you."

"No!"

"Oh yes. Our little Cupid here is a fake."

"But . . . but he is so beautiful." Her eyes grow wide with the news. "And the stone seems so—so old and grainy. As if it had been in the earth for ages."

"Rubbed down with a solution of acid and rolled in the dirt more like."

"Who would do such a thing?"

"A young Florentine artist, apparently. With as sharp an eye for business as he has a hand for sculpture. You are not the only one to be fooled. A certain cardinal who should know better paid a small fortune for him. When he found out he'd been swindled he demanded his money back from the dealer. So I bought him instead. The work of a man cunning enough to fool half of Rome deserves to be celebrated."

She stares down at the melting stone flesh. "I think it doesn't matter how old he is. He is so lovely. Look how deeply he sleeps."

"Exhausted from all the havoc he has caused, no doubt." He slides his hand down the body to where the boy's penis lies curled, a small slug nestled between tender stone balls. "But you, I think, have yet to feel Cupid's arrows, little sister? Despite this 'courtship' of yours."

She gives him a shy smile, the color rising in her cheeks. Since the conversation with her father in the chapel months before, her life has been moving so fast that it is sometimes hard to tell excitement from dizziness.

"Well, am I right?"

"Oh, Cesare, I have not even seen a portrait of him." She sinks down onto the seat, her skirts spreading around her. "What do you know about him, this Giovanni Sforza? Papà says he is a man of substance and civility. Do you think I will like him?"

"You do not have to like him," he says curtly.

"How can you say that? We are already betrothed! The wedding is in less than a month!"

"But there will be no consummation."

"No . . . not immediately." She blushes again. "But one cannot be married for long and not sleep with one's husband."

"Oh, I don't know. There are others around who do it," he says drily.

And now they both laugh.

"She is so lovely, yes?"

"Not as lovely as you."

"Cesare! I was talking about the baby." There is a pause. "I know what you think of Giulia. Don't stare at me like that. It is not so hard. I saw how you looked at her when you visited."

It had been a difficult encounter. Arriving laden with presents for his sister, no one had stopped him, nor thought—or perhaps had the courage—to prepare him for what he would find. It was his first visit to their home in the palazzo of Santa Maria in Portico and he had found them all together. As luck would have it, it had been the day when Giulia washed her hair, and as befits such a mammoth undertaking the room was full of it, stretched out over the backs of two chairs as she sat, regal in her posture, the newborn baby in its crib next to her, Adriana nearby and wet-nurses hovering in the background.

No one had said anything to him about a child until he had arrived in Rome and his father had broken the news. The fact that Pedro had not sniffed it out was not something he could be blamed for. On the contrary, it was proof of how his father's strategies of containment and privacy had worked, though Cesare still feels cheated not to have been told earlier. Well, in the end it is not of great importance. A baby girl means nothing but an expensive marriage fifteen years down the line. No threat there.

He had been courteous, but had taken no interest in the child. Giulia could barely hold his eye. She was, if anything, more beautiful, her body more rounded and womanly after the birth and her face radiant. She had entered his father's life when he was away studying and they had met only twice before. If she had been any other young woman he would have bedded her long ago. But there is something in this recent fecundity that almost disgusts him now, makes him angry in a way he does not understand. She had felt it faster than he did, and as soon as it was polite had excused herself, and she, the baby, the wet-nurses and her endless, endless hair had gone to another part of the palace, so that brother and sister could be alone together.

"She is not my mother," he mutters angrily.

"No. But she is loving and kind to Papà." Lucrezia thinks of the animal sounds in the night. "And he to her. It is not as everyone thinks."

"Ah, Lucrezia, the world would be a lesser place if you thought as everyone else did."

"I mean it. She makes him happy."

"I mean it too. You are a loyal and loving daughter. And sister."

"Oh, Cesare." She laughs in delight, reaching over and taking his hand. "I hope my husband is as fine and handsome as you."

"Such a thing would be impossible." He flips her hand over in his, spreading her fingers out to expose her palm. "See? It is written here.

'Not as handsome as your brother.'" He moves his finger over her skin. "Ah! But I also see that he is not the only husband you might have. And here, here is your lifeline. I can even see when you will die."

"No! You can really see all that? When, when will it be?"

He pulls her hand closer, his fingers running over the mound near her thumb and up toward the underside of her wrist where the skin is almost translucent. She shivers under the caress. "Not for a long time."

"And how many husbands?" she says eagerly.

"Oh, three, maybe four." He looks up at her and her eyes are bright with affection. "But you will never love them as much as you love me. For we are bound in blood and no man can come as close." He grins. "Nor be as handsome."

"That is not how a good courtier should talk!" She laughs, pulling her hand back as if he might be hurting her. "You should keep such dark magic to yourself."

"It is no darker than looking for your husband's face in a pail of water."

"Who told you about that?"

"I know everything about you, remember. You are my sister."

"Well, you had better be careful then. For I am sure I have some secrets about you." She grins and for a moment they are almost children again, unperturbed by the gravity of the world around them.

"Papà says that I will marry in the newly decorated chambers of the Vatican palace," she says at last. "Imagine that. With our pictures on the wall. Though I am not sure they will be finished in time. Johannes Burchard is arranging it all." She makes a face. "He reminds me of a toad."

"Too thin. He is more a lizard. Those flaps under his chin."

She giggles. "And the eyes." She flicks her own back and forwards, cold, blinking. She pauses. "You know that Juan is to give me away."

No, he did not know this. She can see it in the way he freezes slightly.

"But I will dance with you first," she says fiercely. "Well, after my husband."

Across the courtyard, the figure of Michelotto appears, his ravaged face sitting uncomfortably against the smooth velvet of his doublet.

"My Lady Lucrezia." He bows low before her. She nods, dropping her eyes immediately.

"Your Excellency," he says with exaggerated formality. "There is a messenger arrived from Mantua. With news of the horses you ordered."

"As you see, I am busy. Tell him to wait."

He gives another flourishing bow toward Lucrezia, but she still does not look up. After he has gone she sits frowning, picking anxiously at the weave of her dress, a gesture of the young girl she has not yet quite left behind.

"What?"

"Nothing. I—I just did not think that man would come to Rome with you now you are so elevated." She sighs. "He sends shivers through me. He feels . . . I don't know . . . so cruel."

"Not as cruel as the man who made him look like that. Michelotto is my bodyguard now. He goes everywhere with me."

"Well, I would prefer it if he did not come to my wedding," she says impetuously. "I think such an angry face would not be a good omen for my future."

"In which case you shall not see him there." He pauses. "Little sister, you are not to worry about this marriage. If he does anything to displease you . . ."

"Oh, Cesare." She shakes her head. "We are not children anymore. You cannot fight them all."

"No? I would not be so sure."

Chapter 9

FOR ALL CESARE'S SNEERING, GIOVANNI SFORZA IS NOT A BAD-looking man. Tall enough and with a full head of hair, both of his eyes view the world from the same angle and his legs are straight and shapely. He has had the good luck to be born into a family riding high. Though he is illegitimate, bastards of men like the Sforzas are so common that they are seen more as a proof of virility than a lack of morality, and it has not stopped him from inheriting the vicarship of the papal state of Pesaro, with the muscle of his powerful older cousins Ludovico and Ascanio behind him.

The bad luck is that he does not share their rampant sense of ambition. At twenty-seven he has seen enough of life to know that he will never be one of its great players. When faced with any serious challenge, he has a tendency to register it in his gut, which can spasm so badly at times that it is all he can do not to curl up in unmanly agony. Raised on stories of war and cunning, he would like to deny this weakness, but rather like the power of second sight it is not something that one can argue with.

Still, marriage is usually a safe option for a man and he is no stranger to the demands of dynasties. His first wife had come from the confident city-state of Mantua, the sister of the current marquis, no less. While not a love match, they had got on well enough. It might have grown into something deeper, but within two years she was dead in the same bed as her stillborn baby, whose body she had begged to hold as they tried to stanch her bleeding.

The first Giovanni had known of this new alliance was when his cousin Ludovico had given him a fat post with an even fatter salary in the Milanese army. It wasn't until the name of Borgia was attached that the stomach rumblings started. Mantua, at least, has been close to home and the Gonzaga family was of true Italian blood. But what could he do? It would have triggered infinitely worse pains to try and turn down a marriage brokered by a pope, and his own cousins, the Papal Vice-Chancellor and the Duke of Milan. He had been called to Rome for negotiations, and spent the best part of three weeks in a house waiting. The problem was that it seemed his bride was already betrothed to a Spanish nobleman, who had arrived at the same time and gone around rattling his sword, threatening to cut down any other man who staked a claim. On balance it seemed safer not to go out.

Then, suddenly, his rival was gone. The rumor was that it had taken three thousand ducats to buy him off. The amount augured well for the dowry this new wife would bring. His cousin Cardinal Ascanio took care of the bargaining, and sweet words and generous figures were everywhere. The betrothal had finally taken place in February, with his lawyer standing in for him. The man arrived back with tales of an unaffected, fresh young girl who would melt any heart, and a guardian aunt who could talk the hind legs off a donkey. Of her troublesome brothers there was no sign. The dowry agreed was a hefty thirty thousand ducats. He would have the ear of the Pope and, eventually, the body of his precious young daughter. It was the chance of a lifetime. He wandered around the palace, where the ghost of his first wife was fading rapidly. He imagined the echoing rooms newly filled with courtiers, music and laughter. The city would become a center of influence and culture. They would throw banquets for ambassadors and cardinals, even the Pope himself. He would hunt and dance and sit at table with a loving and lovely wife, who would give him a clutch of sons who would grow greater than their father. He spent much of that day in the latrine. Though why, given the evident wonders ahead of him, he did not understand.

But this was no time for stomach cramps. News tumbled out from Rome detailing the most fabulous preparations. His wife's wedding dress alone was rumored to be costing fifteen hundred ducats (separate from her dowry, he was reassured when he asked).

Giovanni's own wardrobe was a problem verging on a disaster. As bridegroom to one of the richest families, he could not afford to be out-shone. Yet without the dowry, which would not come till after the con-summation of the marriage, neither could he afford to shine. In the end he went begging. His ex-brother-in-law in Mantua was in possession of a great ceremonial necklace made by a master goldsmith and fit for the prince that he was about to become. A loan would cost nothing, and any favor could well come back tenfold, given the influence of his wife's family.

The necklace, impressive and heavy as a yoke, arrived quickly. The wedding itself, however, did not. It had been arranged for April, and then postponed to May, then again till June. The palace rooms were not ready. The Pope was still placating other suitors who were pursuing her. But when he plucked up the courage to ask directly if there was a problem, the answer came fast and fulsome. No, absolutely not. She will be yours and yours alone.

In name, but not yet in body. Perhaps this explains why his happi-ness was not unbridled. Of course it is hard to lust for something one has not yet seen. More importantly, since everyone knows that a mar-riage is not really a marriage until husband and wife have got into the same bed together, the official delay in consummation has had its im-pact on his stomach. In short, this union which on paper seemed made in heaven feels compromised from the start.

Alexander meanwhile has better things to worry about than the diges-tive system of his prospective son-in-law. Lucrezia, beloved though she is, is only one of four children he must move across the chessboard. And then there are all the challenges of the daily running of Christen-dom. It is his greatest pleasure when he can address both at the same time. So when the Spanish ambassador, Don Diego de Haro, arrives in Rome in June, the visit cloaked in such obvious secrecy that the whole city is awash with rumor, it seems that God has answered his prayers.

From the splendor of the papal throne, Alexander beams down at the paunchy bustling figure, shiny with the sweat of velvet and nerves, as he unrolls his parchment maps and moves the weights so that the curling pages stay flat enough to give the Sovereign Pontiff a better view.

"You see the island here, Your Holiness, yes, yes? We have called it Hispania. See—there is the name written across it. It is as everyone is saying—a new world! Wondrous enough in itself, but who can tell what lies beyond it?" The ambassador's voice, high by nature, gets higher when he is excited. And today he is very excited indeed. "So—some line of demarcation is essential, as I am sure you will agree."

Alexander nods judiciously, his face impassive though even he cannot help but feel a certain quickening of the pulse. This "new world" is so new that the maps hastily drawn up for the purpose do it little justice. There are two now lying side by side on the floor of the Vatican receiving room. To the east, they show the curving coast of the continent of Europe and Africa and then, across a great expanse of sea marked out by a few ink waves and fishes and the scratch of a few sailing boats with the wind in their sails, a vertical chain of long islands. Down one of the maps a thin chalk line has been drawn through the middle of the water. The other, a copy, is left bare. When Christian nations fight for the ownership of a new land, where else do they come for guidance but to the Pope? He takes his time, savoring God's manifest grace toward mankind by opening up such vistas, but also the aching anxiety of this one little man in front of him, whose life and career now depend on the deal that he can make for his masters.

"Your Holiness, history itself will congratulate you on the decision you take here today," the ambassador says, as meekly as he can manage.

"History, perhaps, Don Diego. But not, I suspect, the Portuguese. Is it not true that they have claims further west than this line?"

"Ah—that is unclear at this stage, Your Holiness, and further details can be negotiated by treaty later. It is the principle that Their Most Holy Catholic Majesties Ferdinand and Isabella beg you to consider now. Our cause is just. You have the words of our own admiral Columbus in front of you as proof."

Alexander picks up the leaves of a letter in his lap. "I must say it is a marvelous dispatch. Marvelous." He grins. "Such wonders. The island of Hispania alone, he tells us, is larger than Spain itself. I hear he has written another, fuller account that is being passed around the courts of Europe," he says drily.

"It is a new world, Your Holiness. Everyone has a great appetite to hear about it. But what he writes there is for your eyes alone."

"Haah. And my eyes would dearly love to see these wonders for themselves. So rich. *So rich!* These natives. Giving back gold for shoe-laces. And their carefree nakedness. It is like the innocence of Eden. Marvels indeed. Hmm. His letter leads one to believe that they are as taken with this admiral as he is with them. They see him as coming from the heavens in fact. I do hope your Columbus is not tempted to set himself up as more than a man."

"Your Holiness! He represents a nation that has expelled the Jews and the Moors and roots out heresy in every corner of the land. The flame of Jesus Christ burns as white-hot in our hearts as it does in your very own. And he is convinced these multitudes are ripe for conversion. No sign of idolatry. Just good spirits. That is what he writes. If they see him as coming from heaven then the truth that he brings with him will take no time to root and bear seed."

"Indeed. So certainly we must consider the request carefully." Alexander turns to Burchard, who is sat with his own pen poised over parchment. "What would you say, Johannes? It should be a papal bull, yes?"

Burchard nods.

"And the wording? Precise and clear, I think. A line of demarcation running . . . so many miles west of—what—the Cape Verde Islands?"

"Yes. Three hundred miles is what Their Majesties of Spain are requesting," Burchard adds quietly.

"Three hundred," the Pope repeats. He gazes at the map. Oh, the pleasure of such moments. He sighs. "Three hundred. That really does not leave a lot of room for others, Don Diego. Such a little line to create such a great empire."

"Which will bring glory to all of us," the ambassador squeaks. This business is of such importance to Spain that he has arrived in the city incognito. And, like Columbus himself, he comes carrying gifts, though of somewhat more value than shoelaces.

There is a short silence. Alexander appears to be lost in thought.

"Your Holiness, I . . . I must tell you how eagerly both My Majesties await the arrival of your son Juan, Duke of Gandia. His offered bride, Maria Enriques, besides being the cousin of the king, is a fine and noble woman, whose hand has been sought all over Europe. Theirs will be a union—"

"Forgive me, sir!" The Pope looks up, indignant. "We are not bartering our son in return for a line in the ocean. He is more worthy and more precious to us than a tribe of pagan souls."

"Of course!" The ambassador laughs nervously. "As is the princess to Their Majesties. No, we are speaking of royal blood. Of the powerful ties that will grow between Spain and the papacy. The advancement of the Church. Of family." He pauses. Is this enough? Apparently not. "And the princess's dowry I . . . I think you'll agree is at least as rich as the lady who accompanies it. Not to mention the lands that will pass into your son's hands." Surely he cannot want more? The ambassador glances at Burchard, who drops his eyes, his fingers offering the merest flutter of a sign.

So subtle. Not subtle enough that Alexander misses it. Wily old fox, the Pope thinks sharply. Burchard has been talking to him behind my back. But the realization is not without admiration.

"Yes, indeed. Church and family, Don Diego. We are united in those two great loves. Very well, the finer points can be discussed later. Three hundred miles then. Burchard, I leave it to you. We had better make the mark on the map in ink. And let us include in the bull some words from the letter of the admiral Columbus to us. To show his care of and loyalty to our holy office."

The Pope nods at the ambassador to dismiss him.

"Your Holiness." He swallows. "There is one more thing."

The Pope stares at him.

"My Majesties have heard . . . well, it is said . . . I mean . . ."

Alexander waits. After a lifetime practicing diplomacy and the culture of blandishments, it gives him an almost childish glee to watch others struggling. "I would spit it out if I were you, Don Diego. We wouldn't want Spain discovering another new empire before you got to the point."

"I am referring to France. The rumor that, with the support of Milan, the new French king has put forward claims on the throne of Naples. This is something—"

"—that would upset Their Spanish Majesties no end."

"Yes indeed. The balance of power—"

"—is delicate. Ambassador, you do not need to tell me my job. I have been balancing power for most of my life. You will tell Your Majesties that while the Pope has entered into friendship and marriage union with Milan, partly in response to most aggressive behavior from their compatriot in Naples—"

"About which we have made our disapproval most clear—"

Alexander stops, making clear his greater disapproval at the interruption, and the ambassador subsides into silence. There are moments at prayer when he wonders if such clear enjoyment of power might border on the sin of pride. Or vanity. But such doubts do not last long.

"However, Don Diego, while we are displeased we are nevertheless willing to be reconciled with King Ferrante in Naples, should he make proper overture. Furthermore we do not countenance foreign intervention in the land. The French ambassador knows our thoughts on this. And they have been relayed in the clearest words to his master."

"Your Holiness, I am deeply relieved to hear it," the little man splutters, though sharp ears might say his voice is not as fulsome as his words.

"Good. And since you are in town, perhaps you would like to make your presence official. Then we might invite you to join in the celebrations of our daughter's nuptials. Oh—and send word to your admiral that we will be most pleased to hear from him again. His stories inform and delight us beyond measure."

Chapter 10

THE LITTLE GIRL BITES HER LIP TO AVOID SHOUTING OUT. HER white teeth shine fiercely against the pomegranate red of the inside of her mouth and her ebony skin. Pinturicchio, who attended yesterday's rehearsals, already has artistic designs upon her. But she is struggling now. The dress they are squeezing her into is too tight around her chest, and she squirms, unable to breathe properly.

"Hold still!" Adriana yells.

The child stops, staring at Lucrezia, who stands with her back to her, a river of embroidered white silk falling down from her shoulders along the ground toward the girl's feet. It is the most beautiful sight she has ever seen.

"Right. Now, pick it up. Bend, girl. There, hold it. Yes, two hands. Further apart. This high up. See. Feel the weight of it." Adriana's voice slips between exasperation and irascibility. "Remember, this is your job. You hold this train and you walk behind Madonna Lucrezia. At the speed we practiced yesterday. No faster, no slower. Don't look at anything or anybody else. When she stops, you stop. When she walks, you walk. And you never, never let it go. Never. Not until I myself tell you to. You understand?"

The girl's fingernails are pale at the edges with the ferocity of her grip on the material. She looks up at Adriana's blotchy face, the white powder eaten away by stress to reveal a forest of broken veins stretching from the trunk of her nose out across her cheeks.

"Do you understand?" Adriana throws up her hands in frustration.

"The child is useless. She's black enough but completely deaf and dumb. I asked for one that was not a savage."

"I think she hears every word, Aunt." When others flap, Lucrezia finds it easier to be calm. "I spoke to her yesterday and her Italian was as good as yours or mine."

She comes closer, the movement wrapped in a rustle of silk, bends down and rests her own hand lightly over the girl's. "Do you understand what my aunt says?"

The girl nods. Lucrezia's fingers, naked and pale, give way to a half-glove, looped over her middle finger, the silk stretching over the back of her hand and into the wrist of her gown, its entire surface encrusted with small pearls, as luminous as the black sheen of the girl's own skin underneath. They both stare, equally entranced at the wonder of the contrast.

The girl looks up. "I walk when you walk. I stop when you stop. I hold on to it until *she* tells me to let it go."

"See!" Lucrezia beams. "Perfect. You look most pretty," she whispers.

The girl stares. And stares. "So do you."

"Aah!" Adriana, if possible, is even more exasperated.

The great room at the top of the palace is a madhouse. It is as if a wandering theater troupe has billeted itself there, late for a king's performance of a chivalric spectacle. Except all these players are young women. Dozens and dozens of them from Rome's great families, to act as maids of honor for the arrival of the bridegroom and the marriage ceremony. By now they are mildly hysterical, chattering and screeching like starlings in the twilight hour. Adriana, in contrast, is a general who has lost control of her troops.

A woman enters the room and whispers something in her ear and she stops, clapping her hands and letting out a great bellow.

"Silence! Silence!"

The room comes to a standstill amid a hushing and shushing of silk across marble floors.

"We are ready. The moment is come. Listen. Listen." She motions to the open loggia at the end of the room.

They stand listening, and there, in the distance, they hear it: the blast of a trumpet, then the curl of pipes and flutes and drums weaving in behind.

"They are on the other side of the river. Crossing the Sant' Angelo Bridge. They will be here within the half-hour."

Adriana rushes out into the loggia, ducking her head over the open balustrade, then ducking back again, her face lit up, younger suddenly than her years.

"Oh, the piazza is full already. Oh my. Oh my. Everyone to their places. Ladies. To the end wall in your ranks. I shall tell you when to come forward. Lucrezia, you go out onto the loggia now. But not so as they can see you yet."

The room clears, the young women scurrying to their places, so the space is empty save for Lucrezia. And her eager little train bearer, who does not budge an inch.

Adriana turns on her. "What? What? Didn't you hear what I said? Get over there with the others."

The child looks up at Lucrezia, but she does not budge.

Lucrezia nods. "What she means is that she wants you to put down the train now."

The girl, biting her lower lip in a gesture of deep concentration, curtsies, bringing the river of fabric to the ground in a slow movement of such grace that both the women cannot take their eyes off her. Then, head high, she marches like a small soldier to the back of the room.

Adriana, who has the vague sense that she has just been upstaged in some way, shakes her head, then throws her entire attention and anxiety onto her niece.

"It's all right, Aunt. I can walk myself. I am ready."

She has been ready for the best part of seven hours. She had woken before dawn without the need of any bell, and lain awake, saying her prayers and asking for guidance in this, the most challenging moment of her life: the first meeting with her husband. By the bed, underneath *The Imitation of Christ* and *The Book of Hours,* lies a small, well-thumbed volume of chivalric tales, deemed uplifting enough for girls of her age and class. Within its pages, pure-born princesses, tricked or betrayed by evil half-brothers or usurping kings, fight their way through wild land-scapes and grisly combat to find their thrones and their true love. While she has no illusions that that is what is on offer here, she cannot help but feel a little dizzy with all the thrills and frills, the heat of so much attention directed at her.

The day outside her shutters had arrived pristine, perfect: Rome in early summer is a sweet season, blue skies and a sun that kisses rather than crushes. On such a day D'Artu might have married his Ginevara. And for a while at least they would be happy.

She turns to her aunt. "How do I look?"

Adriana opens her mouth, closes it again, and then bursts into tears. She too has read her romances. Or perhaps she just has a reason to be upset by arranged marriages.

"Well, it is too late to do anything about it now," Lucrezia says, squeezing her hand. She lifts up her arms and the encrusted pearls glimmer in the sun. "Oh, my gown feels so heavy."

"Wait until you see Juan," Adriana says. "He's wearing half a jeweler's shop."

Lucrezia smiles at the unexpected wit, gives her a hug and then walks out onto the loggia. Though she is careful not to show herself yet to the crowd, someone catches a glimpse and a great roar goes up. It has been almost a year since the public celebrations of the Pope's coronation. Other cities of Italy have great dynastic weddings all the time. Now Rome has its own royal family. The Pope's lovely young daughter. Ripe fruit. Free wine. Time for another Borgia party.

The sound of the music is growing closer. The drumbeat registers in her stomach. This is happening to me, here, now, she thinks. I am nearly fourteen years old and I am meeting the man I will marry. Dear, sweet Jesus, let him like me. Let me love him. With Your help I can do it. She tries to take hold of the feeling, still it, freeze it, pickle it, preserve it in some manner so that she can return to it at will, whatever happens from here on.

Below, the atmosphere is carnival rather than procession: this colorful knot of squires, knights, page boys and musicians attended by fools and jesters turning cartwheels, or gibbering and playing with the crowds, one decked out as a priest offering blessings to anyone and everyone. And in the middle somewhere, the bridegroom.

As the first drummers and flag wavers enter the little piazza in front of the palace, Lucrezia moves forward to the balustrade and every head goes up to look at her. For many it is the first sight they have had of her, this tender young woman emblazoned in silk and pearls, her virgin long hair under a jeweled net falling onto her shoulders. And they are, of course, enthralled. The Pope adores her, it is said. And why not? At this moment she is everyone's daughter. The new blossom on the tree. The spring that promises a great harvest. The kiss of romance. The thrust of lust. Rome is hungry for it all. God preserve the family that brings them so much theater.

The main group of horsemen moves into the square, then peels away to leave one horse and one rider.

He spurs his mount in a slow trot toward the loggia. He comes to a halt underneath. Man on horse: woman on balcony. A chorus of lovely young women can now be glimpsed behind her. He takes off his hat and bows low to the side, his thighs clasping tight to the saddle to balance the move. The reins clink, the horse whinnies slightly.

In response, Lucrezia drops into a deep curtsy, disappearing from view before rising up again. The moment is held. Then he replaces his hat and flicks the reins and his horse joins the others as the procession moves off toward the opening doors of the Vatican palace, where he will pay obeisance to her father.

The crowd howls its approval at a ritual well executed.

She turns back into the room. Her aunt stands, eyes brimming.

"I had the sun in my eyes." Lucrezia shrugs slightly, her heart still hammering out the drumbeat of excitement. "All I could see was a flash of gold on his chest."

Everybody finds it wonderfully funny.

Chapter II

A<small>MID THE DAYS OF CELEBRATION THAT FOLLOW, THE ONLY PERSON</small> who manages to contain his enthusiasm is the indefatigable Master of Ceremonies.

Johannes Burchard orchestrates every element with the same attention to detail that he might give to the Second Coming. With no protocol for such an event—popes do not have daughters, even when they do—he fashions one to fit. The guest list is extensive, mixing family, Church, state and a small invasion of foreign dignitaries, each and every one of whose arrival and placing must be choreographed down to the finest inch of precedent and snobbery.

The new papal apartments have been hastily prepared. Pinturicchio and his gang of apprentices have been banished, the painter moaning fiercely, and tapestries brought in to cover up where his brilliance has been interrupted. The Pope's gilded throne is carried carefully into the main salon, with a lesser seat put in place in the smaller chamber of mysteries so that he may move easily between ruler of Christendom and doting father. Without the religious frescoes that will eventually cover the walls, the most powerful image is that of the Borgia family crest: the rising flame, the double crown, and everywhere the bull, potent and warlike.

Things do not begin well. At the hour of the marriage ceremony Alexander sits magnificent on his throne, surrounded by cardinals, ready to receive his guests, when the doors open on the flock of Lucrezia's gentlewomen who, reduced to starling status again by the thrill of the moment, fling themselves into the room in such high spirits that they forget to kneel at the Pope's feet before taking their place in readiness for the bride. A look of pure anguish passes over Burchard's face, as if that very moment he might be struck dead and his body pulled into hell by a troop of devils. Later, the Pope himself is moved to excuse him of any fault. It doesn't help: it is not the Pope's feelings he is worried about, but the insult to the office. It will be his punishment to survive the incident with his shame intact.

For the rest, well, it is a wedding like any other between two great families: an exercise in status, ostentation, sentiment and pleasure. Many of the guests have never entered—nor ever will again—the private apartments of the Pope, and there is much nudging and gawping. When they are not judging their surroundings they are judging one another. With so much outré fashion vying for attention, the Duke of Gandia's fanfaronade entrance—a chest of jewels masquerading as a suit of clothes—is greeted with remarkable good humor. In contrast, the bridegroom's necklace speaks of both taste and dignity, and Lucrezia's palpable purity and vulnerability as she approaches to kneel beside him on the velvet cushions, the little Negress a shimmering black sprite at her heels, plays on everybody's heartstrings.

It is not her fault if the attention of most of the guests is drawn irresistibly toward an even more dazzling young woman with a cloud of golden hair, who, for the first time ever, is presented in public as the Pope's companion.

Cesare, in formal ecclesiastical dress (unlike his brother he understands the power of watching rather than being watched), stands to the side as something akin to a queue forms close to Giulia Farnese's chair. While the diplomats' pens will no doubt be dipped in poison when it comes to describing the scene, there is no mistaking the approval in their eyes now. Ah, it amazes him how grown men suckle so on the teat of scandal. Still, the more they gossip, the less attention they have for more important things. His own future, for instance. There are plans afoot which will have them falling over themselves soon enough, only when it happens it will be his timing and not theirs.

"Your Excellency. Welcome back." He cannot stop a few of the smarter ambassadors from sniffing around him.

Alessandro Boccacio from the city-state of Ferrara stands beaming at him: face like a fish, nose like a bloodhound, a veteran of the fray but also a man with a seriously leaking diplomatic pouch. "Ten papacies would not satisfy this horde of relatives." Those had been the very words he had sent to his duke. Cesare has been looking forward to this encounter for a while.

"How Rome has missed your bullfighting skills! We all pray your archbishop's robes won't stop you from entering the ring again."

"Happily, Signor Boccacio, I am so busy with Church matters that killing bulls no longer holds the same attraction."

"Perhaps that is because so many of them have been elevated to the skies," the ambassador replies, and they laugh together at this clever reference to the bulls on the Borgia coat of arms, emblazoned over the ceilings. Under one such set the newlyweds sit in their decorated chairs, surrounded by well-wishers, smiling and talking to everyone but each other.

"I must say, the Lady Lucrezia is radiant."

"She most certainly is."

"And the Duke of Gandia. Well . . . he succeeds in dazzling us all."

"Yes, he does catch the sun particularly well today."

"He will make a fine bridegroom himself. Which lucky woman will that be, we all wonder? I see the Spanish ambassador has a big smile on his face. Of course, he has a lot to celebrate. They say it is a whole new world that Their Majesties' ships have bumped into. If I was the ambassador for Portugal I would be most worried about that smile." The Ferrarese ambassador pauses again. Not that he expects anything back now, but he is enjoying the rhythm of his own music. "You do not yearn for it at all yourself, Your Excellency?"

"What? Sailing?"

"I was thinking more of marriage."

"Ah, as you know, I am betrothed to our Holy Mother Church. She sustains me in all my desires."

Except those that are dealt with by a certain young courtesan called Fiammetta, a professional hostess who runs an elegant establishment near the Sant' Angelo Bridge. The silence is long enough for them both to conjure up a pleasurable image of her.

"Your cousin looks well in his cardinal's robes."

"He does." Though in fact Juan Borgia Lanzo, new in the job but old in years, does not look that well at all.

"We have great hopes that more new blood will find its way into the College. You yourself would make a fine cardinal. Were such a thing to be considered."

Ah, thinks Cesare, so this is what all this probing is about. Even now no one quite dares to bring it up directly: how his bastard status will disqualify him from a cardinal's hat.

"You think so? I think I am too old already. It seems the rush is on to promote ever younger blood. Your own duke's young son, Ippolito d'Este, has barely celebrated his fifteenth birthday, I hear."

"Ah, but he is a young man of exceptional virtue and acumen. You cannot imagine how he yearns to serve the papacy. The Este family are holding their very own celebrations today in Ferrara, such is their love and support for the Pope."

"And His Holiness is well aware of it. The heir apparent, Alfonso, brought a whole chest of it when he visited my sister. She says he is a most handsome man."

"And he in turn was overwhelmed by her modesty and beauty."

"The two of them spoke Italian together, I trust?" Cesare says casually.

"I am sorry?"

"I would not like to think my sister welcomed him in . . . Spanish."

"Spanish? No, no, why . . ." he says, evidently flustered.

"Good. It is only . . . well, Boccacio, it seems that rumors persist about how we Borgias lean toward Spain and are besieged by those who demand our favors. Some even say that 'ten papacies would not satisfy this horde of relatives.'" And he plays with the last phrase to show off its quotation marks.

"Oh! That is perfidious gossip indeed!"

Ambassadors, of course, do not blush. It is a requisite of the job that they can sustain any manner of insult without any visible change to their face.

"I shall personally do my best to make sure it is not repeated." He gives a smart little bow. "It is, as always, Your Excellency, a pleasure to spend time in your company."

Which, refreshingly, is meant exactly as it is said. To his credit, Alessandro Boccacio is good enough at his job to know when he has failed in the doing of it. As he drifts away, he is already sifting through the chain of command for the weak link in his postal service. Or how, perhaps, he might exploit it. Either way he has been proved right in his assessment that the Pope's eldest son is a man to be reckoned with.

Cesare watches him go. He is thinking about Pedro and his own informant network, first started to keep lines open between Rome and Pisa, and now sewn up as tight as a nun's vagina. No man in his service would ever open his mouth or his pouch. The rewards are too great. And the punishments too awful. People know what Michelotto can do when he is angry. Anger. He thinks of Lucrezia's description of that face. Except "anger" is not the right word. No, Cesare knows very well that Michelotto's power springs from a darker, colder well. Even as a young boy—one of a group of Spanish children brought in to act as a buffer between the young Borgia and the rest of the world—it had been there: this mix of unquestioning loyalty, bred in his Spanish bone, and the more personal satisfaction of violence. It had started with brawling, a bloody nose for the casual insult (strange how when Italians look at Spaniards so many of them see ex-Jews). But with the family's advancement the fights had quickly grown more serious. Sometimes Cesare joined him. More often he left him alone. He had only known him once bettered: a man in Perugia had taken a dagger to his teenage face in a revenge ambush outside their house, when he was returning home alone one night. The wounds, for which he would accept no salves, had taken months to heal. Cesare had been present when he thanked the man later, as he lifted him up and skewered him on his sword. "People will remember me better now before they die, don't you think, sir?"

It remains Michelotto's only sin of pride: too much pleasure in a job well done. But whether it is a matter of justice or revenge, once it starts, mercy shatters like faulty glass. However loyal or favored you might think yourself to be, it is never entirely a comfortable feeling, turning your back on Michelotto. And since he is so often in the presence of his master, part of that aura has been transmitted to Cesare himself.

Today, however, Cesare has kept his promise to Lucrezia and his henchman's rearranged face is nowhere to be seen. Instead, the honor of guarding him has gone to Pedro Calderón, who is lucky that his enthusiasm for riding has not yet bowed his legs, so that he makes a fine young courtier, waiting in the courtyard or the back rooms to escort his master home.

This duty marks Calderón's first public engagement in Cesare Borgia's service since the household moved to Rome, and during that time his master has done nothing but grow in the young man's estimation. He is amazed by the way he seems to change personality with his clothes: the hunter, the cleric, the athlete, the courtier, with barely a breath in between. Already Calderón knows he would do anything for him. He lies in bed at night imagining the time when Michelotto, for some reason, is absent from his side and there might be an attack so that he could be the one to drive the dagger into an assassin's heart, even if it meant his own death in the process.

The wedding dinner that follows the public ceremony is an intimate affair, family and special guests only, no personal servants allowed. The retainers are put in a modest undecorated room nearby where they are fed and watered as they wait. The high spirits of the party are impossible to miss. The chamber echoes with gales of laughter, followed by bursts of exclaimed pleasure when the favored invitees deliver their presents to the bride and groom. Then come music and dancing, and finally waves of such obvious hilarity that everyone hearing it wonders what is taking place.

The news leaks out fast: how, as the servants delivered the mountains of honey and marzipan delicacies, the guests had started to throw them at one another. Or rather the men started throwing them at the women. Or rather the Pope started throwing his at Giulia Farnese, looping them into her lap or, even cleverer, down the curved front of her bodice. So, of course, everyone else followed suit, until a happy mayhem had taken over. The Pope's mistress, the servants say, was brimming over with largesse and good humor. Not to mention captured confectionery.

But Pedro knows whose lap he would have chosen for his sweets.

Though he has visited their house maybe a dozen times, has smelled her perfume, has heard what he was sure was her laughter once on the stairs, he has not set eyes on her until today. As Cesare's bodyguard he had been close in the throng as she arrived: a young woman on her wedding day, palest skin against white silk set off by a blush of pearls. He gazed at a perfect heart-shaped face, eyes bright and shining with excitement. And such grace. Head held high, she had glided down the long corridor as if her feet were not touching the ground, a cloud of silk floating behind her. Of course he had been waiting for this moment. Any man in love with Cesare is already half in love with his sister. Now, when he shuts his eyes, he cannot see anything else.

As night turns to morning, he catches another sight of her as she is escorted out from the great chamber on her brother's arm, followed by her aunt and two of her ladies-in-waiting. Of her husband there is no sign. She seems smaller now, flushed and tired, with a light cape pulled around her. He stands to attention as they pass. Cesare catches his eye and nods, an instruction to wait until he comes back. She, holding tight to his arm, looks up also. He registers gray-green eyes and a small mouth, puckered, almost like a child's. She gives a nervous little smile, as if they might know each other but she cannot remember how, then looks away and is gone.

Later he and another horseman accompany Cesare out of the Vatican, by Castel Sant' Angelo and across the bridge to the house of Fiammetta. They pass through winding streets strewn with debris—glass, flowers, torn streamers—with men asleep in the gutters or swaying their way home. Rome has enjoyed its own party. Calderón sits, hawkeyed for trouble, one hand on his reins, the other on his dagger sheath. Perhaps it will happen now: a hotblood from the Orsini or Colonna clan, or one of Fiammetta's clients denied access to her bed in favor of her new lover. They will come roaring out of the dark and he will spot them first, launching himself between his master and the sword . . .

They arrive without incident. It is still dark when they reach the house, with its small courtyard on the outside. A young woman appears at a second-story window, as if fresh from her mirror, her tumbling red hair caught in the light of the torches, set further on fire by the wild green of her robe. It is her profession to be awake while others sleep and, while this is by no means her only talent, it is one that suits Cesare particularly well. She lifts her hand in a small wave, and he leaps from his saddle in a single graceful jump and strides inside, leaving the others to settle the mounts.

"How was it, pup?" As Pedro turns, Michelotto steps out of the darkness behind him. "See a lot of flesh and finery, did you?"

"It . . . Ha! . . . I didn't expect to find you here. You startled me."

"Did I? You should have checked when you rode up. I could have been waiting here with a dagger under my cloak. And you, my friend . . ." He pulls him to him and punches him softly up under the rib. "What use would you have been to your master then?"

Pedro laughs. He'd like to ask how any villain would have managed to get this close in the first place, unless Fiammetta had invited them. But it is not worth the energy. The rebuke will fade faster if Michelotto is allowed to win. The change of command has put his nose out of joint enough as it is.

"Look at you. Quite the courtier. Did you get your snout in any ladies' troughs then?"

"Dozens," he says evenly. He has never seen Michelotto with a woman, though stories about girls who like the feel of scars abound in the living quarters.

"That would account for the smell of you." He lets him go and slaps his head casually. "You did an all-right job," he says gruffly, the compliment as always undermined by the insults that decorate it. "Go on. You can get out of here now."

"I was told I was to stay and see His Excellency home tomorrow."

"Yeah, well, it is already tomorrow and I am here now."

They face each other for a second, as if it might be worth making an issue of. Pedro bows his head.

"And watch yourself. The streets out there are dangerous."

Across the city, Lucrezia sits by her bed, her discarded dress across the chest, its pearled arms jutting out like those of a stuffed doll. Her eyes are glazed with tiredness as her maid coaxes the tangles from her hair, then, closing the shutters against the dawning light, helps her into bed. She has already said her prayers, careful to include in them the well-being of her new husband, with whom she has spoken perhaps twenty or thirty words, none of them memorable, and whose face she can barely recall amid a sea of others.

"Such a handsome fellow," her aunt's voice had purred into her ear. Yet when she had looked from him to Juan, or Cesare or a dozen other men around her, he had seemed faintly drawn in comparison. In all her fourteen years she has never been in the company of so many men, nor seen her own bright sweetness reflected back in their eyes. She has been flattered and teased and complimented beyond compare. In return she has smiled and curtsied and laughed and clapped her hands and danced and danced and danced more. Her legs ache, her feet are sore and her head is dizzy. It has been the longest and most exciting day of her life. Yet back in her room, she feels little of it now.

"I look forward to us becoming better acquainted as husband and wife." Those had been his last words; polite, inoffensive, more like the settling of an appointment for a business matter. He had taken her hands and kissed her quickly on both cheeks. She can still feel the dry flick of his lips against her flesh. If she was a little older or more experienced she might have been able to understand his nervousness as well as her own. Husband and wife. Did he really look forward to it? Did she? And is "she" the Lucrezia Borgia who had woken up this morning or the Lucrezia, Duchess of Pesaro, who is falling asleep tonight? The fact is they are still the same person. Lucrezia Sforza. Her mouth finds it hard to even say the two names together; they collide and trip over each other so. How strange that in the space of one day so much can have changed and yet everything still remain the same.

Inside the Vatican, Pope Alexander VI is already fast asleep. Having married his beloved daughter, he has dispatched his young mistress back to her bed alone tonight, so that he might end this of all days in communion and thanks with the other most favored woman in his life. For her part, the Virgin Mother of God watches over him from a glowing portrait over the great bed. If she has an opinion on the day, she is keeping it to herself.

In his book-lined study on the other side of the Vatican palace, Johannes Burchard, Master of Ceremonies, his face set like rigor mortis, dips his ink in the well on his desk and notes down every detail.

Chapter 12

"THIS IS IMPORTANT, JUAN."

"I know, I know, Papà. I have heard it already. Cesare spent half of yesterday lecturing me—as if he knows anything about marriage and behavior! He treats me as if I am a . . . a half-wit."

It is early morning; the summer sun slicing through the open windows and painting columns of golden light across the Room of Mysteries. The walls are still half finished, but the floor is vibrant with new tiles, the emblems of the Borgia crest marked out in hot Spanish blues, so cleverly laid in geometric shapes that they seem to move and shift under one's feet. Any visitor with his eye to the ground and the sound of Spanish dialect ringing in his ears might think he had entered some Moorish or Byzantine palace, rather than the home of the Pontiff of Rome.

"I'm sure that's not true. He is your brother and you are as dear to him as you are to me. But Spain is not Rome. How you live here is not how you can live there. They do not look lightly on foreigners who take liberties with their culture."

"But . . . we are Spanish. That's what you always tell us."

"By blood, maybe. But you were born into Italian ways and unless you are vigilant those ways will let you down. The fact is, you go not just as a husband, not just as a Borgia, but as an ambassador for the papacy itself."

"Oh, they'll know that fast enough." Juan grins. "By the time we reach Barcelona for the wedding, the whole country will be talking about us."

"Yes, but there is talk and there is talk. And what impresses here does not always impress there."

"What? You want me to live like a pauper?"

"There is little chance of that!" Alexander retorts, allowing his exasperation to show. "We have four ships already loaded to the waterline at Civitavecchia. And I gather you have bought up most of the jewels in Rome."

He scowls. "This is Cesare's sour tongue."

"No. The tongue is everyone's."

"I'm the Duke of Gandia, Father," he protests. "You've told me often enough I have a whole palace to fill in Valencia. The gifts for my wife were your choice."

"And I am sure she will be delighted to receive every one of them. Just be careful how you deliver them. Your new family will not applaud ostentation in the way that Romans do."

"Purrh." The scowl collapses into a pout. He has never taken criticism well, this pretty young man. But then he has not been used to receiving much of it, especially from his father. "I thought Spain was interested in riches now. Everyone says her ships will be using gold as ballast soon."

"Yes, the country will be rich. But it will take time for that to sink into its soul. Spain has not embraced the rebirth of art and learning in the same way others have. They have no appetite for . . . well, what they see as frivolities. For them the world is about God and the united monarchy, and both have stricter standards than you are used to. You'll find the court most pious in its religious observations. You should go to church daily, without fail. You must give up gambling and all such games of chance. And when it comes to your wife, there must be respect and discretion. I cannot say this clearly enough, Juan. There can be no running around the streets, bringing contamination back to the marriage bed."

The young man groans, sinking into his chair and picking a piece of fluff off his sleeve. "I think I would rather stay at home and marry Jofré's betrothed. She sounds more fun."

And now the Pope laughs. Because, for all his faults, he adores this high-spirited young man, who is so handsome, with such an appetite for life, and for women. And they for him.

"I heard that she had tutored her proxy as to how to behave at the betrothal." Juan grins, seizing the advantage to turn the talk away from lecturing.

The memory has them both laughing. With wedding fever in the air, the King of Naples has made his peace with the Pope and negotiations over Jofré's marriage have reached the betrothal stage. Such ceremonies are invariably dry affairs, the stand-ins for the participants acting like lawyers rather than lovers. But with Jofré so young—at eleven, it is his first official appearance—this one had an air of mischief from the start. So that when the young noble from Naples, standing in for the bride, fluttering his eyelashes and sending simpering little looks from behind his kerchief, had raised his voice falsetto high for the all-important "I do," the whole company had been reduced to gales of laughter. "If he'd been wearing a dress I would have made him an offer myself."

"And that, my son, is exactly the kind of talk that will not go down well in Spain," Alexander says with severity, though his heart is no longer in it. "I don't say these things just to hear my own voice. Sancia Aragon is an illegitimate daughter of the house of Naples: good enough for a political alliance but not for a royal dynasty. *You* carry the future of the family on your back, Juan. It is worth a little chivalry when you get into bed. As for the country—if you just open your eyes and feel the sun on your skin, you will understand its beauty soon enough. Come. We have little time left. Let's not spend it bickering."

The Pope and his second son embrace. In the last few months, Juan has grown taller than his father. He is doing his best: he has given up his Turkish robes and his lip is clean-shaven, though his body still has the gangling awkwardness of youth about it. While it will break Alexander's heart to see him go, even a besotted father can tell when the wine is too young in the barrel. Spain and the dictates of a fiercer court will help him mature and the boy he sends out will return a man.

When they say their final goodbyes two days later and Juan rides out past the Vatican palace and St. Peter's at the head of his troop, the crowd that gathers is smaller than he might like, but appreciative enough of another Borgia show. His boyish good looks attract as many catcalls from the women as the men, and he plays to the gallery, his pages throwing flowers and hand-kisses as they go. The Pope stands on the balcony watching, tears flowing unashamedly down his face. There is no crime in loving one's children. Nor in having a favorite son. In all his seventeen years, Juan has never been away from home. Alexander is gripped by a sudden anxiety. The world holds so many dangers. The journey to Spain may not be a voyage to the edge of the world, but it is far enough, and who knows when—or if—he will come back?

As soon as the procession is out of sight, he returns to his chamber. Looking out over the gardens and the lines of orange trees which offer their own reminder of Spain for a man who has not seen his birthplace for half a lifetime, he writes a letter, dispatching it with a fast rider to intercept them at the port of Civitavecchia.

My Dearest Son,
I write these words so that they stay with you always, to be read whenever you have need. A few final pieces of advice, and with them a pair of new kid gloves to wear constantly to keep your hands from the sun and the salt air, for as you know, the Spanish love above all things fair hands . . .

He has said it all before. Still, it takes away some of the ache of missing; the idea that, while his voice will die away, a letter might find its way close to his beloved son's heart.

Meanwhile, Lucrezia's marriage to Giovanni Sforza is not going well.

It is not for want of effort on her part—or indeed his. Almost every day since the ceremony the Duke of Pesaro has come dutifully from the house where he has taken temporary residence to visit his wife in the palace of Santa Maria in Portico next to the Vatican. Together they have shared meals, played games, even entertained sometimes. Their conversations have been full of topics: his home in Pesaro, his cousin the duke, her family, books, stories, all manner of fashions and fancies. She has smiled and laughed at things he says, most of which are not so funny, and he has complimented her on every new outfit she has worn, of which there are a great many.

Perhaps within a more traditional courtship, where marriage was yet to take place, all this might have been fruitful: a gradual move from shyness to glimpses of enjoyment, to the promise of something more . . . well, more physical. Alternatively, had there been enough magnetism between them to make obeying the rules as intoxicating as breaking them . . .

But this, alas, has not happened. Whatever the unconventional nature of her childhood, as an only daughter Lucrezia has grown up coddled and cosseted, her innocence a state of grace to be protected for as long as possible. While she has seen enough evidence of a woman's sexual power, she is still at the stage where trying on clothes is more exciting than taking them off. Alone with a man, she has no idea how to encourage him further, even if she thought such a thing was her role. No. She assumes the very fact of her presence is enough. It is not an assumption based on arrogance. Far from it—she is nervous underneath, but about what exactly she does not know.

There are men, of course, who would find this level of innocence enticing, its own aphrodisiac. Juan, for instance, has a reputation for coaxing virgin flesh out of fortress clothing. Sadly, Giovanni is not such a man. As the illegitimate child of a father who largely ignored him and relatives who only notice his existence when they want something out of him, he is no more the natural rake than she is the natural coquette. Like many men of breeding he was introduced to such matters by professional women, who knew what they were doing. His marriage had brought an early pregnancy, where his wife had suffered such chronic sickness that it was hard for her to be safely affectionate for more than a few minutes at a time, and after her death, which had affected him more than he would like to admit, he had lost the zest for conquest and more often than not had found solace in his own company.

Faced with this sweet, exuberant girl, with her hint of double chin, her endless rich frocks and her savagely powerful family, he has found himself almost too . . . well . . . *tired* to rise to the challenge.

Of course there have been moments—before Rome grew too hot and his debts started to mount (no consummation, no dowry). The accidental brushing of flesh against flesh at table or over a book, a certain hold in a dance, where her softness encountered his strength and her breathless little laugh made him feel suddenly potent, one particular afternoon when over a game of chess she had leaned forward to place her queen, her tongue caught between her teeth in unconscious, charming thought, unaware of the rising moons of her breasts, and he had suddenly been moved to slip out a hand to cup her head and bring it forward to his own. There, his lips had encountered those same sharp little teeth as an automatic portcullis, but not without the possibility of the gate lifting if pushed a little harder.

Unfortunately, it was this same moment when Adriana had chosen to walk into the room. They had leapt apart as if they had been on fire. It was hardly Adriana's fault. Her role was to offer them enough privacy to get to know each other while guaranteeing her niece's vital purity until the Pope himself had agreed it might go further. That afternoon she had not even been spying on them. But the possibility that she might strikes both of them. And no better opportunity presents itself.

Eventually the house starts to feel like enemy territory to Giovanni. It is, after all, also the home of the most lusted-after woman in Rome, who just happens to belong to his wife's father. However kind or courteous she herself is, Giulia's presence is a reminder of the potency, in all manner of ways, of his new father-in-law. On days after Alexander visits her, or she has been called to him, her room remains closed until far into the afternoon, after which she emerges, flowing languidly down the stairs into the salon, radiating an aura of deep satisfaction, but also giving off a clear message of *noli me tangere*. Adriana is at her beck and call, as are all the servants, not to mention the wet-nurses, who, giggling and shouting, follow little Laura as she crawls around the house, conquering the world around her with all the cloying sweetness of an adored first child. Santa Maria in Portico is a palace of skirts and there are times when Giovanni feels almost smothered by the weight of rustling silk or the smell of breast milk.

The only respite to this is the occasional visit by Cesare, when, as if by magic, everyone's behavior changes: Adriana becomes unctuous, Giulia subdued, almost angry, and Lucrezia lights up like an oil lamp under his wit and attention. Giovanni—bar the repeated mention of the splendor of his wedding jewelery—is ignored.

In late August things reach a quiet crisis. In the suffocating heat Lucrezia is finding it tedious, spending so many hours at her toilet for what seems like so little impact, and Giovanni is wrestling with the outstanding debt of his wedding expenses, alongside the mounting costs of keeping a second home in Rome with no sign of respite. His audience with the Pope, where he asks for five thousand ducats to tide him over, does nothing to boost his confidence. Alexander, busy dispatching Juan with a fleet of ships loaded with riches, has long since forgotten what it is like to run out of money, and finds it faintly distressing to discuss such matters. It is left hanging in the air. Finally, when the inevitable summer fever starts to bite and Giovanni announces that he is returning home to care for his own people, no one does much to stop him.

Once outside the city walls he finds the air much easier to breathe.

Lucrezia spends a few days moping, only to discover that her life is more engaging with the women gathered back together again. She plays with her enchanting baby half-sister, and starts entertaining ambassadors and suitors to the Pope again, men whose blandishments feel as fresh as if they have been minted that very morning by a clever court poet. But though she laughs and feels more alive again, she is plagued by a sense of discomfort, as if she has been tested and found wanting. She spends time in chapel, asking for help from Our Lady and also Saints Bridget and Perpetua, who as married women would understand the tribulations of earthly love. The advice she receives back is the same as she has given herself: that now she is no longer a child she must be ready to embrace the duties of womanhood. And so perhaps it is her fault that her husband does not seem to find her attractive.

"What did I do wrong?" she says at last to Giulia, some weeks after he has gone, when the day is particularly hot and they are sitting under the loggia in search of a hint of breeze.

"Oh, it is not you, Lucrezia. He is pleasant enough, but he is frightened of his own shadow. No woman can make a man love her unless he has an appetite for it."

"What do you mean?"

Giulia sighs. "It is . . . it is like a fire inside. You can see it in their eyes. In some men it burns so hot that it seems as if it must be constantly fed. I sometimes think it almost doesn't matter who the woman is. In others . . . well, in others the flame takes a certain fanning."

Lucrezia stares at her. She thinks of Cesare, then Juan, and the energy, or is it the heat, that glows out of them. And then she thinks of her father. Which kind of man is he? Only at the same time she does not want to know the answer.

"And Giovanni? What kind of fire did you see in his eyes?"

Giulia pauses, struggling with the formation of the thought. "I think Giovanni may be the kind of man who is more worried about burning himself. But these are silly notions. And you are not to worry, Lucrezia. In none of it are you to blame."

"What will happen to us then?" While there are only a few years between them, Giulia is so very much older. Will she herself ever be so wise?

Giulia shrugs. "Either he will become braver or you will meet someone else."

But we are married, Lucrezia thinks. How can there be someone else? "Is that how it was between you and Orsino?" she asks, because when it had all unfolded she had been too young and now, as a married woman herself, she feels she has the right.

"No, not exactly." Giulia laughs a little uncomfortably. "Your father . . . Your father, well, your whole family, they have a certain way of making the world behave as they would want it to, rather than how it is." And she laughs again.

"How strange. Cesare always says that we Borgias have more enemies than we have friends."

"Among men, perhaps. Not among women."

"I see," she says. Though really she does not. "Did you like him? Your husband, I mean. It is an age since you visited him."

"He is, he was—" She stops, as if she needs to reassess the question. "We have not been granted much time together."

"You sound sad about it."

"Oh, there is no point to being sad about what one cannot have," she says quietly.

But the confusion in her face shows that it is not so much an answer as a reflection of the trouble that the question causes her. Lucrezia watches for a moment, then leans over and embraces her. Maybe Giulia is not so wise after all.

Alexander has his hands too full with other concerns to immediately notice his daughter's distress. With Juan safely dispatched he must now turn his attention to Cesare. Managing his oldest son's future is a delicate business, constrained as it is by facts that contradict each other. The Sacred College of Cardinals is the mainstay of support or rebellion against a pope. To be effective the Pope needs to control it through his own appointments. If his son is to go higher in the Church, he must join its ranks. But Church law is Church law. No bastard can become a cardinal. And Cesare Borgia, as everyone knows, is quite clearly a bastard.

Alexander has had Church lawyers on the case for months, scrutinizing the dark alleyways of canon law, looking at the problem every which way. The solution, when it finally comes, does the job but pleases no one, particularly not Cesare himself.

"Domenigo da Rignano! I hardly remember him. What place did he ever hold in the world?"

"His place, as you know well, was to be married to your mother at the time you were born. I don't find it any more satisfying than you do. But if you are ever to become Pope you must first become a cardinal, and to become a cardinal you must be legitimate. It has all been approved. The papal bull we will issue states that Domenigo da Rignano is your legitimate father and therefore you, Cesare da Rignano, are eligible to be elevated to the Sacred College."

"But at the same time demoted from a Borgia to the laughingstock of Rome."

"You are still my son. Everybody knows that. It is only for the letter of Church law. The purpose of the second bull, which will be dated the day afterward in order to override the official one, makes clear your true parentage."

"But that one remains unpublished. No one will read it."

"Of course. For the first to work, the second must remain secret. Cesare, I have weathered enough storms of petulance and temper from your brother these last months. I need—no, I expect—better from you."

Cesare drops his eyes and stares at the ground. He stands so still that he appears frozen to the spot. The air around him however is alive with tension. Even his father knows better than to interrupt.

"You are right," he says finally, looking up. "There is no other way." He picks up the list of names on the table. "The cardinals will fight you over this, you know. They'll see it as an attempt to pack the College with foreigners and supporters."

"Of course. You think it's never happened before? Every pope does it. The only difference is that not every pope is foreign. But I have not chosen lightly. The Spaniards on the list are all good men and every other name has a pedigree."

"Giulia's brother, Alessandro Farnese?"

"Is a fine churchman."

"You know what they will call him?"

"Yes, yes, I know, the insult is there already: the petticoat cardinal. But those who coined it are fools. Farnese is no puppet, regardless of Giulia, my . . . of his sister."

"And fifteen-year-old Ippolito d'Este from Ferrara?"

Alexander lifts his hands in mock surrender. What else could I do? the gesture says. Sometimes one must take what one can get.

"You are sure you can make this work, Father?"

But if his sons favor their fists, there is nothing Rodrigo Borgia likes better than a high-class political brawl.

In the lead-up to the first meeting of the Sacred College of Cardinals, there is an unseemly rush of apologies from those unable to attend. While a few have legitimate reasons—the young Medici cardinal, for instance, is called to Florence, where his brother's position is grow-

ing more precarious—so many others are struck down by the summer
fever that it seems as if God has chosen to infect only cardinals this
year. "Illness," however, does not stop Cardinal della Rovere from hurling out a barrage of barbed remarks about corruption before keeling
over into his bed.

Alexander, in contrast, remains incandescent with health. And
fury. Over the intervening weeks between the two meetings he makes
clear his feelings to any churchman or diplomat who comes near him.
"There are men on this list who have given their lives for the well-being
and godliness of the Church. There are reformers, holy men and great
theologians from all over Europe. I will have them approved—every
single one of them—or by God, by Christmas there will be another list
even longer. We are surrounded by enemies. Not just inside Italy, but
elsewhere. If we are not united, we are nothing. I am the Pope and until
someone else sits on this throne, my voice will be listened to."

When the College meets again, the room is considerably fuller
than before. Twenty-one cardinals now attend. The atmosphere is
strained as the vote is counted. The result could not be closer. Eleven to
ten. In favor. It is hardly the glorious victory that Alexander might have
wished, but it is enough. With another thirteen of his own cardinals
now injected into the mix, he has taken control of the Sacred College.
And most particularly, the new young Cardinal of Valencia will be his
eyes, ears and voice.

That night he and Cesare dine together in the splendor of the new
apartments. His prayer of grace gives thanks to God for what they are
about to receive. The toast celebrates what he has already got: a daughter married into Milan, a son betrothed to Naples, a foothold in Spain
through a bona fide royal wife and, sitting in front of him, a nineteen-
year-old cardinal with a dazzling Church future in front of him.

Later, as he lowers his knees onto the cushioned stool near his bed
in order to offer further thanks to Mary, Holy Mother of God, he finds
he cannot stop smiling. Ah, the sin of pride. There are times when it is
a challenge even to ask forgiveness for it. But she, whose love and care
he has never doubted even in the bleakest of times, surely she will understand.

———

Like the best politicians, even when matters are going well Alexander has eyes in the back of his head, alert for anything that he is not meant to see. In the final days leading up to the second vote of the Sacred College, Rome has been awash with gossip, with foreign diplomats moving to and fro constantly, realigning their cardinals with the interests of their states. In particular, della Rovere, while too "ill" to attend, has been well enough to take a number of high-profile visits from the French ambassador.

No one, certainly not Alexander, is under any illusion as to what they are talking about. Della Rovere, who favored Naples as long as Milan favored the Pope, is now smelling considerable advantage in changing sides. The forces of opposition are shifting, making allies of former enemies and enemies of former friends. And the phrase "foreign invasion" is starting to move across people's lips.

Alexander sits ready for whatever is to come.

He does not have to wait long.

PART III

Invasion

*I may not be Italian, but I love Italy and
will not see her in any other hands.*

Pope Alexander VI, November 1494

*There is nothing but moaning and weeping.
In the memory of man the Church has never
been in such evil plight.*

Mantuan ambassador to the Vatican, 1495

Chapter 13

IN THE GREAT CASTLE OF NAPLES THAT LOOKS OUT FROM THE HAR-
bor over to the Mediterranean, King Ferrante of the House of Aragon
picks the coldest day of the year to die.

He has been in decline for a while. His gut has grown fat with a
protuberance that isn't food and which presses so heavily on his bowels
that he spends more time than any ruler can afford in the privy trying
to push it out. The less he expels, the more blood comes with it. His
doctors who examine the small black, matted lumps reassure him that,
whatever it is, it is breaking down and evacuating thanks to their potions. When the pains start to rack his lower body, they dither and
argue and prevaricate. Had he more energy he might have them strung
up for treachery—for he sees it everywhere, even in simple mistakes—
but by now he is too busy looking death in the face. It is not the first
time. As a young ruler he survived an assassin's knife and has kept his
throne through turmoil and rebellion. He has gambled his whole life
on stern government. Those who rebelled against him have died ago-
nizing deaths, those who remain loyal have been subject to suspicion
and capricious cruelty. If his court is grown harsh and louche, it is because of his own moral equivocation feeding into the attitudes of those
who dance attendance. Those who come to write the history might say
that the House of Aragon, Spanish by descent, has given in to Italian
decadence and so deserves all that might follow such a man's death.

Burchard, when he hears the news, sums it up with unexpected
poetry. "The King of Naples died without light, without the cross, without God."

Alexander is at dinner with guests in his private apartments when the messenger arrives. He gets rid of them fast. It is too late for him to address the state of King Ferrante's soul, but the crisis which his death unleashes is very much papal business. Within the week the Vatican will be a madhouse of diplomats and spies, but now, for a few hours he can keep his own counsel. It is one of the greatest luxuries a pope can afford himself.

"I want no disturbance unless I ask for it, do you understand?"

The young servant moves silently around the bedchamber, filling the wine jug, loading the fire with wood and covering his master's shoulders with his winter cape lined with sable to keep out the night drafts, then kneeling to kiss the Pontiff's feet before he moves backward out of the room. As the Pope's personal shadow it is his job to be invisible, and by the time he leaves his master is already deep in thought.

Though Alexander's job tonight is to rise to the challenge of the future, he can draw strength from the way he has handled the past. His policy of balancing Milan and Naples against each other has, up until now, worked brilliantly. These two lumbering states have been playing a power game since long before his papacy, with the most efficient chess pieces coming from their own families. Why risk using an army when a daughter or son will do? So five years ago, when Ferrante married his granddaughter off to the young Sforza heir, he had had every reason to think she would eventually become Duchess of Milan. He had bargained without the thug Ludovico Sforza, the boy's guardian uncle, who had usurped the power and then encouraged the French claim on Naples as his way of keeping Ferrante off his back. It was an unscrupulous, cunning and quite brilliant move, but only as long as it stayed threat rather than reality.

Alexander himself has milked it for everything he can get. On the one hand, by resisting the claim, he can set himself up as the savior of Italy, while at the same time using the fear of French invasion to bring Naples to heel. As in many things, the secret—instinct rather than ideology—is pragmatism, working with what is rather than what might be. And with the betrothal of young Jofré to Ferrante's granddaughter the rewards had started to flow.

But the news of the king's death changes the game radically. Because while there is an heir in waiting—a son who has wasted his life in anticipation of his father's death—there is also, temporarily, an empty throne.

He opens his mouth in a huge yawn, stretching his arms up inside his voluminous sleeves to counteract the growing numbness of sitting in the same position. An empty throne. Fortuna. The goddess of chance. The wheel of fortune. The throw of the dice that no one can predict. If the French king really wants to take Naples, now would be the time for him to go for it. With a big enough army no one, not even the Pope, could stop him.

Except . . . He stretches again and now registers the satisfying sound of a small crack somewhere inside his shoulder. Ah, the pleasure of release.

Except for one thing. Fortuna. One man's fall is another's man rise. Because Ferrante's death hands him, Alexander, an unexpected bargaining card. Naples, in every other way an independent state, is, by historical accident, a suzerainty of the papacy. Which means that for its ruler to be recognized by Christendom each and every king must be formally invested by the Pope. In other words, the blessing of Alexander VI is up for sale. What may be a risk for Italy is also, for the Borgias, an opportunity.

A smile starts to play around his lips. Across the lintel of the fireplace, his papal name is picked out in perfectly chiseled stone. Inside the grate, the lower layer of wood collapses noisily in on itself, sending out a firestorm of sparks. He watches as the flames move in on the new thick logs, searching for splits and holes to get their burning tongues inside. Once they catch hold there will be no stopping them.

"Your Holiness, I am here to tell you that your daughter is unhappy. She wanders around the palace and can barely find the energy to sit at her needlework for more than half an hour at a time. It is as if everything is too much effort."

Alexander's face creases with concern. From high politics to family drama: sometimes there is so little time for prayer. "What is it? What ails her?"

"Oh, my!" Adriana allows herself a little roll of the eyes. Though she worships him as Pope and family, he is also a man. "I may speak freely, yes?"

"I would be astonished if you did not, Adriana," he says mildly.

"She is married, but without a husband. From being the center of attention, admired and loved by everyone at the wedding, she now sits alone in the house waiting for a man who, as far as I—as she—can see, has no intention of coming back."

"Ah, I understand. In which case you will be pleased to know that we are in contact with the Duke of Pesaro and, as we speak, he is ordered back to Rome to join his family and take his bride as his wife."

"Oh!" Adriana, who has come prepared to say much more, is taken aback. "I am . . . delighted. I . . . I did not think you had noticed."

"Well." He waves his hand carelessly, as if the credit is not worth the taking. In a perfect world he would let the pouting duke stew a little longer—Lucrezia is not yet fifteen, and he has taken against his son-in-law's spinelessness. But in this new political climate Milan and the Sforzas have to be kept sweet, at least until things turn sour, and to delay the consummation of the marriage any further would, as Cardinal Sforza himself has made clear, be taken as a gross insult.

Under the flowery language of courtesy, Alexander's letter to his son-in-law is crystal clear. You want the dowry? You had better come and get it.

"Tell me, child, how would you feel if your husband was to return?" He is gentler when it comes to Lucrezia.

"Giovanni? I . . . I don't know."

"What? You do not like him?"

". . . No, I like him well enough. Well, the little that I know." She hesitates. Her father is even busier these days, and this visit is both unannounced and unexpected. "I think more he does not like me."

"Nonsense. I am sure he misses you terribly."

"Papà. You do not need to make me feel better. The fact is he could not wait to get away."

"Oh, his leaving was not to do with you. The burdens of finance weigh heavy on a prince and he had business to attend to at home. But he is eager now to return."

"Is this his decision or yours?"

He opens his mouth to lie, but the simple honesty of the question confounds him. "Ah . . . my dear Lucrezia, we are all bound by forces stronger than ourselves."

She nods, as if this is as much as she needs to know. "And when he comes back, where will he live?"

"If it is amenable to you, he will live here with you in the palace." He pauses. He had been intending to leave this to Adriana, for these things are women's business, but . . . "You understand what I am saying, child. You will be husband and wife."

"Yes, of course. I understand." She feels a flush in her face and drops her eyes. "So," she says after a little silence. "So, I will truly be the Duchess of Pesaro. Does that mean that I will go there?"

"To Pesaro? That may happen, yes. Would you like that?"

"I don't know. I have never been anywhere but here. Perhaps. Yes . . . I think perhaps I would."

Little Lucrezia, so young still. He has not bargained on losing her so soon. "Then I am sure it can be arranged." He takes her cheek in his thumb and forefinger and squeezes gently. With so much politicking there has been less time for the pleasures of family. Well, once this is over . . . "For now though you will set up house here, and you will be a wife that any man on earth would be proud of."

"Better than Juan has been a husband, you mean," she says, with sudden mischief.

"Ah, your brother!" He snorts. "If my hair had not been white already he would have turned it so overnight."

Before Naples imploded, it had been the news from Spain that had seen him raging about his private chambers: Juan, despite all advice to the contrary, had been found night-crawling around the Spanish streets and brothels while his new wife was tucked up in bed waiting for him. Alexander's letters had scorched the pouch of the messenger who delivered them. But he has forgiven him everything with the news that not only is his wife now bedded, but that her seamstresses are busy letting out the gathering on her skirts. A grandchild already. Ah, the potency of his sons!

Alexander smiles. "You will have to hurry to catch up with him now, my dearest." And he opens his arms for her to come inside.

This time around there are no parties, no rich dinners, no ambassadors and, perhaps most important, no wedding-night ceremony with the closest relatives accompanying the couple as far as the marital bed. The not-so-newlyweds will be left to consummate their bond in private.

Perhaps because he knows this, Giovanni sets out from Pesaro in more confident mood. He remains largely ignorant of the machinations going on behind the scenes. As far as he is concerned, Milan is riding high, he has stood out for what he wants, and his determination has achieved it. He travels fast and arrives smiling. It makes him almost handsome. He, Giovanni Sforza, will be somebody in Rome now. And a much richer man by the morning. He kisses his wife and gives her a garland of herbs and winterberries picked from the walled garden in his ducal palace. "It is too early for flowers," he says. "But when you come to meet your people you will eclipse all blossom anyway."

Lucrezia, who is so nervous that she has to curb a desire to laugh, curtsies sweetly. "My lord, welcome to your home."

That night, in lieu of the public bedding, Adriana passes by the closed door a couple of times before she retires to bed. The noises that filter through the door seem promising enough. She is not so cynical or so old that she doesn't remember her own wedding night. The most important thing is to be prepared. As surrogate mother she had used the plainest of terms. No point in frills and courtly fancies. Lucrezia had thanked her and smiled sweetly; as if she had perhaps known it all along. Well, so be it. Before she left, Adriana had been plagued with the sudden desire to say more; those things she might have liked her own mother to have offered. "Don't worry. It is not so hard, this joining of the flesh. Yes, it is true that you will never be quite the same. And yet you will not be so very changed either. What is strange or distasteful soon becomes familiar. Almost routine." She might have added, "And though some men seem never able to get enough of it, there are women who never understand what all the fuss is about." Because, if she is honest, that is how she had felt. She had left the room with it unsaid.

In the morning, after Giovanni has left for a hunting engagement, she visits her niece in her bedroom. Lucrezia is still in bed. She looks almost happy.

"So, my dear? You are man and wife."

"I . . . yes, yes," she says. "We are."

In the silence that follows neither of them can think of anything more to say.

It is true that something has changed between the two of them. Now when they pass in the house they smile at each other. He might put his arm on hers at dinner, or reach out and touch her cheek. She blushes but her eyes are bright, and sitting at games together there is chatter, even laughter. Tailors come to measure him for robes. He talks with the vintner about the order of wines from his home vineyards and is in touch with his ex-brother-in-law in Mantua about the purchase of an Arab stallion. As well as a wife, he now has a substantial purse.

When he goes to pay his respects to the Pope, he stands tall in new clothes. Alexander, who would like to believe that he has done right by his daughter, allows himself to be impressed.

"Welcome to our family."

Giovanni sinks to his knee and kisses the papal ring. "I am here to serve."

After that much dowry I should hope so, Alexander thinks despite himself, as he gestures to him to rise.

During all this time, Cesare is nowhere to be seen. He had been on an extended hunting trip in Subiaco at the moment of Giovanni's arrival, and when he returns he makes it his business to visit his father, but not his sister. When they do finally meet, at a wedding of one of the Roman families, he comes late and sits at another table. When Lucrezia sees him there, she is the one to make the journey across the room to greet him, pulling him up and embracing him.

"Where have you been all this time?"

He holds her to him tightly, then pushes her away, but keeps hold of her arm. "How are you, little sister?"

"I—I am fine," she says. Then with mock-sternness: "You have been most remiss in not visiting."

He shrugs. "I have been busy with Church affairs." He glances across the room to where Giovanni sits, intent in conversation. "So, you are properly married."

"Yes."

His gaze slips back toward her husband. As if feeling it, Giovanni now turns and their eyes meet.

"And . . . he does nothing to displease you?" He looks back at her.

"No . . . no." She drops her eyes. His hand stays in place so that she cannot move away.

"Cesare?" She looks up again. "Everything is as it should be. He is my husband. You don't need to worry." She takes his hand off her arm and squeezes it, giving him a bright smile. It is as if she is helping him. "Come and sit with us."

"In a while, perhaps. I have business with some of the men here."

At the other end of the room, Adriana has been watching the encounter. For over ten years she has done her best to care for all of her cousin's children. Cesare, though, she has never understood. Such self-containment in a boy so young made her nervous. It seemed as if he cared for no one and nothing. Except perhaps his sister. With her he had always been different.

"Cesare," Adriana says to him later, when their paths cross after dinner. "You do not need to be worried on Lucrezia's account. You know I will always look after her."

"What? Like you looked after your own son?"

Chapter 14

Inside the Vatican, the great diplomatic game now unfolds just as Alexander predicted it.

No sooner is Ferrante's body under marble than the Neapolitan envoys start to arrive. Alexander sits in his receiving room, listening with studied concentration. Each one brings a further communication from Alfonso, Ferrante's son, the heir apparent. He is, as ever, the Pope's most humble servant. He is also filled with generosity and largesse, eager to unload all manner of titles and lands on his putative son-in-law Jofré and his brothers. All he wants in return is a date for his coronation. After a while the tone grows desperate.

France, for her part, is equally solicitous. Or some might say duplicitous. The real business is not invasion, no! Perish the thought. Rather it is a crusade against the infidels, with Naples a necessary staging post on the way east. How could the Pope not support such a godly mission? Alexander has trouble keeping a straight face as they talk. But it is serious enough underneath and there are times when Vatican officials have to police the flow in the antechambers; when states are on the verge of war, it is important for the ambassadors to remain above the fray.

For the first weeks Alexander is beside himself with the pleasure of it all: to be so courted, so tempted and cajoled. He has waited a long time for such power. But he is not so dazzled that he does not see the deeper significance of what is happening, and by early spring the balancing act can no longer be sustained. His choice is stark. Either he agrees to Alfonso's coronation and offends Milan, or he cuts off Naples and feeds it to the French. He spends the night in prayer. God's voice, through the intercession of the Blessed Virgin, tells him what the politician in him already knows: that whatever he might stand to gain from playing one against the other, the prospect of a foreign army marching through Italy can bring only instability and devastation in its wake for all. He is, it seems, the Church's shepherd after all.

He calls for Burchard. After an hour in his company, the long-suffering Master of Ceremonies retires to his book-lined office to start work choreographing another challenging ceremony on the Pope's behalf: this time the investiture of Alfonso as ruler of Naples, followed swiftly by the official marriage of the new king's daughter, Sancia, to the Pope's youngest son. The Neapolitan ambassador is informed that afternoon, but is told to keep his glee to himself for a few days.

Next morning Alexander dispatches a golden rose to the King of France.

"It has been newly blessed by my own hand this Laetare Sunday," he says as he hands the fat golden stalk with its elaborate gold sculpted blossoms to the French ambassador. "As a symbol of our dear Lord's majesty beyond the agony of the cross, it is the greatest gift we can bestow on a ruler whose friendship we so much value, for it speaks of union and love. You will note the wondrous art of construction in the top rose. When His Majesty holds it in his hand he can open the top blossom to smell the balm and balsam that was poured in, once again by my own hand."

The ambassador, who knows exactly what is going on, takes the rose and flips the lid off the bud. His nose lifts high into the air; but whether this is the impact of the perfume or a show of diplomatic disdain it is hard to tell. Alexander's smile grows wider at the sight.

By the end of the week the news is everywhere and, in his palace next to the Vatican, Giovanni is starting to feel familiar stomach pains. He seeks an audience with his father-in-law.

"Are you happy with my daughter?" Alexander purrs menacingly. While he has been expecting him, he is impatient: he does not need this nervous minnow clouding up the water, when the lake is so full of sharks.

"Oh yes, Your Holiness. Most happy. However, I am wondering . . ."

"What? Tell me."

"Well, it seems that relations with my . . . my family . . . are not so easy now."

"Your family? But you are graciously accepted into ours now."

He hesitates "Yes . . . only—"

"Only what?"

"I am a paid officer in the army of Milan."

"Ah, you are right. How clever of you to remind me." He smiles. If Giovanni knew him better he would read the signs. "I will look into a post for you within the papal forces, as befits your considerable expertise in military matters. It will come with a salary, of course."

"No, no. That is not it."

The Pope pauses. "Then what is it, dear son-in-law?"

"I . . . I am wondering what will happen in the future."

"The future? Of course. It is frustrating. I may be God's vicar on earth but even I cannot see what is not yet come. We shall just have to pray and await it together." He is no longer smiling. "So? Was there anything else?"

Giovanni opens his mouth, but in his gut the biting starts.

"Er . . . no . . . Not as such."

"Then I expect my dear Lucrezia would like you back for the evening."

After he goes Alexander sits for a moment. What a sniveler the man has turned out to be. He never liked him, and it is clear the marriage has brought his daughter no pleasure, which in turn brings him pain. But until they have negotiated the political rapids to come there is nothing he can do.

Easter week arrives, unseasonably cold, and Alexander puts on his ceremonial robes and leads his city in mourning and then jubilation. During the processions through the streets he is tireless, making sure to greet and talk to many in the crowd. His head may be full of politics, but he understands the need for the shepherd to be with his flock.

On Good Friday he and the dignitaries of Church and state attend a Passion play inside the ancient Colosseum. The spectacle is a recent addition to the religious calendar and everyone in Rome, rich and poor, is entranced by it. The cast is huge, with young nobles of the great families dressed in Roman costume competing to take part, playing soldiers and citizens of Jerusalem. It begins in daylight, the great stone amphitheater packed with spectators, and ends with a man strapped to a cross in the middle of the arena as the sun goes down and the torches flare up. To relive the suffering of Our Lord in a place where the very first martyrs gave up their blood for the faith offers a double poignancy, and in the papal box, where the Pope sits with his entourage, as comfortable as any emperor, it is Alexander himself who leads the weeping. The sound of moaning and crying spreads out in waves through the audience. The emotion leaks out onto the street and that night there are incidents in the Jewish Quarter, gangs of young Christian men wreaking vengeance for the crimes of ancestors. Eventually Alexander sends in the papal guard to restore order, but he understands better than most what is happening here. When there is fear about the future, it is comforting to take it out on outsiders who can be blamed for the past.

From unsettled, the weather becomes downright fractious. Amid torrential rain, Burchard leaves Rome for the hazards of the road. Jofré and a bedraggled wedding party follow. In lieu of the Pope himself, the investiture will be done by his cousin, Cardinal Juan Borgia Lanzo. There is nothing to be gained from being coy: Naples is now a family affair.

The rain and storms follow them south, making mudslides of the roads and prolonging the journey. Alexander paces his chambers, waiting. Eventually news comes that the deed is done. Alfonso, having bowed to every demand, including total fealty to the papacy, is crowned king, and Jofré and Sancia are man and wife.

Alexander's delight is muted by reading a further, secret dispatch that arrives soon after. While the lovely Sancia was duly impressed by the trunks of clothes and gems that were flung open in front of her, it appears that she hadn't bothered to conceal her disappointment with the pimply adolescent who brought them. It was common court gossip that there was only one virgin in the couple's marriage bed that night, and that young Jofré had found the whole thing so overwhelming he cried like the twelve-year-old child he still is. When he reads this the Pope has tears of fury in his eyes. Well, such humiliation will cost Naples dear. Both Jofré and Juan are now lords of large territorial lands inside the state, while Cesare is showered with new benefices. One way or another, the union between the two families is satisfactorily consummated.

Cardinal della Rovere, who has effectively removed himself from Rome by retreating to his coastal fortress at Ostia, now uses this moment to set sail for France. It is a clear sign of brewing rebellion from inside the Church. In Paris he is welcomed by the pinheaded king, Charles VIII. Like many young monarchs he is attracted to the glamour of war, though he is also fond of his court comforts and the Alps are a strenuous climb even if one is being carried.

The king and the cardinal spend days closeted together, della Rovere eloquent on the wonders of making history and the glory of pleasing God in the process. At times he grows so excited that his arguments seep out of the palace to the world beyond.

When the messengers arrive back in Rome, no one, not even Cesare, goes into the Pope's chambers for a while. The essence of della Rovere's attack is personal: accusations against the character of Alexander, the corruption of the Holy See, and the pressing need for a great council of reform.

The battle for Naples is becoming a battle for the future of the papacy itself.

Wet spring turns to boiling summer. The Pope and Cesare meet with King Alfonso and his generals and agree on a strategy for the defeat of the foreign enemy. It would be more convincing if their alliance were not so isolated. The Venetian ambassador offers fighting talk but everyone—including Milan—knows that it will never lead to action. Venice did not gain an empire on the seas by wasting her money fighting for land that she has no interest in owning. Meanwhile, worse is happening in Florence, where the Medici are losing their grip on the city thanks to a mad Dominican monk whose sermons pour rivers of hot lava down onto both Pope and government, prophesying the cleansing of Italy through the might of a foreign sword. In Rome many of Alexander's own cardinals now find it safer to express their opinions on the matter only to God. Uncertainty is more contagious than the plague.

Cesare, in contrast, believes in strategy, not prayer. He knows he is his father's closest adviser and, as family, the only one he really trusts. In private, he rails against the impotency of a papacy which owns chunks of central Italy but rents it out for pocket money to half-baked tyrants and imbeciles with as much loyalty as a sack of rats. Had his father been Pope for longer . . . Had he not been forced to spend his life in church . . . Next time . . . If there is to be a next time.

For once in his life Giovanni Sforza, one of those same half-baked tyrants and imbeciles, manages to translate his churning bowels into political strategy. It is possibly his finest hour.

"I understand how deeply preoccupied you are, Your Holiness, but as I'm sure you know, summer fever is on the move again through the city."

"And you're worried you might catch it," Cesare murmurs sweetly from his chair at the side of the room.

"My worry is not for myself, but for your sister, my beloved wife," he replies firmly, ignoring the sarcasm. If he turns his head sharply enough toward the Pope he can cut Cesare out of his vision altogether. "I have to tell you one of the servants in the palace has been taken ill with it."

"When?" Alexander, who has not had the time to visit either of his favorite women for a while now, is immediately anxious. Roman fever can kill within the time it takes a doctor to find his way to a house.

"A few days ago."

"I should have been told!" he roars. "Why was I not told? He or she must be expelled and my daughter and her women need to leave the city."

"It is already seen to. The servant is gone and the packing is begun. The only question is where, given the . . . the situation." He pauses, but not long enough for Cesare to interrupt. "I have what I believe is the answer, Your Holiness. With your permission I will take my wife to Pesaro. It has a good climate, healthier than Rome, and it has been a year since she became the duchess, so her formal introduction to her city is long overdue."

"Pesaro? How long would you stay?"

"I had thought perhaps, until things become . . . well, quieter here. She will enjoy the city and its people. As they will her, I am sure. And as the duke I would be remiss in my duty to delay their meeting any longer."

"And what about your duty to the Pope whose state you govern on his behalf?" retorts Cesare. "Or are you perhaps planning to spend half your time in Milan?"

Alexander throws his son a sharp glance. You are not needed in this conversation, it says.

Giovanni sees it, and slips in fast. "I am not speaking of myself, you understand, only my wife," he says, again addressing only the Pope. "I shall escort her, settle her in and, of course, return if and when you need me to serve in my military capacity. Meanwhile the duchess and her household will remain safe, healthy and protected for as long as they wish."

There is a small silence in the room.

"And my daughter is aware of this plan, yes?"

Giovanni is so pleased now he cannot help beaming.

"Oh yes, Your Holiness, she certainly is. And excited too. I think you will find she is as eager to meet her subjects as they are to meet her."

"It seems my son-in-law has balls after all."

"I look forward to cutting them off. Did you see him sweating? Sweet Jesus, I think—"

"I know what you think, Cesare. And so does he now, if he was ever in any doubt. What is wrong with you? We do not speak of anything that affects our security outside of the family, you know that."

"I'm sorry. I lost my temper."

"So I see. Yet he is no more a fool than many others that you manage to keep it with."

"He is a fool who is husband to my sister."

"Ha . . ." Alexander smiles grimly. "Yes, that is one thing you were right about. I should have married her elsewhere."

"So put him on the battlefield. I promise you he won't survive it."

"No," he says sharply. "It is not the right moment." He stares at him. There are things growing in his son that he does not recognize, things he has never taught him. "One enemy at a time, Cesare. One enemy at a time."

"I still say he will betray us."

"What is there to betray? We barely know what we are doing ourselves."

"He will know about troop movements in the Romagna, and if the French get close to Naples—"

"If they get that far they won't need any help from him."

"What, you think it possible?"

"There is no point in naïveté. When they come, *if* the Neapolitan fleet beat off their ships, *if* we ruffle Ludovico's feathers in Milan, *if* Virginio Orsini stays loyal as the general of Alfonso's armies around Rome, then we stand a chance."

Cesare waits. "And if not?" he asks at last.

"If not?" Alexander's eyes rest for a moment on his own likeness, now captured faithfully, even unflatteringly, by Pinturicchio in the lunette above the door: Pope Alexander VI staring up in devotion toward the risen Christ. How the gold on his papal robes catches fire in the sunlight. The decoration of the Room of Mysteries is almost complete. All it lacks is the scene of the Annunciation; with the figures of the angel and his beloved Mary already marked out on the back wall. Ah, it is everything he could have wished for and it has cost him a small fortune. It does not bear thinking about what would happen to all this beauty if Naples falls and della Rovere manages to force another papal conclave. "If not, we shall just have to outwit them by other means."

"And so we will." Cesare's voice resounds like a bell. "We did not climb this high to fall so quickly, Father. God Himself would not allow it."

God. The word sounds almost strange in his son's mouth.

"Why was I not told there was fever in the house?"

There are packing cases everywhere. "You are not easy to get to talk to these days, Your Holiness." Adriana holds her ground. "She will be ready to leave within a few days."

"Oh yes. And where is she going?"

She hesitates.

"Pesaro perhaps?" he prompts.

She holds his gaze. "Rome is a stew on the boil. Pesaro will be safer than many cities and she is its duchess. If she is to find a place in her life, then let it be there. For now at least."

"Hmmm. Well, she cannot go alone. You will go too, to oversee the journey and settle her in."

"Of course, you think I would desert her?" She pauses.

"Yes. Yes? You have something more to say to me, Adriana?" he says. "Go on—say it."

"What about Giulia . . . ?"

"I do not want to leave you, my lord." That night, for the first time in weeks, they lie together. He stares at her in the candlelight; her eyes are soft with love. Is it true, or simply what she feels she must say? With so much politicking going on in his head, he is beginning to doubt everyone. "I have lived through plagues before."

"That is no guarantee you will live through this one. The summer is wet as well as hot. I cannot take the risk. Rome is not a city for pleasure these days."

"It is true that I barely see you now." She drops her head to one side as if to look at him better and her hair falls and swirls around her. "But Pesaro is so far away. Perhaps I could go somewhere closer. To my family in Capodimonte?"

"No," he says immediately. "If the French invade by the west it will be directly on the route they will take."

"I will not be gone that long. Just till the fever fades."

"Nevertheless, Pesaro would be better," he says again.

She sighs. "Well, Rome without Lucrezia and Adriana will be a most boring place." She smiles sweetly and just for a second it seems to him that perhaps she does not fight so hard to stay after all.

Once the task of packing up the household is complete, the great caravan of horses and carts sets out from Rome amid the usual tearful farewells of the Pope. He sends a cohort of troops to accompany them, but at the last moment Cesare insists that a few of his own handpicked men ride with them as far as the edge of the papal states. While it is a thinly veiled attack on his ability to look after his wife, Giovanni knows better than to refuse it.

Remembering that his sister does not welcome Michelotto, he gives Pedro Calderón the job of liaising directly with the women. It is a happy choice, as young Pedro already knows the household, having been the messenger for the palace letters for many months. Only now he has reason to come into the presence of the Duchess Lucrezia herself.

As she is busy their meeting is brief. But that does not lessen its sweetness for him. They stand amid a roomful of chests, last-minute things that are "essential" for them to take with them.

"You are most kind to be so patient." Lucrezia looks around, distracted. She has buried her anxiety with organization, but is finding the actual leaving upsetting. "It seems there is always more . . ."

"Please. Do not concern yourself. It is my duty and my deep pleasure to be of any service." The words are so full of feeling and then he bows so low and stays there so long that she cannot help but be amused.

"I believe our paths have crossed before. You work for my brother the cardinal, yes?"

"Yes."

"You delivered our letters to him when he was in Spoleto, isn't that true?"

"Yes, yes, my lady, it is."

"I thought I recognized you." She smiles. "And your name is?"

"Calderón. Pedro Calderón."

"Well, Pedro Calderón, my aunt says you ride like the devil with the face of an angel. I am not sure of that, but you are much nicer to look at than that man who usually guards my brother. Though I daresay you are both equally brave."

"In the service of your ladyship you will find none braver," he says, his face flushing pink like a fast rash. "I mean, that is, both of us."

Which amuses her even more.

"Then I hope my life is such that I never have need of such bravery. Tell me, have you ever been to Pesaro?"

"No, no, my lady." He hesitates. "But I have heard that it is a fine city."

"What else have you heard?"

He shrugs his shoulders. "That they are looking forward to greeting their radiant new duchess."

"Oh, but you are a flatterer as well as a warrior, Señor Calderón." She laughs. "Well, I have never been anywhere but Rome. So I am looking forward to it also . . . I think . . . Though I fear leaving my family here with the winds of war around us."

"You are not to worry. Nothing will happen to them. That I promise you." He pauses. "But when all this is over you will return home, I hope. Rome will be a much grayer place without you."

"Thank you." She stares at him. It is the language of common chivalry, the kind she encounters every day from ambassadors and courtiers, yet there is something in its delivery that brings pinpricks of tears to her eyes. Ah, it must be the excitement of the day.

She gives him a bright smile as the room fills up with servants and the business of packing takes over.

Chapter 15

THE BIGGER THE ARMY, THE LONGER IT TAKES TO GET ITSELF ON THE road. Then there is the matter of a mountain range to be negotiated. Summer is ending when Charles VIII and his thirty thousand men, accompanied by Cardinal della Rovere, cross the northwest alpine passes and pour down into Italy.

Like a slow avalanche, they envelop everything in their path. For the first few hundred miles the only conflict is whether they'll find enough food and wine to fill their bellies on the way. In the city of Asti, where the rivers run with sweet sparkling wine, the king falls sick with a bout of smallpox. Though no one would notice a few more eruptions (even those who admire him agree he is one of the ugliest young men ever to ascend a throne), he rests for a few days. It's here that news arrives of the decisive French victory over the Neapolitan fleet at Rapallo. By the time the army reaches Milan it feels as if they have already won the war.

In Rome, Alexander's peace of mind is starting to fracture. He sleeps badly, pacing his bedchamber at night while his servant keeps his eyes propped open, ready for the next demand. With the lack of sleep his temper grows shorter so that everyone, even Burchard, who is usually impervious to moods, tiptoes around him. It is understandable: the kind of behavior one might expect from a man under severe strain. Yet it has little to do with the invasion of the French. No, for Alexander this is more a crisis of the heart.

A few weeks before, his golden-haired Giulia had left Pesaro for her family home, north of Rome, where her eldest brother had been taken gravely ill. The news comes so fast that she is already on the move by the time the Pope learns of it. A dying man's need for a last goodbye: what possible objection could the head of the Church have to such a mission of charity and duty? Only one: the Farnese estate is within easy access of Bassanello, the home of her husband, Orsino Orsini.

The brother dies, the family mourns and time passes. Alexander bombards her with requests to come home. She answers pliantly enough but does not leave. He demands again. She resists. Away from Rome, the taste of independence is unexpectedly sweet. And while her husband's eyes may not always point in the same direction, they are nevertheless full of love for her. Adriana, who has accompanied her, is now also caught between feelings for her son and obedience to the Pope. The situation grows tense. It is made more complex by the fact that while Adriana is a Borgia, her son is also an Orsini. The Orsinis' loyalty to Naples means that for once they are the Borgias' allies, and their support is vital to the war. It is, in all kinds of ways, a delicate situation. Even Giulia's own brother, Alessandro, who owes his cardinal's robes to the petticoat connection, stands firm, suggesting mediation rather than confrontation and warning Alexander against the possible public scandal.

Plagued by his political impotence, Alexander starts to smell conspiracy everywhere and it incenses him further. God's emissary on earth, he is at the mercy both of an invading army and a recalcitrant mistress. He diverts his frustration from one into the other. He will have Giulia back or the devil take them all. *Treacherous and thankless Giulia.* His letter explodes into her lap. *We cannot believe that you would act toward us with such ingratitude and perfidy, risking your life by going to Bassanello with the purpose, no doubt, of surrendering yourself once more to that . . . that stallion . . .* From Adriana he demands penance and threatens excommunication. He is, after all, the Pope.

Still the two women do not set out for Rome. Within weeks he is ready to excommunicate them all. He calls Burchard to start the proceedings. Burchard listens, takes notes and does not say a word.

Cesare, watching from the wings, becomes too exasperated to stay silent any longer.

"You know the gossip among the diplomats, Father?"

"No, I don't," he says bluntly. He is tired and in no mood to be lectured by his son. "Nor do I care."

"That Rome is about to be attacked, but all the Holy Father cares about is getting back his whore. They don't even need to embellish the truth to make it sting. It is a gift of ammunition to della Rovere and he will use it against you sevenfold."

"What, you think he hasn't had women enough of his own? You ask your mother about his poxy cardinal's appetite."

"My mother?"

"Ah!" He makes a dismissive gesture. "Everyone knew about his roaming prick."

"At least he didn't mix it with politics."

"This *is* politics!" he roars. He knows, of course, that he is behaving badly. That it is neither clever nor dignified for a man of his age to suffer such heartache. But for reasons he barely understands himself, this . . . this passion for Giulia has become almost a passion for life itself, so that without her he fears that his energy might be draining away. "My authority is questioned and I am being mocked. How could she prefer that monkey to me?"

"That 'monkey' is her husband."

"Only because I arranged the marriage. He would never have had her otherwise. Giulia Farnese is mine. I found her and she has always belonged to me." He waves his hands extravagantly. "You are too young to understand the power of the connection between a man and a woman."

And you are too old to still suffer from it, Cesare thinks. Or at least to let it show so brazenly.

From somewhere outside he hears the noise of movement. Though they argue in Catalán, instant translations are making it on to the streets.

"With respect, Holy Father, we have more important things to do than row about women," he says quietly, moving across the room. "You give sound advice about not acting on anger. I simply offer it back to you now." And he opens the door quickly to find Burchard standing directly on the other side, a sheaf of papers in his hand and behind him a few open-mouthed apprentices supposed to be grinding paint for the half-finished walls. In his cups, Prince Djem boasts of a tradition in the sultan's palace, where the tongue is cut out from any man who has access to the sultan's inner chambers. He is a mischief maker as well as a storyteller, Djem, but that does not mean he doesn't sometimes tell the truth. Cesare takes a step toward the boys and they scatter like startled deer.

"Your Excellency Cardinal of Valencia," the German says, impassive as ever. "There is news from Florence. I thought it important enough to—"

"Interrupt us. And I am sure it is." Cesare switches loudly into Italian to greet him. "Your Holiness. Would you like me to leave you?" He turns, bowing to the Pope. It is a thin veil of formality, but one they take care to adhere to in public.

"No. Your presence is still required. Whatever the news, our closest cardinals must be kept informed."

Alexander takes the dispatch and reads for a few moments in silence. When he looks up his face is grave, but alive once more. "It seems Florence is no longer an ally. Piero de' Medici has fled and the government is in the hands of the monk Savonarola. He has given the French leave to pass through the city on their way south."

The two other men drop their eyes to the ground. Without Florence, all that stands between them and the French army are the castles of the Orsini. If the Pope's mistress doesn't get back soon, she may not get back at all.

Alexander shakes his head. "God save us from the treachery of mad monks. The messenger is waiting, yes? Tell him there will be a reply within the hour. And I will need other riders too."

"The scribe is outside. I will send him in now." Burchard looks, if possible, impressed.

"You are dining with your mother, tonight, yes?" Alexander says as soon as the door closes.

Cesare nods.

"Tell her to have her things packed and ready. There will be rooms put aside for her in Castel Sant' Angelo. I will send an armed guard when the time comes."

"And the other women?" he asks quietly.

"We will see them safe home before it starts," he says firmly. "Sweet Mary, Mother of God, will grant me that much, I am sure."

The light is starting to fade by the time Cesare and Michelotto ride into the courtyard of his mother's estate in the southeast of the city. It does not stop her from showing her favorite son around her vineyard. It is a long-established welcome between them.

"Well, what do you think?"

He takes another sip from the goblet he has been brought. She stands waiting for his judgment, the last rays of the sun bathing her broad, open face, its age lines written in laughter rather than distress.

"It is good, Mamma. Though still a little young, perhaps."

"Young! We sell that for eight ducats a barrel." She cuffs him affectionately. "You are young in your taste, more like." She slips her arm into his. "Come. It is growing cold. Let's go inside. Dinner will be ready."

They walk together past the neat lines of the vines cut back ready for the worst of winter. He wonders what will happen to her precious homestead if the French come. Whatever arrangements have been made for her safety she will not want to leave. He must be careful how he tells her.

"I had hoped you would come wearing scarlet," she says after a while.

"If you ride as a cardinal, everyone knows who and where you are. One does not need an army to visit one's mother."

"Still, a mother would like to see her son in his finery," she chides. "So, we will eat first and then you can tell me what is worrying you."

"There is nothing."

"Of course not. But we will talk of it anyway."

Michelotto, who has been walking at some distance behind them, now takes his place in a chair by the door. He will eat later.

The food is good and Cesare, who has better things to do in life than compliment his chefs, is careful to compliment her. But then she has always run a fine kitchen. When he and Juan were children, she would often dismiss the servants and his father would sit in his cardinal's finery watching her as she stood tasting and putting the finishing touches to the dishes. Looking back on it now, he is alert to what was clearly an element of eroticism in the domesticity.

She had been old—thirty—when Rodrigo Borgia first set eyes on her, with a ripe body and an unconscious grace, like a cat on the prowl for the best place to settle in the sun. "You have the body of a courtesan and the soul of a housewife," he had once told her, as they bickered casually over some domestic arrangement. It had not been without a certain guile on her part. In a city full of professional women, she had remained unaffected by the threat of competition: never questioning when he left, or when he might return, always offering the same broad smile of welcome when he did. She had understood early that while this lover of hers could have almost any woman he wanted, part of him yearned for the peace and normality of a domestic hearth. She simply gave him what he desired, in all senses of the word. For ten years she excelled in the business of handling Cardinal Rodrigo Borgia and when it was over she grew adept at handling a business of her own. At almost fifty, Vannozza dei Cataneis is a contented woman.

Cesare, who desires women but finds no peace in their company, is, as ever, relaxed in her presence. No doubt that is why, while he keeps no confidant but Michelotto, he comes back so often to visit her. It is a connection that goes deeper than he realizes: the stillness that marks him out to both enemies and friends is a quality inherited from her, though in his case it works to hide rather than reflect what is actually there.

"And business?"

"Oh, business is good. The hostel near Ponte Sant' Angelo is still the most profitable, of course, though unlike some pirates we do not overprice ourselves. There are more pilgrims every year and even the poorer ones can't all sleep on the steps of the church. The centenary jubilee will see a flood of them. The only worry is this war. Is that what you are come to talk about?"

"Partly. Papà says—"

"That if there is trouble, I must come inside Castel Sant' Angelo."

Cesare smiles. "Yes."

"I'm not going anywhere. I didn't build all this for a gang of dirty French soldiers to soil my sheets and drink my profits."

"We will see. If it comes to it, I will come and get you myself."

"They have reached Milan, yes?"

"Yes. And Florence will be next."

"Hmm. Is it true what I have heard—that King Ferrante's granddaughter Isabella threw herself at the French king's feet to try and get her husband back his rightful title?"

"Yes." And it is also true that she was dragged away by Ludovico Sforza's guards, her screams echoing down the great corridors of the castle of Pavia.

"Poor child. She and her husband have been most ill-treated by her uncle."

"Ludovico should have had them killed long ago."

"Cesare! What a thing to say. The boy is the rightful duke."

"All the more reason. Ludovico Sforza will never be secure while he's alive. His very existence will be an excuse for rebellion."

She shakes her head. Ah, young men and their ways. Across the room Cesare glances at Michelotto, who is both listening and not listening. It is something they have talked about before; how such an act might take place.

"Miguel," Vannozza calls out to him brightly. "I think we are safe here now. No poison in the food or assassins behind our curtains. Perhaps you would be so good as to leave us. I would like to spend some time with my son alone.

"I try every time, but I still cannot find it in myself to like him," she says as he shuffles out of the room.

"You are not meant to like him, Mamma. He is here to protect me."

"Perhaps he might learn to do it with a smile on his face."

"Oh, you wouldn't want to see Michelotto smile."

"Well, it is your business. I know only about wine and hostels. So, if you did not come for war, then it must be love."

"You are a wise woman." He smiles.

"I am an old one. And delighted though amazed. Who is she?"

"Oh no, no. Not me. No. It is Papà."

"Your father? And the Farnese girl? She is still in Pesaro with Lucrezia, yes, and he craves what he cannot have?"

"Not exactly."

She sits listening, a half-smile on her face.

"Poor Rodrigo," she says at last. "It seems he grows old like every man. It is strange. They say women are the jealous ones, but I have seen more men lose their minds with it. Don't worry. It will pass. She will come back and he will adore her even more." She pauses. "Though he may tire of her faster now she has given him cause."

"You never felt it, Mamma?"

"What? Jealousy?" She shrugs. "If I did I no longer remember it."

Now, he thinks. Maybe he will ask it now. There will be no better time. "What about Giuliano della Rovere?"

"What?"

"Giuliano della Rovere. Papà said something."

"What did he say?"

Cesare shrugs. "Something and nothing."

"Then we will keep it as nothing."

She makes a move toward the plates, always her way of closing a conversation. He puts out a hand to stop her.

"It is not unimportant, Mamma. He spews up bile against us like a blown geyser. Worse now than ever. He hates the Borgias as if our family has already destroyed his. It makes no sense. Unless . . ." He lets the words trail off.

"Ah, sweet Mary, Mother of God, I wonder sometimes what our dear Lord makes of it all. Forgiveness, meekness, poverty, turning the other cheek . . . the greatest virtues of all, and each one of them is absent from any cardinal that I have ever met." She gives a great sigh, as if it is too much trouble for her to go back so far. "Very well. There was nothing in it to warrant such fury. For a while he was quite fond, yes, though there were others as well as me. And he was not so easy. He had a terrible temper. Terrible. Any woman near him walked on eggshells. Then I met your father. And he . . ." Her face breaks into a smile. "And he made me laugh. No eggshells, no need to be anyone but myself. So,

I left Giuliano and quite soon I grew pregnant with you. And Giuliano, well, he didn't like it. His temper was . . . terrible. But I think it was always more about your father than any contest over me. I had no idea he could hold on to it for so long. Against all of us." She shakes her head. "And now we will never refer to it again. Or my wine will turn to vinegar in my barrels, you understand?" And her voice is fierce.

"However, for now, you may tell your father I will be ready. Though he is not to put me anywhere near this Farnese siren. And before you say anything, there is nothing I am jealous of. Except perhaps her hair."

Events move so fast now that they become history as they are happening. Near Milan, the corridors of Pavia castle are once again awash with the anguished sobs of the young duchess, as this time she nurses her husband through a night of sudden illness. By morning he is dead. Something he ate, it seems. She is still screaming poison and bloody murder when the doctors arrive and deliver her a soporific.

"My nephew was always sickly," says Ludovico, who is now in every way the Duke of Milan. "Mercifully, he is at rest now."

In Rome, Cesare receives the news with a sense of grim satisfaction.

With the enemy almost at the gates, the Farnese family can prevaricate no longer. Giulia and the faithful Adriana say their fond goodbyes and, accompanied by a small troop of men, head back toward Rome. It is not the cleverest of timings. They are barely a day's ride from her home when a group of French noblemen on reconnaissance southward block the road in front of them. Once they open the carriage and see that lovely face emerging from a rich curtain of hair, they know they have struck gold.

Alexander, as he reads the message, goes white and then purple. He is lucky: while the French may be known for their high living and lechery, in a few noble breasts there still beat hearts that appreciate chivalry. Not only are the ladies safe, but for the sum of three thousand ducats they will be escorted to the gates of Rome and handed over to the Pope's own guards.

The money is bagged up and returned with indecent haste. Alexander spends an inordinate amount of time on his wardrobe, deciding finally on black velvet trimmed with gold, boots of finest Spanish leather, and a sword and dagger to show that he can be both the soldier and the lover. The handover takes place after dark. He rides his white stallion to the city gates and waits, ready to be wrathful and full of majesty, but in the end his excitement and her tearful, smiling face as she sinks to the ground at his feet, decide the outcome. The prodigals are welcomed home and Giulia spends the night in the papal bed.

When he wakes next morning Alexander is ready to take on the world. He needs to be: the French king now issues an imperious demand for safe passage through the papal states. The message comes in no less a person than Alexander's old ally from the conclave, Vice-Chancellor Cardinal Ascanio Sforza.

At least he has the temerity to be sheepish about his treachery. "I am sorry it has come to this, Your Holiness. It was never my desire . . ." He trails off.

"Of course not. You know if you have things to confess, Vice-Chancellor, I can always make the time." He has dressed to receive him, his bulk in papal velvet and ermine trim, the fisherman's ring fat on his drumming fingers.

Sforza moves nervously from foot to foot. As rich churchmen go, he is better-looking than many, but the stress of family ambition—and the belligerence of his brother Ludovico in Milan—has put twenty years on his face. Now at least he has a more palpable incentive. If all goes according to plan, when the French take Rome a general council will be formed to depose the Pope and quite possibly set him on the throne in his place, though everyone knows the real power would lie with della Rovere.

"If I may speak frankly, Your Holiness. The French will conquer Naples with or without your support. It would be better if you concurred with King Charles's demands now."

"And for whom exactly would it be better? The king? Me? Your brother in Milan? Or for you perhaps?" Alexander's broad smile smears the words with honey. "Tell me something, Ascanio, how do you like

Pinturicchio's decorations of our papal suite? He has been working so hard of late."

"I, er . . . They are . . . most fine, Your Holiness."

"Yes indeed, I think they are. If you look to your left—I give you permission to turn away from me—there, at the wall directly in front of you. What do you see?"

Under the religious imagery, the lower half of the chamber is now made up of frescoed fabrics, playfully gathered as curtains to reveal painted wallpaper or fake shelves beneath: a little painterly mischief in a room of mysteries. And on one such shelf sits a life-size white and gold papal crown, its three dimensions so perfectly rendered that one might almost lift it off and put it on one's head.

"Clever, don't you think? And so convincing. I daresay you feel your hand itching toward it. Obviously the palace I gave you two years ago is no longer big enough to fit your ambition. God's wounds, Ascanio Sforza, you should be ashamed of yourself." Alexander is rising to his feet now, towering over his old ally, the smile replaced by a bellow designed to penetrate closed doors. "You are a disgrace to the Church. As an elected cardinal and the Vice-Chancellor your loyalty lies here with the papacy, not in the baggage train of French invaders. I may be seen as a corrupt Spaniard by those who like to spread gossip, but by God I am more an Italian than those who betray her now and I will not see this land trampled by foreign troops. You go and tell that to your new lord."

Sforza holds his ground as the tempest rages around him. "I came in all honesty to try and be of service, and now I have my answer."

Alexander roars even louder this time and the door bursts open on five guards armed and ready. "On second thoughts, I'll find someone else to send the message by. You are not a fit churchman to be seen in public anymore. You can see how a room in Castel Sant' Angelo compares with the comforts of your palace. If I were you I would pray that someone remembers to rescue you."

News of Sforza's humiliation is sweet gossip soon enough. The Pope, everyone agrees, has found his courage for battle again. What a shame, then, that he has no army to fight with. In mid-December, with

French soldiers pouring into the papal states, Virginio Orsini, employed as head of the Neapolitan force, and owner of the great castles of Anguilara and Bracciano, which dominate the route into Rome, opens their gates to the enemy without firing a single shot. "Surrender" is too kind a word for it. It is, by anyone's standards, betrayal.

Chapter 16

SHE HAS NEVER LIVED SO NEAR THE SEA AND IT AMAZES HER NOW, how its moods and colors change so much. The thick rope of water she has grown up with, the Tiber, has its own seasonal life, bursting spring banks and sluggish summer pull, but it is dull in comparison. Here the surface can shift from silver to cobalt blue to gray and black within a single day, flat as a table or churning foam, depending on the winds. The sound of it greets her every morning as her ladies open the shutters from the second floor of the ducal palace to the city below, its presence so constant that there are times when she wonders if its moods have not become her own.

They had reached the city amid frantic spring storms. The rain had been so fierce that the celebration planned to greet their arrival had been washed out, the route slippery with ruined garlands of flowers. Still, the people who did come out cheered and cried out her name and she was so grateful to them, and they were all so wet anyway, that by the time they entered the palace and fell off their horses and out of their litters into running streams, there was nothing to do but laugh; laugh and make the best of it that they could. For the first few days the ducal chambers became washrooms, with sodden clothes draped in front of fierce fires, and steam, steam rising everywhere. She had never had such adventure in her life, and because she was the duchess, she found that if she laughed and shrugged off the misfortune, everyone else laughed with her.

With the sun came the leftovers of spring and Pesaro, small but nonetheless lovely if you were not hungry on the streets, opened its arms to greet its new ruler, who as the favorite of a pope could bring only wealth and glory. The vocabulary and dialect of the Romagna is such that there were moments when she could barely understand a word of what was being said to her, but she bowed her head and smiled, and there was such grace and openness in her face that of course they took her into their hearts.

The palace, which had been asleep for years, stirred into life. There were banquets and plays and concerts, just as Giovanni had imagined, and everyone from the estates and towns around made the journey to see this most unusual entourage: a pope's daughter and his mistress, the last even more lovely than the first. And so fashionable, both of them. Even the most renowned of the local nobility, women like Caterina Gonzaga with a reputation for stealing hearts and wearing the latest that the dressmakers of Milan and Venice could provide, found herself upstaged by the rainbow colors of their brocades and the daring cut of their cloth, though the contrast between her milk skin and sea-blue eyes and the sultry olive beauty of Giulia Farnese did not go unnoticed. Letters flew between Pesaro and Rome painting pictures of their social triumphs, detailing the wonders and ennui of provincial life. The more they wrote, the more the Pope demanded to hear. Oh, how he misses his favorite ladies, he moans.

Of course, Lucrezia misses her family too: they are first in her prayers and often in her heart, yet as duchess in her own right there are moments when she registers a lightness, happiness even; the happiness of someone who is both loved and sometimes let alone, where the Borgia in her is matched by being Lucrezia, a young woman with feelings and wishes of her own.

In those early days, even Giovanni seemed to blossom. A hunter who had brought back a catch that everyone could be proud of, he started enjoying what he had, rather than always looking over his shoulder for whoever might want to take it away from him. Though they had separate suites in the palace, as befits a duke and duchess, he would, in the beginning, come quite often to her at night and they would make a kind of love; a little hasty and fumbling perhaps, but one which caused her no pain and gave him such evident pleasure that she herself felt at times quite elated by it. And afterward he would lie with her and call her sweet names, and she would think how comfortable married life might be, though sometimes her mind did slip to wonder about all those other husbands that Cesare had told her were still to come.

This honeymoon, however, does not last long. The ducal postal service is as busy from Milan as it is from Rome, and soon Giovanni is spending days away. When he returns he seems nervous and fretful and does not respond to her welcome. She begins to understand that his earlier unease had nothing to do with homesickness but that he is, by humor, an anxious man, not comfortable in his own skin. Now, even when they are in bed, he seems to have his mind on other things. Either that or there is some obstruction in his stomach, for he often complains of pains. When she asks sweetly (she hopes) what troubles him, he says that being Duke of Pesaro at such a time is not a small thing, and she nods consolingly, though privately she can't help thinking how her father rules the whole of Christendom and yet always has time to joke and smile.

She would like to talk to someone about it. Perhaps their lovemaking has something missing, something that might soothe and satisfy him more. But Giulia by now is absorbed in her own worries, distraught with news of her brother's illness and frantic to get away. Adriana is equally preoccupied because she will have to go with her, and anyway, her advice has already been given. "It is not so hard, this joining of the flesh. What is strange or distasteful soon becomes familiar."

Perhaps nothing is wrong, she thinks. Perhaps this is just how married life must be.

After the women leave for Capodimonte the mood in the palace changes. With less excuse for banquets and the novelty of endless introductions, the pace of life slows, the days grow longer. The citizens of Pesaro go about their lives, oblivious of their new duchess behind the palace walls. It was ever thus. She grows lonely. She had hoped to find a new life here. Yes, there is a court of sorts: a few noble families still eager for invitations, but with little to offer back. She reads her books and brings in the small band of musicians to play music for them in the evenings. But often Giovanni does not stay to hear them, excusing himself with matters of state. She has heard of other cities—Mantua, Ferrara, Urbino, even wild Naples—where men and women gather to read poetry and talk of the new learning and the role of chivalry, late into the night. Where they write sonnets to the sensibilities of their duchess, praising her humor and virtues to the world. Oh, she would dearly like to run a court like that. To be, in effect, the muse of such men.

"Are there poets here in Pesaro?" she asks him one evening.

"Poets? Not that I know of."

"Couldn't we find some, perhaps?"

She wanders around the rooms, looking at the tapestries and the gold plate that is on show. It is a sad little palace really, compared to Rome. There are decorations and a few fading frescoes, but they seem lifeless in comparison to the mischief and majesty of Pinturicchio's brush. Now she has her own home she would like to buy things for it: statues or commissioned paintings, perhaps. There are others who do so. She has heard talk of the eye and the purse of Isabella d'Este, born in Ferrara but married into Mantua, young still, maybe only half a dozen years older than Lucrezia herself. Her palace is said to be a showcase for old wonders and new art. She saw a portrait of her once—most lovely, though she knows from watching her family grow under Pinturicchio's fingers that, while the men need recognizable likenesses to spread their fame, the women must be flattered before they are allowed to be themselves.

Perhaps if the world around was not moving so fast . . . As it is she spends much of the summer defending herself against her father's anger over Giulia's desertion. She charms herself back into his affections, but soon there is further anxiety as the letters speak of growing fear of invasion. Both Cesare and her father want them to return to Rome before things get worse. But Giovanni is busy too. He makes trips to Milan and when he is at home messengers come at strange times of the day and night. Then, from Rome urgent news comes that he is assigned a post in the army of Naples and his presence will be needed so they must be ready to leave at any time. "The state of Milan will be reluctant to give him his money since we are allied to King Alfonso, and Giovanni has no choice but to follow our will," her father writes to her. His tone is so clear she can almost hear his voice in the background.

"We should leave now," she says after she has read it.

"How can we leave when there is a threat of invasion? What will happen to Pesaro if it falls to the French and I am seen to have deserted it? We will go when I have made things safe here."

She, who as yet knows only what she is told about politics, appreciates his anxiety. As duchess she too must worry about her people. Or at least she tries to.

A few weeks later he leaves again, saying he is meeting with the papal forces gathering in the Romagna. She waits anxiously to hear more. When he arrives back he seems smaller than before. His stomach pains are openly worse. She knows he must be torn between his two families. How could he not be? She would like to help him, be a good wife to his agitated self, but increasingly it is not easy to get close to him. Once she wakes in the night and thinks she can hear him moving somewhere in the room. She lights the lamp, but the bedroom is empty. It is late summer now, but still baking hot despite the windows open toward the sea. She soothes her servant back to sleep and goes in search of him. She has an image of wiping his brow, bringing him back to bed and opening her robe so that he might bury his face between her breasts. The image is so strong she wonders if she has ever seen it— maybe a memory stirring from childhood, for the body she imagines under the robe is riper than her own. It both upsets and excites her.

She arrives outside his room to a line of flickering candlelight under the door and pushes it open quietly. He is hunched over his desk, the urgent scratching of a pen on paper, covered pages all around him. When she calls out his name softly, he jumps as if she had shot him with an arquebus, yelling at her for daring to disturb him, then moves his arms over the papers as if to hide them from her.

"I did not mean to disturb you, my lord." She is so taken aback that she fears she might cry, but makes an attempt to stand her ground. "It is only that it is very late and I was hoping you might come to my bed tonight."

"Come to your bed?" he says, as if this was the most deranged suggestion he has ever heard. "But I am busy. Can't you see?"

"Yes, yes, I see, but . . ." And then to her fury the tears come anyway. Because she is fifteen years old and she knows that her marriage is not a success and has spent too long trying to pretend otherwise. He watches her in a kind of horror, then shakes himself and comes over to her, putting his arms awkwardly around her shoulders and pulling her to him.

"I am sorry, Lucrezia. I did not mean to shout. Times are difficult. It is not your fault."

"Whatever is troubling you, you can tell me," she says, trying to stem her tears. "I am your wife."

"Yes. You are my wife." And he laughs bitterly. "My lovely, lovely Borgia wife."

"Is it my family?" she says, drawing away for a moment. "Is there something you have heard that you fear to tell me?" And she glances at the table with its hastily written correspondence.

"No, no. It is just politics. Affairs of state, nothing to worry yourself about."

"You are worried about your family then? That is it. It must be hard to—"

"Lucrezia, this is none of your business." He drops his arms and he does not look at her. "I said it is nothing. I am just busy. Go back to bed."

But whatever she doesn't know, she knows it is not nothing.

After this, he avoids her even more. If you are betraying your wife's family, it is best that you do not pretend love. His bowels become his conscience. He can barely sit through a meal with her and takes to eating alone so he can leave the table when his stomach calls.

The messengers come and go. The French have crossed the Alps. Even the servants now talk of their unstoppable advance.

"My cousin Ludovico is Duke of Milan now," he says one night.

"Oh. What happened to his nephew?" she asks timidly.

"He died," he says bluntly.

"And his wife?"

"I daresay she will enter a convent or be sent home to Naples. Bea-trice d'Este is now duchess. Ha! She and her sister Isabella are queens of both Mantua and Milan," he says bitterly. But then, bitterness is increas-ingly the taste of him now.

Two clever sisters with two great men as husbands. Ah, how she wishes she had a sister whose advice she might call on.

She lives with growing anxiety. The servants whisper about the possibility of the army moving into Romagna on their way south, for the terrain, it seems, would be easier on their feet. That is why there is an allied force of papal troops and Neapolitans waiting for them. But then to everyone's surprise they choose another route, across the Apen-nines and down toward Florence. It is almost as if they know where the enemy will not be.

She waits each morning for news. It is winter now and letters take longer in the mud and the rain. The sea is white froth or death-gray by turns, colored by storm clouds and chaffing waves. There are still no poets in Pesaro and two of the musicians have developed illnesses in-side their chests which means they cannot find the breath for their reeds. The palace becomes silent and cold. She thinks constantly of Rome; of what might be happening there, how there may not even be a family to go back to.

When at last the news comes he cannot hide it from her. After al-most two weeks of silence it is clear there have been reasons why noth-ing is getting through. He breaks his isolation to come into her bedchamber that morning.

"Lucrezia."

Within seconds she is sitting up, the covers grabbed tight under her fingers.

"What is it?"

"I . . . there is a rider. He came in the night." He hesitates. "Rome has opened her gates and let in the French army."

She stares at him in horror.

"When? When did this happen? You should have told me." She is out of bed, calling for her servants, glancing around for clothes.

"Lucrezia, you cannot do anything. It would be far too dangerous to go there now."

"They told us. My father told us to come. They needed our help. What about the defense army you were going to lead?"

He shakes his head at her fancifulness. "Nothing we could have done would have made any difference. The die was cast a long time ago. My dear wife." He makes a move toward her.

"No. Don't touch me. I should have gone. I should be there. What about my father? Adriana and Giulia, my mother. And Cesare, what about Cesare? What will they do to them?"

And once again the bitterness is there under the words. "Oh, I am sure your family will find a way to look after itself."

Chapter 17

HE COULD HAVE FLED. THERE WAS TIME ENOUGH AS THE ARMY APproached, and from Naples King Alfonso had offered him sanctuary in the great southern fortress of Gaeta. But it has never been in Alexander's nature to walk away from a fight and anyway, to leave the papal throne empty would have been an invitation to della Rovere to try his bony rump on it for size. No. However desperate the situation might seem, Rodrigo Borgia is not going anywhere. If anything, as the tension mounts he becomes more relaxed.

The morning when the French messenger delivers the king's demand to enter the city, the Pope is having his bath. The ritual, which takes place every second week, is a semi-sacred time and he will not rush it for anyone.

He sits in the great wooden tub, protected from drafts by curtains on three sides and a tray over the top with a plate of cheeses and sugared figs, and a goblet of hot wine. The temperature of the water is refreshed by a relay of servants balancing heated pails. It is freezing outside and the sense of weightlessness and warmth offer him exquisite pleasure. Rome was once a city of baths. Their ruins speak of a way of living that is lost to them now, when the bathhouse was a great council chamber and the men who ruled the empire sat amid steam and plunge pools, working out strategy and politics. In his youth, when he had a body that drew as much admiration as his mind, he would have loved it. But he is grown so stout that he is loath to show himself to those who do not already love him. Well, when this is over, he promises himself, he will fast for a while. He takes another sugared fig and leans back.

When he finally emerges, scrubbed clean like a huge pink baby and scented with sweet oils, he is gratified to note how filthy and bedraggled the waiting French courtiers appear, and how from under their hurried anointing of perfume there rises the inexorable stink of camp life.

"Oooph! Excuse me," he says waving his hand as if to give himself some air. "The heat of the water is still with me. But I see it is still thick frost outside. Army life is such a challenge at this time of year, no? Why don't you move closer to the fire? You look half frozen," he says brightly, noting how the glow of the blaze shows off the chapped skin on their cheeks. They have barely stopped shivering when he starts again. "Alas, I only wish we could thaw you out longer. But business is business. So, please tell Your Majesty that I will think hard about his 'offer' and get back to him as soon as God has guided me in considering it. Oh—and I have instructed my servants to give you clean towels to take with you. To assist you with the . . . the grime of the road." He brings a finger lightly to his nose. When one is under pressure, one must take pleasure where one can.

The next day he and Cesare watch as the enemy amasses outside the walls. Whatever the bravura of his reply, they both know it is only a matter of time. From the upper storys of Sant' Angelo they look down on the French cavalry grazing their horses in the fields, the artillery rolling to a rest, the great bronze pipes thick as battering rams but nimble enough on their carts. It is the first time such transportable cannons have been used on Italian soil and Cesare, an eager student of war, cannot take his eyes off them. They have already blown holes in any city walls that opposed them and Rome will be no exception.

Fortunately for history, the supplies inside the city are so low as to ensure surrender without the use of force. On Christmas morning, the Pope calls the cardinals and commanders and announces his decision to admit the king. The remaining ragged allied forces leave by the southern gate, and that night three French envoys are admitted to the Vatican chapel to meet with the Pope. They make themselves at home in seats expressly reserved for the highest-ranking churchmen. Burchard, beside himself at the insult, is furiously chastising them when Alexander himself enters.

"You will have us skewered and roasted in our beds if you don't find a way to accommodate them," the Pope hisses under his breath as he sees him to the door.

"It is not right. God will never forgive us," the German stammers, his pain evident.

"Neither will I. And it is me you will have to answer to first," he says, before smiling broadly as he turns to greet the Frenchmen. His charm and the authority of his bulk in ceremonial papal silk have them out of the seats and on their knees fast enough. He wafts his ringed hand for them to kiss. The robes still make the man, as he knows very well.

Six days later the army marches in. The spectacle trumps anything the Borgias themselves might mount, and the whole of Rome comes out to watch. Those who do the counting at the gates will argue for years about numbers. Gossip and terror inflate the size of any army when it is rolling in conquest, and alongside the soldiers come the inevitable camp followers, women and stragglers who have attached themselves like iron filings to a great moving magnet. Certainly modern Italy has seen nothing like it before. At the most conservative estimate over twenty-five thousand warriors troop into Rome that day; swordsmen, pikemen, crossbow men, cavalry, artillery, each group paid to deliver a different kind of death. It takes them so long to reach the Palazzo San Marco, where the king and his principal warriors are to be billeted, that night falls on the way and the last troops march through freezing temperatures to the light of great smoking torches. And in places of honor, next to the king, ride Giuliano della Rovere and the newly freed Ascanio Sforza.

Palazzo San Marco with its echoes of Venetian splendor is more than worthy of royalty. Its inner courtyard is as big as an exercise field and the stone staircase swirling up three or more floors makes a man's eyes giddy trying to take in all the levels. There are stories of how the newly installed young king has his servants carry him up and down lying on a litter, so that he can follow the twists and hollows of its stone flow without risking cricking his neck, for he is, unfortunately, both a hunched and a runty fellow. His behavior is triumphant and nervy in equal measures. He eats every meal with four doctors in attendance in case of the slightest trace of poison, and his wine is served in a cup with a piece of unicorn horn embedded in the bottom to prove the purity of the grape. He is at his most imperious after he has digested successfully.

Three days in, Charles's demands reach the Pope, via a meeting with Burchard, who has been called to attend him. The Roman sky is sack-heavy with rain when the German enters the Room of the Saints, where Alexander sits in conference with Cesare. Whatever news is private to the papacy is public to his son.

"Oh, Holy Father, they have the manners of animals." The Master of Ceremonies is incandescent with outrage. "They treat prelates like errand boys and the palazzo is a pigsty. They have lit a fire in front of the great tapestries, so they are black with soot, and though they were given a great number of clean pallets of straw they have soiled them all already. The filth is such that it is impossible to tell which rooms are for the horses and which for the men. And still they want more. They have a list of houses they intend to commandeer. And—" He takes a dramatic breath . . .

"And your own is one of them?"

Burchard closes his eyes as a shudder of horror goes through him.

"It is most appalling, certainly. But perhaps you might tell us their other demands?"

"Ah! Ah! Here." He thrusts the paper at them. "That you surrender Castel Sant' Angelo. That you hand over Prince Djem as hostage for His Majesty's journey to the Holy Land. And—"

"What about the sultan's payments for his safekeeping?" Alexander has not been balancing papal budgets for thirty years for nothing, and these days he has no vice-chancellor that he can trust.

"Oh, they want the man, not the money. I made sure about that. The payments stay with Your Holiness."

"Good. And what else?"

Burchard stares at him, faltering.

"Come, come—it cannot be so terrible."

"They demand His Most Reverend Lord, Cardinal of Valencia, as a further hostage on their journey to Naples."

In the grainy light of the room, father and son look at each other.

"I believe, I believe . . . that in this way His French Majesty thinks he will secure your Holy Father's anointing of his coronation in Naples, should he take the throne."

"I am sure you are right." Now the moment is come Alexander feels remarkably calm. "Thank you, Burchard, I am grateful for your observations."

"Shall I wait for your answer? I have been deliberating myself, and I would suggest—"

"No. No. You should get to your house and strip out whatever you can carry before they arrive. I will deal with this."

Burchard's long face drops even longer. Inside the disgust, excitement is running through even his veins, and he seems almost disappointed to be dismissed.

"They treat us like serfs who haven't paid their fealty." Cesare stands, arms crossed, by the window, his silhouette framed black against winter sunlight, the air alive with dust. "It's outrageous."

"They are the demands of a king with twenty-five thousand men behind him." The Pope, in his chair, is relaxed, fingers entwined and still. "I daresay you or I, with his advantage, might do the same. Nevertheless, the fact that there are demands at all gives us power."

"Ha! How?"

"How? Think about it. He is negotiating for papal approval for the throne of Naples. What he is not doing is setting out to depose me and put another man in my stead."

"That may be exactly what he will do as soon as he takes Sant' Angelo."

"Oh, we will never give up Sant' Angelo."

"And if he storms us there? Which he will . . ."

"Then, before the castle falls, we will agree to everything else. In which case, he will have what he wants and there will be no reason for a further bloodbath in order to depose us. Put yourself in his shoes, Cesare. If you were leading his army what would you do?"

"I would be on my way south as fast as I could get my artillery out the gates," he says with no hesitation, as if he has been matching it all, move for move. "That many soldiers five months on the road are hungry for a lot more than food. The king is already building scaffolds in the major piazzas to warn off looters."

"So why waste more time organizing a council of reform? It is no small thing to depose a pope. Much more convenient to work with the one you have got." He smirks. "Poor della Rovere. All this way for nothing. I must send him a message of condolence."

"So, what? We give him Djem?"

Alexander blows out a noisy breath. "If we keep the money, there is no reason why not. The king wants to scare the sultan into thinking they are serious in their crusade. But they'll never get further than Naples. Djem is the one who'll be terrified. The great Turkish warrior has been drunk for years to avoid thinking about his brother."

Cesare cannot help but smile. They are fighting for their lives and his father is finding things to amuse him as if they are about the most ordinary of Church business. He thinks back to the man who barely a few weeks before was foaming at the mouth to get his mistress back. The change is a joy to witness. "And the Cardinal of Valencia," he says quietly.

"Ah, yes. The Cardinal of Valencia: him they *do* need. Because, as we know, the Pope is most fond . . ."

"And with him as hostage they force your hand to invest Charles as King of Naples when they oust Alfonso."

"Yes. Burchard is a clever fellow when he stops being pompous. Yes, indeed. I would do that to save my son."

"And they *will* take Naples."

The Pope shrugs as if it is not worth answering.

"So, it would be better if I did not go." Cesare says nothing for a few moments. "But I have to go, for them to believe that we have really capitulated."

"Indeed."

The Pope looks proudly at his son. There are times when he is struck by the beauty of him, when he can see echoes of Vannozza's face, the same generous mouth, the same broad-set dark eyes. And the same beguiling sense of self-containment, whatever the thoughts fulminating behind.

"Everyone says winter is a terrible time to visit Naples," Cesare says flatly, after a while. "I think, if it meets with your approval, I will not go the whole way."

Alexander smiles. "Ah! My hearing is getting bad these days. But I shall not ask you to repeat it. When I shake hands on the agreement it would be best to have honesty shining in my face."

Cesare's gaze flips up to the back wall of the room, where Santa Caterina's disputation in the court of Alexandria is now finished; a crowded scene of magnificence and fashion, its fresh colors more vivid than life itself. Next to Caterina, pretty and fair as young Lucrezia, right down to the hint of the childlike double chin, stands a Turkish prince, dressed to kill, if only through style.

"What about Prince Djem?"

"Ha! Djem is a troublemaker. Let the French deal with him for a while."

The two men look at each other. In these months of growing anxiety they have become, even in disagreement, increasingly at ease.

"You don't think we give too much away, Father?" Cesare says at last.

"No! In truth we could not give away less. Rome remains intact. The King of France will bow his knee to me, Pope Alexander VI. And Giuliano della Rovere and all those who wanted me humiliated will have to swallow their own bile."

"And Naples?"

"We will deal with Naples when it happens. The French have more enemies now that they have trampled all over Italy. Spain is already chafing at the bit. If I was Charles I would loot fast and leave by ship, for I wouldn't rate my chance of an easy retreat."

Cesare glances back up at the fresco. At its center the great arch of Constantine rises up, faithfully copied just as it stands now, amid the ruins in Rome, embossed with gold and reminding all who see it of the triumphs of good government. Though in this incarnation its inscription is dedicated not to an emperor but a pope. Alexander VI: "The

Bringer of Peace." Such an ass-licker Pinturicchio is, Cesare thinks. They all are . . .

He turns to go, dipping his knee toward his father as he always does. But then, almost without thinking, he leans further down and kisses the Pontiff's feet. Alexander lays his hand on his son's head. Pope and cardinal. Father and son. Teacher and pupil.

"Cesare?" He waits till he is almost at the door. "There is something else you should know."

"What?"

"Your mother's house has been attacked."

"When? By whom?"

"Two nights ago. By men from the Swiss Guard, it seems, though I do not yet know for sure. I am telling you because it will almost certainly become known before you leave, and when it does I want you to do nothing about it. Do you hear? Your mother is safe here and the damage will be repaired. We play a longer game than temper and instant reprisals."

Cesare stands, his face impassive. "One enemy at a time, Father," he says quietly. "I understand. But when this is—"

"I don't need to know. I will be too busy raising an opposition to this web-footed French king. Now, I am going to pray. And I suggest you do the same."

"What about my mother?"

"Prayer first. Then I will tell your mother."

Chapter 18

To her credit, when the time came, she had left her house and her vines without fuss or question. She accepted the modest accommodation given inside the Castel Sant' Angelo and asked for no privileges. Though da Sangallo has been at work for near-on two years trying to turn a mausoleum into a home, the deathly chill of stone is everywhere and in the middle of winter the tapestried chambers feel mildewed.

If Giulia Farnese is anywhere close, she does not see her. Neither does she see the Pope. Nor request to see him. She spends her mornings on estate business (she has brought her account books with her) and the afternoons sitting looking out over the city she has lived in all her life. From her window high in the fortifications she has a clear view of her two-story tavern on the other side of the bridge. In her mind's eye she can see herself standing in one of the bedrooms, staring out on the castle itself. There is no better location in the whole of the city. During feasts and holidays the bridge is so thick with pilgrims on their way to the basilica of St. Peter's that you might think there was no stone supporting them, that it was instead a miracle bridge made up of human souls surging on toward God. Many sleep in the piazza or on the steps of the great old church, their backbones and their budgets assuaged by using pallets hired by the night from vendors who line the route. But those who come to God with a slightly bigger purse can make themselves comfortable in one of the six rooms (four beds to a room) that Vannozza's house offers. The doors open at dawn and close soon after sunset, though late travelers who knock politely and pay up front will be welcome if there is a place. In the morning, they can drink watered wine or goat's milk before they head off on their next stage of pilgrimage around Rome's seven great churches, and (if they are not fasting) return every evening to roasted carp and baby pig. In the fifteen years since she bought it from the sale of the jewels given to her by a still-loving cardinal, it has quadrupled its value, and she turns down offers every other month for its purchase. Of course, it is commandeered by the French now. She tries not to imagine the havoc. Two years before, a freak flood took out the ground floor of the tavern, with beds floating down the Tiber, one with a pilgrim who had drunk too much the night before still hanging on to it. The French, like another flood tide, will do their damage and pass on.

When he visits her that afternoon, it is not only because of what he must tell her, but because he wants to see her. Though Giulia's flesh is still as soft and willing as ever, in the midst of crisis he has been thinking of a different kind of constancy, one with—how can he put it?—more sense of a lived life to steady the way the earth is rising and falling beneath his feet.

He was never good at breaking bad news. For all his power, he likes to please more than disappoint, especially women. She, who reads him better than many of his own advisers, knows what he has come to say before he opens his mouth. She listens without speaking, nodding her head once or twice to show she understands. She has not cried for many years and she will not do so now, not in his presence.

"Ah, well," she says at last. "Rome is an occupied city. I am sure I am not the only one to be counting my losses."

He does not tell her that he thinks she was targeted specifically because of her connection with him. But then he does not need to, because she will know that too.

"They will be brought to justice, Vannozza. Of that you can be sure. And any damage that has been done will be made good before you have to return."

"You are too kind, Holy Father." Though there is nothing else she can call him, they both register the inappropriateness of the term on her lips.

He shuffles uncomfortably on the spot. "You are looked after well enough here for now?"

"Oh yes, indeed."

"Good." He looks around. He hovers. There is nothing more to say. Or too much. To leave or to not leave. It was a familiar pattern in their past. "I am glad you were not there when it happened," he says.

They look at each other. He does not want to go, she thinks. He has so much to do and for a while he does not want to do any of it.

"I . . . I brought some of my own wine and olive paste to keep me company away from my kitchens. You probably eat and drink much better fare, but if you wanted to sample some of it . . ."

"Well, yes . . . that would be fortifying." He nods. "It is a hungry business, saving Rome from Christians." He smiles.

She clears her papers from the chair to make a space for him and digs into her chest, removing and arranging things, taking out the glasses, wiping them, uncorking the flask. He watches her move. She has spread over the years, a matron as much as a woman, though her shoulders and neck are still lovely. Her breasts are like great pillows. They would overflow in a man's hands.

She places an engraved-glass goblet down and pours, holding a kerchief to catch any drips. The wine is a ruby red. He imagines her serving men at a great table, one of them moving his hands toward her skirts. Outside, the French king will soon be loading his artillery to send salvos into the walls of the castle, and here he is, playing with fantasies of tavernmaids. Well, even a pope must have some quiet time.

"You look . . . well, Vannozza."

"For my age, you mean?" she says cheerfully. "Yes, I am."

"Of course, I am much older." He waits. But she does not pick up the bait.

"I wonder—would you say the same of me?"

Ah, Rodrigo, she thinks, how little you have changed; never a jot of modesty, particularly when in search of a compliment. She studies him.

While there is still an energy within him, the flesh falls slack on his face and what was once a generous stomach has become a gross one. He is corpulent. No other word for it. He is digging his own grave with his teeth. She wonders what Giulia Farnese thinks as she maneuvers her body out from under the weight of him. Does he know?

"You are a man of even more substance," she says, smiling. "Though you look a little tired."

"Well, I carry the weight of the Church on my shoulders," he mutters, patently disappointed in the level of appreciation.

"Oh, you should not worry. It suits you."

He smiles, better pleased.

Ah, men. However old, however powerful, they still have the boy in them.

"The wine is good," he says.

"And the olive paste?"

"Perfect. Simple. Just as I like it."

He pats the cushion next to him as an invitation. My God, she thinks, is he trying to seduce me? She stays busy with her things.

He registers the hesitation. He gives a large sniff. "So, Cesare says you are a grand businesswoman. As indeed you always were. I am glad you are not . . . unhappy."

"Far from it. I have everything a woman of my age could want." But the sentence does not quite end. And she lets it hang. Well, her house is trashed and her vineyards trampled, and something in her is not willing to play the game in the way she once did.

"You pause. There is an 'except' there, perhaps?"

She shakes her head.

Except for me, he thinks. She would still want me. "Vannozza, you know . . . I could never have done this had we still been together." He smiles, gesturing to the surroundings.

"Oh! I did not mean you." And her laugh is so immediate that he is taken aback.

"What then?"

The unspoken word shivers in the air as it has for so many years.

"Ah, you mean the children."

She looks at him steadily for a moment, and then shakes her head. Even now she does not quite have the courage. She has not become the woman she is by being broken by things she cannot have.

"You know I would have had you at Lucrezia's wedding. But Burchard was adamant—"

"Yes, yes. I know. And of course he was right. Tell me, Rodrigo, how is your gout these days? Does it trouble you much?"

"Cesare visits you. And the others write."

"Ho! Out of formality. Not love," she adds before she can stop herself.

"Of course they love you; you are their mother," he says crossly.

"Don't shout at me, Rodrigo. We are not lovers anymore."

"Well, what is all this anyway? I have a great deal on my mind."

"Then go and think about it."

"I am telling you, your children love you."

"Oh! Cesare is kind to me and cruel to others. Juan—at times—recalls his duty, and the other two were too young. They barely remember me." She pauses. "Or I them, sometimes. I am not criticizing you, I am simply saying how it is."

"Nevertheless . . ." He remains flustered. "You will be mother of a pope, a duchess and two dukes. Many women would give their eyeteeth."

"And how would they chew their meat then? Of course, I am overwhelmed by all the honors I have been paid. I always was." And she holds his eye now, to show him the argument is over. "So, let us not quarrel. Would you like some more wine?"

"I . . . No, no." He gets up, smoothing his silken skirts. "I must go." Yet he does not move. "They were good times between us, Vannozza," he says. "Weren't they?"

"Yes. Very."

"And. And you were always pleased to see me."

"You were usually a great pleasure to see."

"Ha!" He feels happy now, secure enough to take the risk. "And I always satisfied you, didn't I?"

She looks at him for a moment, trying hard to keep the laughter from her eyes. "Like a bull, Your Excellency," she says evenly, choosing the words she would once have used to tease him as they thrashed together in bed. "But we were both much younger then."

"Humph," he says, as if to show how wrong she is. Except that is not what he wants to say. What he came here for. I grow tired in bed, that is what he would like to say. Sometimes I think I might disappoint her, sometimes . . . since she came back, well, I am almost not interested. There is so much else to do. Christendom, the challenges of work. You told me once that I am happier with the fight than the conquest. You were right. The fight never tires me. I can always get it up for a fight. Will you be there at my death? he thinks. Then wonders why he should have such a thought.

"We have come a long way, Vannozza dei Cataneis."

She looks around.

"I do not think you have stopped moving yet."

And so it happens that the next day the Pope defies the King of France and His Majesty Charles VIII rolls his artillery cannons across the bridge and sets them up outside the walls of the fortress of Sant' Angelo. Truth be told, he feels more than a little uncomfortable standing there, a would-be crusader against the infidel, about to shell the sanctuary of the Holy Father of Christendom. The first few halfhearted salvos fail to reach their target, shaking the ground like a small earthquake. The artillerymen regroup and push the guns closer. But as they are reloading noisily, as if in anticipation of the violence, a small stretch of wall further along falls in of its own accord, to the screams of the guards stationed behind it. Mayhem and embarrassment collide. The architect da Sangallo will find his portrait erased from among the spectators to Santa Caterina's disputation if he can't do better than this. Outside, the king, who could order a direct attack now, waits while they retrieve the mangled bodies. Half an hour later, the Pope sends out a messenger, agreeing to most of the key demands and welcoming the king into the Vatican, where he will meet and entertain him himself.

That night, della Rovere growls objections into the king's ear, but the young man is already too busy picking his outfit and taking lessons in papal protocol: when to walk one way or the other, when to bow, when to kneel and when and how often to kiss the Holy Father's feet. It will be a meeting of historic importance for his young Majesty and he does not want to get it wrong. He is still practicing walking backward when della Rovere leaves the city in disgust. When news reaches Alexander he is heard to give a yelp of joy. He puts on his ceremonial robes and waits to welcome the king.

A week ago, one would have been hard-pressed to find a man to take bets on his survival. Now he savors this moment as one of the sweetest. Instructions go out to the kitchens to prepare a great feast for his visitors. It is one of Alexander's great talents: how much he can enjoy life and how, when things are going well, he is happy to invite others to enjoy it with him.

Chapter 19

IT TAKES THEM A GOOD DEAL LONGER TO LEAVE THAN TO ARRIVE. Four weeks of regular food and sleeping on new straw in warm rooms as winter rages outside have sapped their eagerness for the promise of Naples. There is much complaining and groaning and swearing as they hitch up their breeches, stuff their meager belongings into bags and load up the carts in drizzling rain. As darkness falls they are still trudging through the streets toward the southern gates. The city, which has long since lost its respect for men with glinting swords and long pikes, does not come out to see them off. As the palazzi and private houses close their doors, they are already starting fires and boiling water to burn and scrub away the lice. Still, even those who barely grasp the vagaries of high politics have an understanding that they have been let off lightly and that their Pope has shown himself a father to his Roman flock as well as a dupe to his nubile young mistress. As for Naples, well, many go to bed that night remembering it in their prayers.

In the Vatican, Alexander, resplendent in ceremonial robes, bids goodbye to the runty young king whom he has lavishly entertained over the last few days and who has bowed and scraped in front of him (but not so much as to be allowed to feel humiliated). He embraces him as his own dear and faithful son with many tender words before seeing him to his horse at the gate of the private gardens. Along with endearments, Charles carries only the vaguest promises of Alexander's support in Naples; just as well, then, that his hostage is both the Pope's son and a cardinal, ceremonially able to put the crown on his head when the moment comes.

As soon as he is out of sight, the Holy Father, Burchard and other prelates gather at the windows of the newly refurnished corridor which leads from the Vatican palace to Sant' Angelo to watch unseen as the king, joined by Cesare in his Church finery, ride out together like brothers in arms, followed by six magnificent unsaddled horses which the Cardinal of Valencia has just gifted to His Majesty as a token of his affection, while behind them come nineteen chests of his personal luggage loaded on a pack of plodding mules.

When he turns back toward his private apartments, Alexander, for the first time in his papacy, finds himself alone without any of his children. At another time it might have been a moment for sentiment. A few tears, perhaps. At another time . . . As it is, no sooner is the royal entourage out of sight across the bridge than he is welcoming the Spanish ambassador, who has been pacing the floor of the anteroom waiting for the exodus to finish.

Cesare meanwhile is determined to suck some sweetness from the hostage experience. The sky brightens as the army moves south along the great Via Appia, navigable again since Sixtus IV had parts of it cleared and repaved. History stretches before and behind them. The first day they make camp at Marino, where they are joined by Prince Djem, who drinks freely and regales them with tales of piracy and savagery on the high seas (where he never was). They are still eating when news arrives from Naples. Alfonso, king for less than a year, during which time he has not slept for nightmares of doom, has abdicated in favor of his son; and both father and son and the whole court have fled to Sicily. The table rejoices. Cesare lifts his glass along with the others, in the knowledge that his baby brother Jofré is safe.

Unlike Djem, who spends the days in a stupor recovering from the nights before, Cesare is the life and soul of the march. His French is smooth and his sense of humor sharp, and without his cardinal's clothing he appears every bit the soldier as he moves through the ranks of the army, interested and eager for stories of battle. At rest stops he tests the crossbows and the pikes. He rides for a while with the advance light cavalry, impressing them with his horse skills, leaping from one moving mount to another, racing stretches of open road and winning against whoever is fool enough to challenge him. He quizzes cohort commanders and those professional soldiers who sell their services and their troops to the highest bidder. War is a business with its own balance sheets, and a good general needs to master its economy as well as its weaponry. But he is at his most inquisitive with the artillery, running his hands over the rich bronze guns (kept cleaned and primed, ready for instant battle) and regaling the gunners with questions. What weight do they carry? How fast can they reload? What thickness of wall can they penetrate? In short, a more amiable, charming hostage it would be impossible to find, and at night when they dine, the king insists that he sits by his side.

At the city of Velletri they are met by Cardinal della Rovere, whose archbishopric it is. At the banquet he lays on, he and Cesare sit at the same table, raising their glasses in cold politeness. That night the whole company sleeps well oiled, confident of victory and glory ahead of them. It is the waning of the moon and the winter darkness is thick as soup.

Sometime after midnight a figure, dressed in the black livery of the king's stable boys, slips out from a torn flap in the back of Cesare's tent. He moves past the guards, with whom he exchanges a coarse joke in French, toward the field where the royal horses are tethered. He approaches a black stallion, the finest of the six gifted to the king and one who has proved skittish and uncooperative to anyone who tries to mount him. The animal stands still as a statue as the young man slips a saddle and bridle over him, all the time whispering in its ear. Minutes later, the two move in silent harmony through the shadows and out beyond the sleeping camp. They cover the first few miles across fields before rejoining the road. Just before first light, outside a church near Marino, he is met by a masked man waiting with a sword and a change of clothes. The two grasp hands once, then twice, and as the sun comes up on a gauzy gray winter's morning, they gallop off, to be swallowed up instantly by the mist. Before nightfall they will be in Rome.

Back at camp, the king and his entourage breakfast early without the young cardinal. When a guard is sent to rouse him his servant is found in a drugged sleep and his pallet is empty. The king is puce with fury. In the baggage train, Cesare's great chests of luggage remain intact. They are hauled out and broken open on the road in front of the king. Inside, under layers of rich brocade, are revealed great expanses of nothing. The mules, who look burdened even when they are not, stand impassively by as the king jumps up and down on his little feet, spitting fire: "All Italians are scum, blackguards and traitors and the Pope and his poxy family are the worst of them. As God is my witness I will have the Pope off his throne and . . ."

But he and twenty-five thousand men are halfway to Naples and everybody knows there is no going back now.

When the dispatch (the same sentiments with only slightly mediated language) arrives with Alexander, he roars even louder than the king.

"What! Does His Majesty think I would conspire against him, he whom I have welcomed into my heart as my dear son? How dare the Cardinal of Valencia disobey me, his pontiff? His desertion is none of our doing and causes us more pain and fury than it does the king. Where is he? Where? We will scour the city and smoke him out and when he is found he will be sent back immediately."

The French envoy backs out of the room, his ears ringing. Standing behind the closed door, staring up at the bull crest on the beams above, he hears the rant continue through the wood.

"Get me Burchard! Get me the commander of the Papal Guard! We will have the cardinal found if we have to turn inside out every palace in Rome!"

At home in Paris, the French court has a fine reputation for the art of drama, richly performed tales of love and tragedy, but its envoy has never in his life come across an actor of the caliber of Alexander.

Meanwhile, seventy miles to the northeast, in the castle of Spoleto, Pedro Calderón is already delivering orders for the fires to be lit and the bedrooms to be made up in readiness for new guests.

Within a few days two masked men arrive, dusty from the road but in high spirits. To his delight, Calderón is included in the celebration that night. The great hearth spits fire into the darkness as the men gather their chairs close by, the meal laid on trays before them: roasted wild boar in a thick apple gravy with a fat red wine from the local slopes. The alcohol mixes with the exhilaration of escape to loosen tongues, and the talk is all of the skills of war, with Cesare holding forth on the setting and breaking of camps, the superior power of pikes in formation against cavalry, and the onomatopoeic violence of two syllables which have already entered the language to describe the sound and fury of a new siege weapon.

Bom Bard.

Chapter 20

TEN DAYS LATER THE FRENCH ARMY ENTERS NAPLES, TO THE JUBI-lation of a people who are tired of decades of cruelty and negligence, and remain hopeful, as people so often do, that a new ruler will treat them better than the last.

In the royal palace, where he sets up his court, the king welcomes the first flock of Neapolitan well-wishers, along with their wives and prettiest of daughters, all eager to find favor with a monarch whose patronage might also be described as the spoils of war. He is so delighted by the loveliness of what is on offer that he vows to remember every one of his pleasures in a little leather-bound book, which he keeps under his bed. The recording of history comes in many shapes and sizes.

Spurred on by their king's example, the French now settle to some serious lotus eating. Their failing memory is not helped by the loss of their second hostage, Prince Djem. He had been in ill health right from the start, his waking hours spent drunk and abusive, picking quarrels with anyone willing to waste the time of day with him. Alexander, who has watched him disintegrate for years, had been right in his judgment: at thirty-six, the man is a lost cause, bitter and ashamed and now in rising fear that he may, after all, have to face a brother who is more able and at least as unforgiving as he is.

The closer they have got to Naples, the more time he has spent co-matose. Once settled into the palace, he seldom comes out of his room and then only to complain about the rottenness of the food. One morning he does not wake up at all. His servants, grateful for the respite, leave him to it. By the time they think to check, he is barely breathing. The king, who is already having such a good time that he doesn't want to be disturbed, sends his doctors, who sniff and probe and poke, a little more violently than they ought perhaps, but then he has been as abusive to them as everyone else. They get no response. By nightfall he is stiff as a plank.

It doesn't take long for the rumor to spread that Alexander, whose name is now evil incarnate, has had him poisoned to spoil the king's crusade. When the same rumor reaches Alexander, newly reunited with Cesare and scrutinizing each and every dispatch from his spies in Naples, he is caught between fury and celebration at his enemies' stupidity.

"See how such men are swayed by their own thirst for scandal! What possible advantage is there in it for us to have the Turk poisoned? Alive he added forty thousand ducats a year to the papal purse—more as long as someone else was paying his bed and board! Ah well! Someone had better tell Pinturicchio. He might want to erase his likeness from the court of Alexandria now."

Back in Naples, the prince's possessions are distributed among those nobles who have a hankering for oriental fashion, and his great curved saber, which once cut the heads off dozens of true believers (or so he claimed), is given to the king. It is clear even now that this is the closest His Majesty will ever come to the Holy Land. The army lets out a sigh of relief. Who needs rough seas and infidels when they are in the land of plenty?

From underneath the skirts of their Neapolitan hostesses (amateurs fast joined by an army of professionals) the lotus petals unfold and offer up further narcotic sweetness.

Three months later, when the soldiers wake irritated by a gross itching in their groins, Spanish ships from Sicily are already docking on the mainland and an anti-French league has been signed in Rome, negotiated with impressive speed by a pope who, for all his reputation for carnality, knows when to put work above women. The sole object of this alliance: to expel the French and cut off their retreat to the Alps.

They move as fast as an army carrying its own weight in booty on the backs of a thousand mules can manage. Charles heads for Rome, hoping to win over Alexander (despite his treachery he remembers him warmly as the father figure he never had). But by the time they get there, the papal court has moved to Orvieto to avoid him. When they reach Orvieto, the Pope is in Perugia. To follow him any further would be to waste time in what is already becoming a fraught retreat. From Umbria, the French make a dash for home.

The two forces meet on a field outside Fornovo, southwest of Parma. The battle lasts all day. Both sides win and both sides lose. Heavy rain soaks the gunpowder so that the famous French artillery cannot fire. They still manage to kill more soldiers than they lose and break through to head north, but their baggage train is left behind and much of that fabulous war booty falls to the enemy, even down to the king's own chests of treasure, inside one of which is found a little leather-bound book filled with names and dates and coded but pertinent observations.

It is not the only thing they leave behind. Everywhere they have loitered—and in Naples most of all, with its labyrinthine tenements and overflow of humanity—a new disease of the loins starts to spread, to the bewilderment of the doctors called to treat it. Its symptoms, written on the sufferers' faces with angry pustules—a mark of shame for all to see—come and then go, only to return with no warning months later. It is christened "the French disease," and along with "bom bard" it enters the language as another weapon of war.

In Rome, where as yet the population remains smooth-skinned, there is more to celebrate. The Pope has seen off not just an army of conquest but also a direct attack on himself and the papacy by two of his greatest enemies. Cardinal della Rovere slips back to France to lick his wounds and bide his time, but in the south, Virginio Orsini, arch-traitor to the papal cause, is captured by the army of the returning King of Naples and thrown into a dungeon deep inside Castel dell'Ovo on the edge of the sea: an ignominious fate for the head of one of Rome's most powerful families.

In her vineyard, Vannozza is back over her account books, her house and gardens restored. She doesn't ask what happened to the men responsible for their destruction, though she cannot miss the gossip that circulates. It was the misfortune of the Swiss Guard to be left behind by the French king to protect his quarters in case of return. The very day after the league of opposition was signed, a group of them were taking the evening air in Piazza Navona when a wave of Spaniards came crashing out from the side streets and set upon them. Outnumbered ten to one, it is not what anyone would have called a fair fight, and by the time it ended there were some three dozen corpses leaking Swiss blood onto the cobblestones, many of them falling at the hands of two swordsmen, the first in a mask, the other disfigured by scars.

One enemy at a time. The Cardinal of Valencia is a quick learner.

As revenge and celebration mix, the Pope sends instructions for all his children to join him. The family is about to be reunited.

PART IV

Rivalry

*Though every effort is made to conceal it,
these sons of the Pope are consumed with
envy of each other.*

Mantuan ambassador in Rome,
March 1497

Chapter 21

"Oh, it's magnificent. Turn again, faster. Ha! See how the color changes as you move." The young woman pirouettes, her skirts flying out around her, the deep red of her dress breaking into a dozen different shades as her diaphanous overshift catches and filters the light. "How do you get your tailors to pleat the overdress in a way that gives it such lightness?"

"It's made from the same silk as my chemise."

"What? You wear your undergarment over your dress! What do you have underneath?"

"Another one, of course. It is all perfectly respectable. Well, as long as one keeps them on." Her laughter is like a waterfall of gold coins. "In Naples it is all the fashion. Or at least it was until those clodhopping French came in. Do you know they kidnapped our best tailors and took them back with them to France!" She shrugs. "Though not mine or Jofré's. We took them with us when we fled to Sicily."

"How was Sicily?"

"Oooh. Grim. Too hot, too cold and full of wild men and women. I couldn't wait to get home. But then when we got there . . . Oh!"

"What? What did you find?" Lucrezia, who has spent the war in Pesaro, caught between boredom and anxiety, is hungry for horror stories that she can imagine herself into.

"Uuush, it was awful. Awful. Everywhere stink and filth. You would not believe what they did. They took everything—tapestries, pottery, linen, bedheads, the front of carved chests, anything of value that they could fit onto their stupid mules. Even plants. Imagine. Our delicious Arab garden—oh, it was paradise on earth—they ripped the flowers and trees out of the ground. For what? To die in their saddle-bags? The king, my half-brother, cried when he saw it. Really. I mean, we were not supposed to notice, but he couldn't help himself." She shivers theatrically. "Still, they are whipped home now and Naples will rebuild herself. That is what he says. Though I don't know how it can happen with him still fighting rebels everywhere."

"We must thank Our Lord that you are saved from it now. Rome will be a good home until you can go back."

"Oh, I think Rome will be a good home for longer than that."

"What? Even though our fashions are so dull?"

"Not anymore. We still have our tailors with us. You wait—we will have your husband's eyes popping out of his head with your beauty soon enough."

"I don't think he cares much for my clothes."

"No? Well, then it is him and not your clothes that are the problem, because you are quite lovely. As I am sure you know. In which case we will have to find others to admire you."

Though they are the same age, Lucrezia's new sister-in-law is older in all manner of ways. Naples, long before the French, was a city of heat and moist passageways and its court had a reputation for excess. Anyone born into it gains a broad education fast. With royal blood flowing through her veins, Sancia, illegitimate but much loved, has been indulged from an early age. She has a dark, fiery beauty developed from a collision of bloods: olive skin, fine nose, full lips and shining, lapis blue eyes. She has been using it to get her own way for as long as she can remember, the choice of her adolescent Borgia husband being the only exception.

Their arrival, accompanied by what felt like half the court of Naples, has sent shock waves through Roman society. The ambassadors who rode out to greet them, alongside the cardinals and the Pope's family—for this was a political as well as a family affair—had been seduced long before formal introductions, by the flamboyance of Sancia, with her flashing eyes and pert little smile and the overt charms of her ladies riding in fan formation behind her, all laughter and painted faces, such slaves to fashion that they appeared to have chosen their horses to complement their dresses: pale silks spread across black flanks, dark velvets splashed over dappled grays. Pinturicchio, who is already up another scaffold for another patron (always a man for work rather than dalliance), will eat his heart out when he hears, for they make a perfect scene for the arrival of the Queen of Sheba, which is one of his favorite themes at present.

With such competition, Jofré never stood a chance. He rode close to his wife, shorter than her by a good head, and while he was dressed to impress with a ruby-red brocade jacket and contrasting tabard, his hose had been laced so tight to his doublet to favor the shape of his leg that he was having trouble gripping his saddle tightly enough. It was a gift to the satirists among the onlookers: a boy husband who cannot mount his own horse properly. Well, not to worry. It seems his wife rides well enough without him.

The snide jokes are all over Italy within the week. It is not that politics have been forgotten (innuendo is a time-honored weapon of diplomacy) but that there is another, simpler pleasure to be had. Rome has lived through an occupation and the threat of destruction. Those who have weathered the crisis feel both relief and that sense of anticlimax that follows a period of sustained tension. The same ambassadors who now poke fun at the license of the newcomers are themselves craving distraction. Peace, they hope, will now be as interesting as war.

"Though when your father first summoned us, I didn't want to come at all. A city of churches. Goodness knows, we have enough priests in Naples. But Jofré was so excited and Alfonso said we must go because Rome was now a great city for fashion and fun."

"Alfonso?"

"My brother. Oh, and he was right. He would love it here. And you would love him. Every woman does. He rides like the wind, knows every dance and has the finest leg in all Naples. Everyone says we make the perfect couple when we dance the pavane."

"You must miss him."

"Of course. Though I think your brother is almost as handsome."

"Jofré?"

"No!" She laughs gaily. "Cesare. I am sure you missed him when you were away."

Oh, and so she had. The first time Lucrezia had seen him again it had been like the sun coming out after a long winter. Since his triumphant return to Rome he had taken over Prince Djem's rooms in the Vatican directly above the Borgia apartments, and he had been standing there at the window as she and Giovanni had ridden into the gardens. As soon as she saw him she could not stop smiling. He had blown her an extravagant kiss, which she had flung out a hand to catch. The pleasures of theater and chivalry had been missing from her life and she was gleeful at their return. How I love my family, she thought. And yet, though she had been consumed with excitement at the idea of returning home, after a few days she had felt . . . what? Happy, of course, but also strange. There were times, as she basked in the compliments about her new beauty and grace, when she couldn't help but be aware of another Lucrezia sitting next to her: a young woman who had also been away for a long time, and who had missed her family too, certainly, but who had survived without them. Yes, she had cried through some nights, but she had also got up and lived through the next day. And all the ones that followed. She had been the mistress of a ducal palace and had met and been admired by all manner of people. For the first time in her life, this Lucrezia had been more than just an adored daughter and sister. And . . .

"And is it true that he escaped from under the nose of the French army disguised as a groom?"

"What?"

"Cesare? That is what people say about him."

"Yes, yes, he did."

"Oh, that is so . . . so thrilling. If I was a man I know I would have done the same thing. They also say he keeps a courtesan. Fiammetta, that is her name, yes? Have you met her?"

"No."

"I am sure she is very beautiful. Though Jofré says she is not as pretty as me."

"How does Jofré know?"

"He says Cesare took him to meet her." She wrinkles her nose. "But then sometimes he says things just to impress me. Isn't that sweet?"

"What else does he say?" Lucrezia asks, caught between curiosity and a slight sense of the inappropriateness of the conversation. She is used to being the darling of the court, and the arrival of this mischievous, apparently shameless creature has made her feel a little boring in comparison.

"Oh, you know Jofré . . . He is such a boy. Says anything to get attention. I adore him. We all do. Really. Though he can have a temper sometimes." She grins. "As I suspect can Giovanni. I must say at that banquet the other day he looked so . . . so stiff and frowny. Like he had eaten something that monstrously disagreed with him."

Lucrezia smiles. For all her ebullience and daring, there is much that the lovely young Sancia doesn't know and shows no interest in finding out.

The truth is that life in the Borgia court is not so easy for either of their husbands. Jofré has been the baby for so long, adored and neglected by turns, that his pouting and tantrums are fast developing into adult character traits. He is not helped by his wife, who plays with and discards him like a toy, or his father, who can find his pimply insecurity so irritating at times that he has been known to join in the teasing rather than defend him.

Giovanni Sforza, at least, had expected no better.

The duke and his duchess had returned to Rome to find the gossipmongers with their blades sharpened. In the wake of the war the state of the Sforza/Borgia marriage is an irresistible topic for diplomatic speculation. On the surface, the quarrel between the two families is over. In Milan, Ludovico Sforza, like the spoiled child who gets what he wants only to find it disagrees with him, had deserted the French as soon as the tide turned and joined the papal league against them. His brother Cardinal Ascanio has been formally and magnanimously forgiven (*"We wipe away all stain of infamy. Let the past be past and we commence anew"*) and is back in his old job, as passionate in his commitment to the Pope as he had been in his treachery against him. If Alexander feels rancor, he does nothing to show it: every pope needs a vice-chancellor to fill his papal coffers, and on the list of families that have offended there are others higher up. One enemy at a time.

"Ah—look at you. You left Rome a girl and you return a woman." The Pope is overjoyed to see her. "The separation broke our heart a dozen times, yet you have grown more beautiful on it." As she sinks inside the voluminous folds of silk and velvet, breathing in the mix of musk and sweat that reminds her so strongly of her childhood, she can't help also being aware of Giovanni, standing waiting behind her.

"And you too are welcome, esteemed son-in-law," he mutters as he finally lets her go. "We have missed you both."

Across the room Cesare's smile is wide and cold. Whatever the future of their marriage, the bridegroom will be the last to know. Giovanni Sforza's digestive system, however, has long been as effective as a palace full of spies, and he registers both men's welcome as knife-thrusts into his bowels. Or perhaps it is conscience where the blade reaches, for most agree that it resides somewhere near the stomach. Either way, such is his level of nerves that during the first weeks he will not eat or drink anything that he has not seen first pass his wife's lips.

"Oh, my lord. You will enjoy this, I think. Here, taste the sauce. It has a thick Roman sweetness to it, and goes well with the wine."

At their first dinner in the papal apartments, Lucrezia feels his discomfort so profoundly that she makes a virtue of feeding him mouthfuls from her own plate, then cupping arms so that they drink from each other's goblet. His smile, for those who glimpse it, betrays a painful gratitude.

Her kindness reflects the truce that has been reached between them. During the occupation of Rome, their separate levels of anxiety were so consuming that there were days when they barely spoke to each other. But with news of the Pope's victory and the Sforzas' change of sides, it was clear that they too must make their peace. In place of affection they had cultivated civility. It was not so hard. As mistress of a court she had seen worse marriages: open displays of disdain or boredom, the careless lust of roaming husbands. He was never like that. Even when things were at their worst he did not directly insult or abuse her. Nor did he in any way—and in one way in particular—force himself upon her. After the war was over and his nerves had steadied, he still did not return to her bed. She did not ask. Neither did she miss him. It was a compromise agreeable to them both, an understanding without words. It has never been in her nature to hold grudges, and at sixteen she is still in love with the possibilities of life and would prefer to be in high spirits rather than low ones.

"Such a handsome couple. May I take the liberty of raising a toast to welcome them home?" Cardinal Ascanio Sforza's nasal voice rises above the hubbub of the room as he lifts his goblet toward the Pope. "What a joy to see our families so closely linked in friendship again." Across the tables, the envoys scrabble for their wine, amending their dispatches in their heads.

When Cesare quizzes her later, as they sit together waiting for musicians to start the dancing, she finds herself torn between loyalty and a kind of pity.

"We are well enough, considering."

"Considering he is a fool."

"Considering I am married to him."

"I do not see much affection between you."

"Oh, Cesare. Do not make it more difficult than it is."

"I am your brother. I want you to be happy."

"And I am. I am back with you and Papà. You are both safe and the war is ended. I cannot tell you how that warms my soul. I was so worried."

"You shouldn't have been."

Across the room the Pope is settling further into his chair, his face flushed with banquet wine and food. He raises a hand toward them and she smiles back. "You say that, but Papà looks different. He seems older, more worn."

"Fatter, more like. Our mother overfed him during the occupation. She insisted on bringing her own food and wine to the castle."

"At least she was safe." She pauses. "I can't imagine how it was. Is it true that we came near to losing everything?"

"Who told you that? Your husband?" His voice is sharp.

"Do not jump down his throat, Cesare. He was not the only one."

"We were never going to lose. I made that clear in my letters."

"Sometimes people say what they think you want to hear."

"What? Like everyone telling you how much more lovely you have grown while you have been away?" He looks straight into her eyes without letting his gaze falter.

She shakes her head, embarrassed. "You are teasing me," she murmurs. "I don't know what you mean."

"I mean that perhaps they say it because that is what you want to hear. Except it is not true. Not from what I see."

"Why? What do you see?"

"I see a lovely young woman, yes, but with something missing in her."

"What? What is missing in me?" she says, like a child demanding the answer to some question that even the adult cannot know.

"You are unloved."

She continues to stare at him. "Unloved?"

"Yes, unloved. You have a husband, yet you remain unloved." He lets the word hang for a second. "But then traitors are not good at love. And you, dear sister, deserve more."

She feels heat rushing into her face and drops her head so that he doesn't see it. "I cannot hear such things. Please. This does not help."

Across the room Giovanni, who has been in pointed conversation with his cousin, has stopped talking and is looking toward them.

"What things, Lucrezia?" Cesare, who notices everything that is going on around, makes his voice light and normal now. "It is just Roman banter, sis," he says theatrically and as she looks up he gives her his most charming public smile. "You have been away so long you have forgotten how we do it." He takes her hand and brings it to his lips. "But we will not have you leave again. You are far too precious for that." And he pulls her toward him and kisses her fondly on both cheeks. As his lips brush close to her ear he whispers, "You don't need to be afraid. Whatever happens, I will always love you."

As he turns back to the room, he sees that a number of the guests are now looking in their direction. One might almost think he has been courting such attention.

The musicians have gathered themselves and the viol strikes up the opening notes of a dance. He gets up with the intention of partnering her, but before he can do so Giovanni is standing in front of her, his hand outstretched.

"They play to welcome us home, dear wife," he says, altogether too loudly. "Will you take the floor with me?"

She rises unsteadily and puts her hand in his. It is damp with sweat.

Chapter 22

As spring turns to summer, the papal court grows hotter faster than the weather. For the first few weeks Lucrezia and Sancia are inseparable, closeted together in one or the other of their respective palaces with cloth merchants and tailors, picking out fabrics and playing at fashion. Alexander, who lacks only the presence of Juan to make his happiness complete, is charmed by his new daughter-in-law, though her appetite for mischief plays havoc with Burchard's official structures. During one public church service in St. Peter's, she and Lucrezia grow so bored with the interminable sermon that halfway through they break ranks and, accompanied by their flock of brightly colored ladies, clamber up to the choir stalls, where they settle noisily, giggling and preening themselves. It is a small but perfect scandal. The Pope looks on indulgently as Burchard, nailed to his place, suffers a fit of what appears to be hyperventilation. What is news in Rome one day is gossip for the rest of Italy the next.

Like all Sancia's behavior, it is both spontaneous and calculating. She has grown up on a diet of adoration and is at her most relaxed when all eyes are upon her, though at any given time she always knows which particular man's attention she is seeking. As does everyone else, fast enough.

For a while, Cesare is amused as much as attracted. The first meeting between the two of them had been spiced with such obvious mutual appreciation that it felt as if the future had already happened. Nevertheless, he is a busy Church politician these days and his time for dalliance is limited. During the war he had been so focused on affairs of state that his courtesan mistress, Fiammetta, with her professional wit and lack of jealousy, seemed to have won him over to an unexpected fidelity.

The vibrant young Duchess of Squillace, however, is used to getting what she desires. She reveals her charms in all manner of fashionably lovely outfits, coddling and petting her husband while all the time throwing sly little looks in the cardinal's direction. It becomes almost impolite for him to resist. By the second month there is a wager on how long it will take her to bed him.

Fiammetta, who is not allowed at court, could have won the bet easily.

"I see you have come from Naples," she says when he arrives one night dressed in a new black jacket sculpted tight over his chest, its sleeves dramatically slashed to the elbows to allow clouds of crushed white silk to billow out through the cuts.

He laughs. "I wasn't sure you would like it. It was a present."

"I shall not bother to ask in return for what." She pours the wine. "It does not concern you that she is married to your brother?"

"It is not a marriage. She has a lapdog called Jofré."

"Perhaps jealousy will teach it how to bite."

"Ah, Fiammetta, don't tell me that you begrudge me a little fun?"

"I begrudge you nothing. As you know, I am not a possessive type. But I should warn you, I may also be more occupied over the coming months."

Their passion for each other runs hot and fast. They share a fearlessness, which allows them to take risks, so that when it is at its peak you can smell their desire for each other in a room full of people. Out of cardinal's clothing, Cesare is every inch the courtier, with a tongue as fast and sharp as his sword, and their public banter becomes a kind of foreplay. The effect is both shocking and exhilarating. It awakes a certain carnality in the whole court, with Sancia's ladies leading the dance. Some are entranced, others appalled. Jofré reacts by dressing even more loudly and spending more time trying to crawl into his wife's lap. He is not so much angry as glum. It is not the first time and it will not be the last. When he does allow himself to think about it, he becomes fixated on the fact that there is another Borgia brother to come home.

Giovanni, who has taken to spending time in the palace of his cousin, the Vice-Chancellor, is also having trouble breathing.

"Please, stay. You are my husband and we have a position to maintain."

"So come back with me. You are my wife and Pesaro needs you too."

"You know I can't do that. My father has asked for us to be at court with him."

"This is not a court, Lucrezia, it's a bordello. And anyone who doesn't play the game is to be despised. I am barely tolerated here as it is. Have you seen the way your brother looks at me?"

But recently all Lucrezia has seen is the way Cesare looks at her sister-in-law. Alone that night, she cries in a way she has not done for many months. It is hard to know what upsets her most: the behavior of her husband or that of her brother.

One afternoon she calls on Sancia unannounced, only to find her behind the box hedge in the garden courtyard with Cesare's hand halfway up her skirts, her head pushed back and little moans coming out of her mouth.

He sees her first, rising to greet her so fast that Sancia has to steady herself against falling. Lucrezia turns on her heel and is halfway across the receiving room when he reaches her. He puts out his hand to her shoulder but she pushes it off.

"What is it?"

"What is it!" She looks at him incredulously.

"Do not take it so seriously. It is a passing affection."

"Cesare! She is our brother's wife."

"And as family I have grown most fond of her." He smiles.

"Don't," she says angrily. "It does not make it better joking or lying about it."

"I am not lying, Lucrezia. I am telling you not to worry. It is a dalliance, that is all."

"A dalliance? And is that what she thinks it is too?"

"Sancia has grown up in Naples. She knows what she is doing."

"I don't think either of you know what you are doing."

"We are fine. There is no hurt involved."

"Except to your souls," she says.

"Ah, my young sweet sister." He laughs. "No one loves me like you do. Do not fret about my soul."

"And do not treat me like a child. I am neither sweet nor young anymore."

He stops for a second, looking evenly at her. "I know that," he says. "And I also know you care more about me than most of the priests I have ever met. But you must understand that everyone must look after his own soul."

"And do you? Look after your soul?"

"Of course."

"How? How do you do that, Cesare?"

"I confess my sins."

"You take confession. Regularly?"

"Whenever there is need. So, regularly, yes."

"And you complete your penance and are given absolution?"

"Always," he says, allowing himself a small smile. "I am the Cardinal of Valencia after all."

"Oh, Cesare." She sighs, because underneath the banter she does not know how much to believe him. She is well aware of how silly her fears sound when she puts words to them. How young they make her appear. She prays sometimes that she could be worldlier. Understand it all more. But how can one ask God for less conscience?

"And what about Jofré?"

"Jofré is my brother and I would die for him. He has had too much asked of him, too young. But if we are to make the family secure, he must grow up fast. Better to be prodded into it by someone who loves him rather than one who doesn't." He holds her gaze. "And in answer to your next question; no, that is not why I am doing it, but it is true nevertheless. So. Does that satisfy you, little sister? Is there anything else within the family that I can help you with?"

She stares at him. While the words are sarcastic, his tone is not. Is there anything else?

"Will I stay married to my husband?" The question spurts out almost against her will. She expects him to laugh, or at least mock her in some way.

"Why?" he says quietly. "Would you prefer another?"

She makes a fierce little movement with her head, but it is hard to tell if it is agreement or denial. She closes her eyes tight. He takes her hands and holds them for a moment. Before he can say anything they both hear the tapping footsteps of Sancia. It is one thing to be interrupted, another to be abandoned altogether. He turns and offers his arm in welcome. But she stops short of them, slightly breathless though she does not look as if she has been running. Underneath her robes there is perhaps the stomp of a little foot.

She is so very pretty, Lucrezia thinks. She smiles at her. It helps to know there is nothing to worry about.

Of course, it is not as easy as he makes it sound. The fire of sex, once lit, travels where the winds of passion take it, and Sancia, for all that she is a product of the morally feral court of Naples, is not immune to injury. For the first months she registers only the wild beauty of the flame. She has become the heart and soul of the court of Rome, snaring not one but now two of the Pope's sons, and the most handsome and most charismatic man in the Vatican to boot.

Her triumph becomes the center of her life: her days are filled with fashion and fun and the exquisite anticipation of their next meeting. Cesare, in contrast, has many lives to lead, so that when they part, however sweet the connection, he forgets it almost immediately. As the weeks pass, what was once irresistible to him starts to become almost routine.

Within the Church there is some serious business to be done, more new cardinals to be chosen to capitalize on Alexander's recent victory. It is a mark of the Pope's confidence in his son that he leaves much of the deciding to him. But such things take time, and there are evenings when he is late or even fails completely to make their assignations. Sancia, who is not used to being ignored, takes it badly. She pouts and stomps and plays hard to get. He storms the citadel once, enjoying the game, but finds it tedious a second and third time. In her well-appointed white house on the other side of the bridge, Fiammetta, whose job it is to negotiate men's desires without them knowing they are being managed, welcomes him one night when Sancia has closed the door in his face. She listens and laughs and when they retire to bed resists him just enough to make him feel that she is a conquest again.

When the gossip of his straying filters through, as it must, Sancia goes into a rage of hot tears, then recovers, and then collapses again. Where once the court was full of excitement, there is now an undercurrent of anxiety. Alexander himself, who has been indulgent of the situation, now finds it less relaxing being in their company and spends more evenings at work or in private suppers with ambassadors. His withdrawal in turn affects the mood of those who remain. What was once fun becomes difficult.

"She can be rather tiresome. It would be better if she was more of a wife to Jofré," he says one night in bed to Giulia. "It does not help our reputation that he is made such an obvious cuckold." He seems to see no irony in this remark. But then their own relationship has cooled a little since the drama of her self-imposed exile, so that he spends more nights alone than in her bed.

"Your father finds her tiresome." Giulia visits Lucrezia the next afternoon. What she feels about her own gradual fall from favor she does not say. At twenty-three she is as lovely as ever, and with a daughter, a cardinal brother and a receiving room still buzzing with those in need of papal favors she is hardly a woman discarded. Perhaps, like Vannozza before her, she is enjoying having a certain weight lifted off her. "You should talk to her. You know her better than the rest of us."

"What? What should I say?"

"Tell her she must look to making her own marriage more of a success and not make a fuss about things she can do nothing about."

Lucrezia shrugs. "I think she may be disappointed in her husband."

Giulia smiles. "You have developed some of your family's wit while you have been away."

"Actually, I meant it seriously."

"In which case tell her that she is in good company, but that she must learn to be more discreet when she strays."

But Sancia is not in a mood to be told anything. "I am a fine wife to Jofré and love him dearly. As to the Cardinal of Valencia, I have no interest in him. I am a princess of royal blood used to having courtiers around me, not men with the manners of a street cat."

It is a description some might use of her too. "It is just his way, Sancia. He doesn't mean to be cruel."

"On the contrary, I think he enjoys it. But it is nothing to me. It was a dalliance, no more than that. And I was tiring of it anyway."

The silence draws out between them. Lucrezia is uncomfortable and is preparing to leave when a deep sob rips out from Sancia's throat. She waves her hand frantically in front of her face as if to push it aside.

"I am not crying about your brother," she says angrily. "No. He is not worth it. It's just . . . I—I have had some bad news from Naples."

"What? What?"

". . . er . . . Alfonso has been hurt in a riding accident."

"Your brother! What happened?"

"Oh . . . his horse tripped and he fell. He turned his foot. It will be all right. I am just worried about him."

Lucrezia, who is no stranger to the struggle between saying one thing and feeling another, comes up and puts her arms around her. "Oh, Sancia, it's all right to be upset by it all. I think you might be homesick." The young beauty's mouth puckers and trembles like a child's. "Maybe your brother can come and visit us in Rome. I am sure when the time is right Papà would be only too happy to offer an invitation."

"Yes." Sancia nods. "Yes. Then you will see a man whose heart is as fine as his leg. A real courtier." She is almost recovered. "Oh, and is it true that the Duke of Gandia is coming back from Spain?"

Chapter 23

H<small>E HAD BEEN SUMMONED ONCE BEFORE: WHEN</small> R<small>OME HAD BEEN</small> facing the French, the Pope had sent out a plea for his favorite son to return home, as if his very presence might somehow persuade the enemy to turn back. But the Duke of Gandia's life had not been at the beck and call of his father anymore. With a royal wife, a place at court and a piece of Spain to finance his lifestyle, he was a Spanish grandee, held in orbit around the energetic monarchy of Isabella of Castile and Ferdinand of Aragon. It was a sweet enough slavery for him, and Spain's need for a friendly Borgia hostage to secure the Pope's continued loyalty to the House of Aragon in Naples had resulted in all manner of excuses to keep him.

But with Naples now recaptured from the French, Their Most Holy Catholic Majesties can make no objection to his recall. The invitation is irresistible: Juan is called home to lead an army of retribution against his father's enemies. Alexander is finally ready to settle some scores. The Sforzas and the Colonna concern him less—they have been smart enough to prostrate themselves before the victor and can wait. The Orsini, however, with their leader Virginio buried in a Neapolitan jail, remain in the pay of the French and still in control of strategic castles around Rome. It had been the surrender of those very castles that had welcomed in the army in the first place.

The first salvo comes in the form of a papal bull of excommunication against the whole family as punishment for disobedience and treachery to the Holy See. Having scuppered them in the next life, Alexander now sets out to disenfranchise them in this one. To do so, he needs the services of a captain-general of the Church, a man of impeccable loyalty who, when the Orsini lands are confiscated, can annex them into the Borgias' own estates. The only person better qualified for the job is the one who cannot have it. Though that does not stop him from speaking his mind.

"Juan has no experience, Father. Not of diplomacy nor military planning, nor anything connected with the art of war. You read his letters. He barely knows one end of a cannon from the other and the only men he has ever commanded are the servants who move his furniture or the tailors he shouts at when they don't sew enough jewels onto his sleeves."

"He is not a professional soldier, that is true. Which is why we will approach the Duke of Urbino to share command. His name carries weight and our league of allies would support him."

Cesare shrugs. "So then you will have a one-eyed man leading the blind. Urbino is a second-generation condottiere. He runs on his father's reputation. He has not fought a single pitched battle on his own. Nor campaigned for more than a season."

"What are you saying, Cesare? That you have done all of those things?"

"No. But I have lived every minute of this war. I have sat with you over maps of Italy and talked strategy and the movement of men and weapons. I have negotiated surrenders and played off one side against another. I would be a better commander than Juan."

"Even if that is true, you are a cardinal of the Church of Rome. You cannot also be its captain-general. Those who oppose us are vigilant for the ways we misuse papal power."

"We do nothing that the della Rovere haven't done before us. Pope Sixtus sent a priest to assassinate the Medici brothers during high mass!"

"Indeed he did!" cried Alexander, moving between pleasure and exasperation at this sustained attack. "But he did not do it himself. You are my son and a cardinal and you cannot be seen to be slaughtering men in the field."

"No. But I could sit in camp and make sure they measured the distance between the guns and the walls they were bombarding correctly."

"Enough of your sarcasm, Cesare. You are not hearing what I am saying."

Cesare bows his head. "I am sorry. But—with respect, Father—neither are you hearing me. I know about war. I've questioned the artillery commanders who took the fortresses of the south. I've also studied these Orsini castles and I know what is needed for this campaign to work. The smaller ones to the east and northwest of Lake Bracciano will drop into our hands. They have little loyalty to the Orsini and the smell of cannon fire will scare them. Their defense is antiquated." He pauses to make sure he is being heard now. "It is the two that are built on the lake itself that will cause the trouble, because they can move troops and supplies by boat between them. The fortress of Bracciano most of all. It has been refortified and is in the hands of Virginio's sister. She is as much a fighter as her brother and she will see it as a chance to defy us and bargain for his release."

"Ah, you run almost as good an intelligence network as my own. It is a wonder either of us ever finds time to pray," Alexander says drily, though of course he cannot help being impressed. "You are right, my son. You have studied it well. And Juan will know all this before he sets out. As for Virginio Orsini, the matter will be settled another way."

"How?"

The Pope waves his hand impatiently. "You will know soon enough." Since the defeat of the French there are moments in discussion with his son when he wonders who is ruling whom. "You are my confidant in almost everything that we do, Cesare. Some things are better unspoken. What I am telling you now is simply what can and cannot be done."

There is a silence. Cesare sits very still, his eyes fixed on the table in front of him. "In which case release me from the Church," he says at last, his voice quiet.

"No. I will most certainly not. And we will not have this conversation again."

He looks up at him. "I tell you, Father, you will regret it if you don't."

"And you will regret it if you dare to threaten me." Alexander in rising anger brings up a closed fist to slam it on the table, but seems to change his mind, opening his fingers and bringing his hand down heavily so that it lies, palm down, pressing hard into the wood. "God's wounds, Cesare. I am the head of this family, and until I am not, you will do what I say. No dynasty of any worth in Italy has ever succeeded without having either a state under its control, or a pope to conquer one."

He takes a breath to mediate his fury. "Look at what we have achieved since my ascension. Look at the wealth you hold, the benefices and the titles. Look at our land and honors brought through the web of marriages. We are linked to the Spanish throne, we have half of Naples in our pocket and we didn't have to fire a shot to get either of them. Once we have cut loose Pesaro and found another husband for Lucrezia we will be a force that even the Orsini cannot push around. And mark my words, at some point France will need something that only a pope can deliver, and then she too will bend her knee to us. We have achieved in five years that which would have taken fifty without the papacy. I know the Church was not your choice. But at twenty-one you are already in a place where no man would dare touch you."

"The only reason they don't touch me is because of you. If you were to die . . ."

"Ha! Do I look like I am dying?" he yells. Ah, how he hates to be reminded of his mortality. "I will see you strong enough to command enough votes to win the papal crown first."

"Oh, Father. They hate us. Even the ones who vote for us talk about us behind our backs. Della Rovere would see me dead first."

"Della Rovere may be dead himself if we last long enough. I know how capable you are, Cesare. But this is how it must be. Juan will become the Captain-General of the Church and, if he agrees, Urbino will take the field with him."

"And if they lose?"

"They will not lose. The Orsini will be humbled, that I promise you. And now we will move on. Yes? Yes. Right. That young messenger that you stole from me years ago, what was his name?

"Pedro Calderón."

"Calderón. Good. We have a job for him."

"GAN-D-I-A! GAN-D-I-A!"

Thanks to Borgia handouts, the dirty little port town of Civitavecchia raises a crowd to welcome the Pope's son back onto Italian soil. It is the same place from where he embarked three years ago: a callow youth dispatched to sire a Borgia dynasty and gain a little gravitas along the way. The dynasty has come easily: one male heir and another already cooking in the womb. The gravitas is more of a challenge. But in the excitement of his return all the stories of vanity and bad behavior are forgotten. In the days it has taken for the ship to cross from Valencia to the Italian coast, Alexander has worked himself into a lather of anticipation, the court responding around him. "When the Duke of Gandia arrives home" becomes a byword for describing the pleasures of the future.

Cesare, who masks his disappointment well enough, is charming and polite to all. As if to make up for the damage caused, he has recently tucked young Jofré under his wing, taking him hunting and teaching him horse skills and moves inside the bullring. In public, meanwhile, he treats Sancia with exaggerated courtesy. She laughs and twirls her skirts and is so obviously gay that it is clear to anyone with an ounce of empathy that she is not.

Juan reaches Rome on August 10 and is met at the northern gate by Cesare and a band of cardinals and courtiers. The day before, the diplomats lay wagers on the weight of jewels he will be wearing. The new ambassador from Mantua, whose mistress, the great patron Isabella d'Este, demands her politics spiced with fashion, is the winner; but he factors in the horse, which has so many silver bells attached that the duke tinkles like a crowd of lepers with every step he takes.

That night, under a ceiling decorated with bulls, the ladies go mad for him. Three years' absence has turned a gangling boy into a strong young man, his skin aglow with Spanish sun and his pockets deep with exotic tales. He makes a great fuss of his younger brother, picking him up and twirling him around in front of the assembled gathering, as Jofré, who can now pass his cloak at a bull, yelps furiously to be let down. Depositing him at the feet of his wife, Juan delivers her a sweeping bow. The audience applauds. She beams and offers him her hand, which he munches on for a while. Spain's loss is the Duchess of Squillace's gain. Over his head, she glances toward Cesare, who watches impassively for a moment, then winks at her.

Ah, the wonder of a family reunited. The Pope's smile pushes his cheeks so far up into his eyes that he sees nothing of the unfolding pantomime.

"I am a Borgia too. I don't see why I'm not included."

"Because we talk Church business, that's why."

"So why is Juan there?"

"Because he has been in Spain and knows Their Spanish Majesties' minds. No, no, I told you: the weight on your heels, so that you are already turning before the cape moves over your arm. Otherwise you'll have a horn in your gonads."

"I am on my heels," he barks indignantly. "And what's the Spanish king and queen's mind got to do with Church business anyway?"

"Little brother, I am telling you, you cannot be there."

Jofré turns, whipping the cape up and behind him, once, twice, then coming to a stop, throwing his head back and pushing his chest out as he has watched others do. Across the dusty courtyard, a young bull with horns the size of small fists pushing out of his head stands tethered, decidedly uninterested in the spectacle being played out in front of his eyes. "It is not fair. I am not 'little brother' anymore," he says, holding the pose to make his point. "I am Duke of Squillace with an income of forty thousand ducats a year and a post in the Neapolitan army. You know, if Sancia's half-brother was to die, I might become King of Naples."

Cesare laughs. "Not while her Uncle Federico or her brother Alfonso is still alive."

"Well, they could both die too." He swears loudly. It is a habit he has taken to since his return to court, to make him seem older. "Come on, Cesare, everyone knows that we are going to war. If we're going to hammer the Orsini you need me. Now I can fight bulls, I can fight cockroaches too." He prances over to the bull and snaps the cape to and fro in front of it. The animal lets out a low bellow of protest at the unfairness of the provocation. Despite the pain of cuckoldry Jofré has proved eager to be placated; an older brother who can slide along the flanks of a raging bull or leap from one galloping horse to another while barely dirtying his costume is a man to be emulated rather than resented.

"What else do you know about what we are going to do?" Cesare asks casually.

"I know that Juan will lead the troops, with the Duke of Urbino as joint commander, and they will have a cardinal from Milan as legate. I am right, yes? In which case I don't see—"

"Who told you about Urbino and the cardinal? Who?" His voice is sharp now. The Duke of Gandia is barely six weeks in residence and the court is awash with rumors, most of them so accurate that there is only one person who can be starting them.

Jofré shakes his head, suddenly stubborn.

"Who, Jofré? I need to know."

His mouth falls into a familiar scowl. "Sancia," he growls.

"Sancia?"

"Yeah . . . *He* tells her everything."

Pillow talk. Another open secret. From one brother's bed to another's. No wonder Jofré is outraged at his exclusion. Sancia and Juan. It had been like watching ripe fruit fall. She made sure Cesare had a ringside seat, because of course it is her way of getting back at him, as they both know. He is wondering about coaxing her back into his bed, imagining the pleasure of putting Juan's nose out of joint. It would not be so hard a task. Naples and Rome, both cities of alley cats. But he is growing almost fond of his younger brother these days, and would not like to cause him more suffering than is necessary.

"But I knew it all anyway, before she told me," Jofré says defiantly. Since he has learned how to tease tethered animals he has found a new confidence. "Everybody does."

"Then everyone—like you—should watch their tongue. Or some-one might cut it out." Cesare makes a grab for him, slipping the cloak expertly out of his hand, and tackles him playfully to the ground, where he tries to pluck at his mouth as the boy yells.

"Get off! Get off me!" Jofré shakes himself madly to avoid the grab and soon they are both yelping and laughing. Two brothers wrestling in the dust. It is not often either of them is so carefree. "All right. All right. I am only telling you because you ought to know. Ha! If you won't let me in, you should at least pay me to be your informant. You tell me I've got a fast hand and a quick eye."

"And so you have, little brother."

Cesare releases his grip and helps him to his feet.

"But remember. You have to know when to step out of the way, before you sink the dagger into the bull's neck."

Chapter 24

I<small>N THE DINGY LIGHT INSIDE THE OLD BASILICA OF</small> S<small>T.</small> P<small>ETER,</small> J<small>UAN</small> Borgia, newly ordained as Gonfaloniere and Captain-General of the Church, kneels alongside the Duke of Urbino to receive the papal staff and banners of war. After mass, free wine and food help gather a crowd to see them on their way. It has taken time for Rome to get back its sense of pride after the humiliation of occupation, and there are those who think a war between families can bring only bloodshed rather than honor. Others relish the chance to settle old scores. In the Piazza del Popolo a group of Orsini followers start heckling as the troops pass and within minutes a fight breaks out inside the crowd. Swords are pulled and the howls of fury and agony penetrate over the drumrolls into the ranks of soldiers: fitting music to accompany men into battle.

The weather is unseasonably warm for late autumn, and for a while the sun shines on everything. Bunched like a cluster of grapes around Lake Bracciano, the fortresses to the south and northwest fall as easily as Cesare has predicted. By Christmas, Alexander is celebrating the birth of the Christ child along with the transferred ownership of nine castles. The Vatican is full of joy. All that remains is Trevignano and Bracciano, its recently fortified turrets and crenellated walkways reflected into the mirror surface of the lake.

In his private chambers Alexander calls for Cesare's messenger. It is a good choice. Locked in Rome as part of Cesare's bodyguard, Pedro Calderón has spent a frustrating war. There had been his dash to Spoleto, and a few backstreet brawls with French soldiers during the occupation, but the only real offensive had come with the attack on the

Swiss Guard, and the odds had been so far on the Borgia side that he had left the square with a sense of a slaughter rather than an honorable fight. What he wants more than anything else is a mission.

"The Cardinal of Valencia says that you would defend him to the death and that on horseback you can outrun any deer."

The flattery leaves him a little embarrassed. "I do my best, Your Holiness." He has never been so close to the heart of power and his eyes are everywhere at once. Around him the walls and the ceiling pulsate with color, even the floor sings out through its patterned tiles. It is Pedro's destiny to be deeply affected by beauty. Alexander watches the wonder in his eyes and lets the moment linger. Ambassadors and diplomats have jaded palates when it comes to such things. "You find the images around you pleasing, young man?"

"Oh . . . Holy Father, I am sorry. I did not mean . . . I have never . . ." He hesitates. "It is like standing inside the light of heaven," he ends lamely.

"The light of heaven. Finely said." Alexander, who has occasionally wondered if there is perhaps a touch too much gold everywhere, smiles broadly. "The Cardinal of Valencia has chosen well in you. But now we must put you in the saddle. Tell me how long will it take you to get to Naples."

"If the weather is not against me and I change horses, close to two days."

"Good. I need a message taken to a man there."

"It is done, Your Holiness."

"You have not heard all of it yet."

Calderón bows his head.

"You will have a name and place where he can be found. When you locate the man, you will address him by another name. When he nods you will say nothing else, simply hand him the letter. Wait while he reads it. He will then tell you when and where to meet him next. At that meeting he will say the words. 'The meat is well spiced.' You will then ride back to Rome, stopping for nothing. When you get here you will report to me immediately. Is all that clear?"

"Completely."

"Should anything happen either on the road or in Naples to prevent you from delivering the letter it is imperative that it be destroyed."

"Nothing will prevent me, Your Holiness."

From a casket on the table, Alexander hands him a folded parchment closed with the Borgia seal. Calderón opens his doublet and shirt, slips the letter next to his skin and refastens his clothes. All this is done calmly, with quiet precision.

"One more thing. You have never been in my presence, nor gone to Naples nor met the man that you will meet there."

Calderón can feel his mouth twitching to smile. "On my life, Your Holiness." The excitement is leaking out of him. He starts moving backward toward the door.

"Ah—maybe not that way. The palace has more eyes than a sack of needles. There is a door in the back of the next room. The passage leads into the next palazzo. From there you can cross into a courtyard and into the street beyond."

His exhilaration is such that his whole body is tingling as he navigates the gloom of the passage. At the same moment that he opens the door on the other side, he sees a woman entering the room, and turning directly toward him. He recognizes her from his dreams. He pulls his cloak around him and bows low.

"My lady."

"Oh, oh my! Oh, you startled me! Wait . . . it is Pedro Calderón, yes?"

"Yes, my lady."

"What are you doing here? Have you come from my father . . . I mean His Holiness?"

He stares at her. "No. No."

"No. But you have come through the passage? Where have you been?"

"I—I was . . . delivering a letter from the Cardinal of Valencia, but I saw no one."

"So, my father is not in his chambers?"

"I have no idea, madam." And now his discomfort is clear.

"Ah. Ah, I see." And the smile is involuntary. "My, you are elevated in the world, Señor Calderón. So what? Probably I have not seen you either?"

He gives a slight shrug and they stand awkwardly for a moment. Such is the unexpectedness of it all, such the thrill of the moment, that neither he nor she can pull themselves away. "How was the Duchy of Pesaro, my lady?"

"Pesaro? Oh, it was quite fine. Until it was not. You were right, they were most pleased to see me. But I missed Rome."

He nods. He cannot help staring.

"Aren't you going to tell me how Rome missed me?"

"Oh, oh yes, yes. The city was bereft. I . . ." He stops himself, aware of how foolish he sounds. She stands waiting, her lips slightly parted, bright eyes with a touch of mischief in them. There is something in his gaucheness that makes her feel confident, almost carefree. "I am not a courtier, my lady. Words come out badly." He feels the letter close to his skin. It would be better not to stain it with sweat. "But I think any city where you are not is a place in slumber waiting for your return."

"Actually, Señor Calderón, the words come out quite well. Courtiers say flattering things they don't believe. You should not worry about emulating them. I am grateful to you for guarding my brother through the dark days of the war."

"The cardinal guards himself, my lady. I did very little."

"That's not true. I heard you rode ahead of him to Spoleto after his escape."

"How did you hear?" And it is clear he is pleased.

"Oh—I have forced him to tell me everything. Life in Pesaro was as dull as it was alarming. How exciting to have been part of it."

"If I could ever be of any similar help to you . . ."

"I hope I am never fleeing for my life. But thank you. You are a true soldier. I—I must go. My father has asked to see me."

"Of course. May I escort you through the passage? It is dark there."

"You are kind, but it is a darkness I am familiar with. And anyway, we have not seen each other, remember?"

She is still lighthearted from the encounter as she kisses her father welcome.

"My sweet child. I did not expect you so soon. Sit, sit. Here . . . Look at you. You glow as brightly as the room. We are fortunate to have such wonder around us, yes? Here. I am the recipient of a gift of sugared fruits from the new Cardinal of Sevilla. You must help me with them. There are those who say a man can be too stout as he grows older." He pats his stomach fondly. "But it is my intention to be big enough to fit two popes in here," he says gaily, for the world is going well for him, bar a few outstanding matters which he is now addressing.

"So, my dear. I am so busy with this marvelous campaign of your brother's that I have neglected you rather over these last months. The court is full of life, I hear. Do you enjoy yourself?"

She drops her eyes. Watching her sister-in-law move her brothers in and out of bed has been a dispiriting experience for a young woman deserted by her own husband.

"Of course, with the duke away you have less opportunity to shine. Have you heard from him recently?"

"Er . . . no, not for some time. He is busy with business."

"And what business could be more important than a wife? We have summoned him to Rome twice now to join the fight against the Orsini but to no avail. I must say, such behavior makes me fear that there is something deeply amiss in your marriage."

"But—I have been a good wife, Father," she says fiercely.

"Oh, goodness, child. I am not criticizing you. These Sforzas are slippery creatures, as we have found out to our cost. No, no, if anyone must take the blame it is myself. You were very young, of course, but you will remember that you were already betrothed when Sforza made his offer."

"Count Gaspar d'Aversa," she says immediately. There have been moments over these last years when she has wondered if that name would have made her happier than the one she carries now.

"Yes. Excellent fellow. He claimed that the engagement was never formally dissolved. And it is true, thinking about it, that the process was indeed rather precipitous . . ."

"What does that mean?"

"It means, if the Church lawyers agree on it, your marriage to Sforza could be declared null and void."

"Null and void!" The words hit hard. Is it really so simple? Should she have asked before? "You mean I would no longer be married?"

"No. Would that upset you dreadfully?"

"I . . . er . . . if it is your wish, I would accept it." Her heart is beating so fast she can barely hear her voice.

"Excellent. Cesare said you would have no complaints. This Sforza union has brought us nothing but trouble. We will do better next time."

"Does my husband know about this?" She sees him standing before her, a man almost too eager to leave.

"It is a family of traitors, not fools, so his cousins may have picked up a glimmer of some gossip. We have yet to put the matter formally before the lawyers."

"And what if they don't agree?"

He shrugs. "They will earn my grave displeasure. But you are not to worry. It is decided. If it cannot be done one way it will be done another."

"What other way could there be?"

He studies her for a moment, as if deciding whether to proceed. "Well, there is the problem of issue. That after over three years there are no children in the marriage."

"I . . . I am not barren, Father," she says, the words rushing out before she can stop them.

"No, no. I am sure of that. We Borgias could people Rome if we had the time." He laughs. "No, the fault obviously lies with your husband."

"Giovanni?"

"Yes. Tell me, when you are together, does he come much to your bed?"

She colors fast, but the answer is there in the shake of her head.

"What about in the past? Perhaps not then either."

"When? I don't quite . . ."

"Child, I am asking if the marriage was properly consummated."

"Oh! I . . . Yes . . . yes, I think so."

"You think? You are not sure? You know what I am referring to?"

"Yes . . ." Lucrezia is now in an agony of embarrassment. "I mean yes, I am sure it was."

"I wonder. You see, he leaves you so often. That is not the behavior of a man who desires to lie with his wife. And yours was not a public bedding." He pauses. "No one but you—and he—know what took place that night. So, my dear, if there was any doubt . . ."

"But there isn't. It—"

"Let me finish. If there was any doubt . . . if for instance your husband finds such things difficult, as some do . . . then after three years of marriage that would be sufficient grounds for an annulment. You would be surprised how many men are afflicted by this . . . condition."

"Are they?"

"When it comes to ending a difficult marriage, yes." And he is so pleased with himself that he cannot help smiling. "Ah, what charming innocence you have still, my dearest. The next man who stands by your side will receive treasure unbounded. So. The Sforza pup is impotent. Ha! I always suspected as much," he says, the smile growing wider.

"But, Father, I didn't say . . . I mean we *did* lie together. There was consummation, I—I am no longer a maid."

"Well, he may have fumbled a bit. But no one would doubt your word, if you gave it. Your pure heart and a pope for a father will see to that. It may not come to that. For now we will wait and hear what the lawyers say. Either way, his days are numbered. Come, don't look so glum. You will be putting on a new wedding dress before you know it."

She looks aghast. "And who will I be marrying?"

"Oh, there are all manner of possibilities." He leans over and caresses her cheek. "Don't worry. Whoever it is will make you happy. This is the year of greatness for our family. Our enemies will be defeated and we shall triumph in all ways."

He is still beaming as he lets her out.

Defeating the enemies starts well enough. In mid-January, Trevignano's medieval battlements fall to the papal artillery. All that remains is the fortress of Bracciano. The Dukes of Urbino and Gandia are mounting the guns to start the bombardment when news arrives from Naples: in the bowels of the Castel dell'Ovo the jailer has opened the door of Virginio Orsini's cell to find him curled like a salted slug in a mess of vomit. Prison food carries all manner of corruption crawling within it, though many poor souls survive and grow immune to it. More important is the fact that the man who brings and divides the slops each day is no longer to be found anywhere. As perfidy goes, it is politically unsurprising. Indeed, the head of a family dying from administered poison at the same moment that his enemies launch a full-frontal attack on his territories makes so much sense that few can be bothered to be outraged about it.

Except those who love him most. It is Calderón who is given the further honor of taking and receiving news from the front line. When it reaches as far as Virginio Orsini's sister, besieged in the castle, she stands out on the battlement overlooking the lake, weeping and laughing into the wind. For months she has been plagued by images of a man dying inch by slow inch in a dank pit where daylight never reaches. Revenge is a better weapon than anxiety and she will sleep more deeply now, despite the sound of cannon fire in her ears.

In Umbria, where Orsini's illegitimate son Carlo is trying to raise a force to break the siege, fury and grief add urgency to his cause. Using money from the French purse, he buys two of Italy's most effective professional condottieri—one of the brawling Baglioni brothers from Perugia, and Vitellozzo Vitelli, a commander who knows a thing or two about artillery. It is hardly a great army, but its arrival to the west of the lake draws the papal troops away from the siege of Bracciano to meet them on the slopes of Monte Cimone. The military talents of the Duke of Gandia are about to be tested.

As the messenger, it's Calderón's job to ride, not fight, but the sight of the carnage and the wounded has its impact and when he mounts his horse to take the news to Rome he is shaking. In case of bad news Cesare had ordered that he comes to him first.

He listens grimly.

"What should I tell His Holiness?"

"Just what you have told me."

Alexander is at private prayer in the Niccoline Chapel, its warmth and intimacy more inviting than the great emptiness of the Sistine. Since Juan's departure he has found himself drawn to it regularly.

"Father?"

As he registers Cesare's presence behind him he feels a wave of cold shock run through his body.

In the stateroom outside, Pedro Calderón, disheveled and distraught, is already on his knees.

"What? What is it? Tell me."

Calderón glances at Cesare, who nods.

"Holy Father, the news is not good. We have lost the field to the Orsini."

"Lost? How badly lost? What about Juan, the Captain-General of the Church?"

"He ... he is taken wounded. There is no danger ... the doctors say he will live. I made sure of that before I left. He is making his way to Rome now, but he sent me on ahead to let you know that he has withdrawn from battle."

"What of the Duke of Urbino? Is he withdrawn too?"

"The duke was captured early in the battle, Your Holiness. Orsini's son holds him now for ransom."

"Ah! God's wounds. How could this happen? We had them at our mercy. Aah! How many? How many did we lose?"

"Five, six hundred dead, maybe three times that many wounded."

"And the enemy?"

Pedro shakes his head. "The day went to them by more than four to one."

Twilight comes early on winter days. The Pope sits in darkness in his bedchamber. Recently his legs have been causing him trouble. Perhaps he is not used to spending so much time on his knees. There is a long groan of pain down the side of the right calf from the knee and his foot is so swollen that it looks like a tree trunk. His bed servant massages it patiently each night with oils, but his touch tonight brought more pain than relief and he has sent him away. Sixty-six years old. What does he expect? The world is full of old men racked with aches and pains. He can still move faster in his head than many half his age, but then he also knows that the morgue is no respecter of ambition.

He does not regret the decision to have Orsini poisoned. To bring a family to its knees you have to strike at the head as well as the limbs. The man was a traitor and deserved to die. If their places had been reversed Virginio would have afforded him no better treatment. God needs a strong Church with a strong pope, and a strong pope needs a firm foundation of power. The interests of the papacy and the Borgias have been moving hand in hand for so long that he has become used to substituting one for the other: he is doing what is best for all, their survival of the French invasion has proved that. Yet the scale of this defeat and the direct attack on the body of his son gives him a moment of doubt. While he is not a man to dwell on history—the needs of the present take all his time—he finds himself thinking of Pope Sixtus, wily and pious by turns, and how his murderous attack on the Medici had ended in ignominy, the conspirators strung up and dangling from the windows of Florence's town hall. When the news came to him of the failure, and the close escape of his own nephew, did he ever think to question whether it was God's will or just Fortuna?

He cancels his visit to Giulia and orders a vigil in the Niccoline Chapel with a small group of cardinals in attendance. It is a long night. The stabbing up and down his right leg keeps him alert to his prayers. Cesare stands at the back and watches. He has said nothing.

Next afternoon, the Duke of Gandia arrives back, breathless with pain, in the back of a litter.

"They had men with pikes, like the Swiss Guard. As they plunged into the cavalry a giant of a man knocked me from my horse. I thought it was my end."

Alexander pulls his son's head toward him and holds it to his chest. "You are not dead," he says. "That is all that matters."

In the Pope's own apartments half a dozen doctors hover as they unwind a bandage from his torso to expose a livid gash across his chest. The doctors usher Alexander from the room. When they emerge they are hard-pressed to know what to say: not only is the Duke of Gandia in no immediate danger, but with the right salves he might be up and dancing within a few days, for under the blood there is nothing more than a flesh wound.

"I told you that you should not face pikemen with cavalry," Cesare says quietly as father and sons sit together that evening, assessing the damage. His brother's humiliation has left him pleasantly calm. "The horses are thrown by the length of the lances. I have seen it happen myself."

"It was not our intention to meet them that way." Juan rises to the bait. "But they outflanked us."

"And you didn't think to regroup?"

"Enough." Alexander looks weary. "What is done is done. The question is, what next?" He glances at Cesare.

"Without Bracciano, it is not a victory, Father."

"But neither is it a defeat. We hold ten other castles. So we negotiate. They will pay with money rather than blood."

"And the Duke of Urbino?"

"Bah! He has a town full of citizens. If they love their lord they can find the money to pay his ransom."

"He is highly thought of among the other princes. We will make an enemy out of an ally."

"Only one who can't fight. It might teach others to do better."

Juan has the decency to drop his head. "I am ready to go back into the field, Father," he says, wincing ostentatiously as he does so. "We only lost a few hundred men. I could fight again, I know."

"Are you sure?"

He coughs, grimacing again. "Yes, yes. I could do it."

Alexander looks at Cesare again, but his elder son's face still gives nothing away.

"Very well . . . then let's talk about Ostia."

Ostia. A small fortress but a huge symbol, Cardinal della Rovere's strategic castle on the mouth of the Tiber has been in French hands since he fled Italy. It is now the last bastion of their power on Italian soil. To make sure of triumph the Pope has already sent out a call for Spanish help, and a force under Gonsalvo de Córdova, who is in the south mopping up the last of the resistance, is already on its way.

"He is the greatest general of his day, my son. With his infantry and our artillery attacking from both sides, the French don't stand a chance. Isn't that so, Cesare?"

"As long as you do exactly what you are told this time, little brother," Cesare says, the cold smile he has been holding back breaking out at last. "That is all it will take."

And so it does.

In chapel Alexander laughs and cries as he thanks the Virgin for her many intercessions on his behalf, the protecting of Juan from further injury and the fall of Ostia being only the two most recent. Any doubts he might once have had are swept away in the exhilaration of the moment. God favors those who take chances. Even his leg bothers him less as he summons Burchard to give orders for the ceremonies to follow. It is a moment he has been waiting for for a long time: the Borgias have their own military hero to celebrate.

In the Pope's private chambers, amid cardinals and dignitaries, the veteran Gonsalvo de Córdova kneels to receive his reward: a sculpted golden rose, similar to the one given to the French just before their brush-off. Then, wreathed in smiles, the Pope turns his attention to his son, who steps up to be invested, in perpetuity, as Duke of Benevento, reigning over a newly created domain carved out of the lands recovered by Córdova around Naples.

The applause that greets the announcement is peppered by gasps of astonishment. Everyone in the room knows that the victory belongs to Córdova, not the Duke of Gandia: it is one thing for a commander to be awarded the spoils of his own campaign, quite another for them to be given to someone else.

Córdova himself shows no trace of emotion. In gnarled middle age, he is a survivor, a man who earned his spurs in the conquest of Granada, then had the wisdom to help negotiate peace. Like many Spaniards, he prides himself on being a man of honor, as fierce for God as he is for glory, and the smells of corruption that he finds wafting through the corridors of the Vatican have turned his stomach. The diplomat in him will keep his counsel till he reports back to his own monarchs. But once there he will not mince his words: the papacy may be in the hands of a Spaniard, but he is a man who cares more for his family than for the Holy Mother Church.

He is not the only one to spread the word. Over the following days ambassadors sit down to re-create the scene, commenting as they do on the emerging shape of dynastic power in Italy, with the tendrils of Borgia ownership creeping ever deeper into the kingdom of Naples. But the truly sharp-eyed will have noticed something else: that along with all the obvious suspects of the Orsini and the Colonna and the other families who are suffering from the growing power of the Borgias, there are signs of tension within the tribe itself. So that when Isabella d'Este sits at her desk in Mantua reading one of many scandal-ridden dispatches on life in Rome, she will be particularly struck by the thought that, while they may try hard to conceal it, the sons of the Pope are consumed with envy of one another.

Chapter 25

To be lauded as a hero for a battle that everyone knows you didn't win could be a burden as much as a triumph. Juan, however, manages to remain oblivious. Rome has become his plaything and he swaggers from one party to another, barely noticing the smirks and insults that are exchanged behind his back. Inside the Vatican the Pope is so swayed by family triumph that the politician in him is eclipsed by the besotted father.

Out on the streets, the atmosphere is strained. While Ostia was falling to the papal troops, the coffin carrying Virginio Orsini's remains had been making its way through the capital en route to his final resting place in Bracciano and attracting a small army of angry supporters in its wake. Nightfall now sees knots of belligerent young men gathering around the piazzas in search of brawls and knife fights. Not just the Orsini. With the consolidation of Borgia power, the Colonna and the Gaetani also have their noses out of joint. The structures of family influence have been part of the makeup of Rome for centuries, and when the balance is being rocked, as it is now, Rome can become an unstable city.

Juan, meanwhile, has his attention fixed on pleasure. His greatest badge of honor is his fast-healing wound, which gives him even more reason to strip off his shirt for any lady who might take his fancy. There is an army of professionals who would probably undress him for free, such is his status, but he is looking for tougher conquests. His return to court has not gone quite as he expected, as Sancia, far from throwing herself at his feet, has had her mind on other things. In Naples, the

young king, her half-brother, has died and the level of her grief surprises everyone. She has grown up a little in the last few months. Her
fever for Cesare has both scorched and purged her, so that now, as
she grows homesick, she finds herself longing for men who, like her
brother, make her feel safe rather than always on fire. As the court
whirls and dances its way into summer, she retires more to her bedroom, where she and Jofré play cards or games of chance. In bed, when
she is sad he is happy to stroke and cuddle her rather than playact the
rutting animal. Coming in one morning, her ladies find them curled in
each other's arms like sleeping puppies, as sweet as they are still young.

Juan, however, is not used to women refusing him. One night at
dinner, he sits himself deliberately between her and Jofré. The talk
grows saucy and he uses his free hand to test her resistance under her
skirts. She moves herself away and he is about to persist when Jofré
takes his bright silver fork, a new and fashionable weapon, more vicious
in its way than the knife, and plunges it into the back of his brother's
other hand.

Juan roars with pain.

"Oh, I am sorry! I am sorry, brother," Jofré yelps, ducking the return blow. "I was sure that was a cockroach on your plate."

Sancia, on the other side, bursts out laughing. Juan, sensitive to
anyone who mocks him, throws back his chair and leaves the table in
fury.

"Oh, my gallant knight." She hugs her husband, nuzzling his head
to her breast. "You saved my virtue! What a perfect husband."

When Cesare hears the story he cannot help but smile. He is struggling with his own furies. The injustice of his brother's new dukedom
rubs like a hair shirt. It appalls him to see his father so smitten. Not that
he too isn't being favored. A new King of Naples means another coronation, and a cardinal legate to stand in for the Pope. He is clearly too
young and inexperienced in Church matters to be considered, yet Alexander has pushed his name through despite the howls of protest. While
they have enough cardinals in the Sacred College to ensure any vote,
even their own men are finding such blatant nepotism uncomfortable.

In response, Cesare, who is well aware of the mood in the city, has taken to keeping a low profile. When men are angry about injustice it does not help to have their noses ground in it. He would like to slam his brother up against a wall and give him some lessons on how to behave, but he is worried that if he was to start he would not know when to stop. Better to stay out of his way.

It is at this delicate moment that Giovanni Sforza arrives back in town. His Vice-Chancellor cousin may not be the Pope's favorite churchman, but he can catch the wind of gossip as well as the next man. If the Sforzas are not going to go the way of the Orsini, the family need this marriage to continue as much as the Pope wants to dissolve it. Under pressure from both the cardinal and Duke Ludovico, Giovanni is ordered to return to Rome to fight for his wife. By the time he gets there he has become almost immune to the rats that are gnawing at his bowels.

Alexander, who will choose his own moment to deliver the coup de grâce, welcomes him with hearty smiles and backslaps. Giovanni has trouble not falling over.

On the way from the Vatican to his own palace he runs into the Cardinal of Valencia, who is so obviously loitering that it is clear the meeting is deliberate.

"And what are you doing in town, traitor?"

The fear cuts through the pain so sharply that for a moment Giovanni feels almost relief. "I am come to see my wife."

"She doesn't want to see you."

"How would you know that, Your Most Reverend Lord Cardinal?"

"Because no woman wants a man who deserts her," he says sweetly.

But Giovanni holds his ground. They are both attended by servants and neither of them is armed. What can he do? Strangle him with his own bare hands?

"She is still my wife. I would ask you to step out of the way. Please."

"Really. And what if I don't?"

Giovanni says nothing. They both stand rigid, waiting for the other to make the first move. Then suddenly Cesare laughs and falls back.

"You lay a hand on her and what little balls you have I'll cut them off myself," he says to his brother-in-law's retreating figure.

Giovanni does not turn back.

———

Lucrezia is in her bedroom, curled on the window seat in golden afternoon light, working on an embroidered silk for a shawl. Like all women of her class she was trained young in needlework and has a fine eye and a steady hand. While men are called upon to decorate the walls of palaces and churches, the delicate beauty of a piece of embroidered cloth brings another, quieter kind of satisfaction to those who pour their souls into it. At times of stress it can be almost as comforting as prayer. Since the interview with her father, however, she notices that she has been making more mistakes.

"Giovanni! What are you doing in Rome?" Her needle freezes halfway to the outline of a rose petal. "This is not a place for you now."

"So it seems. How are you, wife?"

"Why didn't you send word that you were coming? I have not heard from you in months."

"Well . . . I—I did not think you cared that much."

He looks around. He barely recognizes the room, it is so long since he has been here. "You look well," he says at last. "How are Jofré and Sancia? I hear her half-brother is dead."

"Yes, and she is most affected by it. The court is not as it was. Though Juan has come home bright enough."

"Ah yes, the golden-boy duke. And what about us?" He takes a step toward her and she flinches backward, the needle catching into her finger so that she gives a little cry. He stops. "The talk is that you are trying to slough me off."

"Oh, why do you pick now to return? I have been waiting for months. You didn't answer letters. I thought . . . I can't speak of this now."

"So it is true?"

She shakes her head.

"Then it is not true? God in His heaven knows there is no reason that would stand up in a court, whatever they are telling you, Lucrezia." He stares at her, as if trying to read what she does or doesn't know. Sitting bathed in the light she looks lovely, so young still, even innocent. "Why don't you come back with me to Pesaro? We could start again.

The city needs its duchess. And I need my wife." He can barely believe his own power. It is as if he is a player in a spectacle someone else has written.

"I cannot, Giovanni," she says in a small voice. The pinprick of blood welling up on her finger drops onto the silk. A blood-red rose then. "Even if I wanted to. It's too late."

"I have risked my life to come here. I know things between us have not always gone well. But when we were together in Pesaro we found a way to live. I remember that for a while you were almost gay there. You're not like the rest of your family. You have kindness and love in you that they will snuff out. If they want another husband for you it has nothing to do with your happiness."

"Please, don't say these things. It is not in my hands. It never has been. You should have come when they called. It is too late now. You must get your family to help you."

"Why? What is your father going to do? We are married, Lucrezia. Even he can't change that."

She shakes her head. "You should go home now."

"What?" He looks around him, as if the danger might even be in the room. "Is he intending to have me cut down on the streets? Has it come to that?"

"No, no . . . but . . . I cannot speak for my brothers. They are more hotheaded than him."

"You mean Cesare?"

"Please. Go."

"I tell you, he is a madman, your brother. He can barely keep his hands off you. God help our Church as long as he is in it."

She is not looking at him anymore. Behind him he hears footsteps. He turns in a panic as to whom he might find there. But it is only Pantisilea, her lady-in-waiting, hovering in the background and making signs to her mistress over his head.

"It's all right. I am going. But I give you one piece of advice. Make sure the next husband is one you dislike even more than me. God forbid you should ruin the life of a man you really care for."

———

Giovanni heads back home as fast as his horses will carry him. When his more powerful cousins demand to know why he has fled, he sends anxious, whining letters to both, hinting at dark conspiracies and insisting—from a safe distance—that he will never ever agree to give up his wife, whatever pressure is brought to bear.

His worst fears are realized when, at the end of May, the Pope dispatches no less a figure than the general of the Augustinians to Pesaro to help his son-in-law "understand the choices" at his disposal. In case there should be any doubt, Alexander also lays out the terms in a meeting in Rome with the Vice-Chancellor. The Sforza/Borgia marriage is over; it would be best if his cousin agrees that it had never been valid in the first place. Otherwise they may have to resort to "other" reasons: the Duchess of Pesaro, he adds darkly, is both ready and willing to sign a declaration to that effect. Should their two families not wish a further falling-out, he would urge a smooth and rapid resolution. He is, he hints with a bright smile, willing to be flexible on the return of the dowry.

Ascanio Sforza swallows his outrage. It is a taste he has grown familiar with. He knows that one way or another the Borgias will get what they want. Better for everyone if they can be persuaded to take the first course. He will get nothing out of Alexander, or his eldest son, whom he is beginning to fear as much as the Pope himself. The beloved Duke of Gandia though is easier to approach, assuming one can find a way in through the layers of preening. What is clear is how much he likes a party. So the Vice-Chancellor now goes out of his way to organize one: another celebration for the glorious hero of papal victories.

The guest list is extensive and the menu large: a man used to eating at the private dinner table of the Pope is always appreciative of more luxurious fare. The animals and birds are slaughtered on the day to ensure the freshest meats. From France comes a new recipe for calves' kidneys mashed with eggs and spices, while another pan bubbles on the stove like boiling blood, pork juice thickened with flour and a sack of cherries. When our hero is tired of meats there will be fish, and pasta stuffed with oranges and pine nuts, ricotta tarts filled with every fruit in season, and a table of cheeses. You could eat all night and there would still be more to taste in the morning.

The company starts off as exclusive, but the word spreads and as the evening progresses there are not enough guards to see off the groups of men, clerics as well as youngbloods, who find their way into the highly decorated salon and courtyard. Twilight turns to darkness and on such a sweet summer evening everyone gives way to pleasure. Juan arrives late; rumor is that he is courting a young beauty due to be married to another man, and therefore a perfect challenge to his vanity, and that he has been trying to get himself into her bedroom while her father is looking the other way. At least he enjoys the food, and the wine, which he drinks in quantity too fast to notice how much of the Vice-Chancellor's money has been spent on it. As the hero of the moment, at least in his own mind, he does a few laps of honor around the room, receiving compliments from those alert enough to remember to pay them. The number is perhaps less than usual, but then the food is so rich that after a while it is easier to lie down to digest it. Juan, evidently frustrated by his inability to get into his sweetheart's bedroom, starts to feel unappreciated. He moves past a group of young nobles tossing out insults as if they were high wit: phrases like "stuffed bladders" and "lounging Roman gluttons" are thrown like stray punches. One of them hits back. The words "Spanish bastard" come out loud enough for others to hear. An exchange of slanders: a common enough dance on the night streets of most cities.

Juan, however, snaps around in instant outrage, and there is a sudden hush as the room holds its breath, waiting for a weapon to be drawn. Instead the duke, flushed and unsteady on his feet, flings down his goblet and marches out of the room. By the time the Vice-Chancellor gets to the courtyard, his honored guest is on his horse and out on the streets, hammering toward the bridge and the Vatican. Ascanio Sforza returns, a nervous smile on his face, and waves the guests back to enjoyment.

But Juan Borgia is not finished yet.

The Pope is sitting through a less than enjoyable foot massage and drinking his after-dinner fennel-and-mint infusion when his son storms into his chamber, ranting about insult and violation. The servant is dismissed, Juan's voice ringing in his ears as he backs out of the room.

"Roman scum!" the Pope says when he has heard it. "I thought we had silenced their crowing. If I had a ducat for every ill word spoken against us, we might have made our fortune quicker than we have. You were right to walk away, my son. It is beneath a duel. We will deal with them later."

"You don't understand, Father. I've come here because later will be too late. The attack was directed at me but it was aimed at you. Because I am your heir. It is you he was insulting. And such disrespect should be paid for immediately."

The door opens on the Cardinal of Valencia. The servant's fast exit and the raised voices have caused commotion outside. Juan scowls, but his brother is already in the room.

"What is it? Are we attacked?"

Alexander shakes his head. "Your brother has been severely wounded by words."

Cesare listens. When the story is finished he can hardly hold back his sneer. "So where were your sword and your men?"

Gandia turns on him. "I'm a general, not a thug. I don't grapple and brawl like some."

"How many of them were there, brother?"

"Four, five . . . what does it matter?"

Cesare's look is its own answer.

"This is not about me," he roars. "It was deliberate provocation against the papacy."

Cesare opens his mouth, but Alexander silences him with a look.

"It is justified anger, Juan. And it will not go unmarked. We will have an apology or people in jail by tomorrow morning."

"Tomorrow it will be all around town. We should hit back now, hard, so they get the message that we are not for playing with. They will be laughing behind our backs already."

"No doubt about that," Cesare says under his breath.

"So what would you have us do instead, my son?"

"Fight fire with fire. Send in the Papal Guard now and string up the man for all to see as a warning to others."

Cesare lets out a hiss of a breath. Juan turns on him.

"What—you don't have the stomach for that, Cardinal?"

"It is not to do with stomach. The Vice-Chancellor has immunity in his own home. It would be a breach of Church law."

"Oh—Church law!" Juan says, making it sound like a petticoat game. "That would be your business, yes? Except I am talking family justice in the face of treachery."

"Ah, grow up, brother. It was common insult, not treachery. It just got you where it hurt, in your vanity. An easy hit. All you do is make enemies. The wives you chase, the husbands you insult, the way you swagger around. Half of Rome hates you already. If you send soldiers in to do your dirty work, the other half will feel the same tomorrow. Yes, Father, I know you want me to stop, but someone has to tell him," he says quickly. "If it hurts so much to be called a bastard, Michelotto will come out with you tonight and see this man doesn't go home with his insides still in his body. My household never sleeps till dawn anyway."

"That's your way, not mine. You do things in the dark because you're in Church robes and you don't want anyone to recognize you. You don't need to worry. You might be important in here, Cesare, but I tell you, out there on the streets no one has heard of the Cardinal of Valencia. *I* am the one who holds the honor for this family. It's *my* sons that will inherit half of Naples. Thanks to *my* victory on the field."

"What? A few Spanish fucks and a botched battle and now you're a hero?"

"You dare—"

"Sorry. Have I insulted you? Poor Juan. You want to fight me?" And he moves closer. "Or maybe you should just get Father to do it for you."

"Cesare!" Alexander's voice cuts into them both.

His eldest son takes a deep breath, his eyes cold as a cat's. "I am sorry, Your Holiness." He lifts up both his hands as if in surrender before stepping back. "We are talking family business and I thought you might want to hear my advice on the subject. I wish you well, brother. I will be in my rooms if I am needed."

And he turns and walks out, leaving the door open behind him.

"Cesare." Alexander's voice reaches out through the door into the room beyond. "Cesare!"

But he does not stop.

"He's a bad loser," Juan says sourly. "He always was. But he is wrong about this, Father. I was there and he was not. I know what we should do."

The Pope looks at his son's angry, handsome young face and the insult he has sustained becomes his own. Spanish bastard! How dare they abuse the family thus after all he has done for Rome? It is, indeed, insupportable and must be punished.

His beloved Juan cannot be denied.

In the Vice-Chancellor's palace there is madness and mayhem. The co-hort of papal troops, with Juan at the head, break their way in past the guards. The screaming starts even before they enter the room, men and women running for cover, the offending young man, desperate to save himself, hiding behind chairs and tables. Furniture is smashed, food and wine flung everywhere as they try to root him out. A couple of other youngbloods draw weapons and there is a short battle among the debris of the night. One of the guests takes a wound, the others scatter. In the end they find him: a woman is trying to hide him, or maybe he is just clinging to her skirts. As they drag him away she begins to yell, a high-pitched howl like a wounded animal, and he joins in. By the time they get him out of the palace, half the neighborhood is awake and watching. Anyone who is anyone in Rome is now either in the palace or on the streets. They fling his bound body over the back of a horse as he thrashes violently, and ride a few blocks to the river, at the edge of which there are trees of suitable height. As they throw the rope he lies crying for mercy, begging Juan to forgive him. They string him up and he hangs awkwardly for a second, choked yells coming out of him. One of the guards grabs his legs and pulls sharply. His neck snaps and the body slumps, swinging madly to left and right. Behind on the bank a small crowd gathers. As the soldiers mount and ride away a few throw stones at them, though from far enough away that they will not hit. The mix of fear and outrage is palpable.

Next morning half the city comes down to gawk at the sight. The early-summer sun parboils the flesh, and by nightfall the corpse is already turning putrid.

Chapter 26

In the Vatican, business goes on as normal. Having made the decision to stand by his son, Alexander does not waver. If Burchard has views on the incident he keeps them to himself. In the Papal Consistory the attack is not referred to, though there are loud murmurings about the further favoring of the Duke of Gandia with what should have been papal lands in Naples. Alexander, now as sensitive to criticism as his son, tells them if it were not for him Rome would be half French by now and most of them poisoned or dead in a ditch somewhere to make room for new blood. He will do what he pleases with the land that has been recaptured. The session ends in angry silence.

Juan keeps to his apartments until things have calmed. When he does go out a few days later, no one comes near him. Even the fake compliments have stopped. The lesson has been learned, I am respected now, he thinks. His swagger and his appetite for erotic adventure return.

Alexander might have found time to urge a little caution on his son's behalf, but he is consumed now by the vexed question of his daughter's marriage. Despite his bullying, the Church lawyers are finding no credible reason why the union was not valid in the first place. If it cannot be done one way, it will be done another. Lucrezia must now lodge an appeal directly to him, the Pope.

The Latin text that Burchard draws up is formal but explicit: *Lucrezia, Duchess of Pesaro, attests that she has been in the keeping of the family for more than three years and that the union is still without any sexual relation, without nuptial intercourse or any carnal knowledge. She swears to this fact and is prepared to submit herself to the examination of a midwife.*

All it needs is Lucrezia's signature. Thank goodness for the loving obedience of his daughter.

"Papà, I cannot sign this." She looks up from the paper, her eyes awash with tears. Ever since she has learned from Adriana that an examination will be called for she has been in dread of this moment, but seeing it here now in black and white the terror is even worse. "How can I swear before God to such things when they are not true?"

"Don't think of it as true or untrue," he murmurs. "It is simply a way to help the Church lawyers, who like me care greatly for your welfare, to find a solution to this . . . knotty puzzle. Here, here—take the pen."

She stares at him, swallowing hard, but even as she reaches out her hand the floodgates open and soon she is crying so much that he has to rescue the parchment lest it soak up the salty rain. Oh, there is nothing he hates more than to see a woman cry . . .

"Very well, very well," he counters patiently, "it does not need to be done today. I shall leave it here so you may think more on it. The Lord God will help you with the decision. But do not take too long: these Sforzas are slimy vermin and they will use any hesitation in their defense. Shall I send Adriana to you? Or Sancia? Or Giulia, perhaps? They are women who know a thing or two about marriage and may be able to soothe your fears."

But Lucrezia, now inconsolable, wants no one. Infected by undercurrents of sexual jealousy and intrigue, life at court has lost its shine and since the flight of her husband she has retreated into the company of her own entourage, led by her lady-in-waiting Pantisilea. The more she frets the faster her embroidery grows. The flecks of blood are overstitched with scarlet thread and new flowers emerge under her fingers, bursting with life and color. Days pass and she starts to feel calmer. The declaration, however, remains unsigned.

Alexander, growing impatient, calls for Cesare. He understands that his son is angry with him, and it is beginning to cross his mind that he might have been a little hasty in defense of Juan's reputation. Still, what is done is done. Cesare above all others knows that he is not a man to apologize—unless he doesn't mean it—and for that there has to be something to be gained from the pretense. Instead they will make their peace by putting family business first.

"You have a way with her. You always have had. She loves no man better than she loves you. If you explain it to her again, I am sure she will agree. I don't think I can suffer another storm of tears. Women! They do feel such things so deeply. When I think of Christ's crucifixion, sometimes I cannot help but be moved as much by the grief of Our Virgin Lady Maria herself. Ah, the power of love for one's children."

Cesare, who has little time to dwell on the Lord's death—or even much on his life, for that matter—bows his head in acceptance of the task.

"I am sure you know that you are a great support and source of strength to me and I depend on you for many things."

"Yes, Father," he replies, with no evident sense of rancor. "I do know that."

Despite herself, Lucrezia is pleased to see him. They begin with gossip, for even in distress she has not lost her appetite for that. Rumors of Juan's bad behavior have seeped under the firmest-closed doors, but in her isolation she has missed the color of detail. Cesare is a fine story-teller and before he is finished she is cowering in the Vice-Chancellor's palace, watching in horror as the young unfortunate is pulled scream-ing from under her skirts to his fate.

"Oh, Cesare. He is my brother and I would not see him insulted for the world, but as you tell it I feel sorry for the man."

"You and half of Rome."

"So people will be angry with Papà now as well as Juan."

For all that she is a girl, she has always been sharper than the others when it comes to understanding politics. "It is spilled milk and we will just have to lap it up. We have risen high in a city that never welcomed us, and it is not done by making friends."

"No," she says, "I think I have realized that now. And you? Are you angry with Juan as well?"

"Ha! If he wasn't my brother I'd strangle him with my own hands." He laughs as he sees the look on her face. "It's all right. It is a thought, not a deed. Confession will handle it. We are family, remember."

"Yes, we are family." She sighs. "You are here to get me to sign the letter, aren't you?"

"I am here to do whatever it takes to make your future happier than your past. You deserve better than that . . . that fop."

"What happened when he was here, Cesare? He was very frightened. Did you threaten him?"

"No need. He shits himself every time anyone looks at him." She winces slightly at the crudity. "Ah, sister. You know as well as I do that he has never been the right man for you. The sooner he is out of all of our lives the better."

"And it has to be this way?"

"It has to be a way that works. And this is it."

"Even if it is not the truth? It is not a fair way to fight, Cesare."

"What, you think *he* fights fair? You are too kind. Your husband is a coward and a sniveler and he has betrayed you and the family a dozen times over."

"What do you mean?"

"You really don't know?"

"Know what?"

"The man is a traitor, Lucrezia, a spy and a conspirator. We almost lost the war thanks to him. He betrayed us to Milan at every turn. We gave him a position in the army and he paid us back by giving details of our troop movements to Duke Ludovico, so that when the French headed for Rome they knew exactly where not to go. He carries the guilt for the occupation on his miserable little shoulders."

"No! No . . . He didn't do that."

"You think not? What else was he doing all that time in Pesaro? He wasn't in bed making love to you."

He throws it out and immediately it hits home. He can see it in her face. "Think about it. Your letters to me were full of the visits he was making this way and that. Don't tell me you didn't notice anything?"

Except now, of course, she remembers. That night when she had gone to him and found him in his study, writing, the table strewn with letters and maps. The way he had flung his arms over the papers so that she could not see what he was studying.

"Whatever is troubling you, you can tell me. Is it my family?"

And his voice, gruff with anxiety.

"No, no. It is just politics. Affairs of state, nothing to worry yourself about. Go back to bed."

Yes, she has known it somewhere. "Dear God, Cesare, I should have told you."

"You did. Your letters were as good as his confession. He doesn't deserve any pity. If he had had his way, what do you think would have happened? We would have been strung up or poisoned by now. And a new pope would be dissolving your marriage on the grounds of your barrenness."

"Oh . . . oh." She closes her eyes, bringing her fists up to her chest in a gesture of angry helplessness. As the tears come, Cesare reaches out and takes one of her hands, pulling it down to rest within his. He says nothing, just lets her weep.

Except she doesn't want to be crying. As in that night in Pesaro when she had confronted Giovanni, she is angry as much as she is sad, because none of these things are of her doing. He had understood that. He had got up from his chair and held her in his arms; held her and called her his wife, his lovely Borgia wife. Only the words had been like wormwood in his mouth. A lovely Borgia wife. That is what she will always be. A poisoned gift. Too difficult and too dangerous for any man.

She is crying not only for her past but for her future. "You don't understand, Cesare. In his way he did love me. Or tried to. And if I sign this I will have to go before a court and lie. Lie! Before men of the Church. Before God."

"It is not so serious as you make out. Such things are a formality."

"On oath before the Church! A formality! And what about the examination? Because they will examine me. Is that a formality too?"

"In its way, yes. It will take place behind closed doors. And the midwives will find whatever we tell them to."

"But they will examine me, yes? And how can they too lie? I am no longer a maid, Cesare."

He flinches at the words, his eyes suddenly cold.

"Oh sweet Jesus, I wish I still was." The words burst out and with them come sobs, gulps of self-pity and pain. He pulls her to him and holds her tight, and she gives in to him, burying her head into his chest as she weeps and weeps.

"Ssshh. Hush," he murmurs, rocking her to and fro. "Don't think about it. It will be all right. No one will hurt you in any way. I would never let that happen. You know that."

But the more she tries to contain herself, the more she breaks down, as if the tears are all the things that she can never say; the humiliation of it, the strain of living so close to other people's desire yet never feeling her own, of being a young woman who is adored but not loved. Whatever that word means. The tears soak into the velvet of his coat, her skin hot and clammy against the cloth. She has always felt safe inside his arms, this beautiful, powerful elder brother, whom so many fear but who has always been as tender as a lover with her.

"There. See. It's passing already." He is moving his hand over her hair now, long gentle strokes. As the storm subsides he moves her away from him a little, his eyes fixed on hers. "Remember how when you were little and you used to get frightened at night"—he wipes away a few soggy strands of hair that have become plastered to her face—"you would run across the room and get into my bed? Remember what I told you then. No one will hurt you, Lucrezia. I will never let them. Remember that?"

And she nods, a half-smile breaking through her distress. "You said you had a sword and that even if it was the devil under my bed, you would skewer him. Then you would light the candle and we would go and look together. But there was never anything there. Because you said they knew you were coming and had run away."

"So they had."

"And in the morning the servant would find us asleep together and tell Aunt Adriana and she would be cross."

"But we would take no notice." He laughs; lifting another wet strand and smoothing it back into place. "See. I am here and it is the same. No devils anywhere. Nothing to be frightened of at all. I won't let them hurt you. Not ever."

She takes a breath, the tears finally stilled now. "I love you, brother."

"And I love you, little sister." He lifts her right hand and brings the palm to his lips to kiss.

"Aha!" She laughs a little, and then returns the gesture. He uses both his hands to hold her head, bending it slightly to kiss her on the forehead, almost like a father to a child. Then on both cheeks. Then he brushes her lips. He breaks away to look to her. Her face is flushed, naked, and she is utterly still, though whether it is because of how firmly he is holding her is not clear.

"Cesare?" she says, on a half-breath, just before he kisses her again. Only now the kiss continues. His tongue moves around the edge of her lips, then slips softly inside. She lets out a tiny breathless moan but does not resist. Her eyes are tightly closed and her hand hovers close to him, as if not knowing where to go. He lifts his mouth from hers. "It's all right," he says and his voice is very gentle. "There is nothing to fear. My beautiful sister, my love."

But as his lips come back, she flinches, as if jolting herself awake from a difficult dream. "No, Cesare!"

The protest starts as a flutter, bird wings against glass, becoming fiercer when he does not respond, so that now she is pushing, trying to get her hands between them. "No, no—we can't . . ."

Abruptly, he lets her go and she jumps up and away from him. He leans back against the side of the window seat, a strange half-smile on his face. She stands staring down at him, her breath coming in fits and starts. He lifts his hands in mock surrender. It is a gesture she knows well from when they were young: a way of swallowing feelings so they are hidden from anyone watching.

"You have the sweetest lips, Lucrezia," he says lightly. "So sweet, they deserve kissing. And only a brother who loves you . . ."—he hesitates—"as deeply as I do, has the right."

"I . . . You should go now. I . . . Sancia will be here any moment. We have agreed to do some sewing together and it is better at present if you two do not meet."

He stares at her, because of course he does not believe her and she knows it.

"Very well." His eyes fall on the declaration that lies crumpled on the small wooden table before them. "But you must sign this for me before I do."

She stares at the paper, a dense forest of letters in a perfectly inscribed hand. Then she picks up the pen and quickly, without thought, dips it into the ink and signs her name. Lucrezia Borgia Sforza. An elegant flourish. She takes the sand from the container, sprinkles it onto the words and waves the parchment in the air for it to dry. It is done. It is done. It is done.

"See, I said you would feel better." He reaches out for it, but she does not respond, putting it back instead on the table.

"Take it. Give it to Papà straightaway. He will be pleased. I . . . I need to be alone now," she says, the excuse of Sancia already forgotten. "I want you to go." And the break in her voice tells him the urgency.

He stands up. "Nothing happened, Lucrezia. It was a moment of love, that's all." But though the words are light, there is something in him that is not. He moves to the door, like a man in a semi-trance. Before he leaves he turns. "You will be all right if I leave you?"

She nods, but with her head down so as not to meet his eyes.

With the door closed she sits, hands clasped in her lap, staring at the floor. She lifts her fingers to her mouth, holding them there as if to feel the burn mark that he might have left. Then she slides a finger inside.

"Pantisilea!" She is on her feet. "Pantisilea!"

The lady-in-waiting is there fast. "What? What is it, my lady? What's happened?"

"It is done. The declaration is signed," she says. "The Cardinal of Valencia—" She breaks off, shaking her head. "I want you to pack some things for the household. And tell the head groom that we need horses and a carriage ready to drive as soon as it grows dark. But that he is to tell no one."

"To drive? Drive where?"

"Close to the southern gate of the city."

"But where are we going, my lady?"

"To San Sisto. I am no longer to be a married woman. We are going to the convent."

PART V

A Father's Grief

*Rather, had we seven papacies we would
give them all to have him alive again.*

Pope Alexander VI, June 1497

Chapter 27

M ID-JUNE. THE DAYS ARE BALMY AND LONG, SWELLING HEAT UNDER brilliant skies, but with enough of a breeze to bring respite. Deep in the cellars of the greatest palaces, servants are lowered into the ice store to chisel scrapings for the making of lemon sorbets or the chilling of summer wines. There is a bean harvest in the markets and the last of the apricots melt like honey in the mouth. The sewage-filled river sparkles under the sun and the boatmen, stripped to the waist, take their time as the slow barges pull wood and supplies between landing posts, while away from the center of the city, shepherds and goatherds lie half asleep in the grasses of various ruins as their flocks munch contentedly at the leftovers of history.

In her vineyard near the ancient baths of Diocletian, Vannozza is overseeing preparations for a family dinner. The news of Lucrezia's flight a week before has upset everyone, but there is little she can do to help. Her daughter had been taken from her when she was barely six years old, and unlike Cesare, she has retained no closeness. Vannozza has learned to live with it. Now, however, she tastes the loss again: a girl who flees to the convent of her childhood as her marriage disintegrates is in need of a mother's care. She writes a careful letter. *I understand that you must bow to your father's wishes, but sometimes such a thing is not easy to do. I, more than many, know that. Should you need me . . .*

She signs herself, as she always does: *Your unfortunate mother, Vannozza dei Cataneis.*

As yet there is no reply. She has heard that Alexander, furious at Lucrezia's unauthorized leaving, has sent a cohort of the papal troops to follow her and bring her home, but he bargained without the stalwart Dominican prioress of San Sisto, who met them at the gate using God as her shield: "A young woman seeks sanctuary with us. It is not for us to deny her that right. Tell His Holiness that we will protect her with our lives and care for her until she is ready to leave." Not even Alexander VI can storm a convent and get away with it.

The glee of the gossip is everywhere. The Pope's daughter is to become a nun! Marriage—or something more unspeakable—has turned her to God and the Pope is beside himself because he cannot get her out.

"Foul slander!" Alexander bluffs in response to Vice-Chancellor Sforza's worries over what is happening. "I sent her there myself because a convent is a proper place for her to be until your recalcitrant cousin makes up his mind. Perhaps you would tell him that. Or shall I? I cannot believe you and the Duke of Milan would put his miserable concerns before the deep and necessary friendship between our two families."

In Pesaro, Giovanni puts his head in his hands and groans. The Augustinian preacher, whose best has not been good enough, sets off back to Rome. This problem calls for stronger arguments than God can provide.

Vannozza lays an elegant table under a long pergola. Whatever worries she has about her daughter, she lays them aside. She does not enjoy the company of both her elder sons very often and tonight they will come with the Pope's cousin, the Cardinal Juan Borgia of Monreale, and a few close relatives.

It is a perfect summer's evening. Supported by their grooms and the ever-present Michelotto, Cesare and Juan arrive together in full fashion and finery: two young lions in their prime, a fitting complement to their mother's aging beauty. While at other times they have been known to spat in her presence, tonight everyone is well behaved. Juan is in a haughty, happy mood, cracking jokes and magnanimous to others if paid enough compliments himself. Cesare, in contrast, says very little. Vannozza is accustomed to her eldest son's moods: times when his mind seems so active that the stillness of his body is almost unnatural. Tonight, though, he seems more relaxed. Almost dreamy. And so beautiful. In less than two weeks he will be donning his papal-legate robes and crowning a king in Naples. Whatever other ambitions he might have had, this is greatness enough for now. Vannozza cannot take her eyes off him. Dear Lord, she thinks, how blessed am I? And with Your further benevolence, I may yet live to see him clothed in more glory. To be the mother of a pope; me, the daughter of an almost-nobody. And she, who is usually so sensible and levelheaded, finds herself burying her face in the lengths of Venetian silk that he has brought her as a present.

When the talk turns to Lucrezia, he is reassuring.

"The dissolving of the marriage is not easy. She will have to present herself before a court. It will make a better case if she is seen to come from the sanctuary of a convent."

"But it was so sudden. And she takes no visitors. Not even you, I hear."

"No." He hesitates; because it is true Lucrezia has refused him. "But then, can you see me in a convent?"

The table laughs.

"I could do it," Juan interrupts. "Though they would have to lock all the nuns in their cells first."

"Is that to keep you out or them in?" says someone else, and the laughter grows dutifully louder.

"So there has been no contact with her?" Vannozza pushes.

"Not directly. But we've appointed a messenger: a young Spaniard who has worked for Father and now works for me. He rode out with her when she left for Pesaro: a good man, honest and silent, who can be trusted with family matters."

"Well, I hope she is not in too much distress."

"What she needs is a good husband to see to her." Juan laughs. "Women, eh? More trouble than they are worth."

"You sound like your father," she says mildly.

It is close to midnight when the evening breaks up. Juan has remained the center of attention, not least because toward the end of the meal he is joined by a bearded man in a mask who takes a place at his end of the table but offers no introduction.

"It is a pleasure to welcome any friend of my son's, but are we not allowed to know your name?" Vannozza, like many parvenus, has always been fierce in the upholding of manners.

"Alas, Mother, my friend has taken a vow of silence."

"And anonymity," someone else adds.

"Everyone needs a little mystery in their life." Juan laughs. "He is my new and wondrous bodyguard." And he slaps him on the shoulder.

"He looks more like a procurer to me," Cesare says, but with no apparent malice. "Who is it to be tonight, brother?"

Juan smiles. "Ah, I have so many invitations."

"That is enough of that," Vannozza retorts briskly. "I do not lay a fine table in order to hear my sons' indiscretions. If this is indeed to do with a woman, I would hope you treat her with honor. You are a married man."

"But with a wife in Spain, alas," he says, and they all laugh, she included because the atmosphere is too jubilant for her assumed displeasure to last long.

"Come, children, it is getting late, and with the city so fretful it would be better for you all to leave while there is still respectable traffic on the streets."

"She worries that this is not a good district, don't you, Mother?" Cesare says playfully. "You need not fear. We will all leave together, filled to overflowing with your hospitality, most especially the taste of your own grape."

"Oh, you are too much the flatterer." She stands on tiptoe to ruffle his hair as he comes to embrace her. It is a gesture that no other living soul would risk.

When the goodbyes have been said, they mount their horses, the masked man riding behind Juan, as it seems he has brought no animal of his own.

At Ponte Sant' Angelo Juan's horse, along with that of his groom, peels off from the rest of the party. "A matter of a well-defended fortress that needs besieging," he calls as they head northeast along the river.

"Do you need artillery?" Cesare calls after him. "I can offer you Michelotto—he's as good as a dozen cannonballs. Bom bard!"

But all they hear is the sound of laughter swallowed up in the darkness.

A few hours later the city yawns and rumbles into life. The hours before the heat begins to bite are always the busiest of the day. In the Vatican the Pope and Burchard are up early, in consultation over arrangements for the upcoming coronation in Naples. Cesare joins them midway through the morning. There is much to be done before he leaves.

It is afternoon when a Spaniard from Juan's household comes with news that his master has not arrived home. The Pope registers a twinge of anxiety: since the incident in the Vice-Chancellor's palace he frets more over the whereabouts of his son. Still, Juan is a man used to waking up late in someone else's bed, and with Rome all ears and eyes for further Borgia scandal it has been drummed into him that he must cover his romantic tracks with darkness. If only I still had the stamina, Alexander thinks to himself, and tries to put it out of his mind.

But as afternoon turns toward dusk, there comes a report that the duke's horse has been found wandering the streets with one of its stirrups cut. And then his groom is discovered unconscious near the Piazza degli Ebrei, blood bubbling from his mouth and a deep knife-thrust in and up through his lungs. Whatever his story, it will go with him to the grave: the man is dead long before they get him home.

Alexander, now frantic, sends out patrols of Spanish Guardsmen. The sight of their swords on the streets brings out other family gangs, alert for any new threat, and suddenly there is a terrible urgency abroad. The Duke of Gandia is missing. *Missing.* The word contains all manner of horrors. Traders close early and family palazzi bolt their great wooden doors. The night brings skirmishes and brawls but, crucially, no further news. The Pope barely sleeps.

Next morning, the troops accost anyone and everyone in the area of the Piazza degli Ebrei or Santa Maria del Popolo who might have seen something. From along the Tiber, a Slav boatman called Giorgio

Schiviano comes forward. He owns a woodpile by the hospital of San Girolamo where the Dalmatian community gathers, and he sleeps every night in his boat among the reeds to keep guard against thieves. The story he tells is so vividly drawn that when Alexander hears it read out, word for word, by the head of the guards he lets out little moans, as if it is happening right there in front of his eyes.

"I was lying awake in my boat in the hours after midnight when two men came up out of the alley by the hospital to the open ground by the river. In the half-moon I could see their figures but no faces. They looked up and down to check there was no one about, then they disappeared. Then two more followed and did the same thing. One of them made a signal back toward the alley and a rider on a white horse appeared. There was a body slumped over the crupper behind him: head hanging over one side, legs on the other, with the first two men walking next to it, holding it so it didn't fall off. They got as far as the river's edge, the place where people throw rubbish, and then the horseman turned so the horse's backside was to the river. The men pulled the body off and swung it with all their might into the water.

"Then the horseman said to them. 'Has it sunk yet?'

"And they answered, 'Yes, sir.' But the dead man's cloak was still floating on the surface and when he turned he saw it. 'What's that?'

"'His cloak, sir,' they said, and they all threw stones and bits of rubbish at it until the water pulled it down. They stood watching to make sure it didn't rise again then turned and went off where they came from. I watched for a while, but I didn't see anything after that."

And so the fishing starts. Within hours, the Tiber around San Girolamo is clogged by boatmen from all over Rome, trawling and poking the muddy waters, spurred on by the promise of a reward. It fast becomes the joke of the day: the Borgia Pope, whatever his reputation for corruption, has turned out to be a real fisher of men. His enemies laugh hardest of all.

The river proves only too eager to disgorge its grotesque treasures. The first corpse comes up fast: a young man, half dressed, with a fat knife wound in the chest: the flesh of the face swollen and nibbled by fish but still recognizable. Except that no one knows who he is.

Not long after that a shout goes up as a trawling net snares a sodden mass of velvet and flesh. And now, sure enough, it is Juan, Duke of Gandia, who rises from the foul water, decorated with bits of debris and fully clothed down to his shoes, gloves and purse, still heavy with ducats, hanging from his belt. He might be ready for a night on the town, save for the fact that his legs and torso are riddled with stab wounds and his neck is a gaping grin of slashed flesh. Behind his back, his arms are tied fast. Whoever did this clearly enjoyed themselves.

Chapter 28

Even though he knows his son is dead, when they bring the news Alexander lets out a rolling howl, like an animal snapped in the jaws of a trap. The mutilated corpse is brought by boat to Castel Sant' Angelo, where it is washed and cleansed and dressed in full finery with a neck high enough to cover the slash, and at dusk a funeral cortège sets off over the bridge toward the Borgia family chapel in Santa Maria del Popolo, the bier surrounded by a hundred torchbearers and a sea of nobles, chamberlains and churchmen. Their open prayer rises like a cloud of melancholy into the air, pierced by the Pope's discordant wails, which sing out from the open Vatican windows even as far as the mourners on the bridge.

Inside his bedchamber, refusing all sustenance or solace, Alexander is a man pulled halfway into hell. The demons of grief have sunk their claws deep into him. He sits propped in his chair, his body rocking to and fro to the jagged rhythm of his own sobbing. Juan is dead. His pride, his joy, flesh of his flesh, is murdered. His beautiful, beloved son tortured and thrown into the river like a dead dog. Moans pour like vomit from his mouth, his face swells with tears, his eyes and nose clog so that he can barely see or even breathe. Juan is dead. God in heaven, how could anyone deserve this?

"Sweet Mary, Mother of God, help me . . ." Stumbling forward from the chair, he falls onto his knees, a broken old man praying like a child. "Forgive me my sins and have mercy on me. If I have offended . . . I will do better, I promise. Just bring him back to me, bring him back, please. Please."

But she, his own dear Virgin Mary, who has been with him through triumph and sorrow, understanding and forgiving him all manner of compromise or behavior, she who knows the agony of a son's death better than anyone, is no longer there. Her warmth, her sweetness and her boundless comfort have been withdrawn from him. He is indeed forsaken. Juan is dead and he is thrown to the devils.

He cries long into the night, the pain sliding under doors and out through windows so that everyone who hears him, be they servants lying on their pallets or cardinals tiptoeing down corridors or standing in anxious silent knots, registers the sound with the strange sense of constriction in their own chests. Pity, yes. Certainly there is pity. But also awe, and fear, that such a powerful man could be brought so low.

He torments himself over and over with the same questions. Why? How? Two nights ago his son was alive. Two nights. So little time. If this is punishment it is also the cruellest trick of Fate. Abandoned by his precious Virgin, he becomes consumed by an image of time as the great rolling wheel of fortune running ever onward. He spreads out his hands blindly in front of him, seeing himself grabbing hold of the spokes of the wheel, wrenching and wrestling it to a slow, grinding standstill, then using all his bulk and heft to force it, inch by inch, backward; reclaiming the body of his son from the water, back through death into life, back to the bridge where Juan had left his brother, back to the light and laughter of a summer banquet, back as far as their last encounter that same afternoon: a smiling, vibrant young man in slashed silks, standing in front of him, dismissing all concern for his well-being as he kisses him goodbye ready to head off into his fate.

"Don't go to your mother's tonight. Stay here with me instead." Alexander howls the words into the darkness. "I need you. Stay with me."

But the wheel is already groaning under the strain of its enforced stillness, and he can hold it no longer, so that it bursts out of his hands, time rushing to catch up, events unfolding, each irrevocable step on the road back and forward to death. Now, in retribution for his arrogance in trying to play with Fate, he seems to see the worst in most detail. Juan's horse with its two riders, weaving off from the riverbank into a complex of alleyways. The rush of men emerging from the shadows, dragging him from the saddle on to the ground, the push and pull of him through a dark entrance into a back room or cellar already prepared. He sees the rope lashed around his wrists and then watches as, supported from behind, his body is forced upward to meet the man whose pleasure it is now to deal out death through an orgy of knife-thrusts. Nine wounds, they say. Each one delivered for a different insult, a litany of grudges. And as the blade thrusts in, Alexander groans as if it were his own flesh being punctured, until at last the man gestures for the head to be yanked back and held so that he can start work on the throat. His final gargling scream collapses into another wave of sobs. Juan is dead.

Outside the barred door, a small coterie of his supporting cardinals wait in relays, alert for a break in the terrible music of suffering. They are joined by Burchard, who stands tall and still as a stork, his grim face set even grimmer. Eventually there comes a moment of silence and someone knocks tentatively, calling through the wood, begging for His Holiness to take some nourishment, at least some water, for the summer air is thick and hot and he will do himself damage. But they are answered by a low wail of resistance. "Leave me. Leave me be."

It does not even sound like the Pope's voice anymore. No one would wish such pain on any man. Even Burchard's granite face crumbles with compassion.

It is close to dawn when the Master of Ceremonies climbs the stairs to the apartments of the Cardinal of Valencia above the papal suite. The receiving room is dark and empty, a further door shut. As he knocks he hears movement, then Cesare's voice demanding who it is before calling him in.

"Your Most Reverend Lord Cardinal." He finds him sat at his desk, fully dressed, a piece of paper in front of him. "His Holiness the Pope . . ."—he hesitates—". . . Your father . . . is in the deepest of distress."

"I can hear each cry as clearly as you." Cesare's face in the glow of the oil lamp is strained, almost ghostly, another man who has not seen his bed for nights.

"The fear among the cardinals is that he will make himself ill." He stops again. "I . . . I thought perhaps . . . if you could talk to him . . ."

"Me? No, I don't think he would want to see me," he says flatly. "I am not the right son."

For the first time Burchard feels something akin to pity for this arrogant young man whom he has never liked, nor ever will. "I am sorry for your brother's death, Reverend Lord Cardinal—it is a terrible crime."

Cesare nods, his face creased in a strange half-smile. "In which case you are in select company, Signor Burchard, since we both know that half of Rome is celebrating behind closed doors. Tell me, when you come to write your account of this affair, what will you say?"

"My . . . account?"

"What? You keep a diary, don't you? That is what people say."

"A diary? No. No . . . I . . . sometimes I record details, the protocol of papal affairs, that is all." And Burchard is seeing the hiding place in his study, slipped between the heavy volumes of Church law, and already thinking about finding a more secure place.

"Protocol? That's all? No thoughts? No opinions?"

"I don't quite . . ."

"I am wondering whose names you might put on to your pages as being responsible for my brother's death."

"Oh no." He shakes his head. "I am a servant of the Church, Reverend Lord Cardinal. It is not my job to speculate about such things. Only to record facts."

"Of course. Well, then I hope you will record this: that the Pope is a man with a great heart who feels his loss most deeply, and takes us with him into his grief."

"No one would doubt it." Burchard is already turning, eager to leave.

From below, Alexander's voice lifts again, breaking on the wave of a sob. They both listen in silence.

"Don't worry," says Cesare softly. "He will not cry forever."

———

With the Master of Ceremonies gone, Cesare sits for a while staring into space. From the darkness outside the throw of the lamp come two sharp knocks. He gets up and opens a door at the back, its edges lost in the decoration of the surrounding wall, then turns back into the room as Michelotto follows him.

He is fresh from the streets, his clothes crumpled and stained, face streaked with sweat. He carries an unbuckled sword and a light cloak, both of which he throws down on the chest. The scabbard bounces off the wood on to the floor beneath, the metal clanging on the tiles.

Cesare hands him a goblet of wine and he downs the liquid in one. He pushes the jug toward him and watches as he refills.

"So?"

"A fat sack of nothing. The city is closed as tight as a Jew's purse. There are so many boarded houses you'd think the plague had come."

"What about the families?"

"All behind bolted doors. The Sforzas are so nervous that they're shitting themselves—the Vice-Chancellor has moved out of his palace and in with the ambassador of Milan. If there is anyone cheering you can't hear it from the streets. Everybody's waiting for the Pope to stop crying."

"And the boatman?"

"Is back in his boat."

"Is his purse any bigger?"

"If it is, he doesn't spend it on himself. He smells worse than the river."

"What about his story?"

"Exactly what he told the guards. With a few extra stammers when it looked like my knife might slip."

"You believe him?"

"He's too stupid to lie. He lives only for his wood and it's given him sharp eyes for anything and anyone who comes near it."

"So why didn't he report it?"

"Because according to him, if he reported every body he'd seen dumped there, he'd never get any sleep at all." Michelotto laughs. "It's fair enough. The place is hardly a secret. I've been on that bank a few times myself over the years."

"But you don't ride a white horse and have four grooms with you."

"More's the pity." He rubs the heels of his hands into his eye sockets as if to clear his sight. His face looks even wilder when he takes them away, the crosswork of scars rising in jagged ridges out of sallow skin. "The horse doesn't get us anywhere. Just like you said, every great family has a white purebred in its stables. Virginio's bastard, Carlo Orsini, rides one, I know that much, but everyone is saying he's out of town. I daresay you'd find other Orsini mounts, as well as a few inside the Colonna or the Sforza palace."

"And the masked man . . ."

"Dissolved into the air. The duke's manservant says he visited the house six or seven times over the last month. He never heard a voice, nor saw more than the edge of a beard. He could be five hundred men and counting."

Cesare waves his hand. "What about the woman he was offering?"

"Which one?"

"You tell me. Whichever one my brother couldn't have."

Michelotto snorts. "From what I hear there are barely any virgins left in Rome since he got back from Spain."

But Cesare is not smiling. Over their years together, Michelotto has grown accustomed to not always knowing what his master is feeling, which, in its own way, is a kind of knowing in itself. Certainly he is not surprised by his apparent lack of grief: there was little love lost between the brothers, and the Pope's greed for sorrow has sucked up all the available tears. What does surprise him is the lack of anger. Perhaps it is buried too deep or blunted by exhaustion; for they have both been awake for as long as Juan has been dead.

"There is talk of one. Filamena della Mirandola, daughter of a count. Ripe and ready. With a father who prized her dearly." He pauses. "Their house is close to where the body went in the river."

"And?"

"That's where it begins and ends. His reputation is spotless. And he owns no white horses."

"Of course. The woman was always only the bait. The real question is who was doing the hunting."

They fall silent. Michelotto pours himself more wine. The tiredness is beginning to prick at him and he moves around the room, massaging his neck to and fro as if to free it from some permanent crick. His eyes fall on the table and the paper sitting there. He looks up at Cesare, as if to ask permission. He is given it.

He gives a low whistle. "This is a rich harvest. Are these names in order?"

"You tell me."

"The Orsini," he reads. "No one would argue with that. Only question is, which one?"

"Which one would you say?"

"Ah, we're spoiled for choice. Everyone knows Virginio was poisoned before we hit them in their castles. Carlo, the son . . . his nephews Paolo and Giulio, they all know how to carve up a body. His brother-in-law, Bartolomeo. Even that loving sister of his; if she didn't plunge the knife herself she could well have instructed others. If I was in her pay I would have done it for her."

"I don't doubt you would. It's a clever double blow. Kill the son and at the same time torture the father."

"Number two: the Sforzas?" He shrugs. "Why not? The Duke of Gandia insults the Vice-Chancellor in his own home. That by itself warrants a knife in the belly."

"You can cross him off. He has already given up the keys of his house for us to search. He's acting too guilty and terrified to have done it."

"What about Giovanni? You always said he didn't have the balls."

"He hasn't. Except we're going to force him to admit that fact in public soon enough. If he has heard a whiff of that it would be reason enough for revenge."

"Gonsalvo de Córdova? You got a Spaniard's name on here?"

"You didn't see his face during the ceremony when the Pope gave his war spoils to Juan. The insult was palpable."

"Except he's a soldier with a reputation for honor."

"This *is* honor we're talking about."

"And the Duke of Urbino? What? Because we didn't pay his ransom?"

"You know how long he rotted in the Orsini jails? Close on nine weeks."

From below, the Pope's keening rises up again, low, broken wails, like a man trying to wake from a never-ending nightmare.

Michelotto looks down at the rest of the list and his face comes up amazed. "You're not going to show him this?"

"At some point he will stop grieving. When he does he is going to have to decide what comes next. Everyone is waiting. He needs to consider anyone who had a score to settle or something to gain."

Michelotto stares at him and a slow smile crosses his face. He lets the paper fall on to the table and yawns. "Well, if you don't need me anymore tonight, I have to sleep."

Cesare waves him away. He leans back in his chair and stares at the ceiling.

At the door Michelotto turns. "The last name? Is that there because of a score to be settled or a gain to be had?"

But Cesare already has his eyes closed. Whether he does not hear, or just does not choose to answer, is not entirely clear.

Chapter 29

IN A WELL-RUN CONVENT EVEN THE MOST DRAMATIC NEWS TAKES A while to creep under the doors of the cells, and San Sisto, under the leadership of its abbess, Madonna Girolama Pichi, is very well run indeed. Unlike most city convents, where every other raised voice can jump over the walls, its ancient setting on the Via Appia near the southern gate means that these days it is surrounded by open countryside. It was built close to the spot where great men preached and gave their martyred bodies to God, and their devotion has soaked into its very stones, making silence easier to bear.

So far away is it that, unless there is an express reason for a nun to be informed of something, it is usually only when the riders gallop out toward Naples that the more sharp-eared have reason to hear the thunder of hooves and wonder what new Roman gossip they might be carrying in their saddlebags.

In this case, though, they do not have to wait long. Pedro Calderón, who in the past has kicked up enough dust as he rides past the convent's bolted doors, is dispatched the moment the funeral cortège reaches the church. With the Pope incapable of making decisions, Cesare writes the letter. It is imperative that Lucrezia does not hear it first from any other source.

Calderón is shown into the abbess's receiving room. Though a little sweaty from the road, he is still a most lovely young man. Not that the abbess notices such things. Or if she does it will certainly not affect her behavior toward him: this is a woman who has already seen off a cohort of the Papal Guard.

"You have entered a place of sanctuary and worship where we have few visitors, and though I am sure your news is as urgent as you claim, I would ask you to respect that."

In contrast, he is palpably nervous. But nuns often do that to men, and he has much to be nervous about. "It is urgent indeed. I also carry a letter for you, Reverend Mother. From the Most Reverend Lord Cardinal of Valencia."

She takes it, breaks the seal and reads. A short gasp leaves her lips and the horror on her face moves quickly to pity. "Oh, how dreadful. This will affect the duchess deeply." She looks up. "Perhaps I should be the one—"

"No. No," he says quickly. "Thank you . . . but my instructions are that the letter must be delivered by my own hand."

He had said the very same thing five years ago when standing in a dusty courtyard in the middle of Siena, and from that moment of courage everything else had flowed. Then the words had been true. But Cesare had not issued any such explicit instructions to his messenger. It is the first lie that Pedro has told in this, the great affair of his heart.

"Very well. I will send for her. It would be best for you to meet in the garden. The sisters are at individual evening prayer and you will have privacy there. I will show you there myself. When you are ready to leave, ring the bell at the door and the watch sister will collect you." She slips the letter into a drawer. Then says, almost abruptly, "Tell me, how is our Holy Father?"

"I . . . he is in great distress."

"Yes, yes, of course." She nods quickly. Not even the abbess, it seems, is totally inured to the temptations of gossip. "The ways of the world can be cruel. I am sure you are well picked for your kindness."

He bows his head. "I am the most humble servant of the duchess."

She studies him for a second, and then moves on to lead the way.

The sun is setting and the garden is bathed in softest gold. It is well cared for: rows of clipped box hedge around a small pond where sun-lazy carp glide in and out under lily leaves. Trained fruit trees and banks of herbs give off a mix of medicinal and summer smells, a rich illustration of God's handiwork, as useful as it is lovely. He stands awkwardly in the middle, waiting. Waiting. He, Pedro Calderón, who was taught duty by a Spanish father but learned romance from an Italian mother so that it took him till the age of seventeen to lose his virginity, to a professional, while he continued to wait for the woman of his dreams. His Laura, his Beatrice, his Ginevara. His princess. His downfall.

She comes clothed in white; a simple day dress, her hair caught in a loose gold net with a few strands flying free. She walks quickly, head held high, and he remembers the first time he saw her, resplendent in her wedding gown, gliding down the corridor as if her feet were not touching the ground.

She gives a laughing little smile, her face aglow in the light. Whoever summoned her has not warned her that it is bad news. "Pedro Calderón!" And she is almost running now. "Oh, I am so pleased. They did not tell me it was you." She reaches him and takes his hand impetuously, slipping into the Catalán tongue of childhood intimacy.

It is the first time they have ever touched and they are both aware of it.

"Madam, I . . . It is an honor to see you again. You are well?"

"I am well enough. Learning to be quiet." She shrugs. "Though it is not an easy lesson. And you? You bring me news from home?"

"Yes—"

"What?" Now she is looking, she sees it immediately. "Oh, what? What is it?"

"I—I have a letter."

He holds it out, but she is still staring at his face.

"What is it? Is it my father? Oh dear God, it is my father, something has happened to my father."

"Madam, I— No, no, your father is well."

"Then it is Cesare . . ."

"No. The letter is from him. See the seal. Here. Please. Please, you should read it."

She gives a little laugh of relief. "Oh, then it must be my marriage. Very well."

Yet as she puts her hand out to take it, she knows that it is not her marriage. Her fingers fumble with the seal, and in her haste she nearly drops the letter. Her eyes scan the first few lines, the loving thoughts, the gentle way in, and then . . .

When she has finished she stands still, her eyes fixed at the pond. She sees fish flashes of silver and red, notes the way a breeze tickles the surface of the water. Nothing has changed. How could that be? Juan is dead yet wind still blows and fish swim. Juan is dead, but there is nothing in the world to mark his extinction. The thought makes her feel dizzy.

"My lady!"

Immediately she sways and he is there, his arm around her waist, a hand under her elbow, moving her toward the edge of the garden and a stone bench under the wall of high cell windows. She allows herself to be taken.

He sits stiffly next to her, his hand still supporting. At her feet, the flagstones are blurring through tears. But tears are too easy for such horror. She pulls them back as she sits frozen in the moment.

Finally she looks up, frowning, almost as if she had forgotten he was there. "You know what is written here? Oh, yes, of course, of course you do. My brother says it was murder. Murder! But how? Who did it? What happened?"

"Should she receive you herself and should she ask you further, tell her no details. The duchess feels things deeply and women like her do not need to know more than is necessary." Cesare's voice is clear in his head.

"I don't— I mean it is not for me to . . . ?"

She stares at him. "Oh . . . Cesare has told you not to tell me, yes?" She shakes her head. "He's wrong. He thinks because I am a woman— He doesn't understand that it is much worse not to know. I will hear it from others soon enough and the gossip will be more foul. It would be better if it came from you, Pedro Calderón. Please."

From the first lie to the first disobedience. What else can he possibly do? He makes it brief, dwelling as much on the care as the violence, painting a picture of the majesty of the cortège, the perfection of Juan's body on the bier after the beauticians of death had worked their magic. "So peaceful—his face as perfect as if he was still alive. That is what everyone who saw him said."

"Yes." She listens, never taking her eyes from his face, nodding, deep in concentration. "Yes, I can see it. I think I have even seen the river somewhere near that place." She shivers, then looks down at the letter again, as if she knows there might be more solace in the words now.

"Will you answer me another question, Pedro Calderón?" she says after a while.

"Yes, my lady. If I can."

"Have you ever killed a man?"

"Me?"

"You are a bodyguard for my brother, yes? I think there must have been times, fights . . ."

He is back in the Piazza Navona with the Swiss Guard; all is panic and mayhem, with screams of fury and pain as blood sprays across the cobbles. He would prefer to keep his counsel on this as it is not something he is proud of, but a man of honor cannot break his promise to the woman he already loves. "Yes, there have been fights. And men have died. One fight in particular. I know I killed one, maybe more."

"And as he was dying . . . did he know?"

"I don't understand . . ."

"Did he know he was dying? Was there time for him to pray?"

"Pray?" Prayer? Had there been prayer in the scream for mercy? Did that count? "I don't know. They spoke another language."

"Ah! Well I pray that before Juan died he had time to ask forgiveness for his sins. I would have him at peace more than I might wish him back again here on earth." Her eyes fill with tears again. "My poor father . . . the Pope . . . This letter comes from Cesare because he is in too much grief to write himself. Is that right?"

"I think it possible, yes, my lady."

"Oh, I wish I was there to comfort him." She shakes her head. "Well, I am not going to cry. Juan needs prayers more than tears," she says firmly, taking a deep breath and straightening up, her chin high, only the merest, sweetest touch of puppy fat around the jawline. They sit in silence for a few moments. He can feel his own pulse inside his head, tapping out the passing of time. Let me stay here forever, he thinks.

"It is close to this very convent that Saint Sixtus was martyred," she says. "Did you know that? He was beheaded on the orders of the Roman Emperor, and even as they wielded the sword his face was filled with joy. Because in death he knew he would find eternal life. The abbess speaks of him often and when she does all the nuns cry. Everyone knows that it makes this convent, built in his name, special for prayers of intercession." She is talking faster now, as if she is trying to convince herself. "So I am in the right place to pray for Juan, do you not think?" She does not wait for his answer. "I mean he was . . . he was rash sometimes and I know he was not liked by everyone—but he was so filled with life, and much was put upon his shoulders. He was God's child and underneath it all his heart was pure. I know that. So if I pray here then surely Our Lord will hear me."

"I am sure He will, my lady."

"Yes, yes. I think so too," she says with perfect earnestness.

They sit further, the light draining away under a gaudy pink- and apricot-streaked sky. They are both aware that their hands, though no longer touching, remain too close. She moves hers away, self-conscious now. "Thank you," she says. "I—I am glad it was you who was sent to tell me."

He nods. "I . . . I will go now . . . if you wish."

"I . . . If you don't mind, would you sit a little longer? The nuns are very kind but . . . my cell grows gloomy after sunset and it is so beautiful here." And she lifts up her face into the light, so that her skin glistens.

"My lady, I will stay here till night ends and the day comes again if it would help."

"Ha! I am not sure the abbess would allow that. You sound like a knight in a romance tale, Pedro Calderón."

"I did not mean—" He drops his eyes.

"No, no. It is not a bad thing to be. I think the world would be a lesser place without the bravery of Buovo or the love of Lancilotto and Ginevara. When I was a child I loved such stories. I—"

She stops, realizing suddenly what she is saying, how just for that instant she is no longer thinking of the horror of Juan.

Neither is he. No, right now he is imagining instead what a wonder it would be to be sitting at her side in the fading light sharing romance stories. How, if that might happen, he would surely die happy.

Career Spaniards, alas, are not so in thrall to the wonder of Dante that they read him as diligently as educated Romans. So this dreamy young man has not spent time in the fifth circle of hell, marveling at the burning wind of agony which sweeps sinners in its path, or hearing the plaintive tale of Francesca and her brother-in-law Paolo, whose mutual appreciation of chivalric poetry pulled them into sin and an eternity of such cruel punishment that even Dante himself was brought to tears.

As for Lucrezia? Well, Lucrezia knows that story well enough. But as much as she dreams of heaven after death, she also dreams of just a taste of it on earth. She is seventeen years old with one brother cruelly murdered, another who loves her too much and a discarded husband who does not love her at all. She sits caught inside a vortex of grief, fear and yearning. Yet whatever the confusion, life is worth living. Ah, Juan . . .

Across the way, the door opens, silhouetting the figure of the watch sister. The convent is on its way to bed and visiting, even for its most powerful guests, is over. They are both on their feet immediately.

"I am grateful to you, Pedro Calderón," she says quickly. "I would wish to send word back, but it is late now and I must compose my thoughts . . ."

"I could return again in the morning, my lady. I am the appointed messenger between the Vatican and the convent."

"Oh, then . . . you will come back?"

"Without fail."

He drops on to his knee and takes her hand.

"Tell my brother and my father that my heart is with them, and with God's help I will find the words to comfort them."

At a small window on the second floor the abbess stands, watching their leavetaking.

It is always a challenge when a convent opens its doors to noble-women in distress: in the time it takes for their trunks and maidservants to enter, the ways of the world slide in with them, sending tremors through the hard-won calm of regulated worship. In her time, Abbess Pichi has overseen all kinds of dramas played out inside the walls and has grown adept at reading the signs. In the search for future nuns, it is her job to distinguish the spiritual from the sensual in young girls, not always an easy task when their bodies are as full of turmoil as their hearts. When the young Lucrezia had left to take up her place in the world she had prayed that God would preserve her from too much temptation. But His will often works in ways that even His most humble children cannot divine. That night she remembers her again in her prayers. And makes a note to talk to the watch sister about an occasional inspection of the garden during the evening hour of private prayer.

Chapter 30

FINALLY, ON THE AFTERNOON OF SUNDAY JUNE 18, AFTER THREE days and three nights of grief, Alexander calls his manservant in to wash and dress him. With much coaxing he agrees to take a little soup and watered wine. Burchard is then allowed to enter. Through him he sends a message to his waiting cardinals, thanking them for their sweet vigil and asking them to leave him now for the comfort of their own beds. He will address them all in closed Consistory of the Sacred College the next morning.

When the hour comes the great room is filled to bursting, the only absences being della Rovere, still in self-imposed exile in France, and the Vice-Chancellor, Ascanio Sforza, who clearly does not feel safe enough to leave the house of the Milanese ambassador. The Pope arrives leaning heavily on his servant's arm. They all fall to their knees as he enters, then rise quickly to take in the sight of a man who seems smaller than they remember. Alexander, for so long propelled through life on an energy greater than his years, appears suddenly vulnerable, even old. His son, the Cardinal of Valencia, the most handsome and dandified cleric in the room, looks grim and tired. Everyone waits.

"The Duke of Gandia is dead." His voice is strong with emotion. "A worse blow could not have been dealt us because we loved him above all things and valued not more the papacy nor anything else. God has done this perhaps for some sin of ours, and not because he deserved such a terrible or mysterious death. Nor do we know who killed him and threw him like dung into the Tiber—"

He falters for a second, looking around him. The cardinals sit locked into the drama. It is clear they have no idea what words will come out of his mouth next.

"There are many rumors, but this we will say now. We absolve our Vice-Chancellor of any suspicion of guilt and would ask that he return to his home and our service, and lay aside any fears for his own safety that he might have. Equally we are convinced of the innocence of our son-in-law, and of our former compatriot in arms, Guidobaldo da Montefeltro, Duke of Urbino, both of whose names are being carried on the winds of gossip.

"The investigation for the perpetrators of this obscene crime will continue, but we will move forward in a resolve to lead a new life for ourselves and for the Church which it is our privilege to rule over. In future, we will pay scrupulous attention to the appointments of all sacred offices. Benefices will be conferred only to those who merit them, with all nepotism renounced and a commission of ecclesiastics to oversee a new era of reform. If we had seven papacies, we would give them all to have the Duke of Gandia alive again, yet nevertheless we will go forward under God's clear and watchful eye."

And now, at last, Alexander's gaze falls on the Cardinal of Valencia, who sits impassive, his eyes cold into the distance, as if there is no longer any connection between father and son. Such is the shock of it all that afterward the cardinals, who can scarcely believe their ears at this turn of events, wonder if this cocky young Borgia has lost not only a brother but also the approval of a father who has done so much to advance his career.

What they do not know is that by the time Alexander walks into the room, father and son have already been in conference, feeling their way toward a strategy to deal with the chaos into which the family has been plunged.

It was close to dawn when Alexander, pulled from fitful sleep back into a fog of grief, secretly called for the Cardinal of Valencia. Cesare had been waiting for the moment: he, who could face a goaded bull and feel no fear, registered an unfamiliar lurch in his stomach as he entered the bedchamber.

"Ah, my son!"

The air is stifling. In the gloom he makes out the figure of his father sitting heavily on the side of his bed in a linen robe, his head bare, no papal regalia to give him stature. He rises up and opens his arms, swaying slightly on his feet. As they embrace Cesare feels the sweat on his body and the gasping breaths of a man who still has more tears to shed.

"Father." They stand entwined, as if Alexander has not the strength to support himself alone. "Father, your suffering is inside us all. The palace has been in fear for your well-being."

"Ah, what is my pain compared to his?" He breaks away and sinks back toward the bed, his hand grasping the thick carved bedstead as a crutch. "He is dead, Cesare. Juan is dead; tortured and thrown like a dog's corpse into the Tiber."

"Yes, Father. I know."

"And I . . . I have been in hell."

"But you are back now," Cesare says firmly. "Which is only right and proper, for as God's vicar on earth you are sorely needed here. The whole of Rome is holding its breath waiting for your response."

"Yes, yes, you are right. I am needed. You know when I was lost, even Mary Madonna, Mother of God, would not heed my cries. She who has supported me through all my triumphs and tribulations. Ha! But she came to me in the end. When I had no more strength she took pity and offered me her hand. Oh, the sublime comfort of her blessing. And now, as you say, we must go forward. And make amends. Our behavior has offended God, Cesare."

"That may be so, Father," Cesare says carefully, moving to stand in front of him. "But I think it was not God who plunged the dagger into Juan's body."

"No, no. Still, it is to Him we must make amends."

"And He will listen and bring us all to peace."

"Yes, all of us. Oh, I have been selfish in my pain. Your mother? Ah, who will tell Vannozza that her son is dead?" He grabs at his son's hand, squeezing it hard. "And Jofré? And my sweet, sweet Lucrezia? Lucrezia, who loved her brother so."

"The news is delivered to all of them, Father. Our mother will find solace in God and Lucrezia will be better cared for in the convent than she would be here." He pauses, never taking his eyes from Alexander's face. "We must look to ourselves now. Whoever did this intended to destroy you as much as Juan. But they will not succeed. You are too strong for them."

Alexander nods heavily, staring at the fiercely colored tiles on the floor in front of him. His face is sagging flesh, as if the bones beneath have melted; a man collapsing into himself.

"Father?"

"Yes, yes. I am still here," he mutters. And slowly he pulls himself back from the slump until he is sitting upright. The head lifts last of all. "So, tell me, Cesare. Who is it, you think, that we have offended more than God?"

"Everything marks it as a revenge killing: the precision of the trap, the cruelty of the wounds, the insult of the disposing of the body. I would say the Orsini."

"The death of Juan for the death of Virginio Orsini? Ah! The man was a sniveling traitor. That they should dare! You are sure?"

"The Sforzas perhaps have as much motive, but I think less courage." He pauses. "But there are others."

"Is this how you buried your grief, my son? With thoughts of revenge? Did that help you with the horror?"

Cesare gives a slight shrug. "It has been three days. And you have been crying for all of us."

"Still, I hope you found time to pray. Whatever power a man has in this world, there is no comfort without God, and a cardinal cannot live within our Holy Mother Church without prayer. That is an offense in itself."

"I am what I am, Father," he says quietly. "The Church was never my chosen profession."

The Pope grunts as if this is not something he wants to hear. "So? Who are these others?"

"Perhaps this is not the time—"

"Agh, it will never be the time. Nothing we do will bring him back. And I have promised God that my eyes will be directed to penance, not revenge." He stops. "However . . ."

Cesare takes the paper from inside his sleeve and puts it into his father's hand. "The names written there denote motive, not guilt. You should know that before you read it."

He looks at it and his face grows pale. "I don't understand. What does this mean, these names at the bottom?"

"It means that a deed this foul will breed gossip as fast as corpses breed worms. And everyone who has been in this palace has witnessed things they will talk about. Not least of which is Jofré's jealousy on behalf of his wife."

"Jofré? Jofré! I do not believe it for an instant."

"Neither do I, Father. But he has grown a temper along with his manhood, and when tongues start wagging it is best we are prepared."

"And you? You, Cesare. Your name is on this list. God in heaven, why do you put yourself here?"

"Because if I don't, others will. Juan and I quarreled over many things, Father. You have seen it yourself. Our antagonism is well known. I have in my time envied him the place he held in the world." He pauses. "And the place he held in your heart."

Alexander sits staring at him. Cesare waits. If it is a risk, then it is one that needs to be taken.

"But you are so precious to me. You know that, surely," he says at last.

"I do, yes. Which is why we must speak of this now. There must be no doubt between us, Father. So. Ask me. Ask me now and I will tell you the truth."

"Oh sweet Jesus." Alexander shakes his head and his eyes fill up with tears. The silence sits heavily between them. "Very well," he says at last. "Did you kill your brother?"

"No. No, I did not. I swear to you on my mother's life. Though there have been times I have come close to wanting to."

There is a quiet knock on the door. "Your Holiness. The time is come." His manservant's voice is gentle, unsure. "The cardinals will be gathering for the Consistory soon. May I enter and help you dress?"

"In a moment . . . in a moment."

Alexander gets up and embraces his son heavily again. Is it possible that Cesare's answer has stanched the bleeding from a wound that he himself had not yet been aware of? "I shall speak to Jofré and send him and his wife from Rome. They may find a stronger connection away from the temptations of the court. And I will write to Lucrezia. Ah, I fear I am being punished for my overfondness of my children."

"What about the divorce?"

"The divorce?" He gives a small sigh, for a second resistant to the call back to family business. "I will talk again with the Vice-Chancellor."

"You'll have to coax him out of hiding first. He is so sure we think him guilty that he has disappeared."

"All the better. It may make him more malleable to our will."

"And the Orsini?"

"Ha! The Orsini. Damn their souls." His voice breaks apart with fury. He shakes his head to collect himself. "If we revenge ourselves now it will start a greater war in the streets, which would only play into their hands."

"You are wise even in grief, Father." Cesare, who has been eager for a sign that this new piety will not last forever, smiles. "I will go to Naples and squeeze what concessions I can from the new king to make up for . . . for some of what we have lost."

"Our loss, yes." The thought catches again in his soul. "Ah. The new Duke of Gandia is a two-year-old boy hidden in his mother's Spanish skirts. Where is the Borgia future now?"

"Don't worry, Father. We will survive this. One enemy at a time. Just as you always said." He takes his hand and kisses the ring.

"Ah, my son," Alexander murmurs. "My beloved son."

It is hard to know which one he is referring to.

Chapter 31

IT MIGHT HAVE BEEN EASIER IF CESARE *HAD* KILLED HIS BROTHER. Then he would have had some plan ready in the wake of the chaos that now surrounds them. As it is, he must make it up as he goes along.

Fate. For him it has always been a more compelling deity than God. When did his allegiance to one overtake the other? If asked, he would probably not be able to remember. Even as a child the passivity of prayer—the humility of the asking and accepting—had felt not so much unhelpful as unnatural, and with adulthood, privately it had fallen easily into disuse. While others gained comfort and guidance by appealing to a force outside themselves, Cesare found everything he needed inside himself, and the shift from thinking to action came so naturally that it fast became who he was: in argument he would use his wits, with women his charm, and in the hunt or the bullring physical agility and strength. What the world sees as confidence, bravery, even arrogance, is, for him, simply being Cesare. God has nothing to do with it.

Given the whirlwind of gossip, it is inevitable that some will ask the same question that he has just put before his father. Did he kill his brother because he stood in his way? Except Cesare knows it is the wrong question. The more accurate one would be, why did he do nothing to stop it?

Over the eleven months since Juan had set foot in back in Rome it had become clear that he would almost certainly kill himself. His dalliances, his violence, his military incompetence were all bound to incite revenge, while his vanity and Alexander's fawning love had made them both blind to the increasing danger he was in. Why else would Juan have allowed himself to become the willing servant of a masked man? To go with him after dark into Rome's murky streets with only a single groom for protection? That night by the bridge, as the dinner-party guests had parted company, Cesare had come the closest he could to protecting him when he had offered Michelotto as a bodyguard. But Juan, eager to be seen as wilder and braver than his brother, of course had refused.

To be given so much, only to throw it away. No wonder Fate had turned against him. When the news came through of his horse found with one slashed stirrup it had been fury not grief that Cesare had felt: fury at the stupidity of such a degrading end. As Alexander lay battered by the winds of grief, leaving Cesare to police the city and try to fashion some tactics to go with this new reality, the anger had only grown. How dare his brother have so unmanned his father, have brought such humiliation on the family?

By the time Cesare walked into the Pope's bedroom that morning he had forged a strategy of sorts. He must somehow coax his father back from the quicksands of grief, for nothing can be done without his energy and consent. In time the crime will be avenged, but the first priority must be to address the damage.

With Juan's death, so die the family's dynastic and territorial ambitions in Spain. If they are to survive, they must now find a similar foothold in mainland Italy. If Cesare had an army at his back, the papal states would be where he would go. He has studied each and every one of them and most are ripe for the picking, cities ruled by petty tyrants with no allies of any size to protect them. If Juan had been a better commander or been more careful with his wooing. If . . . well, there is no use in ifs now. They must work with what they have. And what they have is a stake in Naples: a state reeling from invasion and once again dependent on papal support to crown its new king, Federico. Jofré's marriage has already bought titles and lands there. The faster Lucrezia's ties with the Sforzas are severed the faster she too can be woven into the dynastic web. In a perfect world he would go one step further. Federico has a daughter, Carlotta, of marriageable age. If she was to become Cesare's wife, Naples would be closer for the taking. Except, of course, cardinals cannot marry.

One enemy at a time. As for the rest—he will wait for Fortuna, which has taken such cruel revenge, to turn her smiling face toward them again. And when she does, he will be ready.

Naples: closer to Rome than many of the great cities of northern Italy, yet more foreign than any of them. Wars of invasion and centuries of sea and sun have turned its dark-skinned population even darker, so that when courtiers take to the streets with their artificially whitened faces, they look bloodless against those they rule over. Inland from the glistening bay, the city is cramped and labyrinthine: teeming alleys populated like anthills, longer streets with running loggias and deep cornices offering shade from the relentless sun. It is not enough. When summer bites, the heat grows so humid that it feels as if flesh is melting. Inside this cauldron, the city is pulled between piety and sin. As many convents as there are brothels, that is what they say about Naples. The balance may tip in favor of God, but with poverty rising like its own stench from the gutters, it is the discordant music of orgasm rather than the mellifluous singing of nuns that most travelers remember. No wonder the French could not resist it.

For the first few weeks, Cesare plays his part as a man of the cloth. The youngest ever papal legate to crown a king, he is regal in his ceremonial robes and cultivates a gravitas alongside his charm, so that even those who would prefer to mock him take him seriously. In the celebrations that precede and follow the coronation, he and the new King Federico, a man of sturdier backbone than his predecessor, spend long hours in conference, bemoaning the parlous state of Italy and laying plans to bind Naples and the papacy closer together, to withstand the appetites of Milan and Venice.

Outside the council chamber, a network of spies help him to build up a picture of a land as troubled as it is corrupt: large swaths of territory run by squabbling baronial families and beset by brigandry, making it so wild that civic government is well nigh impossible. In short, a state ripe for the taking, if one could find a way into the center of power.

By the end of the first week Cesare has secured a marriage proposal for his almost-divorced sister and prepared the ground for an even more audacious suggestion: that should a certain cardinal be able to revoke his clerical vows (with the support of the Pope nothing is impossible) he would be most interested in the hand of the king's own lovely daughter, at present at the French court being groomed for whatever future her father's diplomacy might bring her. The king listens and does not disagree. It would be politically impolite to do anything else.

With the diplomacy successfully concluded, Cesare slips off his cardinal's robes and allows himself some pleasure. His prospective brother-in-law, Alfonso, a natural charmer, proves the most accommodating of guides. The pull of beauty amid languid heat does the rest. He moves between the attractions of the palace and the city. He falls in courtly love with a coquettish young duchess, showering her with attention and presents, until her virginity can barely stand the strain, then leavens the drawn-out challenges of courtship with the thrills of open lust.

The only difficult moment comes a few weeks before his departure, when he wakes to excruciating shooting pains in his legs and shoulders, so that he can hardly breathe or walk, and then his flawless skin breaks out in pustules. For a moment he feels panic. This is not the time for him to succumb to a plague, even one brought on by pleasure. Luckily, he has his own Spanish doctor in his entourage. Gaspare Torella is a medical scholar as well as a priest. He is also a man who makes it his business to study all new ailments, and there is none so new and challenging as the French disease.

"You are not to worry, Your Lord Cardinal. There are things we can do to address it." He diligently notes down the symptoms (which now include a small canker on His Most Reverend Lord Cardinal's penis) and recommends special unguents and a course of steam baths to open up the pores and led the morbid humors out.

In a few weeks the sores have started to close and a handsome young courtier returns, barely a trace of scarring to mark the adventure. As Cesare mounts his horse and leaves Naples, it feels as if Fortuna is once again with him. The doctor, riding behind, keeps his thoughts to himself.

Back in Rome, Alexander makes sure that the public welcome he offers his son is one of cool protocol, as befits a pious pope to an appointed papal legate. He even shows his distance by keeping him waiting for an hour.

It is a more pragmatic Alexander, however, who arranged the private meeting the night before, where, if he is to be honest, he found the fruits of Cesare's diplomacy almost as rewarding as prayer.

PART VI

A Very Papal Divorce

*I have known her an infinity of times, but
the Pope has taken her away to have her for
himself.*

Giovanni Sforza, Duke of Pesaro,
autumn 1497

Chapter 32

It is difficult to know how much jubilation a good Christian should admit to when someone he hates is violently dispatched. But when the news of Juan's death reaches Giovanni Sforza in his palace in Pesaro, he has no problem celebrating. He might have preferred that it was another brother-in-law butchered and thrown into sewer water, but over the last months he has suffered from the rough tongue of Juan as well as Cesare, and there is no doubt that the death makes his spirits rise.

Alas, the euphoria does not last long. Halfway through the night he wakes with crippling stomach pains when he realizes that even now they must be discussing who might be responsible for such a monstrous act and that his own name cannot be far from anyone's lips. When tales of the Pope's wailing through the night reach him he is in a panic lest anyone might hear the word "Sforza" rising up from within his howls. His cardinal cousin, he learns, has already given up the keys to his house to be searched for evidence and has fled in fear of his life.

There are moments when he wishes that he *had* done it, had had the courage. What would it have taken? How much money? Which contacts? Which men? The world is full of ways to carve a body into pieces without being the one to wield the knife. But you would have to be sure of the loyalty of your employees: that they were more frightened of you than of the victim's family. And he has never commanded such a following.

The news of the Pope's emotional collapse and public repentance is so extraordinary that Giovanni almost envies his father-in-law his capacity for feeling. He spends so long on his letter of condolence that by the time it is dispatched he is already hearing how many others have been received. The papal choir will soon be rehearsing the most delicately felt motet on the death of David's son Absalom by the Pope's own composer, and even His Holiness's most passionate opponents have been moved to try to comfort him. The mad monk of Florence, Savonarola, who spends his life launching thunderbolts at the Vatican, sends a fulsome sermon on love and God's infinite compassion, while from France no less an enemy than Cardinal della Rovere writes such a feeling letter that the Pope cries all over again when he receives it. One might even believe that political rapprochement is not impossible after all.

As the Sforzas are publicly absolved and received back into the Vatican fold, the names of further suspects speed out of Rome amid clouds of summer dust. In Venice the word "Orsini" is everywhere on the Rialto, while in Florence they are even whispering individual names: Paolo, nephew to the poisoned Virginio. Or his brother-in-law, the bellicose Bartolomeo. But everyone agrees that whoever is responsible, the Borgias will have to swallow their pain and bide their time. The arrogance of the murder speaks of threat as well as punishment, and there are those who wonder if the family will be able to survive the blow. It seems even the Pope understands that: by August he has officially called off the investigation, claiming that he is leaving the matter to God.

The gossip gives Giovanni hope that his own fortunes too may change and that in all this newfound holiness his marriage might be given a second chance. At times he is not sure what would be worse, to be tied forever to this vicious, violent family or shamefully shrugged off. But as long as Alexander is Pope the answer is clear: as the ruler of a city that is also a papal state it is better to be inside the family than out. To help things along he even prays: for the soul of Juan (safe enough—it will take more than his prayers to keep him from the fires of hell), and for his own future.

He gets his answer soon enough. While his Vice-Chancellor Ascanio Sforza is received with open arms and given the honor of private consultations by both the Pope and the Cardinal of Valencia, the warm welcome soon gives way to cold reality. The marriage is over and the Pope now wants it done with. The longer it takes, the less chance there is of him keeping the dowry.

The matter is deposited firmly into Giovanni's lap. Or rather a little higher in his anatomy. Ascanio's letter spells out the depths of humiliation that await him, paraphrasing as it does the wording of Lucrezia's declaration of non-consummation.

He reads the first lines and then explodes with fury and outrage. How could they do this? They, who are already reeling from the effects of their corruption. What infamy, what nerve. How dare they? He rages around the palace, his servants running after him. After months of silent moroseness there is worry that he might be tipping into madness. Entering what had once been Lucrezia's rooms, he overturns chairs and smashes vases, tearing the covers from the bed so that he can imagine better the sight of her, her chaste nightgown pulled up over her thighs as she opens her legs to let him in. Non-consummation? He, who had lain with her a dozen times in the first few weeks of their arrival in Pesaro alone. He, who had a child by his first wife. What do they take him for? An imbecile, a coward, a man without balls? Well, they have picked wrongly. He is cousin to the Duke of Milan. He will not give them what they want. Without his agreement, while they may force an annulment, Lucrezia's declaration will be seen for what it is—a diplomatic lie—and make her damaged goods when it comes to remarriage. Cometh the hour, cometh the man. He may not have what it takes to cut his enemies' throats, but he can stand up to this deceitful, immoral, conniving upstart family.

A flurry of correspondence moves between him and Cardinal Ascanio. But each reply is more dispiriting than the next. Eventually he packs his bags and sets out incognito for Milan. If his cardinal cousin is too compromised by his connections to the Pope, then surely the Duke Ludovico will have the guts to support him. By the time he arrives at the Sforza castle he is enjoying the sense of adventure that comes with disguise and subterfuge, and once safely inside the great modern fortress palace it is impossible not to feel braver.

———

But for all his belligerence, Ludovico Sforza has troubles of his own. Having unleashed the demon of foreign invaders into Italy, the all-powerful ruler of Milan is now living with the consequences. The French, once so keen to be his friend, have developed a taste for easy pickings and are now looking to find a claim on Milan itself. Ludovico needs to make Italian allies as fast as he once made enemies. And pleasing the Pope is high on his list.

The first thing he does is to instruct his young cousin to take off his ridiculous disguise, put on his ducal finery and come around to the main entrance as an official visitor. With spies everywhere he does not need to be found negotiating behind the Pope's back. Once the Duke of Pesaro is formally acknowledged, he throws him a small banquet, gives him a state bedroom and, before he allows him to retire to it, sits him down and tells him the facts of life.

"They will have this marriage dissolved by fair means or foul. The longer you prevaricate the harder it will be on you in the end."

"But it is not fair," Giovanni wails.

"No," the duke muses, thinking back on how often he had heard that same phrase from his brother's son, the one whose dukedom he usurped before delivering him a dose of something nasty in his bedtime drink. How these spineless young men do whine.

"What can we do?" Giovanni sighs, looking out through the windows to where a gigantic clay horse stands in the summer twilight, so fine, so lifelike, its right foreleg lifted boldly into the air, so that at any moment one might expect to see it move off into a trot. When it is finished it will surely be a wonder of the world. "The monument of the great horse is still not cast, I see?"

"Ah, he has too many ideas, that man da Vinci. His mind works faster than his hands." The duke waves an arm to the blaze of color on the half-frescoed walls around him. "If I had waited for his brush in every room, most of the palace would still be bare plaster. Your grandfather Francesco will be turning in his grave to see how long his memorial is taking. Well, he will have to wait longer now. We will need bronze for casting cannons, not horses, if the French come back."

"These are parlous times."

"Ha! What times aren't?"

"Still, I think a man should stand up for what he believes in. Which is what I intend to do. This attack on my masculinity is an outrage."

Ludovico, who with his swarthy looks and belligerent manner has never had any problem with potency, public or private, cannot help but be amused. "So you are saying that it is not true that the marriage was never consummated?"

"What? No! Of course it is not true. As God is my witness, no. I have known my wife an infinity of times."

"An infinity, eh? Lucky man. In which case it's a pity she is willing to swear the opposite."

"If she signed that declaration of her own volition then she is a liar and a whore."

"That's as may be. But they have circumstance on their side. Three years and still no issue to prove your version of the story."

"But the proof is that my first wife died in childbirth."

"In which case you should know there are rumors that someone else had a hand in that."

"What? Who? Who is spreading such filth?"

"I can't imagine."

"It is them! That family. Nothing can survive their corruption. You should see how they behave, all of them! Kissing and caressing. It is an affront to God's modesty. You cannot keep them out of one another's arms. I tell you, the Pope only wants her back for himself."

"Back for himself? My! You have reason to be angry, but you had better be careful what you say in public, Giovanni. Or get yourself some more bodyguards fast."

"I . . . I will not—not be downtrodden," he stammers. "I have four men already. Do you think that is enough?" He shakes his head. It is a trial being both scared and brave at the same time. "Anyway, what I say here is not in public," he says, wondering as he does so how many others he has told already.

"No. But we all know how news travels. The Duke of Gandia may be dead, but the real viper in the Borgia nest is still very alive." Ludovico gives a mirthless little laugh and fills both of their glasses. "Let it go, young cousin. Everyone knows it is politics and not your prick that is the problem."

"I don't understand." Look at him, Giovanni thinks. Such bulk, such bravura. No sign of constipation or twisting bowels here. Instead, with threats building all around him his manhood glows even brighter. "I have come to you for help. My name—which is our name—is being traduced."

"Very well. I do have a suggestion. Though you may not warm to it."

"Tell me."

"Ascanio will ask that Lucrezia leave the convent and be taken under his protection to his estate at Nepi, where you can join her. There, with both sides as observers, you can prove that their assertions about your manhood are wrong."

Giovanni stares at him in disbelief. Ludovico's proclivity for black humor is something that does not run in the family. "I—but that's preposterous. Anyway, they would never allow it."

"In which case we'll do it without them. I could set something up here. A few professional women . . . We could invite the cardinal legate, the Pope's cousin, to adjudicate."

"Are you trying to humiliate me?"

"I don't need to, Giovanni, you humiliate yourself. The world is full of bigger problems than your manhood. Stop being a fool and accept the inevitable."

"I . . . am not a fool."

"Alas, that's exactly what you are, cousin. Always were and always will be. The problem is that now you are a dangerous one. So let me put it plainly. You have a choice. You can lose a wife and a little public honor, but keep your state and the dowry; or you can keep your honor and lose everything else. Because be assured, when the Pope sets out to crush you, which he will, I will not lift a finger to help. Now, can I get you anything else before you retire?"

Chapter 33

Back in Rome, Alexander prays for the soul of his dead son daily and does his best to stay humble for God as the pleasures of politics whisper temptation into his ear like the snake in the Garden of Eden. Meanwhile, in the real garden of San Sisto, a similar test is taking place. Summer is turning to a golden autumn. The sun has kissed the convent fruit trees and the figs are blush ripe, so rich and lovely that the invitation to pluck and sink one's teeth into their sweetness is proving almost overwhelming.

It has been a gentle courtship, the early encounters taking place on the same stone seat under the shade of the vine, exchanging letters refreshed by a breeze that ripples the water in the pond and cools the skin, if not the hearts, of those who sit there. As the light dies away they have lingered sometimes, talking of this and that, safe in the feeling that no one is watching. If they have done anything more, a brush of hands, maybe a brush of lips, it has been fast and breathless, almost as if it has not taken place at all. Even in the world of knights and princesses there are consequences, and they both know that this shy, sly affection that is growing between them is forbidden and perilous. Which means the mingling of joint laughter or the imprint of a kiss carries an excitement equal to a much greater sin.

By mid-July, the roar of summer heat had driven them inside, to the merciful relief of thick cell walls. In itself, there was nothing amiss in this. As a noble visitor Lucrezia has a small suite of rooms to house herself and her maidservant and it is certainly not the abbess's job to supply additional chaperones. Nevertheless, the atmosphere of the convent seems to shift a little. The balance between talking to God and listening out for worldly gossip is a delicate one, and to have the fashionable young daughter of a pope licking her marital wounds at the same time as playing court to a handsome young messenger has made the younger nuns almost flighty. In response, the abbess's eye has become more eagle. So that when she comes across Pantisilea in the chapel, praying during the same work hour when her mistress is entertaining her visitor, she decides it might be prudent to visit her guest herself.

Had she come a little earlier she might have found greater evidence. That day there have been a number of more ardent kisses and the lacing on the top of her dress has become loosened so that rising full moons of creamy skin are exposed. Each has been expecting the other to pull away, yet somehow it hasn't happened. It is only as their hands take on a will of their own and she starts to utter little moans as her skirts lift that the enormity of the transgression comes home to him and, like the good knight he strives to be, he desists. Just.

By the time the abbess knocks—and then chooses not to wait until she enters—they are sitting together, a book in their hands, trying unsuccessfully to settle their hearts back into their bodies. It looks blameless enough: a young man and woman together, intent on a story. Except the second he sees her he is on his feet, knocking the book to the floor, and suddenly they are both ducking to pick it up and all is flutter and nerves. A more guilty innocence would be hard to find.

"Mother Abbess. You startled us."

"So I see. I was looking for your maidservant," she says evenly. It has always been her belief that God will forgive a white lie if it leads to the saving of souls.

"Oh, I think she went to the chapel. Pedro . . . Señor Calderón has brought me a letter from my father. All goes a little better in Rome, it seems. I am so pleased."

"And His Holiness has sent you a book too?"

"Oh, oh no; it is one I brought with me. We were speaking of history and there was a story in it which seemed apposite."

"Yes. I remember that as a boarder you had a fondness for chivalric tales."

And now both of them are blushing. The abbess moves her eye from Lucrezia to the young man. The look she gives him would freeze fruit on the vine. It is a chastisement well known among the novices and it works just as well on him now.

"My lady Duchess. Mother Abbess. I will take my leave. The letter will be in your father's hands within the hour, you may depend on that."

The same letter that presumably is already in his pouch, giving him no reason to remain.

"Thank you, Señor Calderón," Lucrezia says lightly. "Godspeed you on your way."

"Mother Abbess." He bows low.

She bows high. He cannot get out fast enough.

She waits until the door is closed behind them.

"My dear Duchess—"

"Señor Calderón, as you know, is the most trusted of my family's messengers," Lucrezia interrupts gaily. "He and I knew each other a little before I came here. He is a noble, honorable young man who lives only to serve."

"Yes, I see that very well."

As befits a woman in charge of so many young souls, she is a subtle judge of character with an excellent memory of all who pass through her hands, especially the more noble ones. Even at twelve years old Lucrezia had an infectious appetite for life, along with a desire to please God as well as her family. She was, however, never good at telling lies.

"And along with the letters he brings me other small morsels of news. Which is important for when I return. And also gives me pleasure, because—well, there is so much pain, and so much that I miss. Though of course I am quite content here . . ."

It is a satisfaction, of sorts, to find that she is still better suited to telling the truth.

"My dear Duchess . . ." she begins again, more firmly. "It is an honor to have you housed under our modest roof once again. You are delivered into our hands by no less a man than the Holy Father himself, and it is our job, and our joy, to protect and keep you safe, both in body and in soul."

She pauses to let the words rest around them. She must be careful now: this young woman is a power in the land, even if she herself does not choose to be, and it would be a disaster if, under her watch, some scandal should take place. But equally it would not do to offend her.

"This is a difficult time in your life, as we know. We pray daily that God will find a way to release you from your unfortunate marriage and establish your purity in the eyes of the entire world. In the pursuit of which, I think it advisable for Señor Calderón to spend less time on news and more on the simple business of delivery and collection of letters."

"I—I think how long he stays and what we speak of, Mother Abbess, is not your business," she says hotly.

"With deep respect, I believe it is."

"We do nothing but talk!"

The abbess watches her flushed, pretty face. A lifetime ago she herself had been in love with life and the clang of convent doors behind her had been a bitter sound. But she would not change places with her now. "It is not always what one does, my dear. But what one feels."

Lucrezia stares at her. "I . . . I pray fervently every night."

"I know that. You were always eager to be in God's company, Lucrezia. I remember it well. And He is always waiting to help you. I will have someone find your maidservant and send her to you. I trust her prayers have been granted."

"Mother Abbess?"

"Yes, my child?"

"You will . . . you will not say anything about this." It is hard to know if it is an order or a request. "I mean . . . to my family."

No, indeed, she would not change places with her now. What a burden to be so tossed by power and fortune. "I speak only to God," she says. Though as she says it she feels a slight disquiet, as if even the contents of prayer sometimes have a way of seeping out into the world at large.

Chapter 34

WHEN DOES CESARE BECOME AWARE OF IT? NOT FOR A WHILE CER-
tainly. For a while he, who loves his sister more than any other woman,
is deep in the business of men. Since his return from Naples he is filled
with a fierce energy. His skin is smooth again and when he puts on
Church robes he moves more like a hunter than a cardinal, the heavy
cloth trailing after him as if trying to catch up. As for Lucrezia—well,
she is safe, the correspondence between the Vatican and San Sisto is
regular and he is often in conference or elsewhere when the letters are
picked up and delivered. As long as what is said between them does not
find its way onto the streets, there is no reason to doubt the loyalty of
his servant.

Others are a good deal less careful with their tongues. Giovanni
Sforza's formal capitulation takes place in November, when litterloads
of doctors and theologians descend on the ducal palace of Pesaro to
stand witness as the hapless duke publicly signs away his potency. Privately, though, he has never stopped bleating about the monstrous injustice of it all, so that by now half of Italy seems to have heard the
rumor that Lucrezia is more whore than virgin and loved best of all by
her father. The Pope, who has recovered much of his bonhomie, laughs
off the outrage. They have won, and bad losers have foul tongues. Cesare's reaction is darker. No one insults his sister. More than that; within
a few weeks she herself will have to stand in front of the Church court
and proclaim her virginity to the world. It will not do for the Sforza
obscenities to penetrate the convent walls. He calls for Calderón.

"You won't get much sense from him," Michelotto says casually.

"What do you mean?"

"Apparently he's sick as a dog with love for some maid or other. Writing verses even."

"Who is she?"

"No idea. The boys can't get anything out of him. But whoever she is she obviously won't have him or he wouldn't be shitting poetry. Hey, maybe it's a nun! Some of the stories you hear about convents—"

"Why wasn't I told about this?"

"What's to tell?" Michelotto shrugs. "He still rides faster than any-one else. And his mouth is sewn tight. What else do you want from a puppy messenger?"

How long is it since he talked to him last? He thinks back but re-members only the usual mix of attention and devotion. This time he is more careful.

"So, tell me, Pedro Calderón. How do you find San Sisto?"

"The convent? It is a . . . a calm place."

"And when you are there, who takes you to the duchess?"

"I . . . er . . . there is a watch sister."

"With dispensation to greet you."

"Oh yes. Though she does not do much greeting."

Cesare laughs. Pedro grins. Men's talk. He feels a rising sweat, as if his body is detecting a fear that his mind has yet to identify.

"And the abbess? A lioness, no doubt."

"Indeed."

"Good. We are in need of a safe place for our dear sister at this time."

"Oh, there is none safer, Your Most Reverend Lord Cardinal."

"And the duchess herself. She seems well to you?"

"I . . . I think so, yes."

"She is recovering from our brother's death."

"I . . . I believe she has found some solace. She is a lady of the great-est heart and sweetest soul."

He stops, but Cesare has seen the light in his eyes. Poetry, eh?

"I had rather hoped that as our go-between she might have con-fided in you. She speaks so highly of you in her letters."

"She does?" Since the abbess's intervention his visits have been shorter and more careful, but this has done nothing to dampen his longing. If anything the marvel of the unobtainable has increased.

"I wondered if she might have opened her heart to you a little?"

"No, no, my lord." And Pedro now feels himself suspended above the ground, dangling on a hook. For a moment the shock overwhelms the pain. "I am simply a messenger."

"Still, as my messenger I would like to think you might have offered her some comfort."

"I . . . have done my best. It is my life's work to do my lord service."

"And my lady also?"

"My lady . . . you mean the duchess? Yes, of course," he murmurs, each response now digging the hook in deeper.

The door opens quietly and Michelotto slides in with a quick bow and an easy wave, as if he has always been expected. Pedro bows back and looks up into his wide smile. The sight is ghastly.

"Well, I must thank you for your loyal work over these few months. And tell you that there is good news. We will not need your services anymore. The duchess is called to give evidence before the Church court and will leave the convent soon to prepare herself."

"Oh, so the annulment will go through!" And for a moment he cannot keep the excitement out of his voice.

"Yes."

"The duchess will be . . . be most happy to hear it."

There is a pause. Which turns into a silence. It is unclear who is waiting for whom. Cesare is smiling. On the hook Pedro is now in so much pain that it seems almost a relief to move. Until he does. "I would be . . . I mean, it would be a privilege for me to take this last news to her. I know that she will be delighted to receive it."

"Yes. However, it will not be necessary. The letter gives her only a date when she is to be collected. So it has no need of a reply. Michelotto can take it and give it to the watch sister. They will probably find some solace in each other's faces."

And now there is a large laugh from both of them.

Pedro Calderón bows to take his leave. As he reaches the door, Cesare calls.

"How long is it that you have been in my service, Calderón?"

"Five years and three months now, Your Most Reverend Lord Cardinal."

"And in that time you have always served me faithfully."

"With my life."

"Then we must look for some reward for you."

After he has gone, Cesare sits with one hand on the table, the fingers playing restlessly over the surface. "I need to know what has been happening inside the convent," he says at last.

"Inside the convent? How?"

"There are ways. It is stuffed with the daughters of noble families and I daresay they all squawk like magpies at visiting hour."

"Why not ask the abbess?"

"Because, my dear Michelotto, if she is any good at her job, she will be truthful with God and double-faced with everyone else."

Michelotto stares at him. "You don't think—"

"I don't think anything yet. But I will."

It is close to Christmas when Lucrezia appears before the dignitaries of the Church court. She travels from San Sisto the week before and is housed within the Vatican, where she spends the time memorizing the composed address that she must give and deciding which outfit will offer the best message of purity. Whatever heartache she might suffer about lying in front of God's tribunal is now overcome by the fear that she might not do it well enough. Her marriage is ended and there is no going back. Alexander, who inspects her before she enters the court, sheds tears as he embraces her. "Ah, you are a sight for the sorest of eyes. Like a virgin saint standing out before torture to reach God." Since his recent brush with religiosity he has become accustomed to a certain flounce of language. But the idea appeals to the fantasies she once indulged in as a girl, and she enters the room head held high.

In front of a bank of gold-embroidered elderly clerics, her youth (she is yet to celebrate her eighteenth birthday), natural grace and word-perfect Latin work their charm. What might have been a grimy duty becomes, for many, a pleasure, and there are those in the room who feel a sense of outrage that a young woman so fresh in body and spirit should be the target of such monstrous slander, while at the same time remaining intrigued by the idea. After the interrogation comes the examination: a small chamber where two nervous midwives lift her skirts and probe gently in the direction of her most private places, though never quite stepping over the threshold.

When she returns to the court, it takes no more than a few moments for the verdict to be announced: she is *virgo intacta* and her marriage to Giovanni Sforza herewith annulled.

That night they dine in the Room of the Saints inside the Pope's private apartments: she, Cesare and Alexander. When she arrives, the table is laid and the room lit by dancing candles, illuminating the brilliance of the lunettes on the vaulted ceiling. Each saint is placed inside a different landscape, bursting with life and color. Never have the tribulations of martyrs seemed so vital, so contemporary. With Alexander still in conference, it is Cesare, still in full cardinal dress from the court proceedings, who greets her. Cesare, whom she has not seen face-to-face for seven months. And whom, of course, she cannot but love all over again.

"Ah, sweet sister, what a performance. The judges are comparing you to Cicero, with him the worse for the comparison. Convent life clearly suits you."

"I think it is divorce that suits me," she says gaily, the exhilaration still coursing through her. "I can hardly believe it is over, Cesare. And you? You have crowned a king since we were last together. Imagine that!"

He shrugs. "It was not such an imposing head."

"Not like yours, you mean." She reaches out to touch a small scar on the run of his cheekbone. "What is this? You have not been fighting?"

"It's nothing: a leftover from a fever I caught in Naples."

"Oh—how was it?"

"Hot." He laughs. "And the convent?"

"Quiet."

"And the messenger we chose for you? He was faithful to the task?"

"Oh yes. He did his job admirably," she says lightly. "How was it with Father? Please tell me. It must have been terrible. I spent so many hours in prayer over Juan."

"Just as long as you did not feel in any way neglected."

"What?"

"In the convent. I would not have wanted you to feel unloved in any way."

No one else would spot it. But then no one knows her brother as she does. "Unloved?" She repeats the word with an open smile on her face. In the lunette above him, Santa Barbara stands sweet-faced, golden hair streaming out, freed from her prison by the miracle of God's grace. As long as one's heart is pure. "On the contrary." She smiles. "I was exceedingly well cared for. The abbess is a wise woman and you remember that San Sisto was once my school."

Of course she has wondered, worried, about Pedro's unexplained absence. But with it had come the news of the court hearing and there has been no time to dwell on it. So much has taken place since brother and sister were last together. Their letters had never referred to that last meeting in her chamber, so that now it is almost as if it had never happened. She can barely remember the touch of his tongue between her lips, replaced as it has been by the feel of another. Does he somehow suspect? No, no, how could he? The abbess is an honorable woman, and anyway, what is there to be guilty about? Heaven knows there were moments in her marriage when she felt more shame than she does now. Thinking back to the stone seat in the convent garden, she can already detect sadness inside the pleasure.

"Your Excellency?" The knock on the door is followed by the sight of Burchard's granite face. "Ah, Lady Lucrezia."

Lady Lucrezia. No longer the Duchess of Pesaro. His is the first public tongue to confirm the change. She feels a small thrill pass through her. "Signor Burchard. It is good to see you again. I hope you have been well."

"Yes, my lady, quite well. I . . . the Holy Father says I am to tell you that he will be with you soon, but that should you be hungry, dinner can be served without him."

"Is he with Naples or Spain?" Cesare asks.

"Naples, I believe." He turns to go, then stops. "It is a pleasure to have you safely returned."

"My, you have stolen even the lizard's heart," Cesare says drily. "Perhaps I should go to a monastery for a while."

"Ha! Heaven help all women when you come out."

They make small talk while the manservants bring the dishes: winter-bean soup, cut meats, stuffed pasta, the Pope's favorite simple fare. After they have said grace, she pulls the conversation toward Juan and the days that followed his death. "Tell me everything. The convent was full of stories about Father's grief and his renewed faith. How was he? Is the Church much reformed under his zeal?"

"Ah, a few corrupt officials imprisoned. A council to discuss reform. Everyone agrees until it's their own job under scrutiny and then suddenly they lose interest." He shrugs. Above the door of the room, a naked Saint Sebastian writhes under a hail of arrows, his sacrifice almost dull compared to the athletic youths in fashionable dress who load and dispatch their crossbows. "It will take more than zeal to clean these Augean stables."

"And Father?"

"He is . . . he is more himself now. And you, beloved sister, how has it been for you?"

"You know it from my letters, I think," she says, picking her words more carefully now. "They were dark days at first, but with God's grace I found peace."

"And did God also make you laugh?"

"What?" She frowns, deliberately not understanding.

"I have heard there was laughter."

"Ah, men have strange thoughts about convents, Cesare. They can be quite happy places, you know. I may well have laughed. There were tears enough for laughter to be its own relief."

"And poetry. Was there poetry?"

"Poetry?" Not the abbess. She would never have betrayed them, surely? So who? "Why do you ask about poetry?"

"Just a brother caring for his sister's well-being. Did you entertain in your cell?"

"Entertain? How could I? My only visitors were the abbess and your messenger," she says hotly, though inside she is cold. "How did you hear such strange things?"

"Oh . . . a few birds flying overhead."

"Then I must tell you that their eyesight was malicious." Even as she says it she amazes herself with her confidence. "I am your dear and loving sister as I have always been. I have wept and prayed for my brother and in the end, through God's help I have found a way to smile again. I have given my evidence in court and thrown off my husband and been declared pure by the Mother Church. What more would you ask of me, brother?"

"Brava," he says as behind them the door is flung open and Alexander, all puff and bulk, flings himself into the room with arms outstretched. "Let's hope your eloquence is enough to stop the gossip."

"What—not more gossip, Cesare!" Alexander's booming voice is filled with love as Lucrezia rises from the table and throws herself into his arms. "Your brother spends his life measuring the levels of slime that surround us. But you, my shining daughter, have emerged as white as purity itself today, despite all the grimy slanders of your poxy ex-husband."

"Slanders? What slanders?"

"Oh, we will not speak of them. You are a virgin from a convent and it would make you blush to hear even the words. No, there will be no talk of the past. Come, come, eat, eat. I am starving. You have said grace already, yes? Then I must add a few more words. For we must raise our eyes to heaven to thank God for His care of our good fortune."

He sits and slaps his big hands together, his elegant ringed fingers entwined as his head bends and the words flow out. When he looks up there is a huge smile on his face.

"So. You have not breathed a word to her?" he says to Cesare.

"No, no. We have spoken of other things."

"Excellent. Then it can be spoken of now. Though only between ourselves, in a room full of saints as our witnesses." And he waves his hand generously to the ceiling as if to include them all. "We have much to celebrate, Lucrezia. Your homecoming—oh how we are happy to see you. The end of your marriage. And a reward for all your patience and suffering."

He leaves a pause, so they can all appreciate the suspense.

"I am to have a new husband," she says.

"Ah no, but someone has told you already! Who? Who? It wasn't that young messenger of ours? No—how could he know?"

"Your messenger was beyond reproach," she says firmly. "No one needed to tell me, Father. After night comes day. As it must. May I know the name of the man?"

"Oh, he is less a man than a young god. Handsome, courteous, educated, gentle, brave, with the finest leg and a reputation as the best dancer."

She finds herself thinking of Pedro and feels a short sharp pain in her chest. "But, Father, I cannot marry my own brother," she says instead, and is taken aback by her own coquettishness.

"Alas, no." Alexander laughs. What an exquisite pleasure it is to have his daughter home. "But you can marry your brother-in-law."

"My brother-in-law? You mean Sancia's brother? Alfonso?"

"Yes. Yes, the very same. Are you pleased?"

"I—" She hesitates. She has a vivid memory of the way Sancia's face lights up every time she talks of him. "Is it arranged then?"

"It is decided, certainly. Cesare did much of the work in Naples and I have come this minute from a meeting with the ambassador. Now you are free the offer is firm, though we will pretend it is not for a while. There will be others making their bids and it is as well to let them think they have a chance. What do you think?"

"I think that if Spain is lost to us, we must have our heart set on Naples."

"Ha. Listen to her, Cesare. Such cleverness in a beautiful woman is hard to find. She is a Borgia to the last drop of her blood."

"But . . . but I don't see how. I mean, Jofré is married to Sancia, but that gives him no claim, and neither will my marriage to her brother, since both of them are illegitimate."

"Ho. You have been practicing politics in that convent. Everyone says the best abbesses are as canny as foxes. The fact is that there will be other opportunities for marriage in this new royal family. But all that is in the future." And he glances conspiratorially at Cesare. "For now you have yet to say if you are pleased. You will most certainly like him, wouldn't you agree, Cesare? You have better knowledge of him than me."

"One would hope so," he says quietly. "He is a most pretty man."

"Then I shall look forward to meeting him. Sancia I know will be pleased. She loves him dearly."

"As a good sister should. And so will we all," says the Pope, reaching over for another helping of stuffed pasta.

Chapter 35

SEVEN MONTHS IN A CONVENT AND THE WORLD HAS CHANGED IN all manner of ways. Returning home to the palace of Santa Maria in Portico, she finds its wealth disconcerting after the simplicity of an enclosed life. The parrots that decorate the frescoed walls of the receiving room, their bright green plumage growing out of the pink and ochre patterns of branches, are too noisy now. Would she really prefer the silence of bare walls? Adriana is noisy too, but then she goes everywhere accompanied by the tap-tap-tap of a stick. "Inside my knee little bits of bone have come away. Ah—how they grind and throb. I should rest, but how is one to live sitting down with so much to do?" Though, as always, she enjoys the complaining.

And Giulia? Well, Giulia, it seems, is too ill to take visitors at all.

"What? Does she have the contagion? You said nothing in your letters?"

"No. More a problem of digestion. We would have told you, but we did not expect you home so soon."

"Well, I am back now, Aunt, and of course I will see her."

"Haaah . . ." Adriana's protest dissolves into a great sigh. "Very well then—we are family after all."

Giulia, curled lazily on a daybed under a mound of velvet with a fire spitting sparks into the freezing air, looks rosy, one might almost say plump, with health.

"Alas, I cannot embrace you, dear Lucrezia. As you see, I am confined to bed."

"What is it? What do the doctors say?"

Giulia shrugs, registering Adriana's sharp warning glance. "Oh, let it be, Mother. Whom will she tell?" She sighs, leaning back against her cushions. "There is no need of doctors for what ails me, Lucrezia."

"Oh!" She stares at her, her face still serious. My, how life does go on. "So on what date do you think you will be well, my dear cousin?"

"God willing, toward the end of March."

And now their laughter rings around the room. Adriana starts to shush and hush, but Giulia waves her away. "How much more secret can we be? Counting my maidservant, there are five people in the world who know, and three of them are in this room now. I have been lying on this bed for what feels like half of eternity. I think I deserve to laugh sometimes."

"And the fifth person?" Lucrezia says slyly.

"Ah, well, let us say it is not my husband."

"But . . ." Lucrezia shakes her head. "March?" The mathematics is not hard. "I mean . . . everyone said that . . ."

"That the Pope was in despair and dedicated to reform. You are right. And he was. In *such* despair. And his penance was real. No, I am afraid in this business I must bear the blame. I was the temptress." She sighs. "I think it must sound strange to hear it, yes? But you were not here, Lucrezia. His grief was terrible. It would have broken your heart to witness it."

"Yes indeed, terrible." Adriana supplies the chorus. "Terrible. There was nothing anyone could do. We feared for his sanity."

"Some did, yes. But I knew it was his heart and not his mind," Giulia says quietly. "At first he would not see me. Imagine that. I sent messengers every day: a token, a few words, my prayers. And then, finally, one afternoon, he came. And though he cried I also made him smile. I don't think—ah . . . Ah, oh, feel!" She grabs Lucrezia's hand and pulls it under the cover, placing it over the well-concealed rise of her belly. "There, there! Do you feel him?"

And she does, the thrust of something hard, like an unripe peach or an apple, sliding up and under her fingers.

"Oh, he is always so busy! He moves quite differently to Laura. So restless and forceful. Ha!"

"What? You know it is a boy?"

"Yes, I do. I can feel it about him. And it would be a fine thing, don't you think? A boy to help relieve the loss of his beloved Juan. That would be a gift such that God might forgive me a little for the act itself."

"Oh, I don't think God would damn you, Giulia. You are a good woman."

"That's not what the scandalmongers would say if they got hold of it. You have not been here, Lucrezia. Since Juan's murder the city is all Borgia tittle-tattle. You of all people are most lucky to have been in the silence of the convent."

"What do you mean? Has something been said about me? What is it?"

"I wouldn't bother with it. Gossip is a pauper's entertainment: the people who pay are those who are slandered."

"Not in God's eyes," Adriana jumps in, busying herself with the covers and calling for the servant to add more wood, as the winter wind whistles in around the fabric of the windows. "In God's eyes slander slanders those who produce it. And we will have none of it here."

If no one will tell her, then she must find out herself. Her fear, of course, is that it is to do with Pedro. If Cesare suspects something (but what? and how?), then might others? She has risked her soul declaring a virginity she no longer possesses. How would it be then if she were damned as a whore for something she has not actually done? It is not long before the news finds her.

"No! But why? Why would Giovanni say such a thing?"

"I cannot tell you why, mistress." Pantisilea has barely had to walk the streets to hear it. "Only that he said it more than once, so now everyone is saying it."

"I have known her an infinity of times and the Pope has only taken her back for himself." How could he be so cruel? She thinks back to the last time she saw him, trembling in front of her, fearful of his own shadow. "You must go now, Giovanni." Who knows what might have happened if he had stayed? They had not been happy together, certainly, but she had cared for him as best she could. God knows, without her intercession he might well have found himself dead in a ditch some-where with the imprint of Michelotto's hands around his neck.

Her father wants her for himself. Is that what people believe of her now? When she welcomes ambassadors—as she will again—will it be in their minds when they kiss her hand or make small talk about the world? That same afternoon when she sees the agent of the Duke of Gravina, who is sniffing around for her hand in marriage, there are mo-ments when she cannot help but blush at what he may be thinking. Yet there is nothing in his face but kindness, and what feels like a genuine appreciation of her courtesy and good humor. That night she spends longer at her mirror: if it was true, then surely it would show on a wom-an's face. Of course such things happen. The world is full of stories. Everyone knows that in Rimini old Sigismundo Malatesta, whose name is still a byword for evil, kept both his daughter and his son for his own enjoyment. She thinks of her father's bearlike embrace, the pungent smell of his body inside his clothes, the slap of his fond kisses. But that is all they are—fond kisses from a fond father. How dare anyone think otherwise? Then she thinks of Cesare's fierce love and the probe of his tongue. What? Is there perhaps something in her family that loves dif-ferently from others? Is it a Spanish way?

"Slander slanders those who produce it." She hears Adriana's voice in her ear. Fine words. But she and Giulia are still concerned enough to be concealing a belly full of secrets. The fact is, it is not what you do or don't do, but how convincingly you can be accused of it.

Over the next few weeks she keeps to the house. There is little op-portunity for diversions anyway as the winter is abnormally foul. After days of torrential rain the banks of the Tiber break just before dawn, sending a giant wave of water through the town, taking the contents of cellars and stables with it, so that days later horses are found wandering miles from home and farmers wake up to full barrels of wine washed up on to their farmland. And downriver near the city gates a body is found with two heads and five legs. Or that is what they say around town, for no one who repeats the story has actually seen it, though ev-eryone knows someone who knows someone who has. The wonder and horror of nature. She and Pedro had talked about such things in their stories. Pedro. It has been almost two months and still she has heard nothing. But when she sends for Pantisilea to find some news of his whereabouts, the young woman shakes her head.

"I don't think that is a wise thing to do, madam."

"What do you mean?"

She shrugs. "Just that—well . . ."

"Well what? Is there something you haven't told me? Because—"

"It is not my fault, madam. I never said a word to anyone, I swear it on my mother's grave."

"You may say that, but how can I know if I believe you unless you tell me?" she says fiercely. "What have you heard?"

"That he has been put in prison because of things they say he did with you."

"Things? What things?"

"I don't know." The girl gives a hopeless shrug. "People say that Lady Adriana has started looking for midwives. However hard you try, you can't keep that kind of thing secret for long."

Cesare and her father are in conference together in the papal throne room when she demands that Burchard announce her. The door is barely closed behind him before she speaks.

"Whatever you have heard about Pedro Calderón and myself is slander and calumny. He was a good friend to me when I was in need and has done nothing that deserves prison. I want you to release him." She realizes she is trembling and tries to still herself.

"I told you she would be upset," the Pope says mildly.

Cesare, lounging close to his father in the leather-backed chair that he has made his own, says nothing at all.

"Come, come, my dear. These are not things that should concern you."

"Not concern me? A man is in prison because of me, Father."

"My child, it is more complex than you know. This is a most delicate time for the family. With God and fortune on our side, this marriage of yours to Naples will be the stepping-stone to much greater things for your brother. However, King Federico is a man of strict beliefs and the character of his new daughter-in-law is important. I am sure your dealings with Pedro Calderón were innocent enough—but somehow or other petty gossip has trickled out and to prevent it going further your brother thought it would be circumspect to remove him from the scene."

"Really! If we're talking gossip, I'm surprised anyone thought it was worth noting, given that most of Rome seems to think I am a young woman who is best loved by her father."

Alexander scowls and swats the words away like a fat fly. "Oh, no one believes that. It is simply the poisonous dribblings of an idiot."

"And the rumor of a pregnancy in our palace?" she says, quietly.

"Ah, yes; it seems we are hostage to timing there. It had been our hope to keep the secret at least until sometime after the birth. It is unfortunate that such gossip has leaked out so soon after your return to Rome."

"In which case by arresting Pedro Calderón, you will make it seem that the slander against me is true."

"If we don't take him off the streets, someone else will," Cesare says quietly, watching her all the time. "And then who knows what stories he might tell about what the two of you have been doing together?"

She turns, staring directly at him. Out of Church robes he is the consummate man about town: his velvet doublet sculpted to show off his chest, the purple hose over his legs as fine as another layer of skin. All he needs are more jewels sewn into the cloth and he will be flaunting it as richly as Juan. She thinks back to the abbess with her shift and sandals. "I have told you already, brother," she says. "I have done nothing wrong."

"You also told the judges that your husband had never touched you."

"No! No." And suddenly the injustice of it all is too great. "Don't listen to him, Father. I was unhappy and alone and in distress. Pedro Calderón was a courtier toward me. Kinder and gentler and more honorable than any that I have come across in a court yet. Yes, I enjoyed his company. What is wrong with that?"

"Everything." Cesare will not let it lie. "You were in a convent to keep you pure while your asshole husband went around slandering you to anyone who would listen. Your defense was to be seen to be without stain."

Without stain! How many women have you bedded in the last six months? she thinks. She almost wants to say the words out loud, but there is no point. Every woman who walks through the world knows there are two roads: a wide, triumphal route for the men, and a second mean little alley for women. Freedom is so much men's due that even to draw attention to it is to make them angry.

"Cesare, Cesare . . ." Her father's voice is gentle. "I know how much you care for your sister. But she has been through a great deal and I—"

"I love her more than anything in the world, Father," he says brusquely. "As she well knows." It seems he is enough the adviser now that he can interrupt both his father and the Pope. "But that is not an excuse for her offering herself up to some Spanish stable boy."

And now it is there in his voice for all to hear. Oh sweet Mother of God, he is jealous, Lucrezia thinks. My brother is jealous. This is what this is about. Oh, but I should have realized! She glances toward her father. But he seems oblivious of the confession that his eldest son has just let slip.

"Ah, Cesare, listen to you," she says lightly over the pounding pulse in her ears. "You sound almost as rabid as the gossipmongers you condemn! Better you should believe your own sister than the rabble, for why would she, who loves you above all things, lie? That 'stable boy' is a man that you yourself picked as a safe courier and I tell you, he respects and admires you more than life itself. Whatever you seem to think he has done."

Now she turns away from him to Alexander himself. "To defeat this scandalous suggestion, surely it would be helpful for me to be seen by the world more. Perhaps a dinner with the Neapolitan ambassadors? So they can be reassured I am without child. Otherwise when the baby is born and Calderón is still in prison, everyone will be encouraged to think it is mine."

"Yes, yes, indeed, it is already in our minds. Don't worry. As for the baby, there may be a flurry of gossip, but it will die down as soon as there is nothing to stoke the flames. I will own paternity when the moment is right. Let us only get through this marriage and the business with your brother."

"What business is that?"

There is a small silence. The two men look almost shifty.

"I think if I am family enough to risk blame for a child that is not mine, I might have the right to ask about my brother's future."

The Pope laughs out loud. Given that women's path is narrow and mean, she knows it is a risk being so forward, but Alexander has always liked his women to speak their mind. As long as they love him.

"When the time is right, Cesare will give up the purple. He will leave the Church to free him for marriage."

"Ah!" She stares at her brother. And now he smiles. It has something close to coyness in it. It does not suit him.

"Can it be done?"

"With God's will and a little politics, yes," Alexander says. "Though once again you are joined in family confidence here. It would not do for it to get out."

"And this is the union that will take Naples?"

"The hopes are high, yes."

"Well, then we shall be related in yet another way. How close can we be, brother?" And she comes up to him and kisses him on both cheeks. It is hard even for her to know how much she is pleased and how much playacting, such is the nervous exhilaration in her. "I must say you have always looked more the bridegroom than the cardinal."

He rises and pulls her to him. She feels the hardness of the body underneath the velvet. The Pope beams. It is so painful for there to be discord when there can be happiness! The embrace continues, then, gently, she releases herself.

"I shall look forward to my new sister-in-law," she says gaily, as if they are already reconciled, with or without his agreement. "And, since the matter is now resolved," she adds lightly, "when it has all taken place, perhaps you will let Pedro Calderón go free?"

The Pope glances at Cesare.

"I am your loving and loyal daughter, Father," she says, standing her ground. "I ask humbly that you do this for me."

Cesare keeps his eyes on a spot on the floor near his father's throne.

Alexander's voice is soothing, always wanting to please: "I promise you that if it can be done, it will be," he says. And though she is pleased to hear it, when she recalls the moment later she finds herself chilled by the precision of the words.

The baby comes in the middle of March, a bonny boy, arms and legs waving like mad little windmills until they are strapped fast into swaddling clothes, at which point he yells his dissatisfaction to all around. Adriana bustles around giving orders while Giulia lies as still as she can to heal the tears he inflicted as he fought his ebullient way out. Within a few days he has developed an appetite to challenge even the wettest of wet-nurses, and with so much to-ing and fro-ing, it is not long before a few nosy ambassadors are confident enough to send birth notices out to their gossip-hungry employers. A new Borgia baby. A boy, no less.

Just as the Pope predicted, the infant Romanus, as he is instantly referred to, starts a frenzied guessing game. A healthy baby means one brought close to term. Conception mid-June then. Or, at the latest, July. The smartest money is on the Pope and Giulia, though there is the issue of when he might have found the time to stop crying. Cesare, meanwhile, must have sired a dozen up until now, though if that is the case, why bother to give a good home to this one? Which leaves Lucrezia again. Lucrezia, the virgin whore whose husband had known her an infinity of times, but certainly not on this occasion. Lucrezia, who has been wearing her dresses high, as is the fashion, so that the cloth flows generously as she walks. June/July. Before or after the convent? When the abbess hears, she delivers a richer sermon than any priest on the power of silence and the devil's work through gossip, but it comes a little late. The name of Pedro Calderón, faithful retainer to the Pope and his son, is already known. But, whatever he did or didn't do, no one will be able to ask him about it.

It is not in the Pope's nature to refuse his daughter anything. Nor to be vindictive for its own sake. But her passionate plea had come too late for further discussion. What some might call fate, others would call timing. The day after her frantic visit to her father, Johannes Burchard, neat and tidy in all things relating to papal matters, sits down at his diary and composes his entry for February 14, 1498.

The servant Pedro Calderón, who last Thursday fell—not of his own will—into the Tiber, was fished up today. Concerning which affair there are rumors running through Rome.

When Lucrezia finally hears the news, she rolls her sorrow up into a small tight ball and swallows it down deep inside her. She is eighteen years old and the future will roll out whether she wants it or not.

PART VII

Throwing Off the Purple

Iacta est Alea
THE DIE IS CAST

Inscription on a sword made for Cesare
Borgia, summer 1498

Chapter 36

APRIL 1498: A GENTLE SPRING DAY IN THE ROYAL HAMLET OF
Amboise in France and runty King Charles VIII with his good Queen
Anne of Brittany set out to visit an extension to his chateau built by a
Neapolitan architect whose work had so impressed him that he had
brought him back as war booty. The design is an ambitious one and
everyone is excited to see the king's reaction.

Perhaps it is the excess of anticipation—for the king is very eager.
Perhaps it is carelessness, or perhaps (God forbid) the man is not up to
the job and has got the dimensions wrong. Whatever the fault, His Majesty rushes in through a new door, stumbles on a loose floorboard and
cracks his head on the wooden lintel. The thwack is heard by all around
him and though he laughs after he groans, he is taken to bed seeing
stars. One can only hope it is a good augury and when he wakes up he
is indeed in heaven.

It is upsetting that such a silly death should befall the conqueror of
half of Italy. Upsetting particularly for the house of Valois, since this
sickly man has already presided over the deaths of his only four children in infancy. The crown of France now moves toward the closest
living relative, Louis, Duke of Orléans. But those who stand to gain
most from this cruel trick of fate do not have a French bone in their
bodies. When the news reaches Alexander in Rome, his smile is as wide
as the mouth of the Tiber. At some point all good Christian monarchs
need something from their Pope, and though Louis may now have a
crown, to keep his country intact he also needs help with a marital
problem. The timing could not be better.

"Where is the Cardinal of Valencia? Bring him to me. I need to see him immediately."

The Pope's son, however, is not in his rooms, nor anywhere else in the main palace. Neither is he to be found at early mass, though this is a surprise to no one; in recent months the cardinal is so seldom in church that Burchard has taken to recording his appearances in his diary.

"I believe, Your Holiness, that he may be in the courtyard of the Belvedere. He . . . exercises there some mornings with men from the Papal Guard."

It is a routine that Cesare has been following slavishly, some might say religiously, for a while now. If he is indeed going to renounce his cardinalship (and the only question is how will he finance his lifestyle without the generous thirty thousand ducats a year that his revenues and benefices bring him), then he must be ready for his new profession: war. When he is not in the saddle he is practicing swordsmanship: both the rapier and the two-handed battle sword, a steel monster that needs as much stamina to wield as it does skill to land the right blow. This hard-chested, hard-hearted young man who can be so unforgiving with his servants is, in other ways, unforgiving with himself and there are times after particularly strenuous workouts when he can barely move for the groaning in his legs and arms.

With the rapier it is a more precise dance. The morning they come looking for him he is testing chain mail. Rome is full of master crafts-men vying for the privilege of protecting his precious body and as he moves around the courtyard the snake-ripple shine from a vest made of a thousand tiny woven steel loops is so mesmerizing that a couple of his opponents miss their steps. Or maybe they are feigning inadequacy, for it is a risky business fighting the Pope's favorite son.

"I thought you said they were soldiers!" he shouts to Michelotto, who is standing in the shade making notes as the last one leaves. "No one is even trying."

"What do you expect? They are being paid to fight, not to win."

"So pay them more and have them try harder."

"And what happens when you take a wound? Do we give them a bonus or string them up for skewering the Pope's son?"

"Then you fight with me."

"With pleasure."

"Double-handed swords."

"Ah, it's too hot for more armor."

"Is that an excuse for you to lose?"

They put on breastplates and helmets and prowl around each other, feigning and parrying until one makes a lunge and the swords slam together, holding like fat magnets as they shove and stagger trying to get the better of each other, finally flinging themselves apart in order to start the whole ungainly dance again. The voices of clashing steel along with accompanying grunts reverberate around the gardens and it isn't long before they grow weary from the mad effort of it all. But Cesare will not be the one to stop.

"Enough!" Michelotto yells at last, stepping back and dropping his sword on to the ground. He takes off his helmet and shakes the sweat from his hair, his latticework face grinning. "God knows, you had better throw off the purple soon. I don't think I can take much more of this 'pretend' warfare," he says as the Pope's messenger puffs his way into the courtyard.

"You have worked up a hard sweat." Alexander sits admiring the gleam on his forearms and half-bare chest. "I will call for a robe. You should not risk a chill, even in clement weather."

Cesare waves his hand. "It can wait. So . . . you are sure that Louis will give us what we want?"

"Why would he not?"

"They say there is a cunning streak in him."

"Cunning or not, even a king cannot dissolve his own marriage. I tell you, Cesare, we will have an offer of a dukedom for you or Louis will find he has only half a kingdom to rule."

It is partly the symmetry that so delights Alexander: the way a problem can be so elegantly solved to the satisfaction of all parties. King

Charles, for all his faults, had been smart enough to cement the union of French lands with those of Brittany by marrying its queen. Now Anne is a widow it is possible she might be tempted to assert the territory's independence again. Obviously for the sake of France the new king must marry her himself.

A man could wish for nothing better, for she is lovely and still has juice enough in her loins to start a new dynasty. It is the perfect answer. Except for the fact that Louis of Orléans already has a wife.

The Pope wrinkles his nose. "Of course, there will have to be a church commission to look into the matter. He is adamant that he was forced into the union against his will. Apparently his wife is 'deformed'—certainly everyone says she is exceedingly plain—but who knows what goes on under her skirts. Haaaa. The wonders of women."

"He wants an annulment on the grounds of non-consummation?"

"Hmm. Yes. Most likely that is what it will be."

They sit for a moment in silence. The Pope's mind flicks to Lucrezia. How she has turned somewhat inward herself these last few months, since the death of Pedro Calderón. She goes out of her way to avoid gatherings where she and her brother will be in the same room. It pains him to see his children estranged.

"Tell me, how are things with Lucrezia?"

"She is struggling to hate me as much as she loves me," he says quietly. "Don't worry. It will pass."

"The sooner young Alfonso arrives the better. Women should not be left too long alone."

It takes eight weeks for their plans to unfold. While everyone knows that the annulment will not come cheap, the details of the negotiations remain secret until the end. That the Cardinal of Valencia intends to leave the Church is common gossip now in Rome, but when it reaches Spain, Their Spanish Most Holy Catholics Majesties are choleric with rage. Such a course of action would be an offense against God as much as the Church and their ambassador takes pains to relay their voluble horror. Alexander, who has never taken to being lectured by men less powerful than himself, snarls quietly under his breath. Let them stew in it.

When the deal is finally hammered out, it is so perfect that Alexander might have dictated the details himself. This time the conversation between father and son takes place in the open air, strolling amid the orange trees of the papal garden, with no chance of the walls listening in.

"Louis will give you the Duchies of Valentinois and Diois."

"Is that enough?"

"In land and prestige, certainly. In revenue, possibly not, though he will make up any difference himself. It is done, Cesare. You will have your titles and your income."

"What about military support?"

"We shall mention it when the time is right."

"And my suit to Princess Carlotta? That is as vital as the money."

"The king knows that well enough. He will bring pressure on both her and her father. Don't worry. She will come around. It is only a matter of time."

During these months of waiting, Cesare's proposed marriage into Naples has hit problems: Carlotta herself, who is under Louis's care at the French court, is proving unexpectedly recalcitrant. By rights her father should bring her into line, but though he was all smiles and acquiescence when he bent his head for Cesare to put the crown on it, King Federico seems less enamored of the idea now. To supply a bastard nephew to Lucrezia is one thing, but delivering his legitimate daughter into Cesare's hands would be opening the royal nest to allow a scorpion to crawl in. As long as the Pope's son still has a cardinal's hat on his head he can put off the confrontation.

"Louis should threaten Federico with invasion." The warrior in Cesare is growing restless with nothing to test his skills on. "That would concentrate his mind on the offer."

"Don't even say it out loud, my son. When the French come this time we need them to stay north of the Apennines."

"When the French come . . ." Alexander picks his words carefully.

The wonders of inheritance. At Louis's coronation the list of titles that had followed his name included not only Naples—a surprise to no one—but also Milan, over which his Orléans lineage has a particular claim. (Go back far enough in the tangled webs of marriage and everywhere is half owned by someone else.)

Milan. Not only richer than Naples, but so much closer: a quick sprint up and over the Alps and the momentum of the slide down the other side takes you almost there.

"Who would have thought it, eh?" Alexander chuckles to himself. "That a small dent in a king's skull could cause such a mighty headache for Ludovico Sforza. One moment he is offering the French Naples on a plate, the next they are taking Milan. There isn't a man in Italy who will shed a tear on his behalf. You should learn from this, Cesare. Make enemies if you have to—and you will—but always make sure the most powerful stay your friends."

"I know these things already, Father," he mutters, slightly impatiently.

"Then it will not hurt you to hear them again," Alexander says good-naturedly. "Come, give me an embrace. We have great things ahead of us now, and it will do me good to feel the sweat of exercise on the body of a soldier."

Cesare comes as he is bidden and opens his arms to his father. The distance he must stretch his hands is larger now. Since Juan's death, Alexander has both grown and diminished. At sixty-eight he carries the weight of two men and is developing a stoop to compensate for it. As he moves from room to room, sometimes you can hear him huffing and puffing. When the business of his own future was still much in the balance, Cesare would watch him and wonder how much time they had to remake the world around them, and feel a chill that it might not be long enough. But Alexander has never wavered. It is as if, once the mourning was over, Juan's death had spurred him on. His avowed religiosity, as sincerely felt as his grief, had faded naturally as the scale of the task became apparent. A penitent pope was novel for a while, but whoever heard of humble cardinals? For many, reform was more shocking than corruption, and while they stalled, Alexander returned to family business.

Cesare is his Juan now, and this news from France lights an extra fire in his belly. As for his age—well, he doesn't celebrate birthdays anymore. Sixty-eight is only old if you intend to die soon. And death is not on Alexander's agenda. His continued survival is the greatest revenge he can take on those who sought to destroy him.

He marks the anniversary of the murder with special masses for the dead, and visits his son's tomb in the Borgia chapel of Santa Maria del Popolo, weeping unashamedly. But there is too much to be done for him to cry for long. With his ambassadors en route to France and the Duke and Duchess of Squillace back in Rome, the Vatican is already plunged into preparations for Lucrezia's second marriage.

Sancia is all of a tremor at the prospect of her brother's arrival. She spends hours with Lucrezia, painting pictures of Alfonso's perfection and imagining their lives together at court, and their renewed friendship is a balm to both of them.

She has returned sunnier than she left, her exile having gone some way to heal her wounded pride in the affair with Cesare. During their first public encounters she goes out of her way to show that she cares not a fig for him, and is a little disconcerted when he is attentive all over again. But the feral cat in her smells deceit and she remains brittle in his presence. She is right, of course. Cesare has no feelings for her (which is not the same as disliking her, though she will read it as such), but as long as he has his sights set on Naples, he must show affection for the whole family.

He has already done his best to charm Alfonso in the weeks they spent together after Federico's coronation, and he is now determined to make his welcome to Rome a rich one. It is not just strategy: Cesare is in high spirits. As soon as the details are hammered out between the diplomats, the date will be set for the secret Consistory of Cardinals where he will make his move to leave the Church. Finally he is a man in control of his own destiny.

Wooing back Lucrezia has proved a trickier process. When she continues to avoid him, he makes the first moves. Their initial encounters are painful. He comes with gifts: rich fabrics, books of prayer and poetry beautifully illustrated (he can be an attentive suitor when he chooses), but their conversation is marked by guarded politeness and raw silences. It is not that she sets out to resist him; rather that she cannot help herself. Seeing him makes her think of Pedro, so that she wants to rage and cry at the same time. But then, once he leaves, neither can she stand the feeling that she no longer loves her own brother. Because, of course, she does.

"Lucrezia, we must make our peace over this." On the fourth meeting he confronts it directly. "You will know by now that when you asked for Calderón's life that day, the matter was already out of my hands. You may think my behavior was unjust, but in everything I did, your honor was uppermost in my mind."

She sits upright in her chair, looking at him intently as the tears drop onto the bolt of new scarlet velvet in her lap. Later, when the fabric becomes a cloak, she will remember this moment each time she puts it on. She squeezes her eyes tight shut. This crying is futile, she says to herself sharply. It can change nothing.

"I know that. It just seemed so . . . so cruel. Pedro Calderón committed no crime."

"That is not true. His crime was his betrayal of me. And equally cruel is the damage that scandal inflicts on a woman's reputation. Not only for herself but for her whole family."

"In which case, the fault was mine as much as his."

"No. Calderón was in my service. He knew the rules of loyalty well enough, and what to expect if he disobeyed them. But it is over, Lucrezia. We survived the storm. Your new husband is more a man than Sforza ever was and his coming, along with my marriage when it happens, will make the family secure. If there is a wound between us let it be healed now. You are my beloved sister. There is no woman I love more than you."

She smooths the nap of the tearstained velvet with her fingers. There are many things she could say. But none of them will bring back the dead. When she looks up at him she sees echoes of Juan in his face. To resist him will be to have lost two brothers. What does that leave her with?

His eyes are clear and steady. If they lie about the past, they do not lie about the present. He is right: no one loves her as he does.

"Oh, Cesare," she says.

To resist him is to resist herself. It cannot be done. The struggle is over.

Chapter 37

Alfonso of Aragon, newly created Duke of Bisceglie for the purpose of his marriage, arrives in Rome in the middle of July 1498. He comes incognito to spend private time getting to know his wife-to-be: which means that everyone knows he is there, but they must pretend that he is not. The first day he spends at the Vatican. The next he visits his bride.

Sancia is beside herself with anticipation. The two women, along with Jofré and Cesare, gather together in the upper loggia as his entourage rides into the courtyard below. He barely has time to dismount before Sancia has broken ranks and is down the steps and flinging herself into his arms. He picks her up and whirls her around, so that Lucrezia, watching from above, can make out only flying silk and infectious laughter. She remembers the pomp and ceremony of her first husband's arrival and the informality delights her. He deposits Sancia on the ground and puts an arm up in greeting, bowing low to the delegation above, before taking the stairs two at a time.

"Lady Lucrezia." He drops to his knee and his head comes up with a smile so full of play that she cannot help but respond to it. His resemblance to his sister is remarkable: the same mane of black hair, the same intense blue eyes, bright as the Madonna's dress, so piercing that it seems as if he is looking straight into you.

Oh, thank the heavens, he is as pretty as everyone says, she thinks, at the same time remonstrating with herself for such shallowness.

He puts his hand behind him to welcome Sancia, who has followed him up the stairs, before moving on to embrace his old, young play-mate Jofré, who squeals his delight. And then at last there is Cesare.

"Brother!" They embrace warmly, shoulder to shoulder, chest to chest, so filled with energy that they seem as capable of play-fighting as greeting. Two more handsome young men it would be impossible to imagine. The last time Lucrezia watched Cesare grasp a man like this it was their own brother and the sight of it makes her heart leap. What a wonder it would be if he could indeed make the family complete again.

Unlike her gaudy first wedding, the ceremony is a quiet affair, with not an ambassador or diplomat in sight. Outside the Vatican, they grind their teeth and open their purses to anyone who can bring them the stories needed to keep their rulers happy. Never let it be said that the Borgias disappoint. The ceremony takes place in the private apartments, and as the guests process into the Room of Mysteries, a row breaks out between Sancia's and Cesare's entourage as to who holds precedence of entrance. It is the bad blood that has been waiting to flow for a long time. Moving swiftly from insult into blows, there is suddenly a free-for-all in the antechamber, with two bishops punched to the ground and the Pope himself trying to hold men apart, until they have to bring in guards to separate the fray. Like so many things in this papacy, the like of it has never been seen before and it makes for a glorious story.

There is more to come.

In August, five years after Alexander shamelessly bullied the College of Cardinals into accepting his son, he now bullies them again into letting him go.

The first task is to get enough of them in the room to make the vote worthwhile. In the fever cauldron of a Roman summer they have the perfect excuse to be absent, but Alexander has always shaken his fist at such weakness and he will not accept it now. "A matter touching the good of the Church and Christianity" is how the meeting is trumpeted. One of them actually manages to die en route rather than attend, but finally an acceptable number drag themselves into the Consistory, leaving their consciences outside.

When the Cardinal of Valencia stands for the last time in front of them, he is surprisingly nervous. The papers he holds tremble slightly in his hand. There is a certain irony in the fact that some of what he says actually comes from his heart.

"It is a difficult thing that I ask of you today, but I would have you bear in mind that not only is the honor of the Holy Mother Church at stake, but also my soul. I was taken into the Church young. It was not my choice. The vows I said at that time were from my mouth but not from my heart. Though I have tried hard to adapt myself to its demands I have never had a vocation for the religious life and I stand before you now, begging permission to give off my vows and, for the sake of the salvation of my soul, return to the lay estate.

"Should my request be granted I intend to dedicate my life to the service of the Church by other means. My first act will be to travel to France to intercede with the king so that he should not bring an army into Italy, and in the future I will do everything in my power to protect papal interests."

In the short silence that follows no thunderbolts crack through the roof, no demons rise out of the floor to hook their pitchforks into his dress. The cardinals vote (their mumbled yeses have never come so fast) to refer the matter to the Pope and an hour later Cesare leaves the Consistory a layman. He walks straight into a meeting with the French envoy, who has arrived that very morning carrying letters of patent to invest the now ex–Cardinal of Valencia with the title of Duke de Valentinois, along with forty thousand gold francs a year and the secret promise of troops—lance and cavalry—whenever and wherever he might need them.

So Valencia becomes Valentinois, the words so similar that they slide together on the Italian tongue. And thus Duke Valentino is born.

There is no time for celebration. Both King Louis and Cesare are men eager to get married. At the French court Carlotta is still holding out, but then she has yet to meet Duke Valentino. On the off-chance that his charisma may not be enough, he invests in a little luxury. Rome hasn't witnessed such a Borgia shopping spree since his brother Juan set off for

Spain. But for Cesare, the best of all is the parade sword he has made for himself. Meticulously engraved with the Borgia coat of arms and scenes from Roman history, it is imperial, in both design and intention. Julius Caesar's exploits are everywhere. Caesar and Cesare. Not a letter to separate them. The river Rubicon that Caesar crossed from Gaul, against the will of the Roman Senate but to his own glory, still runs across the northeast of Italy, only now it is inside the papal states, where the right soldier might forge a new empire if he had the backing of the Pope and an army to go with it.

"The die is cast." The inscription works for both men.

Cesare's future is irresistible. How upsetting, then, when a week before he is due to leave he wakes with his legs in spasm and his skin erupting again. Not pustules this time, but blotches, like a rash of raspberry birthmarks all over his face. "Get me Torella!"

The doctor is out of bed and in attendance within minutes.

"I thought you said it was over. That I was cured."

Gaspare Torella, who has been busy with correspondence and notebooks on this very subject over this last year, shakes his head. "I had hoped so, my lord, but it is such a new disease, we have yet to understand its journey through the body. It first appeared in cities where the French army went, though some say the men who brought it had been in the service of Admiral Columbus in New Hispania. I have made a study of it and—"

"Forget the history," he interrupts. "How do I get rid of it?"

"It comes in phases. The first is the open sores and the second these . . . these flowery blotches. Steam baths and mercury have been shown to help. I have made up new herb compounds in differing strengths."

"And then what?"

"Then we do not know exactly. For some it seems to go away entirely."

"Then I shall be one of those. You'd better bring me the unguents."

"It is not so bad, my lord," he says cheerfully. "At least there is no breaking of the skin."

"Not so bad! My legs scream as if they are on the rack and I am going to woo a wife. Would you sleep with this face?"

"May I ask, is there anything further down?"

"God's blood, Torella, just get rid of it, will you?"

"I shall do my best."

"How long?"

He hesitates. It is always hard, judging the gap between what he knows and what a patient wants to hear. "When do we leave for France, Your Lordship?"

"The week after next."

"It cannot be postponed?"

"Ha! Someone better get me a mask."

He props the bone-handled mirror in front of the window. The black velvet covering his face is as soft as skin. His eyes, in contrast, are bright: young man's eyes, blazing with life. The mask looks good on him, suggesting a certain insolence along with the mystery. When he wears it during Carnival he winds in women like a ball of wool. But it is not carnival season now.

He slips it off and looks back into the mirror. How do ugly men make their way through life? He thinks of Michelotto. When he walks down the street men take half a step back from him. But he, Cesare, wields a different power. His face has always been his first weapon. Look at me, it says. I am what you see: easy on the eye, strong to the taste, a man with substance, someone to admire, for how can beauty this natural lie? But now . . . What will they make of him now? Even if this is not a plague from God, everyone knows the soil these flowers grow from: those moist, corrupt places where careless appetite is king and honor has little to do with anything. A man with this face may not keep his promises. A man with this face is not the kind of husband that a good king would want for his child. A man with this face might not even like himself.

Well, it will not last forever. The sea voyage will take the best part of two weeks and then there is the journey from Marseilles to meet the king. If that is not long enough he can always wear more jewels to dazzle their sight. He chooses not to think of Juan and the arrogance that goes along with such behavior.

Back in his room, Gaspare Torella's pen scratches rapidly across the page.

Second stage. Return of pain and rash of purple flowers.

Records are essential to the understanding of the body's ills: what, when, for how long and the effects of what treatments. He is writing a treatise on this new plague and has been exchanging letters with doctors and scholars from Ferrara and Bologna, where the universities have the best medical men in Europe. This contagion has spread further and faster than any they have heard of before, bar the great plague itself. It appears to transmit through intercourse and its symptoms attack more men than women. Some say that the Jews brought it to Naples, others that it has traveled from the New World, others still that it comes direct from God as punishment for an age of fornication. Yet one scholar has discovered its symptoms in the works of Hippocrates, and another has recorded the disease in young virgins and old, sexless men. For many the answer is bloodletting or the use of hot irons applied to the back of the skull to release the buildup of bad humors. Torella himself thinks bloodletting is of little use and recommends mercury, but only in small quantities. Too much and the cure is worse than the disease. The fact is, no one knows. Some men die fast, the stages of agonies and eruptions coming within months of each other, followed by a kind of mania until their brains seem to boil and they lose their minds. Others hold it at bay forever, or at least for as long as their records show.

It has been over a year since Cesare Borgia was first afflicted. Before the first attack, Torella had never known a young man so healthy or so strong. It was as if illness itself was afraid of him. With such a disposition, and good treatment, he might well die in his bed with his grandchildren around him. Or . . . well, that is not for him to say. While Torella is a scholar he is also a priest. In Dante's inferno there are doctors herded in with the soothsayers, their heads twisted on their bodies so they walk into eternity backward, their bitter tears falling into the clefts in their buttocks. No one predicts God's future but God.

He puts his books aside to prepare more salves for the journey.

Chapter 38

A GREAT HOUSEHOLD ON THE MOVE IS LIKE AN ARMY WITHOUT weapons. It is still night when the Vatican gates open. After the first bodyguards rides Duke Cesare himself, surrounded by nobles, Spanish and Roman, his doctor, his secretaries and all his household officers. Then come cohorts of grooms and servants like foot soldiers, then the pack mules, heads down as if in resigned despondency at the hardships to come, and bringing up the rear an endless line of loaded baggage carts thundering over uneven cobbles. Those few Romans who are up, or woken by the noise, watch amazed; it looks as if half the Vatican is on its way to France. The hour is deliberately unsocial: the throwing off of his vows and this "affair" with the French king are not to everyone's liking and it is best not to draw too much attention to them. The stealth suits Cesare as well, for his face is still in full bloom. It is a shame, since his natural coloring goes well with the red and gold of his new livery, and with his nobles and pages all dressed the same, once the sun comes up they will be on fire against the dirt and drab of the streets.

Cesare's going brings an immediate change of atmosphere in the Vatican. Without his restless dynamism the Borgia apartments feel heavy, almost sleepy; as if the air itself has to readjust to the lack of him. The Pope finds it hard to propel himself into business and there are moments, reading dispatches or preparing to quiz ambassadors, when he misses the certainty of his son's quick mind, the instinctive cat-pounce onto unsuspecting prey.

But the feeling passes and as he relaxes so do others around him: churchmen, palace officials, servants, even the indefatigable Burchard all feel a little less harried, more appreciated and therefore more appreciating.

The change is most noticeable inside the family. With less male strut and banter, the hush of silk skirts and the sweetness of women's laughter expand to fill the Pope's private rooms. His two darling daughters (for that is how he also sees Sancia since her return) both let go of the breath they are not even aware they have been holding, and take advantage of their position in the court. Together they arrange dinners, entertainments, music, concerts and dancing, fussing around their father like handmaidens, delighting in his delight. Giulia, who has never been at ease with the Pope's eldest son, joins them sometimes, with young Laura and the baby at her side; because of course she is family too. Jofré, always in awe of Cesare, finds his own voice again, and Alfonso, who has had no option but to match his brother-in-law's aggressive good humor toward him, is allowed to be more himself. Despite the onset of winter, the Vatican seems a warmer place than it has done for years. Without naming or in many cases even knowing it, they come to feel how much tension there is inside Cesare's insistent energy and how their world is a gentler place without him.

Lucrezia in particular, though she shed tears at his departure, is soon dancing on air. But then Lucrezia is a happy woman. She is also a lucky one, for she is that rare thing in a world of arranged marriages: a bride who loves her husband.

In the end it was quite simple: a young woman yearning for love marries a handsome, lively young man with a proclivity for pleasure and a soft spot for women with pale skin and fair hair. Any fear this Adonis might have had about penetrating a pope's daughter had been allayed the minute he set eyes on her. The mind behind those startling blue eyes has little interest in politics or even malicious rumor. He simply likes what he sees. The attraction is immediate, and though he does his best to be chivalrous, in the weeks leading up to the wedding he cannot help but let it show.

Lucrezia, still nursing guilt that it is she who led Pedro Calderón on, is excited and nervous by degrees. She is not used to men outside the family being so open and at ease with her. For the first few days she watches him as closely as he does her, so that often they can't help but catch each other's eye and have to laugh to avoid embarrassment.

Alfonso laughs a lot. She likes that; likes how easily he enjoys himself, how he and Sancia are so relaxed and playful together. It reminds her of how it used to be between her and Cesare. Cesare: he is her other fear, of course, though she will not let herself admit it. His bonhomie toward Alfonso feels real enough. And yet . . . it is almost as if she cannot allow herself to become too fond in case Cesare will then become less so.

But as France beckons, Cesare has his own life to lead and even he cannot be in all places at once. With Sancia and Jofré as their unofficial chaperons, the courting couple is given enough space to let the attraction flower and the anticipation grow.

In the marriage bed that first night, he is so full of desire that he asks if they might keep the lamp burning as she removes her embroidered nightshift so that he might see her properly. She blushes deeply, fumbling with the ties, until he takes her hands away and undoes them himself. Her nerves act as their own aphrodisiac.

"You are very lovely," he says thickly, laying his hand on the pale rise of her stomach.

She laughs. "Am I?"

"Oh yes . . . yes, you are."

"So are you," she replies.

Because he is. She has long been smitten by the wonder of his leg—such a test of a man and in him the perfect union of strength and line. Naked, however, his beauty is more shocking: the tension of muscles running through his calves, the long powerful pull of the thigh reaching high into the torso, framing his rising penis. Above, his chest is a thicket of curls. Nervously, she slides her fingers in among them: rich and dark. As dark as she is fair. The flesh beneath is firm, almost hard. As hard as she is soft. He smiles down at her and in the lamplight his eyelashes are as full as a girl's.

"Don't worry," he murmurs, moving his hand skillfully downward. "It is more fun even than dancing."

At nineteen, blessed by blood and beauty, Alfonso is a young man overflowing with optimism and confidence. After Giovanni Sforza, it is like being loved by a god.

Later that night, the guard whose job it is to keep watch over the stores and cellars is disturbed by strange noises coming from the kitchen (vermin in great houses often come human-size). He picks up his staff, fat enough to counter kitchen knives, and, carefully lifting the iron latch, pushes open the heavy door.

The shadows of hanging pots and pans flap like heavy bats around the room, their dance set off by flickering candles. At the great table in the center of the room an impromptu banquet is taking place: the Duke and Duchess of Bisceglie sit side by side in their nightrobes, hunks of bread, cheese, dishes of preserve and a bottle of cellar wine and metal cups laid out in front of them.

It is hard to know who is more taken aback.

"Whoa. Did we wake you?" The duke, his bare feet curled over the rungs of the rough stool, is first to recover. "We were trying to be quiet, but I dropped the carving knife."

He waves it in the air and beside him Lucrezia gives an impish smile, her face framed by a cloud of pale, tousled hair.

"Marriage is a hungry business." Alfonso laughs, raising his glass to the man's stunned look. And she laughs too. So that now the guard can do the same, only nervously; the loss of the cheese and wine will be noticed immediately.

"Don't worry. We will wipe away the evidence. And keep a note of everything we eat so that you are not blamed for the loss."

The man nods, embarrassed but satisfied as he backs his way out of the room and closes the door. What a story. Who will ever believe him?

"I'd like to see his face when he tells the cook tomorrow," Alfonso says. "When we were children, Sancia and I did things like this all the time in the palace."

"You were allowed?"

"No allowance needed. We did as we pleased. The cooks grew so used to us they would leave out pickings for 'the royal mice' . . . Ah, what games we played."

In the half-light she smiles at him. "You get on with everyone, don't you?"

He shrugs. "Why make enemies? Life is too short. My God, wife, you have given me an appetite." And he slices off another sliver of cheese, covering it with fruit preserve.

"I wish Cesare felt the same way about people," she says.

"Oh, your brother is a fine man."

"You like each other."

"Why should we not? We both care for you and want to see you happy."

She nods, and her heart feels fit to explode with happiness.

They sit watching the shadows jump, enjoying the transgression of the moment. He eats the cheese and licks his fingers, sticky with the preserve, and then he dips them back into the jam and offers them to her. She slides them in and out of her mouth, all the time watching him watching her. Oh yes, she is eager to learn about love, this fine young bride of his.

"We will be content together, don't you think, Alfonso?" she says at last, looking fondly at him.

He yawns and stretches out his handsome arms. "I don't see why not."

By the end of the year she is sick to her stomach and happy as a lark. There will be a grandchild in Italy by the summer. Alfonso d'Aragon and Lucrezia Borgia. Man and woman. Husband and wife. Family and dynasty. As simple as that. In Rome, at least.

Chapter 39

In France, Cesare's courtship of Naples has only just begun.

Princess Carlotta of Aragon is a particular young woman. Born on the right side of the blanket to a strict father, there had been no running wild in the palace kitchens for her. She laughs less than her tearaway cousins, and when she does she cups a hand in front of her face, a coquettish gesture in some, but in her case more to hide her teeth, a set of crooked tombstones fighting with each other to fit into her mouth. Of course Cesare is courting royalty, not beauty, but one cannot help noticing such things. She is tall, head and shoulders above the queen's other ladies-in-waiting, and her face is long and rather flat. Though not as flat as her chest. All this he has taken in across crowded court gatherings. Now, face-to-face for the first time, his overriding impression is of a piece of dough that has been rolled too thin. The French word "crêpe" comes to his mind. Duke Valentino and his pancake princess. He smiles to himself. Ah, the price a man pays for family.

"Princess. I have ridden day and night, crossed rough water and stony ground, spurred on by the promise of our meeting. But seeing you now in front of me, I would do it all again for the pleasure of this moment."

There is a grain of truth in his pomposity. It has not been an easy journey. The sea crossing from Ostia was bilious and an early winter had soaked and then frozen the French roads. Disembarking at Marseilles, they were met by the king's agent with warm words of welcome and a demand for the letter of annulment so it could be sped to Paris, where the king was waiting impatiently to divorce his wife. Except

Cesare doesn't have it. Alexander, a stickler for canon law when it is to
his advantage, had calculated that a delay in this trump card might concentrate the king's mind on his side of the bargain: the softening up of
the princess for the attentions of his son. It is a rare miscalculation on
the Pope's part. By the time their next letters cross, the document is
already halfway across the Alps.

In the papal state of Avignon, the city comes out in celebration. It is
a party to rival any that the Borgias used to throw. Waiting to greet him
at the steps of the old papal palace stands their oldest and greatest
enemy, cardinal and now papal legate of France, Giuliano della Rovere.

"Valencia and the Sacred College have lost a fine cardinal but
gained a finer warrior," he booms, arranging the features of his hatchet
face into a smile.

The last time Cesare had been in della Rovere's company was at the
banquet in the town of Veltri, the night he slipped his hostage reins.
They had hated each other then and the years in between have done
nothing to improve matters. But both of them know that if della Rovere
has any hope of becoming a player in time for the next papal conclave
he cannot afford to sulk any longer in voluntary exile. His first overture, a letter of condolence after Juan's death, had been well received.
Now he offers something solid: as a friend of the French Crown, he will
use all his influence on behalf of the Pope's son. With both sides watching their backs, it may work for a while. Cesare's return smile is prettier
but equally insincere.

"You do our Holy Mother Church proud, Cardinal. Avignon shines
under your government."

"It was once the seat of popes." The irony of his rejoinder is lost on
neither of them. "One has a duty to the past."

"And to the future."

Though the cardinal has aged in exile, he remains an imposing figure. If one did not know better, one might think they were father and
son. Certainly they have the same appetite for life and the same ruthless desire to drink it dry. They share something else as well.

Gaspare Torella notices it straightaway: the telltale purple buds decorating their faces and hands, disappearing up inside the folds of their clothes. The doctor in him is already measuring out the mercury, the priest is more resigned: Lord, how these Roman cardinals do love their ladies.

As they set off for the king, they are besieged everywhere they go, people flooding in from the fields and villages, shouting, openly gawking at the spectacle the duke's entourage presents. Nobles bejeweled like kings, pages dressed like nobles, horses so decorated in precious metals that it's a wonder they don't shit gold. France has never seen anything like it and people don't know whether to cheer or jeer. What passes for sophistication in Rome evidently conveys a different message outside it. In the cities, the more educated can barely conceal their ridicule. *Mon Dieu!* How can any man carrying a French title exhibit this level of crassness and vulgarity? If Italy breeds such parvenus then it is no surprise that she is fresh meat to foreign conquerors.

Cesare realizes fast enough how badly he has misjudged the situation. But what is to be done? He can hardly strip the gold leaf off his horse's saddle, or send back all the clothes and the jewels. That would have them laughing behind their hands even louder. In such an atmosphere, his charm becomes unctuous rather than winning, and by mid-December, when he reaches King Louis's court, he is a sullen, angry man.

He decides to brave it out, marching into the city of Chinon, where the king is holding temporary court, in full splendor. Louis watches the performance from a tower inside the city walls. "My, my," he is heard to remark when the city gates finally close behind them, "altogether too much, one thinks, for a little Duke of Valentinois."

When the gossip reaches the Pope's ears back in Rome his much-vaunted tolerance dissolves into rage. "What makes the French so superior, when everyone knows it was their troops that soiled Rome's sheets because they don't wipe their asses properly?" he yells. "How dare such poxy men mock my son?"

The insults are about nationality as much as family; the Spanish and the French have long fought a war of manners, finding each other crude or affected by degrees. It touches Alexander more deeply than he might choose to admit, because underneath his pragmatism he is still a Spaniard at heart, and this new alliance with France is making him anxious in ways even he does not quite understand.

With the annulment of his marriage now in his hands, King Louis is instantly transformed into a more gracious host. The "little duke" becomes the Pope's beloved son and his dear cousin, a man to be royally entertained day and night. As to the business of Cesare's courtship with Carlotta, well, there is no time for it just yet. As lady-in-waiting to Louis's future queen, Carlotta is too busy preparing her mistress for the wedding.

"Don't worry, dear cousin. Let her feast her eyes on you for a while. That will get the juices going." And the king nudges him in the ribs. He has good reason to be so sunny. Anyone with the wit to understand politics can see he has scored a double victory: he now has the Pope's son as semi-permanent guest, and a wife who carries part of a kingdom between her legs.

Cesare, who sees it too, takes his impatience out on the hunt. The royal forests are groaning with game and there is no one who can ride or throw a spear to match him. Smooth-skinned now, with his falcon on his arm alert to his every whisper, he knows that once again he is a man to be watched and admired. And when he has ridden and killed to his fill, there are court games to be played, with pretty ladies eager to partner him in the dance. By the time the princess is ready to meet him, he is the talk of the court. What a fortunate young woman she is.

"I would do it all again for the pleasure of this moment. I look forward to a long and fruitful acquaintance between us," he says, slipping into intimate Spanish as his smile widens to greet her.

"That is most kind of you to say, Duke Valentinois," she replies in formal French. "However, I did not ask you to make such a journey on my behalf." Her long thin face shines like a waning moon in the candlelight. "I know you to be a very busy man and I do not want to waste your time."

"Perhaps you should let me be the judge of that."

Over her shoulder he sees the broad, intelligent face of Anne,

Queen of Brittany, and now again Queen of France, watching him carefully. Who exactly am I wooing here? he thinks.

"It seems she is in love with someone else."

"Who?"

"Some Breton nobleman, kinsman to the queen, I gather," the Pope murmurs, lifting his eyes to the ceiling.

"Oh, Papà. He is nobody compared to Cesare."

"Less than nobody. But the lady is unshakable. I gather she is as forthright as she is plain."

"It could be that Queen Anne supports her in this. The princess is in her care and the man is a kinsman."

"Ha! Your brother is of the same opinion. In which case the king should tell his wife to keep her nose out of it. Alliances of state are men's business."

"Nevertheless, Papà, women—plain or pretty—do have feelings," Lucrezia says gravely.

"Indeed they do. Still, I did not come to burden you with such things. How are you?"

She is lying on a daybed in the receiving room of her palace, lovely though a little paler than usual. "Oh, you do not burden me. It is good to have something to take my mind off things. Anyway, I am better. Only a little sad now and then."

"Have you dismissed the maidservant yet?"

"It was not her fault, Papà. I was the one who fell. I was just feeling so . . . so full of the joy of it."

Happiness has its drawbacks. It had been one of those tender days toward the end of winter when the sky is a bolt of blue silk and no one can bear to be inside anymore. On the spur of the moment she had arranged for herself and her ladies to ride into the country along the riverbank. After eating, they had been playing and she had started to run, because her energy had returned and she no longer felt sick, because the day was so beautiful, because she was eighteen and in love and going to have a child and wanted to celebrate all of it. Long skirts, muddy grass, tree roots. At any other time it would simply have been a tumble and the girl behind falling on top of her a cause for breathless laughter. At the moment it happened they had indeed laughed, but she had registered the flash of worry in the girl's eyes and by the time they were on their way home there was a gnawing pain in her abdomen and everyone knew something was wrong.

It was too early to tell the sex. Too early to tell anything in the clump of black blood that she passed later in the night. Such things happen all the time, both the doctors and her women assured her. A clean expulsion. Nothing to prevent the next one. But she had been taken aback by the desolation that followed, and even Alfonso's brightness could not bring back her laughter. Her father's bear hug and the very smell of his love had brought more comfort, so that over the last weeks, when the worst of business is over, he has taken to visiting and sharing the gossip of politics with her.

"What about King Federico in Naples?" she asks. "What does he say about this other man?"

"Nothing." The Pope scowls. His moods these last weeks have been much affected by the news from France. "He buries his head in the diplomatic sand and says nothing at all. The fact is he wants this marriage as little as she does, but he doesn't want to say it out loud. Which makes him twice the fool."

"I am very sorry to hear it. You know Alfonso has written to him many times telling him what a fine man Cesare is and what a great match it would be."

"Hmm." He nods distractedly. While he enjoys his new son-in-law's company head and shoulders above that of the idiot Sforza, not least because he has made his daughter so happy, the Duke of Bisceglie's grasp of politics has proved disappointingly superficial.

"Perhaps you should bring Cesare home and find him another wife," she says. "Cardinal Sforza has a number of suggestions for the right bride."

"I can imagine. You see more of my Vice-Chancellor than I do these days."

It is true that, since Cesare's departure, the Milanese faction have taken to using Lucrezia as a way of trying to get their voices heard by the Pope. Ascanio Sforza's letters to his brother Ludovico talk of a sharp mind inside her studied graciousness.

"He says nothing disloyal, Father. He is simply worried about the future of Milan."

"Then he should have thought about that five years ago when his brother invited in the French in the first place."

The Sforzas are not the only ones complaining. Since Cesare's departure Alexander's audience chamber has become like a fish market with so many raised voices. The Spanish ambassador has gone so far as to accuse the Pope of compromising the independence of the Church with this reckless alliance. As the Pope roared his response, the ambassador exited so fast that he almost hit the hovering Burchard in the face. Tales of the row had been halfway around Rome the next day.

"Papà?"

"What?"

"Are you all right? You look so angry."

He smiles. "Yes, yes. Just thinking about business."

"Can I help?"

"You do already, just by being here. I must go and you should rest."

But at the door she calls him back.

"If this courtship does not work, you will find him another fine wife, yes? I mean . . . whatever happens, Alfonso and Sancia will still be family, won't they, Father?"

"You are not to worry about such things, Lucrezia," he says, because he does not want to think about it either. "Just get well and give me that grandchild."

Chapter 40

THE TRUTH IS, ALEXANDER WOULD LIKE NOTHING BETTER THAN TO bring the duke home and find him another wife. But Louis has no intention of letting him go. He has given away a prime piece of French real estate to unite the houses of Orléans and Borgia in this great enterprise of Italy, and the last thing he wants is for his dear cousin to return to Rome, where who knows what political pressure might be brought to bear on the Pope to make him question his support for the invasion?

As the courtship staggers from bad to worse, Cesare, caught like a fly in a dish of preserve, curses himself for not seeing it sooner. He is reliant on Louis, not only for a large slab of money (yet to come), but also for the troops he will need when they return to Italy. He can hardly spurn the king's hospitality and march his whole household out of France. But neither can he leave without it. There is no slipping out of the tent leaving empty baggage chests this time. The guest is more a hostage than the hostage ever was. It is a mistake he will not make again.

At the beginning of March the king tries once more, organizing an intimate meal between the reluctant lovebirds with just Their Majesties as chaperons. It is an excruciating affair: Carlotta does not speak unless spoken to and Cesare stares across the table at her flat face, imagining it as the wall of a fortress town, more suited to cannonballs than compliments. It doesn't help that his humiliation is so public that the law students of Paris, always an irreverent bunch, are presenting an entertainment on how the son of God cannot find any woman to marry him, poor thing.

"Lawyers! In any language they smell of other people's shit." Michelotto, never at his best at court, is itching to take it out on someone. "Let me take some men into the streets of Paris and every one of them will have higher voices when it comes to pleading their cases."

If only, Cesare thinks. If only . . .

Next morning, the king orders the Neapolitan ambassador for an emergency audience. Voices are raised and it does not last long. That afternoon Cesare vents his frustration on the hunt. With his own pack of bay and catch hounds, he breaks ranks from the main party and moves off alone further into the forest.

The dogs plow through the winter undergrowth, tails in the air, noses to the ground for the first good scent. They have traveled all the way from Italy with him and he knows each and every one of them by name. A few of them, the bullmastiffs and the boxers, he has watched being whelped from bitches that were catching boars when he, Cesare, was still a boy in the saddle. His hunting master says that he has never worked for a man who had such a way with them: that what is skill in some, in him is instinct. Cesare, who has an advanced nose for the odor of flattery, is not so sure. But what he does know is that when his head feels fit to burst with the intransigence and stupidity of men there is always room to breathe out here, where his horse and his dogs, like the best fighters, anticipate the next command almost before he gives it.

Away from the body of the hunt, the only noise is the rustle and snap of the scrub underfoot. The late-winter sun slices in through the canopy of trees, so there are moments when it feels as if he is riding through the nave of a French cathedral, the soaring space lit by arched windows halfway to the sky. Some say God enters a man's heart differently in such churches; that because the light is so precious the very architecture pulls your head up toward Him. Cesare has spent the winter freezing his balls off inside such places and longs for the comfort of Rome. The Vatican chapel may be big but its walls are alive with battles and stories, most of them so realistic that you might think you could climb into them. He has done some of his best strategic thinking in there.

God's blood, he thinks, I am tired of this country. I want to go home.

The dogs are howling. The bays have picked something up. With a fresh enough scent, they can outrun the swiftest deer. Boars move more slowly, but their battering-ram bodies can smash through smaller openings and into deeper undergrowth. The chase runs for two, maybe three, miles. He hears the royal bugle calling from somewhere in the distance. The main hunt is nearer than he'd realized, maybe they have picked up the same scent. But this is his kill. He urges his horse on, flattening himself against the saddle as they jump fallen trees and speed under low branches.

The bay dogs are further ahead now, throwing themselves deep into a thicket and suddenly there it is, breaking cover: a full-grown male boar, fat head, stumpy legs and thick bristling body. It is big; 150 pounds at least, with fully grown saber-curved tusks thrusting out and up from its bottom jaw.

It hurtles faster into the forest, driven by panic, but not fast enough for the bays; within minutes they have it surrounded, harrying and corralling it toward a patch of open ground, the catch dogs ready, straining and howling but holding back until they are called.

Now he gives the order and they pile in, snarling, snapping, jumping to catch a tail or an ear in their teeth, all the time dodging the tusks. There is a cacophony of sound, barking, squealing. The boar flings itself this way and that to throw off the dogs. Breaking free for an instant, it puts its head down and charges, a tusk catching the underbelly of one of the mastiffs, lifting it off the ground and hurling it to one side. The dog's high-pitched screams are everywhere. Cesare launches the first spear while still mounted. It embeds itself deep and low in the animal's back flank. There are vital organs in there, but the pain will make it mad before it kills.

He flings himself off the horse, the second spear, with a crossbar a third of the way up, already poised as the boar twists and howls. There are twenty, maybe thirty, forty paces between them. He settles his feet into the ground and braces himself. His blood is pumping and he can hear a kind of singing in his ears. The best place would be the neck, but wherever it is, there will be no second chance.

The boar is charging now, moving at frenzied speed, head low so the tusks will get leverage on flesh. He has seen men half disemboweled by the goring if the spear doesn't hold.

"Come on!" he roars at the top of his voice. Even braced against impact, he is thrown off center as the whole weight of the animal rams onto the spear. For a second both man and beast are staggering. The man recovers first. All those hours of slamming, battering contact with battle swords have run rods of iron through his body and the spear has plunged in as far as the crossbar, so however hard it pushes the boar can get no closer. The tip has entered through the back of the head, deep into the body, and with Cesare at the other end holding firm, the beast can do nothing but squeal and squirm in furious agony. He calls in the dogs again and they hurl themselves upon the trapped body until finally the boar is brought to its knees. Only now does he let go of the spear and go in with the hunting dagger. The beast tries to rise, but it is too wounded. It is lying half on its side now, its great bulk juddering. This time he gets close enough to feel the brush-bristles of the hair. He picks his spot and slams in the long blade, hitting an artery so the blood whooshes up like a fountain into the air, soaking his clothes, spraying his face and hair: the gush-gush of a life extinguishing.

As it lies twitching heavily, its blood pumping out on the ground, he slits open the stomach. The dogs hold back, growling, muscle straining, impatient for their share of the kill. Even the injured one has pulled itself out of the bushes to try to join the pack, half its own innards trailing the ground. He cuts out some offal from the boar and throws it the first piece. As he stands aside to let them in, the dogs go mad with joy.

The chase and the kill. There is nothing in the world to compare to it. He has not felt so present, so filled with life, for months. Like any other man he has a yearning for the snug warm tunnels of women, but if heaven lets in men like him, then his eternity will be spent hunting, not copulating.

The first horses from the main hunt are galloping into the glade, the king, of course, in the lead. He reins in his mount, amazed by the sight of this beautiful young man, drenched in blood. The royal hunt dogs pour in, snapping at each other in territorial dispute over the kill. No one else moves.

Finally the king dismounts, motioning everyone else to stand back. "Valentinois," he shouts, striding up to Cesare. With the boar still twitching at their feet, he grabs his face between his hands and pulls it toward him as if they are going to kiss, then at the last moment embraces him, holding on until he too is thick with blood. But Cesare is still in communion with death and his laughter is more bestial than courtly. "Valentinois," the king says again, as if to remind him who and where he is. And now the shout is taken up, like a chant behind him. "Valentinois! Valentinois! Valentinois!"

"Sweet Jesus, you look like a pagan. God help your wife on your wedding night," Louis laughs, throwing an arm around his shoulders and turning him toward the hunt, inviting his men to enjoy the spectacle of their bloodstained intimacy. "Come, leave the butchering to others. They will reward the dogs and bring you back your tusks and hooves. You and I have work to do."

Back in the palace, Cesare, bathed and dressed, attends His Majesty for a private dinner in his bedroom. Thick brocade curtains cut out the drafts, and there is a healthy fire in the open grate, the apple wood spitting sparks into the room. As his servants pour the wine, black as boar's blood in the candlelight, the king can barely take his eyes off his guest.

"Like you, my great, dear Duke, I am a man who does not admit failure lightly." Louis is bullish from the start; Cesare's blood lust is still strong in the room and the king is energized by it. Such virility is wasted on court intrigue; only put him at the head of a cohort of cavalry and this fiery young warrior will shine brighter than any armor. "I have done everything I can, but it seems Naples does not want you as a son-in-law. What can I say? Believe me, it will be their loss. But you are our dear ally and even dearer cousin and I will not have you disappointed. I promised you a royal wife called Carlotta. And that is what you shall have. I offer you a toast: to marriage and war." He lifts his blood wine and their silver goblets clash together. "Now. There is someone I want you to meet."

Charlotte d'Albret is young and lovely, and the blood in her veins runs as blue as that of her unlovely namesake. She is the sister of the King of Navarre, with a claim on the French throne itself. She has high, melon-ripe breasts, a smile to melt ice, a quietly religious sense of duty and a father whose only concern is the need for some extra cash. Maybe the king has had her waiting in the wings all the time. Who knows?

"What is Naples anyway but a hellhole of deceit and disease, eh? This way you will have not only French lands but also a royal French wife." They walk together through the royal garden, the air growing milder with each passing day. "Once married, there will be nothing to stop us marching together and subduing the renegade Milan. With the city taken, my army will be your own to do with as you wish. God help the fortresses you march on, Cesare," he says, seeing again the boar's insides bloody and steaming in his hands. "As for Naples . . . well, there is always our own French claim on it. Revenge, dear cousin, can be taken in many forms."

Cesare, who has looked in the mouths of many gift horses, knows a good enough mount when he sees it. Back in Rome, Alexander, who has been suffering his son's humiliation as if it was his own, is jubilant. The marriage is negotiated, signed and celebrated in the queen's own chapel at Blois on May 12, barely six weeks after their first meeting.

Cesare's envoy gallops out when it is still dark. Seven hundred miles and a mountain range separate father and son. He reaches the Vatican four days later. Before he can open his mouth his knees buckle under him and Alexander gives a mere servant permission to sit in his presence. When he starts to talk his larynx is so coated with dust that his voice cracks. Food and wine are brought to help him recover.

Four hours later, when the man is still answering questions, the Pope joins him at the table. No detail is too small, no triumph uncelebrated. His new daughter-in-law is a vision of beauty, her new wardrobe overflowing with Borgia gowns and jewels. Cesare is the most handsome bridegroom the court has ever seen, the marriage breakfast the most sumptuous, and the King of France so enamored of his cousin that he showers him with even more titles and gifts. As for the wedding night—oh, the wedding night . . . No sooner has the messenger staggered home to sleep than Alexander invites others in to hear the news all over again. And so it is that Cesare's sexual prowess enters history: twice before dinner and six times afterward.

"My son. My son! Eight lances broken in a single night," he reiterates gleefully with each retelling. "He has bettered his own father in that!"

It is a family triumph and everyone must rejoice with him.

In the forecourt of the palace of Santa Maria in Portico, the Duchess of Bisceglie orders a bonfire to be lit to commemorate the event. Inside, however, the celebration is muted.

When the Pope visits, the couple receive him in Lucrezia's bedchamber, a bowl for sickness discreetly stowed close by. As with her brother, family duty is pleasure for Lucrezia these days and the new baby she is carrying will be born in late autumn. Halfway through the story of Cesare's triumph, her smile starts to tremble and tears slip down her cheeks. She tries to laugh them away, but they will not stop.

"It is the baby," Alfonso says, squeezing her hand. "She feels everything most acutely these last weeks."

Alexander nods understandingly.

But it is not the baby. Cesare is married into France, and Naples is no one's ally anymore.

"*Whatever happens, Alfonso and Sancia will still be family, won't they, Father?*"

"*You are not to worry about such things, Lucrezia.*"

The words, exchanged lightly only a few months ago, now sit accusingly between them. The Pope, who cannot bear to have his joy interrupted by the problems to come, kisses her on the forehead, before making his excuses to leave on further business.

As the door closes, Alfonso puts his arms around her. "It is all right. You are the Pope's daughter and everything will be all right."

"No. Don't you understand? This marriage makes your family our enemy. And that exposes you and Sancia."

"What? Will he try and divorce us both? I think not. I may not have performed as publicly as Cesare, but no one can doubt we are married. In a few months I will be the father of the Pope's grandchild. However angry he might be with my uncle, he will not take it out on me. He loves you too much for that."

She stares at him: such eyes, like cut sapphires. One would think that they could see through anything.

"I am sure you are right," she murmurs. "I am being foolish."

She holds him tighter. There is no point in telling him that it is not her father she is worried about.

Chapter 41

July, and the French army is on the move. Cesare leaves his new bride in tears as he takes command of his squadron of cavalry. The king greets him publicly, embracing him, calling him brother and warrior and finding yet another French decoration to add to his list of titles.

When the news reaches Rome, Vice-Chancellor Ascanio Sforza leaves immediately on a hunting trip, his baggage train altogether too large for such a short stay away. Milan is doomed and he can expect no help from the Church to save it.

Even if the Pope had the will there is little he could do about it. Half of Italy is in France's pocket anyway. Venice has signed her own treaty and the smaller states of Ferrara, Mantua and Savoy are already banking on the favors they will get from supporting King Louis. Whatever patriotic dreams Alexander might have had for his adopted homeland, the unpalatable truth is that the country is a sack of spatting cats that have learned nothing from the past. The only justice will be a poetic one: the man who started the tide turning five years ago will be the first to be swept away by it. As Alexander predicted, nobody is crying for the Sforzas.

Before the Vice-Chancellor leaves he makes a last call at the palace of Santa Maria in Portico to say his goodbyes to the young couple who have been the nearest he can get to the Pope over the months of escalating tension. He sits nervously, as if the door might open on soldiers at any time.

"Must you leave?" Lucrezia asks anxiously.

"The lines are drawn. There is no place for me here anymore." He pauses. "And if you want my opinion I would say this is no longer a safe city for your husband."

"But I am the Pope's son-in-law," Alfonso says automatically. It is a phrase that has already lost much of its comfort.

"You are also the King of Naples's nephew. If I may speak freely, my lady?"

Lucrezia nods. She has learned fast these last few months and knows that allies can only be friends when the political moment allows. Nevertheless, she has developed a certain fondness for this Sforza cardinal. Though he lacks a taste for the kill, he is more able than many and with a different brother might have made a greater career for himself.

"Once the French have taken Milan, they will revive their claim on Naples. By refusing Cesare's marriage to Carlotta, King Federico has thrown not only himself but the whole house of Aragon to the wolves. Your brother will get French troops to carve out a state for himself in Italy, and Naples is the price the papacy will pay for it. Being married into this family is no longer a privilege but a liability. I speak as someone who knows only too well."

No, no, she wants to say. No. This is not the same as last time. How could it be? She crosses her hands across her belly in a gesture of unconscious protection.

"I am sorry, madam. It is what I think."

Lucrezia stares at her husband. Neither of them speaks. They are both thinking the same thing: It has started already.

It is partly Jofré's doing. In his struggle to get his father's attention, in recent months he has taken to imitating Juan, dressing in jewels and carousing around Rome at night with a band of Spanish reprobates. Crossing Ponte Sant' Angelo a few days before, he was confronted by the Sheriff of Rome and in the brawl that followed someone fired an arrow into Jofré's leg. He'd been brought back to the palace howling murder as the blood spouted and Sancia, terrified by the sight, had raised the alarm as far as the Vatican, pulling the Pope out of bed in her demands for revenge.

But Jofré's pain can never pierce his father's heart in the way that Juan's did. After calling both sides to put their case, he excuses the sheriff and sends his son to Castel Sant' Angelo to cool his temper in a cell. When the news reaches Sancia, she explodes with fury.

"It is an outrage. Jofré almost bled to death."

"That is not what the doctors say. According to them it is a flesh wound."

"That's not true! He was beside himself with the pain."

Alexander sighs. Up to his eyes in high politics, he does not need this now, but Sancia has never learned the art of softening up her prey before she pounces.

"How can you pardon the offender and punish Jofré? This is not justice."

"If Jofré draws his sword and attacks the sheriff's men, then he deserves what he gets."

"But he is your son!"

"In which case he should act like it."

"That is not what you would have said if it had been Cesare. Or Juan."

Juan. The word hangs heavy in the air. The fact is, nobody mentions his dead son in the Pope's presence. He has made it clear that he does not like to be reminded . . .

He stares at her: this dark little beauty with her piercing eyes and flamboyant ways. Four years of marriage and not a hint of a pregnancy. He would be willing to believe it was Jofré's fault had she not bedded all of his sons with not even a miscarriage to show for it. Maybe it is she who is the problem. If he needs to find Jofré another wife . . . ah! For now, it is not worth the trouble.

"This audience is finished, young lady. Go back and look after your husband."

"Will you come and see him?"

"I am a very busy man."

"But he is your son!"

"*If* he is indeed 'my son' then . . ." He waves his hand in blind fury. Oh, how he is tired of being lectured by hysterical Spaniards.

She stares at him, both of them immediately aware of what has been said.

"What a madam you are," he says, collecting himself. "You should learn to hold your tongue."

But she has always been impetuous and when she is scared she has to fight to get over the fear. "I am sorry, Holy Father. But where I grew up we were allowed to speak our minds."

"Then perhaps it would be best if you went back there."

"What do you mean? You would send me away from Rome? What about Jofré?"

"Oh, such drama! Go to your husband, woman. I want no more of you."

He sits fuming after she has gone. He is the Pope, the heart and head of the Holy Church, how dare she rage at him? Holy Mother of God, he should command more respect. He sighs. He is expecting the Ferrarese ambassador at any moment. The man will stride in huffing and puffing, demanding reassurance that wherever Cesare takes his army after Milan, it will pose no threat to the noble house of Este. Ferrara, Mantua, Bologna—oh, they are all worried now. Letters crisscross the Alps between father and son: the most secure postal system in Europe, thank the Lord. The future of the dynasty is at stake. So much to be done, yet he spends his life surrounded by people who either cannot stop complaining or think they can raise their voices to him.

Somewhere inside himself, Alexander understands that he too is overreacting. It does not suit him being so bad-tempered, but then this sudden shift of allegiance away from Naples and Spain has made his life difficult in all manner of ways. He would like to talk to Lucrezia, because in the past she has been a discriminating listener. But not now. Now she stares at him with big mournful eyes. What? Is it his fault if the King of Naples signed his own death warrant? God damn them all.

Sancia is close to collapse when she arrives at the palace, throwing herself into Alfonso's arms and crying that they are about to be displaced—or worse.

"You should not have angered him, sister. He is under much pressure."

"And we are not? I tell you, Alfonso, we are disowned. You should have heard what he said. He does not even care for Jofré. To listen to him you would think he only had one son, that monster Cesare."

"Do not call him that," Alfonso says quietly.

"Oh, you are such an innocent, brother. Cesare never liked you. It was all pretense. He only cares for people when they're of use to him. He would swat you like a fly if the 'family' would gain from it. Talk to Lucrezia, she will tell you."

But when he repeats Sancia's story to Lucrezia he does not press her further about the past. She is nearly five months pregnant now and he does not want to alarm her. Instead he takes up his pen and writes to his uncle. Even when a husband loves his wife as much as he does, his first loyalty is to the family he comes from. It is simply the nature of things.

August: too hot to move, too hot to think, almost too hot to pray. French troops are sweating their way up the foothills toward the summer passes of the Alps. By winter there is no telling where they will be. The feeling of impending doom is made greater by the fact that this will be no ordinary winter. Fourteen ninety-nine is drawing to a close and with it, not just the end of a century but also the end of a half-millennium. Fifteen hundred. It is such a cleavage in the passage of time that for many it brings on a kind of spiritual vertigo. Invasion, war and this new sexual plague, so clearly a sign of God's wrath, all add to the whispers of doom that are spreading like fire in bracken across Christendom. In preparation, sinners everywhere (and who, after all, is not?) make plans for pilgrimage. Their destination will be Rome.

What is panic for some will be profit for others. It is a fortunate vicar of God who presides over such a windfall of revenue, and Alexander is already busy rebuilding. In the cauldron of heat, the work goes on: men ripping down the barnacle growth of houses and shops that have sprung up along the long route of pilgrimage between the great churches of Rome. From Castel Sant' Angelo to the steps of the echoing old Basilica of St. Peter, an elegant new thoroughfare is emerging: Via Alessandrina. In his mind it is already teeming with faithful souls, filled with God's love and the majesty of His church on earth. The papal coffers will be full, Rome will be seen to be a great city again and they will travel back to towns and hamlets all over Christendom with the name of the Holy Father who presided over it all on their lips: Rodrigo Borgia, Alexander VI, a Spaniard by birth, but a pope carrying history on his shoulders. Of that he is sure.

In her palace next to the Vatican, Lucrezia starts to feel the child move inside her. She sleeps sometimes in the afternoon now, heavy deep sleep, like a drug sucking her down underwater, while the baby flips and rolls like a fat fish. When she wakes, her mind is sometimes so glued that it takes her a while to remember what is happening. The movement comes again and she claps her hands over her belly. "Hush, hush, it will be all right. You are safe."

At the beginning she had prayed constantly: "Let it be a boy, dear God, if I am worthy of being granted anything in Your mercy let it be a boy." She said the words so many times that she began to feel it was a fact already. Then, fearing that her certainty was arrogance for which she would be punished, she asked forgiveness. In the last weeks she has rearranged her bedchamber so that everywhere she looks there is a devotional painting. Rome is filled with great artists who celebrate the beauty of man, but not all of them capture the spirit as well as they do the flesh. She searches for the images of the crucified Christ where his suffering has the most pity in it. When faced with half a dozen Virgins-and-child she picks the one where the serenity is as great as the joy; this way when she wakes she can move her gaze between the two. In the midst of the growing chaos it helps to be reminded.

With the first troops flooding over the passes, news comes from the court of Milan. Ludovico Sforza, a man who poured scorn on those who ran their life by astrologers, has looked into his own future and is seizing everything that is not nailed down in readiness for running away. The fear is contagious. Two days later, Lucrezia wakes to find her husband has made the same decision. The letter he leaves tells her he loves her and that he will write when he reaches Naples. She does not know whether to laugh or cry.

"This is King Federico's work," Alexander roars when he finds out. "If he is so keen to have his family reunited, let us make a clean sweep of it. Tell my daughter-in-law to pack her bags. He can have her back as well."

When Sancia refuses to go, he threatens to have her expelled by force. The whole court is thrown into disarray with his temper. After tears and pleading from both Jofré and Lucrezia, Sancia goes on her miserable way.

A few days later the Pope's spy service intercepts a letter from Alfonso to Lucrezia, urging her to leave Rome and join him.

Lucrezia is reading it—badly resealed—when Alexander arrives unannounced. "I have come to see how you are," he opens in blustering fashion.

"I am six months' gone with child and my husband has left me." She has prayed and cried and prayed some more. And now, to her surprise, she feels almost calm. She folds the letter and hands it to him. "In case you have not read it already."

He is taken aback by her self-possession. "He should not have gone in such a manner," he mutters. "Without permission."

"He was frightened for his safety."

"There was no need. As your husband he is under our protection."

"What, like Giovanni Sforza?"

"That is different." He sighs, as if he is the wounded party and the world is conspiring against him. "I am not here to fight with you, Lucrezia. On the contrary, I have come because I need your help."

"My help? In what?"

"I am in need of a governor for the cities of Spoleto and Foligno; someone who can do the job with strength and fairness."

She stares at him. "Me? But it is a post for a cardinal, surely."

"In the past, perhaps, yes. But the coming months will see our fortunes change dramatically and I need people around me that I can trust. There is already unrest through many of the papal states in anticipation of what may come. Spoleto remains loyal, and her loyalty must be honored by a good governor. You have an aptitude with people and with politics, Lucrezia. I have watched it grow."

"But . . . What about Jofré?"

"Jofré! We both know Jofré is not capable of peeling his own fruit. Though I will send him with you, for companionship."

"And my husband? Will you bring him back to me?"

"It is the king's decision, not mine."

She waits.

The art of bargaining: whatever his motives for the offer, his admiration for his daughter's growing acumen is not false. He sighs.

"Very well. I will try."

She refuses the silk-lined palanquin the Pope has arranged for her to ride in, and, despite her pregnancy, does much of the journey on horseback. She feels so healthy now and she remembers the road: it is the one she once took to Pesaro and she loves the way the landscape, at first wooded and dense, gives way to a long fertile plain with spectacular hill-towns poking up their stone-clad heads in the distance on either side. Wherever they stop people flood out to greet her. The sins of the Pope's daughter are ripe gossip and those who meet her are amazed to find her such a gracious, modest figure. Her belly is big now, catching the light on the silk of her gowns, and women in particular press to get close to her, many in the hope that her fertility may pass to them. Others bring flowers or amulets to have her hold and bless. On the road into Narni, with its sculpted Roman bridge and rippling river water, a bent old woman shouts from the front of the crowd.

"A boy, the duchess is carrying a boy! I can see him, my lady, swimming in your waters."

"She should know," someone else yells. "She's delivered hundreds and never got it wrong."

The crowd roars its appreciation and the baby rolls and slides inside her as if in answer.

The castle of Spoleto sits perched like an eagle above the hill-town, the great viaduct below a memory of ancient splendor. Once inside the fortress, the gates are bolted behind them. As she is helped off her horse, she can feel her heart beating hard against her chest. She has no illusions about the velvet trap her father has set for her. A pope's daughter governing a city cannot be a wife running off to join her husband in exile. But Alfonso is safe and she is in that blessed stage of pregnancy when many healthy young women find themselves filled with unexpected energy and well-being. While the post may be a prison as much as a privilege, she is exhilarated by the challenge.

The household is still unpacking, flinging open windows and doors to ventilate the stifling chambers, when Lucrezia welcomes the dignitaries of the town and starts taking petitions and hearing complaints. She can do this. She is a Borgia.

PART VIII

Women at War

*The Pope plans to make him no less than
the King of Italy.*

Gian Lucido Cattaneo,
Mantuan envoy, 1499

Chapter 42

THE ARCHER'S UPPER ARM TREMBLES WITH THE STRETCH OF THE bow. The arrow, a high whine of wind, hits the great horse's left ear full on, shattering it on impact. The shot is greeted with a howl of approval, then one of derision as the next narrowly misses the other ear. A dozen others follow, slamming into the animal's neck and flanks, and sending chunks of clay flying, crashing, smashing everywhere.

"Ssssforza, Ssssforza," the archers chant and cheer as they load and reload until the air grows dark under the onslaught.

"Poor da Vinci. Ludovico should have employed him to design weapons not statues." From a window high in the Sforza palace, Cesare stands watching the carnage. Before long the horse's tail is severed from its body. "Look at them. Even pissed stupid they shoot better than most Italians. Well, they had to sack something."

Beneath the plinth, servants run head-down around the hooves and under the belly, dodging the falling debris to gather up the used arrows and return them to the archers. Three months on the road and when the army finally reached Milan, itching for a fight, they had found the gates of the city open, waiting for them to march in, Ludovico Sforza having fled with his tail between his legs and a cartload of treasures behind him.

Another cry goes up as the stallion's head takes a series of direct hits, the sculpted nostrils splintering and crumbling. Cesare leans out of the window and shouts something in French. The captain looks up and yells back. A few of the archers raise their hands in salute: Cesare is now the darling of the troops as well as of the king.

He turns from the window. In dark silhouette, with the Milan sky the color of a dirty sheet behind him, he cuts an impressive figure. It is not just the light. Cesare Borgia, Duke Valentino, now dresses only in black: black cap adorned by dyed-black feathers, black cloak, black hose and black doublet, with just the barest sliver of gold silk ripping down through the sleeve. The man who left Italy in blazing color has returned dark as the devil. How well it suits him.

"So, gentlemen," he says, moving back into the room. "We have a deal?"

A fast murmur of assent goes around the table. There are four of them sitting there, hard, weathered faces incongruous above the soft velvet of court robes. They are fighting men all of them, condottieri with mercenary troops at their beck and call. In peacetime, you would not trust them to cut a pack of cards without sliding an ace out of their sleeve, but when it comes to war they are loyal to the highest bidder. And right now, no one is offering more than Cesare Borgia. He has picked carefully. The small wiry Vitellozzo Vitelli is the nearest that Italy comes to having its own artillery expert. Next to him, Oliveretto da Fermo is a hungry thug but a well-trained one; while across the table sit two Orsini brothers, Paolo and Francesco. Orsini. Cesare would as happily string them up as employ them, but between them they hold a small army of men and until he is ready to take his revenge it is better to have them fighting with him. And while his father is still on the papal throne, each and every one of them is happy to lick his hand and do his bidding.

"You have a question, Vitelli?"

"How many men will you field besides ours?"

"How many men?" Cesare repeats, smiling. He knows it is what they have been waiting to hear. On the triumphant entry into Milan King Louis and his Duke Valentino had ridden side by side, and since then they have been publicly joined at the hip, hunting, feasting and entertaining. Anyone in any doubt that the history of Italy is being written between them has only to look at the language of their bodies: bent heads, whispers, shared laughter, more like brothers than "dear cousins."

"I will lead a force of two thousand French cavalry, three hundred

French lancers, twenty-seven artillery guns and four thousand Swiss and Gascon infantry." He stops to let the numbers sink in. "With the troops that our Holy Father the Pope will send from the Papal Guard, alongside the men you bring, the army will be ten thousand strong."

Someone lets out a small hissing sound between his teeth. The silence lengthens. The Pope's son has just become the commander of one of the biggest forces ever to move across Italian soil. Cesare glances toward Michelotto, stationed behind the table like an ugly bulldog, and his henchman pulls a paper from his jacket and spreads it out on the surface in front of them.

"And this, gentlemen, will be our route of campaign."

The Via Emilia. Even on the map it stands out: a road as only the ancients built them. Beginning in Piacenza in the north, it moves straight as an arrow southeast through Parma and Bologna, running along the eastern edge of the Apennines and then on as far as the Adriatic coast at Rimini. Exactly when it was first built is conjecture, though it must have been well before the birth of Christ. Its reconstruction under Augustus and Tiberius is better known, for there are dated milestones and a set of the finest bridges in Italy; sweeping arched spans of stone, their surfaces worn and pitted by centuries of feet, hooves and cart wheels, though most of those who walk the stones now couldn't care less about the history of the ancients or even the name of the great Roman general who crossed the Rubicon before them. No, like most people they are too busy working to stay alive in the present.

The poets—who work hard in their own way—liken this elegant artery in the body of Italy to a string of pearls laid out on a table of green velvet. It is a fitting simile: the pearls because along its length are threaded a number of city-states, each rich enough to have its own ruling family, greedy, squabbling and committed to lining its pockets at the expense of those it governs; and the green velvet because on its unswerving way to the sea the road runs through one of the most fertile plains in the country. It is said you only have to throw a handful of seeds in the state of Romagna, as it is known now, and within a year you will have enough bread, fruits, vegetables and oil to feed an army.

All this in itself would be enough to tempt a new young Caesar looking to secure himself a place in history. But there is another accident of history that makes this area ripe for conquest and explains why Cesare has had his eyes on it ever since he was old enough to read a map. Because in law these city-states do not belong to the families that rule them: they are rented rather than owned. The landlord to whom they belong sits in Rome presiding over the Holy Mother Church. And Alexander VI has already made it clear that he is intending to evict a number of tenants in favor of his own son.

The first attack has been a spiritual one: a bull of excommunication against five of the rulers of papal states in the Romagna on the grounds of non-payment of tribute to Rome. Robbed of God's protection and the support of any bigger allies (no one is willing to fight the Pope when he has the King of France in his pocket), these five named towns sit close enough together to offer the foundation for a larger single state: Imola, Forlì, Rimini, Faenza and Pesaro. Though the choice is as much strategic as malicious, everyone in the room knows that the ousting of his ex-brother-in-law, the Duke of Pesaro, will bring with it a special satisfaction.

"We will start here." Cesare places his index finger on a point on the map. The stones in his rings glitter even in the half-light. Their captain-general is wearing the price of a small estate on one hand. "The city of Imola, and then Forlì. Vitelli?" He turns to the weasel-faced veteran. "You are a man who knows your artillery. How many cannonballs do you think we need to blow holes in Caterina Sforza's fortresses?"

Vitelli grins. "I think that will depend on what the lady is wearing at the time."

Chapter 43

WHEN LUCREZIA WELCOMES BACK HER HUSBAND, THE CHILD IS SO large inside her that it comes between them as they embrace.

"Look at you. It has made you even more beautiful. Naples is full of women dark as roasted chestnuts, while you are lilies and thick cream."

"Ha! I smell a man who has been indulging in courtier's talk."

"Untrue. There is not a moment when I was not thinking about you. My God, I have missed you, wife."

And she knows it is true, because she feels it too. She holds his face in her hands, pushing his cheeks together so that his lips, those full fleshy lips, are squeezed and open. She stands on tiptoe to kiss them.

"We have done it," she says, laughing as they break apart. "We have brought you home."

It has taken almost two months and a crosstrail of envoys and ambassadors, with neither side willing to give in: Rome because it has too much to bargain with and Naples because it has nothing.

King Federico had always known that his stand against the Borgias would sever the alliance with the papacy and open Naples to the French, but he had banked on Spain's outrage to provide him with protection. He is, alas, an idealist in an age of pragmatism. Their Most Holy Catholic Majesties Ferdinand and Isabella, watching the French walk into Milan and realizing that Naples is already lost, are making secret overtures to King Louis.

Such is Federico's isolation that he feels chilled even when the day is hot. If he is to stand any chance of survival, he would do better to appeal to the Pope's Spanish blood and give him what his daughter wants most—her husband's return in time for the birth of their child. And while he is at it, they might as well have Sancia back as well.

When the decision is made, he is, at least, honest about it. "I do not like it, nephew. But I have no option." His eyebrows are so used to being knotted together in worry that they seem to have fused, so that now he peers out at the world from under an overhang of hair. Some of his courtiers are beginning to wonder how far it is obscuring his vision.

"I know that."

"The Pope's bargaining is always the same: he offers you a warm coat, until you put it on and find it has open razors for a lining. I have no power against him. If you go, I must tell you I cannot guarantee your safety."

"I know that also."

The king sighs. In the past he never had much time for his bastard niece and nephew, feeling them to be tainted by the decadence of their father. It had been almost fitting when they had found a place inside an even more corrupt family. But it seems this marriage to the Borgia hussy has given Alfonso unexpected dignity. His own plain daughter is newly married to her Breton nobleman; a man with as little charisma as he has ambition. She will never return to Naples. Well, God grant her a long and happy life. It is more than he has to look forward to.

As soon as it is decided, Alfonso rides north with an armed guard, by-passing Rome and moving straight on to the papal city of Spoleto, where Lucrezia and Jofré have made a home of sorts. While the city has good reason to be grateful for the Pope's protection (especially when it is being so brutally withdrawn from others), it has also taken her to its heart, impressed by her diligence and grace. Now, with her husband at her side, together they can inspect outlying areas of her governorship.

It is a glorious autumn, balmy after the mad heat, and the forests are starting to take fire. For the first time in their married life they are their own masters. They both know it is a freedom that cannot last, which makes it all the sweeter. They are welcomed everywhere they go: the Duchess of Bisceglie may be a Borgia but she represents a softer face of power and her deliberations in Spoleto have earned her a reputation for fairness. Besides, who can resist such fecundity: a young woman ripe with child and so clearly in love with life itself?

By the time they are summoned back to Rome she is within weeks of giving birth.

Alexander, who sent away his children only to become lonely without them, is beside himself with pleasure at her return. Giulia, who has been away visiting her family for much of the summer, has become more resistible with time, and there are moments when he feels almost sentimental for a less arduous kind of love. His daughter's particular beauty fells him completely. In this last stage of pregnancy, she has come to resemble her own mother in her youth. She brings a glow into every room. The baby rides so high in her now that when she walks she must hold herself backward to accommodate its weight, putting a hand in the hollow of her own back for extra support, and when she sits she gives a slight breathless laugh, as if she can hardly believe her own condition. Such gestures trigger a flood of other memories in Alexander: Vannozza's full breasts, the sheen on her skin, the sense of voluptuousness in her weariness. When he had experienced it the first time it had been so powerful that he could barely wait for her to drop the child so that they might set about making another. Even Giulia, at her most exquisite, never inflamed him in the same way. It was as if there was something about Vannozza's beauty that had been bred to make babies, and the force of it plucks at his heartstrings even now. Well, why not? It is good for an aging man to be reminded of his potency and anyway, God knows, he loves his daughter deeply and it is impossible not to be touched by her happiness.

He is also proud of her. The letters from his representatives speak of a curious and serious mind, a willingness to listen but not to be shaken from her decisions by spurious argument. Of course such observations are inflated with flattery, but even so . . .

Jofré, on the other hand, affords him little pleasure. Since his brief sojourn in Castel Sant' Angelo, he is sulky and aggressive, like a pet animal neglected and gone to the wild. He is only bearable now when in his wife's company, for she has always been partly the mother he didn't have, chastising and cajoling by turns. Sancia herself, despite all the vicissitudes of life, has retained both her appetite for pleasure and an inability to disguise her feelings. It makes her almost refreshing in a world dictated by subterfuge.

Inside the palace of Santa Maria in Portico, the talk is all of births and babies. The kitchen buys in doves and young calves ready for the knife for the celebrations that will follow. A gilded crib is put into the bedroom under the portrait of the Virgin, the new linen embroidered ready with a space for the first initial. In the morning of October 31, Lucrezia goes for a walk with Alfonso in the courtyard garden. Coming back inside she feels a sharp stab and then her waters break, a flood that soaks her skirts, sending Alfonso running in panic for assistance. The midwives and women swoop in, shooing him away as they take charge, supporting her to her rooms and closing the doors. After a few hours, when nothing more has happened, the chief midwife starts massaging her belly with scented oils, sliding well-practiced fingers up inside her to encourage dilation. By sunset labor has started. Her groans rise up throughout the palace, and the Pope, who is informed of the progress when he comes out of a meeting with the new—and rather more pliant—Spanish ambassador, swears that he feels her pain himself. He refuses all food and drink and orders prayers throughout the Vatican for her safe delivery.

In the early hours of November 1, after a final stage of labor which leaves them all breathless with its speed and intensity, the Duchess of Bisceglie is delivered of a baby boy, in rude health and good voice. After a prolonged suck at the wet-nurse he is put into his mother's arms, suffused with an air of self-satisfaction.

He is given the name Rodrigo after his esteemed grandfather and, as the winter dawn creeps in, Lucrezia falls asleep safe in the knowledge that she has achieved the one thing that might save her marriage: a male heir for the Borgia dynasty in Italy.

For his part, the Pope is so elated one might almost think he had fathered the child himself. He holds a mass of celebration to thank God and then calls in Burchard. Having presided over two papal weddings, three betrothals and a divorce, it is now his job to orchestrate a baptism. Fortunately, the Vatican has a chapel that will do nicely for the event.

Chapter 44

THEY SAY THAT THE BLACKSMITH WHO MADE CATERINA SFORZA'S battle dress was invited into her bedroom so that there could be no mistakes in his measurements. Anyone who has seen her in her armor would agree that her engraved breastplate fits her womanly body most eloquently. They say that sometimes she wears the breastplate with nothing but silk petticoats underneath, and that they blow up in the winds as she strides across the battlements. This last fact is stated with particular confidence, because it is a well-known story that ten years ago, when the city of Forlì rebelled against her rule, murdering her husband and holding her and her children hostage, she managed to escape and make her way into her fortress, where she paraded herself on the battlements, lifting up her skirts and shouting to the conspirators below.

"You think I care what you do with them? Look—I have the means to make many more."

By then she was twenty-six and already famous. As the illegitimate granddaughter of the warrior Francesco Sforza she had been excellent marriage fodder for one of the great families. She had been nineteen when the death of Pope Sixtus IV had triggered a wave of carnage in Rome, much of it directed at her new husband, the Pope's nephew. As the mob attacked their palace, she had saddled up a horse and galloped, seven months pregnant, through rioting streets across the bridge to take Castel Sant' Angelo and hold it against all comers till her husband arrived back in town. That and many other remarkable exploits have earned her the sobriquet of "Virago." For most women it would feel

like a term of abuse, denoting manliness in body as well as temperament, but Caterina Sforza rejoices in it. She has never been one for simpering or blushing; as she soon discovered, a woman who finds herself
ruling over men is better served by fear than courtesy.

At thirty-six, she has outlived three husbands and given birth to
nine children, the last still a baby. She has survived more than one rebellion and her appetite for revenge is legendary. When the killers of
her first husband escaped the city, she punished their eighty-year-old
father instead. In a display of imaginative cruelty she had the sick old
man tied to a plank behind a horse, his head dangling free, then sent the
animal galloping around and around the city's cobblestoned piazza. But
while she is without mercy to those who oppose her, they say that when
the right man desires her she can be as seductive as a siren, with a cat-
purr voice and skin soft as sable fur. Such beauty, they say, comes from
her practice of the dark arts of nature: unguents, oils and pills which
she concocts herself, keeping her secrets in a book hidden under her pillows at night. She can make dark skin pale and black hair blond, and
whiten the foulest of teeth with a paste of ground marble and charcoal.
She has recipes to help make babies and others to wash unwanted ones
away. They say the bottles lined up along her shelves contain aphrodisi-
acs, poisons and perfumes, but that only she knows which ones are safe
and which lethal, for they carry no labels, and that when she starts to
prepare death for someone, the man or woman for whom it is intended
feels a terrible shiver run through them, as if they have already been
touched by the clammy cold of the grave.

Or so they say.

They say a great many things about Caterina Sforza. But though
there is much fun to be had making up gossip about bad women, the
most amazing fact of all is that quite a lot of what they say is true.

In the second week of November, as the Sistine Chapel plays host to
cardinals, diplomats and noble Roman families, all craning their necks
to witness the baptism of the Pope's beloved new grandchild, the
Virago of Imola and Forlì (who of course is not on the guest list) is busy
dictating a letter to be signed by her most prominent citizens.

"But, my lady, this is a petition offering the surrender of both your cities to the Holy Father, the Pope!"

"Well done, Signor Naldi. I always knew you could read, but it is your signature that I am after now," she says sweetly.

When she has all the signatures she needs, she takes the parchment into her dispensary and with a needle pricks dozens of holes, so fine as to be invisible, on to its surface. Then, putting on gloves, from a leather pouch she extracts a generous square of cream muslin, marred by a number of small marks and stains. She sprinkles lavender essence to counteract its rankness and then presses the parchment into it, carefully rolling it up in the material until it is encased within it. She slides the package into a cane tube and returns to her council chamber.

It will arrive too late for the papal christening, but then Caterina Sforza's gift is not intended for the baby.

"I swear I felt something; it was on the evening of the baptism. A deep shiver—tremor, more like—through my whole body. Burchard was standing next to me. He says my skin was white as chalk and my eyes went blank. He moved people away so I could get some air. I may have even lost my wits for an instant. That must have been when she was preparing it."

"It could be that you were drained from the festivities."

Cesare, who has as little time for witchcraft as he has for miracles, is suppressing his own exhaustion. He had been camped outside Bologna, days away from the march on Imola, when the news of an attempt on his father's life had reached him. He and Michelotto have ridden two days and nights to get to Rome, entering the city incognito and brought secretly into the Pope's private apartments. It is hardly the triumphant homecoming he had envisioned for himself after so long away.

"Whatever it was, the Virago wanted me dead. The gall of it! To try to poison the Pope." Now he is safe Alexander is rather enjoying the drama of it all.

"Desperation, Father, not gall. Even if this so-called assassin had delivered the petition, you would never have opened it yourself. It would have gone to one of the secretaries first."

"But they would have handed it on to me. The contagion would still have worked. She may be desperate, but the woman has never been a fool."

Certainly it had been a clever idea: a citizens' petition wrapped in cloth cut from the shroud of a man who had just died from the plague, the fabric still rich with his sweat and pus. Had it found its way into the Pope's hands it would have done the job most admirably: no foaming at the mouth, no fire in the throat or pitchforks in the gut, nothing indeed to give her away. Instead, a few days later, His Holiness would have developed a raging fever and the telltale eruptions of the skin. It would have seemed like the hand of God placed on a man's shoulder—for who can really know His ways, and why or how the plague singles out one over another? What everybody does know, however, is that with Alexander dead, the ambitions of his son would have crumbled into the dust.

"This would-be assassin. Where is he now?"

"He is residing in the dungeons of Sant' Angelo."

They had been lucky. The chosen messenger had turned out to be a lesser man than his mistress: far from a professional killer, Tommaso da Forlì was a lukewarm patriot who earned his living as a singer and musician in Jofré's small court orchestra. His mission had pressed so heavily upon him that the day the petition arrived he had blurted out a few wild details to a fellow viol player from his native city. Thirty-six hours later a supper concert at Jofré and Sancia's apartments had been interrupted by the Papal Guard and all too soon Tommaso was singing his heart out to quite different instruments.

"When your men have finished with him I want him."

"He'll be of no use to you. He has nothing more to say. He does not have a tongue anymore." Alexander's voice is almost compassionate. "It's a bad end for a man who earns his living from his voice."

"And Caterina Sforza—does she know she has failed?"

"Not yet. But I entertain both Venice and Florence tomorrow. Her treachery will be all over Italy by the time you reach her walls." He grins. "Perhaps we should 'uncover' a few more assassination attempts from Rimini or Faenza or Pesaro, eh? Though when she denies it I dare-say they will accuse us of making it up anyway."

He sits back against his great chair. They have talked their way into dawn. He closes his eyes, though there is little enough time for sleep now: the first ambassadors will be arriving soon.

Cesare sits, studying him. The year they have spent apart can be read in his face: lines etched deeper, jowls more sallow and sagging. He has heard that Giulia spends time out of Rome with her husband these days, and that the Pope no longer frets so much about getting her back.

"So, how is your health, Father?"

"Hm?" He opens his eyes.

"This . . . fainting moment that you described after the baptism. Have you had it before?"

"What? Is this some comment on my failing powers? I have never been better. I could ride out with you tomorrow if Rome didn't have such need of me." There is nothing like an intimation of weakness to invigorate him. "Ha—this . . . this Virago thinks she can take me out in a shroud. She has forgotten how she used to make eyes at me when she was a favorite of Pope Sixtus. Give her my regards when you blow her fortress to smithereens. Tell her I look forward to hosting her in my dungeons." And he laughs, rubbing his face to wake himself up further. "So, no more talk of illness and death. Since you are here, let us cele-brate birth. Tell me, when is your son due?"

"I am not sure. January, February."

"Ah ha! I knew it. Those first lances hit their mark. What will you call him?"

Cesare shrugs. He had taken pleasure enough in his wife when there was the time to do so, but a warm bed in France is now a long way away. "Cities I can give you, Father. When it comes to the sex of my children, you must speak to God."

"Of course it will be a boy. With that heat of conception how could it not? We will bring him and his mother to Rome and he can grow up with Rodrigo. Ah, my son, you should have seen him at the baptism: half of Rome watching and he didn't utter a cry, not a murmur, even when trembling old Cardinal Carafa almost drowned him in the font. But when they handed him to Paolo Orsini—as we agreed, so everyone could see the rapprochement of our two families—he took one look at his treacherous face and started to bellow. Didn't stop until they took him away. My God, ten days old and my grandson already knows who not to trust. There's a Borgia for you."

Cesare says nothing. While he has no illusions about the Orsini, he needs their men and weapons until he can raise enough of his own, and he has not ridden day and night to talk of babies, especially not one born of a Neapolitan father.

"And Lucrezia?" he asks after a while. "How is she?"

"Like the Madonna herself: radiant and serene. Though a little weak still from the birth."

"And this plot against you?"

"She knows nothing of it. I would not wish to worry her. You will visit her and the baby before you leave?"

"I have no time. Since you are safe I will sleep today and leave in the morning."

"She is your sister, Cesare. And the child is your nephew and my grandson."

"He is also the son of Naples." The words come out despite himself. It has suited him not to dwell on this matter, since the irritation it brings up in him is something he cannot easily control.

"If you feel so strongly, you need not meet Alfonso. I will have him here this evening to give you time alone," the Pope says firmly.

"That is not the point."

"Ah, Cesare, be realistic. This thing is not so simple."

"On the contrary, Father, nothing is simpler. King Federico refused us. Naples is our enemy. It will not survive this invasion. And when we have taken all the cities along the Via Emilia we will need to consolidate our gains with a marriage."

The Pope waves an impatient hand. "Your sister is a new mother and happy wife. For now I suggest we concentrate on the campaign. When that is done we can talk of all this again."

"Just so long as we do, Father," he says, rising abruptly to his feet. He is suddenly extremely angry. No doubt the tiredness has rattled his temper. "With your permission I will leave you now. I need to sleep."

"Very well. Cesare?"

He turns at the door.

"You do know that your sister will never forgive you."

"For what?"

"If . . . if she finds out you were here and left without seeing her," he says mildly.

In the end he cannot stay away. When he wakes it is dark again. He sends a message to the palace to make sure his brother-in-law is not there, but the Pope, as good as his word, has called him away.

Lucrezia is asleep. She contracted a mild fever after the birth and has been bled and cloistered, cared for by her women and two midwives. The one who is attending her now is a middle-aged Roman with firm hands and a reputation for holding her ground when it comes to protecting the mother's best interests.

"She is weak." She greets him outside the bedroom, putting herself between him and the door. "Sleep is a most precious medicine. Tomorrow would—"

"Tomorrow I will be halfway across Italy. I have no idea who you are, but if you do not stand away from the door I will remove you."

Later, when his reputation marks him as more feared than hated, she will recount this moment to others, explaining that she had intended to resist him but found herself stepping aside anyway, as if propelled against her will by the intensity of his gaze.

The bedroom is frescoed to resemble the fall of brightly colored curtains and lit by the night oil lamp, which makes it feel warm despite the cold. He steps up on to the platform of the carved bed that dominates the room. She is lying propped up on its pillows, her lips slightly open, waves of hair fanning out around her. The bleeding has left her very pale so that at first glance she might almost be sculpted from marble. Her face is thinner than he remembers, its puppy fat replaced by finer contours of jaw and cheekbones. He puts out a hand to touch her, to reassure himself that this is sleep rather than death, and as he does so she opens her eyes.

"Ha? Cesare?" she says with almost no surprise, and the childlike smile that crosses her face has no time to take in the complexities of what may or may not be to come. "Ah! I . . . I was dreaming that you were here. But . . . Is it really you?"

"Yes, sweet sister," he says. "It is I."

She frowns, closing her eyes, and for a second it seems that she might slip away again.

"Lucrezia?"

She rouses herself and he helps her upright on to the pillows. Her body is damp from the sweat of slumber. Her breasts have been bound tight to subdue the flow of milk, and as she settles she winces as if there are places inside her that are still wounded. A woman postpartum: it is not a state he knows nor has ever wanted to think about. He has an image of Alfonso in his place, moving his hands over this ripe flesh, knowing that it is his more than ever now. The fury is so sharp that he makes himself laugh to disguise it.

"You have been busy since I left."

"A little. But . . . but what are you doing here? I thought you were with the army? Is something wrong?"

"No, no. I had final business with Papà, that is all." He pauses. "Anyway. How could I stay away from you at such a time?"

"The baby?" she says quickly. "Rodrigo . . . is . . ."

"With your women. Safe, I am sure."

"I'll call for them to bring him."

"No. No. Not yet. It is you I came to see." He leans over and pushes a lock of damp hair from her forehead. Does she flinch just a fraction? "So, tell me, what were you dreaming?"

"I . . . oh, oh it was horrible. You were with Father in the Room of Mysteries and you were both laughing, laughing so loudly, and I came with the baby in my arms, but Papà said that I must only talk French because that was all you spoke now. So I did, except you didn't seem to recognize me. And when I showed you the child . . . you said you could not touch him because he was a . . . and you used some word which I didn't know." She smiles apologetically. "When the milk came in, I could not sleep for the pain so they gave me syrup, and it brought on strange dreams . . . Two nights ago I dreamed that that mad Turkish prince, Djem, came back from the dead and cut off Father's head with his curved sword." She shivers. "They say after birth women's minds are prone to such things."

"And they are too free with their potions," he says, pleased to find he is not singled out. "If I took everything prescribed for me I would suffer more from the cure than the disease."

"What? Is your affliction returned?"

"No, no, I am better."

"Still, you must be careful, Cesare. One of Papà's cardinals died from an excess of treatment, they say."

"So I have heard. But he and I have different physicians."

The story had reached as far as Gaspare Torella in Milan: it seems the cardinal had been in such agonies that he had risked a new remedy brought in by some Portuguese doctor. But for every moment of relief it gave him, it added tenfold to his suffering later, and he had died screaming. Torella has been involved in a battle of words ever since. Cesare, well for so long now that he is convinced he is cured, is more interested in the vacant place in the College left by the death. War is a costly business and cardinals' hats are a reliable form of income. "But we are talking of you, not me. You are too thin. They are not feeding you."

"Oh! Far from it. I am like a stuffed goose for the table."

"You look tired."

"There is little enough wonder in that," she says, laughing now. "I have labored. I must tell you, Cesare, Eve's sin is indeed a great burden. I don't think many men could bear such pain easily."

The image of Caterina Sforza with her skirts up against her breastplate flickers through his mind. "Ah, but then you are a Borgia. And we can bear anything. I have missed you, sister."

"And I you, brother. So. Will you see him? . . . The baby, I mean."
She rushes on in case there is any misunderstanding. "Papà says he
looks like you. I will call them to bring him now."

And her face is so eager that he cannot refuse. "Quickly then. I ride
at dawn and there is much to do."

But now he is leaving she suddenly wants him to stay, to use their
closeness to try to repair the damage that she knows lies underneath.

"Papà showed me a likeness of your wife. She is most lovely, yes?
Does she adore you?"

"I think she is not dissatisfied."

"And you will be a father soon too. You must bring her to Rome.
Then we can all be together. The children will be—"

But there is no time, for the door opens and the matron comes in.
She approaches the other side of the great bed, getting her own back on
Cesare by not letting him too close. She lays the bundle in Lucrezia's
arms.

The baby is deeply asleep. He has been in the world for eighteen
days and is still greedy for the blind containment of the womb.

"Isn't he beautiful?" she whispers.

Cesare has never seen a baby so close to birth and he is disconcerted
by the contrast of flesh and fragility. The swaddling holds him fast,
framing his face. His eyelids read like faint lines drawn on to the skin.
There is a sprinkling of tiny white spots around his squashed nose and
his lips are puckered, as if in disapproval. As ugly as a newborn pig, he
thinks, even as his hand goes out to touch him.

"Can you see the resemblance?" she adds teasingly. "At the baptism
he was as silent as an angel until they gave him to Paolo Orsini and then
he yelled his head off. Papà said—"

"I know what Papà said."

"You may hold him if you want. He will not wake," she says, gently
offering him up to him. But Cesare has already pulled his hand away.

"Not now. I have a war to fight and I should have left already." He
leans over the bed, avoiding the child and kissing her on the forehead.

She closes her eyes to hide her disappointment.

Chapter 45

LONG BEFORE THERE IS ANYTHING TO SEE, THEY CAN HEAR IT. DIStant thunder. The men in the fields pull the oxen to a halt, putting down the forks and spades, clambering across the half-turned earth until they are closer to the paved road, though not so close as to attract attention. The women stay where they are, calling to the smaller children, making sure they are safe behind their skirts before they too lift their heads and squint into the distance.

The sharp-sighted now make out a blur on the western horizon. They wait patiently as the rumble grows and the mass gains shape and definition. First they see the phalanx of steel horses glint and shine through rising dust as they march toward the morning sun. The thunder breaks into a mass of individual sounds, horseshoe metal on stone, animals snorting, steel plates clashing: the noises of war. The metal giants, horse and man fused together by armor, ride six abreast, line after line, too many to count. A few children, wide-eyed in wonder, shout out and are cuffed into silence by their parents.

Behind the horses come the pike carriers, the first rows picking their way through fresh piles of dung. They keep the same pace as the cavalry despite the weight of their great timber staves; impossibly tall men with matted hair falling onto leather jerkins, worn pouches and water bottles slung around their shoulders. Now it is the turn of the infantry and regular foot soldiers. Each man carries the same rations as the Roman legions did when they tramped this road fifteen hundred years ago—half a gallon of watered wine and a quarter-loaf of bread, all bought at market prices, fair and square: generous enough to have become gossip; generous enough to tempt the young in the fields to think of throwing down their spades and joining them. Fathers hold on to their sons a little tighter as they pass.

They keep on coming and coming until the great road of the Via Emilia is filled both in front and behind as far as the eye can see. With the kitchen carts and supply mules the mood changes: drivers whoop and laugh, big leering smiles as if they have been at their own wine supply. Most of what they say makes no sense; French, Italian, Spanish, German, Gascon; there are so many tongues glued together here that a new diced, spliced language has been created from them all, its vocabulary sufficient to the needs of war: fighting, eating, defecating, sleeping, plundering.

After a while the women turn away, back to the earth. It is an army. They have seen it before and they will see it again. The men are waiting for the guns.

They are buried in the midst of more infantry, mounted on carts pulled by teams of horses as strong as any oxen and able to move twice as fast to keep up with the pace of the army.

"Boom. Bom. Bard."

The chant is a drumbeat in time to the footfalls of the gunners who march beside the carts, their dress as black as the cannons.

"Boom. Bom. Bard."

The first gun is the biggest: La Tiverina, named after the great river in Rome, nine feet long with a mouth wide enough to spit out stone balls bigger than a man's head. They say that when the guns have all been shot and a city taken, the commanders send in special soldiers to find where the cannonballs have fallen, scraping off the blood and the brains and heaving them back on to the carts to use them another time. Thrift and death: men who work the land understand the combination better than most.

"Boom. Bom. Bard."

The voices roll on under the wheels of the carts. A few of the younger men at the side of the road join in, as if the repetition of the words might ward off the terror. They are still chanting as the gunners disappear into the distance and the final carts clatter by, accompanied by a crowd of hangers-on: old men, boys too young to fight and a bevy of scrawny women, yelling invitations to the laborers, their language and gestures cruder than any of the soldiers' before them.

The Borgia army is marching the Via Emilia on its way to war.

By the time the cavalry reaches the city of Imola, the scouts have already announced its arrival to the town's custodians and picked a site close to where the towers of its fortress back up against the city walls. The latrines are dug, the cooking pots are belching the smells of stewed mutton and in the commander's enclave the wine has been poured when a small delegation arrives.

They are shown into Cesare's official tent, sparsely decorated with trestle table, chairs and stools. He is alone except for Michelotto, his shadow now but always at a slight distance, and the veteran leader of the French force, Yves d'Alegre.

The man who leads the handful of citizens has a clean-cut face and is fashionably dressed, a silk sash over his velvet jerkin and a plume of feathers in his cap. His boots, however, are filthy.

"I am Giovanni Sassatelli," he says. "I am—"

"I know who you are, Sassatelli," Cesare cuts in easily. "Imola has no older nor finer family than yours. If we are to go to war to bring the city back under the papal banner, then it will be my privilege to fight you."

Sassatelli nods in acknowledgment of the compliment. When a man is about to swallow humble pie it helps to have some honor to ease its passage down the throat. "There will be no need for fighting, Duke Valentino. We are here to offer you the surrender of the city."

Cesare is careful not to alter his expression. "And what moves the good citizens of Imola to make such a wise decision?"

"We have heard of your magnanimity, your sagacity, your fairness. And we wish to commend ourselves into your hands."

"And your ruler? What does she think of this generous gift on her behalf?"

"Caterina Sforza left for Forlì ten days ago, putting the city in the hands of myself and the governor, Dionigi da Naldo."

"Ah yes. Also a fine fighter." Cesare pauses. "He does not come with you?"

"No. As governor he is also the castellan of the fortress." He hesitates. "The duchess has his children as hostage."

"Ah." Cesare glances toward his French counterpart. "Then we must see that his surrender does not bring them to any harm. Our guns will be in place by the day after tomorrow. We will need some local knowledge as to which walls are the weakest."

"There is a master carpenter who worked on the refurbishments a few years ago. I . . . I have spoken to him already."

"Excellent."

"You should know, my lord, of Imola's great distress over the plot against the Holy Father. It was none of our making. We have not flourished under Sforza rule."

"I know that, Sassatelli." Cesare gets up and puts his hand on the man's shoulder as he guides him out. "Rest assured I have not come to replace one tyranny with another. You are brought into the hands of the Church and there will be fair government here from now on, as well as opportunities for a fighter like yourself to earn glory elsewhere." And he offers him his most charming smile.

Returning to the table, he notes a wry grin on the Frenchman's face.

"What? You would prefer slaughter?"

"Certainly not." D'Alegre waves his hand. "I am enjoying myself too much. Truly, my dear Duke, there is no better country to make war in than Italy. Everyone is so . . . so reasonable when it comes to avoiding battle."

"You think it is a lack of courage?"

In reply, d'Alegre purses his lips, as if to prevent himself from agreeing.

"I think rather that they see life for what it is and know when a ruler isn't worth fighting for."

"Or that the next one will be better," the Frenchman says, knowing how fond his king has grown of this confident young warrior. "Nevertheless, what is good for the people is not always good for the army."

It is a mark of Cesare's passion for his new career that he does not take offense at d'Alegre's patronizing attitude. He knows that this veteran of the French campaign in Italy is aggrieved at having to share the field with an inexperienced twenty-four-year-old. He has gone out of his way to show him respect, engaging him in war talk, drinking in his stories of bombardments and battles, which he then revisits move by move in his head while others sleep. He has learned a great deal. But not all things need to be taught. The mood of the army is clear enough. He would like to see action as much as the next man—more, perhaps, since he knows he has something to prove—but he also has his father's nose for politics, and with so many cities to be taken in so little time, stealth is as wise a strategy as glory. The last few days have brought rumors that the defeated Ludovico Sforza is planning a return into Italy. If he finds the troops to support him the king will call his army back and the Borgias' great plan will have to wait.

Imola does not take long. On the carpenter's information, the north wall of the fortress is breached within a day and its governor, da Naldo, having failed to receive the troops he asks for, surrenders and takes up the offer of service with the Borgias. Should he find his children slaughtered, he will at least have a way to take revenge: family is one thing that is always worth killing for.

With the city and its leading families in pledged obedience to the Pope and Borgia rule, the army moves on to Forlì. It is close to Christmas and the Virago is ready for them, embedded in the great fortress of Ravaldino inside the city walls. Safe in the knowledge that they will never again have to face her wrath, the nobles of the town ride out to offer formal surrender. The soldiers, driven on by the prospect of warm beds, strike a fast pace and arrive ahead of the artillery.

The triumph of entry is marred by hellish weather: lashing rains churning the streets into liquid mud, with intermittent artillery fire from the battlements of the fortress chasing them on. Discipline holds while the troops are billeted but by the time the artillery arrives the atmosphere is sour. As usual it is the Swiss and Gascon forces that set the pace, refusing to pay for what they can take for free. Six months on the road and it is Christmas after all. The first cry of plunder is followed by a wave of violence which d'Alegre does not try hard enough to stop.

"Who do they think they are, damn them!" Cesare vents his rage at Michelotto. "I gave the leaders of the town my promise that this would not happen."

"What does d'Alegre say?"

"What do you think he says? 'It is most unforetuneight.'" Cesare pouts his lips in imitation. " 'But it is how souldjiers behave in war.' I tell you, if we didn't need them so much I would plunder them myself. Imagine the satisfaction it brings *her,* watching her citizens slaughtered for deserting her."

"Ah, if she's as canny as they make out, she'll be more interested in the size of the cannons rolling up to her walls." He grins in his inimitably ugly way. "You know what soldiers say about her? That because she's got teeth inside her cunt the only way to enjoy her is with an iron prick and stone balls."

It is one of many obscenities circulating, some of them written down and sent by slingshot over the walls. Whether or not the lady reads them it is hard to know. She is a law unto herself. Her former citizens speak of a palace built around the keep with vaulted ceilings and tiled floors, a summer loggia frescoed with paintings of vines and surrounded by fruit trees and a herb garden for her precious cosmetics and unguents. Every twilight she parades herself for the world to see, walking the battlements between the towers, the setting sun making a fiery halo around her wild loose hair, lighting up her armor and her unsheathed battle sword as she goes. The artillerymen setting up the guns below follow her progress in a kind of awe. The French commanders, weaned on stories of combat and chivalry, are no better. Those hoping for a glimpse beneath her skirts are disappointed. Her children—even the youngest, barely a year old—have been dispatched to safety and she is no longer, it seems, interested in making more.

Before the bombardment starts in earnest Cesare makes an attempt at negotiation.

"It's a waste of time. She'll never surrender," Michelotto says.

"I know that. I'm not doing it for her."

At an agreed time, and dressed with the scarlet colors of Valentinois over his chain mail, he rides to the edge of the moat in front of the ramparts. Behind him, the troops stand eager for whatever entertainment is to come.

"The humble fortress of Forlì is honored to be the object of your ambitions, illustrious duke." A melodious voice, ringing out through a speaking-trumpet from the turret above the drawbridge, reaches past Cesare into the army behind. "What would you have from us?"

"The surrender of yourself and your men to His Holiness the Pope and the Church." Cesare's voice unaided is loud enough to be heard by all without amplification.

"And in return?"

"In return I guarantee you safe passage to join your children and an invitation to your brave troops for their further employment in my army."

"It is an honorable offer." The silence that follows enhances the theater of the moment. "Perhaps we might discuss it in person."

The drawbridge groans into life, cranking its way away from the wall and falling forward by juddering degrees. The horse whinnies slightly as it looms above them, but Cesare has judged the distance accurately and both rider and mount hold their spot as the wood slams to the ground, an arm's length or so from its hooves.

A view opens into the fortress, revealing an empty courtyard, not a single soldier in sight. Now comes the lady herself, striding out on to the drawbridge, skirts the same scarlet color as the sash flowing over her breastplate, bare arms despite the winter frost and waves of chestnut hair over her metal shoulders. She stops almost halfway across, planting her feet firmly and holding out her arms in a gesture of welcome, aimed as much at the whole army as at him.

"So here I am, Duke. Ready to talk," she shouts into the wind. "Won't you join me? I have had many hours of pleasurable intercourse with men even younger than yourself."

Behind him the men roar their approval. Italians, Spaniards, French, Gascons, whatever their nationality, there is only one man commanding them right now and they are waiting to see what he will do next. He lets them wait. Then slowly, each move conducted with exaggerated grace, he dismounts, running his hand down the horse's neck as if to communicate something, before turning and stepping up on to the drawbridge to face her. How far is there between them? Twenty, thirty paces? He is in the forest again, attention focused on the dance between hunter and hunted.

"Duke Valentino, I see your leg is even more shapely than they say."

She takes a further few steps toward him, smiling broadly. He does the same. They stand in silence. Not close enough yet. What next?

She moves again. Three steps now. He mirrors her move.

Suddenly she lets out a girlish cry. The jolt of the rising bridge does little to disturb him since he has anticipated it already. She is turning almost before it happens, the descending incline between her and the fortress entrance easily negotiable as she runs. Above her the battlements are suddenly full of soldiers, yelling and screaming. But he is not listening. There is a familiar ringing in his ears as he too turns: he has nine—at best ten—paces to judge both the angle of the jump and the gap as it grows wider.

The horse, as bidden, has turned its back to the moat, ready for him, so that he will land the right way in the saddle. He propels himself into the air. There can be no mistake here, to enter the water would in its own way be as disastrous as being taken prisoner. How many times has he practiced such trick leaps, from windows to courtyards below or one moving horse to another? But he has never done this before, and whatever the skill, there is always risk. Why else would one do it?

It is closer than he would choose. He lands clumsily half on, half off the saddle, the jolt shocking his body deep into his groin as he grabs the mane to right himself. The horse rears up in protest, but he is safe now and can make a spectacle of it. What is imperfect to him still looks superhuman to others. The screaming and cheering from the bank is deafening and soon both sides are at it: howling across the water at each other like packs of rapid dogs.

As he rides past d'Alegre and Bailly de Dijon, the head of the Gascon force, Cesare raises his hand nonchalantly. The citizens of Forlì will sleep more securely in their beds tonight. Plunder may have its attractions, but for soldiers looking for action it is nothing to the excitement of the enemy goading them on.

Chapter 46

In ROME, THE YEAR 1500 BEGINS BENIGNLY WITH BRIGHT SKIES AND a crystal frost. In the south of the city, the paths and wasteland around the cathedral of St. John Lateran are crammed with pilgrims, ready to greet the Pope and his beloved daughter, Lucrezia, Duchess of Bisceglie, who rides in place of honor inside a cavalcade of churchmen and nobles. The service they attend in the cavernous old church of Constantine marks the official start of the great jubilee year. Later, as darkness falls, the battlements of Castel Sant' Angelo are lit up by wheels of fizzing, spitting fireworks that squeal their way into the night sky, exploding over the city like showers of comets.

Two hundred and fifty miles to the northeast, outside the fortress of Forlì, another kind of firework display is about to begin. It is still dark when the boys from the supply carts hand out small beads of tallow to the men of the artillery. The helpers and shot handlers press them quickly into their ears, securing them with rag bandannas to soak up the worst of the sweat to come. The gunners are more careful, playing with them like rosary beads, softening them between the pads of their fingers so that they will mould better into the ear. A few offer a fast prayer to St. Lucy, the virgin martyr of the blind who carries her eyes before her on a tray, a reminder of the torture she suffered before execution. Such is the hatred for this new mobile artillery, raining death from the skies with no respect for the skill or courage of the men it crushes, that captured gunners have been known to have their eyes gouged out as punishment. With their hearing already damaged by the blasts, they become walking dead men.

Now, though, their sight is the sight of the guns, accurate enough to pound any fortress wall to smithereens. The cannons are lowered into position, the powder poured in. The balls are rolled into the breech—the rounder they come, the better they fly—then rammed into position hard against the wad which covers the charge, while the gunner pours more powder into the touch-hole. A group of young boys stand ready with burning torches: the only heat in the bitter cold of a breaking dawn. As daylight stains the eastern sky, the first boy hands a taper to the first gunner, who lights the charge, waiting to check that it has caught, and then moves out of range fast in readiness for the violent recoil of the cannon.

The roar rips through the morning silence. Then another. And another. By the time the tenth cannon is fired, the first is already halfway to reloading, men shoving the sticks with swabs of soaked cloth deep into the bore to clean the sides and extinguish any lingering sparks, making it safe for the gunpowder again.

Soon the iron dragons are all belching fire and the air is filled with thunder and the screaming smash of stone on stone. From the top of the towers the smaller fixed guns blaze back, but their range is too short and with no room for maneuver they are more vulnerable to direct hits. The smoke from the cannons merges with the exploding clouds of debris. In the perpetual twilight they create it becomes impossible for even the most sharp-sighted gunners to assess the damage.

The bombardment goes on unabated until early afternoon, when a halt is called to bring up further ammunition and the men, now black as their guns, rest awhile. From their vantage point on an elevated tower to the side of the artillery, Cesare and the other commanders wait as the air clears. The shattered outline of the battlements to the left of the drawbridge comes into view. There is no one in sight, though as their ears adjust to the silence, a soundscape of human shouts and cries becomes audible. The top of one tower is in ruins, the guns disabled, small fires breaking out everywhere. The walkway of the battlement and the walls beneath are holed and pockmarked. But there is nothing as conclusive as a breach. Cesare turns to d'Alegre and Vitelli. They nod. As the first men emerge up on the tower, buckets of water in hand, he sends the order down the line for firing to begin again. This time it is only darkness that stops them.

The fortress, for so many years impenetrable, takes another full day of punishment. Then on Sunday morning, as snow begins to fall, in a single thunder crash a great section of the outer southern wall collapses into the moat, the chunks of masonry and debris throwing up a makeshift path halfway across the water. On Cesare's side the rafts are ready. The men cram onto them, the Swiss and Gascon troops pushing their way to the fore, punting across the water and clambering over the stones, so that before the remaining guns inside can offer any resistance the breach is taken.

Wave upon wave of men flood into the fortress, their hunger for victory in bloody proportion to how long they have been kept waiting for a fight. Corpses pile at their feet. Inside the fortified keep where Caterina and her officers have taken refuge, the order is given to set fire to the stores and magazines. But in the chaos that follows, the smoke and fire blind the defenders more than the attackers and the Gascon soldiers and swordsmen are soon storming their way in, wielding a battering ram against the door of the spiral staircase. Above, Caterina Sforza and her entourage are barricaded in, waiting.

The rest of the army now streams over the lowered drawbridge, cavalry first, Cesare and d'Alegre riding at the head. The temperature is dropping rapidly as the horses move through flurries of sleet and snow, picking their way over bodies and rubble. But once inside the keep, Cesare finds himself frustrated: the door to the prisoner's room, though smashed open, is blocked by a dozen bloodstained Gascon fighters.

The Bailly de Dijon, their leader, hurries forward to greet him, bracing himself for the fury that will follow.

"I . . . It is the rule of war, Duke Valentino. It was my troops who took the citadel, and the Duchess of Forlì has already surrendered to my own constable on the understanding that she would be a prisoner of Fra—"

"Ah, you wouldn't dare," Cesare shouts in his face. "I lead this army and you and your poxy constables are fighting for me."

"Sire, we are Frenchmen first, and our loyalty is to our—"

"Duke Valentino," d'Alegre, at Cesare's side, interrupts smoothly.

"As a great noble of France you know it is military law that a woman cannot be taken as a prisoner of war. The Bailly de Dijon's men only hold the lady in the name of King Louis. Under whose protection she now resides."

"'Protection!' God's blood. Officers' plunder, more like." Cesare gives a bitter laugh. "You want money. A ransom. That's what this is about." Even d'Alegre looks sheepish. Had they been planning it from the start? No wonder they had fought so hard to be the first in. "I had forgotten—you are an expert on such things. It was you who took 'care' of Giulia Farnese and my aunt when they were on their way back to Rome before the invasion, right?"

D'Alegre shrugs. He is not to be embarrassed by this. "It was my pleasure as well as my duty to accept their surrender and keep them safe under the king's jurisdiction until I could deliver both ladies back to His Holiness. Safe—and very much sound."

"Oh yes. So—would you say this 'lady' upstairs is worth more or less than them?"

Three thousand ducats. That's what his father had paid. He remembers it well because the joke on the streets was that it was a cheap price for the Pope's courtesan; implying that, in his chivalry, it was d'Alegre who had been robbed. No doubt he intends to make up for it now. You laugh at us behind our backs, Cesare thinks. But I wonder if it is as hard as we laugh at you. He turns back to the Gascon leader.

"Six thousand."

"What?"

"I'll take her off your hands for six thousand ducats."

Just behind the Bailly de Dijon a man, evidently the constable himself, splutters, his eyes wide as saucers.

"I . . . I don't know—"

"Very well, five thousand."

"But—"

"It goes down with each refusal. Be careful. You had better be sure that when this reaches the king's ears he does not come to take my side over yours. Five. Or do I go lower?"

The head of the Gascon troops glances anxiously to d'Alegre, but it is clear the negotiations are over. The Bailly de Dijon steps aside and Cesare's men throw themselves up the staircase. There are raised voices and the floorboards thump. A chorus of women starts howling, a high-pitched ululating, as if murder is taking place, and the struggle grows louder as the men stagger down the spiral stairs, holding a screaming, kicking, flailing Caterina Sforza between them.

"Scum bastards," she screams as she is dragged across the room. "I surrendered to the King of France, and no one else. You will all rot in hell for this dishonor."

The nobles drop their eyes. Though ransom is a valued perk of war, the erotic possibilities of chivalry that this magnificent Amazon has aroused have become an open secret in the tents of the French commanders: as if such a woman might be persuaded to give freely what others would have to forcibly take.

She is still screaming as they pull her out of the door.

The celebrations go on into the night, the thumping pulse of victory running through everyone. The men who took the breach are exultant with it, each with his own near-death story to tell, some showing off wounds, the narcotic of battle numbing them to injuries which will bring agony by the morning. Cesare moves through the makeshift camp, talking and laughing with the troops, embracing the soot-stained gunners and their handlers, eager to relive the beauty of the bombard-ment, edging it toward legend with each retelling.

By the time he and his guards ride back into the town, it is deep night and the streets are empty except for a few drunken stragglers, the coating of snow now freezing into ice. The quiet after so many days of deafening cannon fire feels unnerving.

The woman who once ruled two cities is held in a boarded-up room on the top floor of his billeted palace. Cesare does not bother to wash or change his clothes. He cannot remember when he last slept. But the conquest is not finished yet.

The next morning his receiving rooms swarm with well-wishers, town leaders, French nobles, even a few of his own condottieri, each man nursing a curiosity greater than his hangover. A dawn dispatch rider is already halfway to the Apennines with news of the spectacular victory, but another stands waiting for whatever further details might be worth the extra journey. The Pope's appetite for every breath his son takes is well known; but when the exploits are so glorious, the longer the wait, the better the story.

When the door to Cesare's room finally opens, it is not the duke but his most faithful fellow Spaniard who comes out, closing the door firmly behind him.

"Gentlemen, gentlemen! I am to bid you welcome and good-morning from Duke Valentino, ruler of Imola and Forlì. He is grateful for your good wishes and sends them back manyfold. But at present he is busy on dispatches to his father. And when they are finished he will rest for a while. It has been a . . . a very busy night," he says carefully, and a leering cheer goes up from the men. "As I am sure you can imagine."

"And how 'busy' was it for the Virago?" Vitellozzo Vitelli's voice rises up from the rest. If a man's prowess is to be judged on numbers alone, Vitelli would be more lauded than he is; but more often than not these days he is plagued with blotches over his face and sword-stabbing pains through his whole body. War booty. It brings with it all manner of riches. "Come on, Michelotto. You can't send us away empty-handed. There are ten thousand men out there who risked their lives to make it a memorable night. Give us something to offer them back."

Michelotto shrugs. "One does not like to sully reputations," he says, playing the courtier with more verve than usual. "But the duke did have something to say when we met earlier this morning." And he re-peats the words to them now.

There is a howl of laughter around the room. Oh, this is exactly what they wanted to hear. Michelotto watches the vicarious pleasure it brings. There will be no need of a dispatch rider now. It will be halfway around Italy by the end of the week.

"I couldn't care less, but you have to give them something," he had said as Cesare had flung himself on the bed, an avalanche of sleep ready to engulf him.

"What? Testimony? Is that what they want? So—tell them that the duchess defended her fortress better than she did her virtue."

He had closed his eyes and within seconds was asleep. Yes, Michelotto thought, "her fortress better than her virtue." That will go down well. Though knowing his master as well as he does, he wonders how far it is from the whole truth.

Chapter 47

How could it not have been a contest? Anything else would have been an insult to them both.

According to the guards, she had spent the first hours shouting abuse, hammering at the door, demanding that they bring her candles, food and clean linen, that they light a fire against the cold. If they had been less frightened of their own commander they might have done it, for there was no doubt she was used to being obeyed. Eventually, when she had got nothing, she fell silent.

She is not, however, asleep.

As he locks the door behind him and lifts up the lamp to scatter the darkness, she is facing him, sitting in a chair by the empty grate, the covers dragged from the bed and draped around her shoulders like a grand cape. She seems to be inviting study. Her great mane of hair has been tamed, twirled and knotted over itself high at the back of her head, a few stray curls falling free. Her forehead is high, the hair plucked away in current fashion, a network of fine lines running across it marking out her age. Her eyebrows arch perfectly over deep-set eyes, and her lips are full and fleshy. Though her skin is streaked with dirt, her cheeks have a blush to them, as if she has just pinched them to bring up the color. Could it be that she has made an effort for him?

Her breastplate is lying carelessly discarded on the floor halfway across the room. He imagines her breasts without it: creamy and ample, like soft, hanging fruit. He sets the lamp carefully on the table. The hardening of his prick cuts through his tiredness. There is no question as to what will happen between them. She has lost and he will write his victory on her body. He thinks of the parchment petition, rank with the plague, sent to his father, the drawbridge juddering upward as she skipped laughing away from him, the Frenchmen's eager faces as they argued for her. Five thousand ducats: Jews' bollocks, she is the most expensive whore he will ever have. Anger sharpens his lust as he throws his cloak off and moves toward her.

But she is already inside his head as well as his loins.

"Don't come near me," she growls, no melody to woo suitors. "Whatever rights you think you have, they do not include my body."

Only, as she says it, part of the cover slips down to reveal a naked shoulder, pale and firm.

No one thrives on fear. Or if they do, then it is not fear anymore. Caterina Sforza has felt it enough times in her life to know that it is what you do with it that counts. She has witnessed its impact on others, has watched grown men fall to the floor in front of her, sobbing like children as they beg for mercy. The first time it happened the sheer turmoil it triggered in her meant that she offered the man his life. Eighteen months later, when he was up to his neck in another plot, she had thanked him for curing her of such female weakness. If cruelty was what was called for to survive, then it was cruelty she would cultivate. After his public execution, his body cut down from the noose while still vital enough to register the agony of dismemberment, she had walked back into the palace to play games with her children. It was he who was suffering, not her. She did not feel anything. She was simply doing what had to be done.

As she is here, now, in this room. She knows as well as he does what must come next, has played the whore often enough to be familiar with the part. Her first husband disgusted her so much she had taken to closing her eyes the minute he came near her. When he had drunk enough to give him the courage, he would hit her to make her notice him. Her humiliation had been part of his pleasure. As his enemies had sliced him into bits and thrown his corpse into the square, there was a part of her that was cheering them on. But instead she had played the devastated wife, weeping and pleading, giving herself enough time to think through a strategy of survival. Doing what had to be done. Survival. It has become her speciality.

She has learned everything there is to know about this pretty young man. She has heard the stories of iron in his soul: his greediness for greatness so that no triumph will ever be enough. She knows why he is here: that he needs to take the city all over again, this time on his own. And though of course he will win, it must not be given too easily. What glory would there be in that? Her challenge is not to be humiliated: to judge the line between resistance and surrender and to give him what he craves without him realizing that his lust is being managed. That way, though he may take her body, she will have a kind of victory in defeat.

Cesare is so close now that he can smell her, the scent of sweat, and something else, something stale, putrid almost. A duchess without her perfume bottles is no sweeter than a common whore. The idea excites him intensely. How could it not? He rips away the remainder of the cloth and her bodice and chemise rip with it, freeing her breasts, which, just as he imagined, fall full and pendulous.

She cries out, pulling up her hands to cover herself, she who has gone half naked to the world when it suits her. How dare she? Now he hits her, the back of his ringed hand hard across her face. She falls halfway off the chair, her head turning sharply with the blow, so that he cannot see the light in her eyes as she recovers herself, biting down on her lip to accentuate the damage. When she turns back blood is welling from her mouth.

"I am a duchess of the Sforza family," she says, her voice low and trembling. "You dare to touch me again and I will scream your new city awake with your cowardice and shame."

"Scream away, lady. When they realize it is you, they will be shouting for more."

He grabs her hands, lifting her up out of the chair, kicking it away and slamming her against a wall. Even if she was fighting with all her strength now she would not be able to free herself. He pins both hands above her head using only one of his own.

"Nooo!" she howls. He uses his free hand to hit her again.

"What? Has the Virago of Forlì lost her appetite for the fight?" he says, using his other hand to wrench up her skirts, tucking them into her belt so that her belly and legs are free. "Not got the stomach for it anymore?"

But, at the same time as he knows he has the better of her, she is already ahead of him. I have you now, she is thinking. You can't help yourself. Oh yes, I have you now.

She clasps her legs fast together so that he has to work for it. As he separates her thighs and finds her, plunging his fingers inside, she hears him growl his triumph. There it is: the sound of desire, fat and mindless, melting iron into garden-variety male madness.

"Why don't you put your prick in me and find out?" she says fiercely, looking straight at him. And his desire is so naked that just for that second she allows the triumph to show in her eyes.

She would swallow the words back if she could, for she feels their impact immediately, sees him freeze, watches as his dazed eyes focus into something else. She has lost him. His fingers slip out of her. She cries out, closing her eyes and struggling. But this time he does not hit her.

Instead he is staring at her, an expression close to disgust on his face. He brings his cupped fingers up in front of him. They are black and wet, the soot of the guns stained with menstrual blood. Of course! That had been the smell: Amazons in battle have no time for clean linen. He lets go of her, her arms falling suddenly free, as if there might be some kind of infection in her very touch.

She stands there, breathing heavily, trying frantically for a way to bring him back. But with warriors as finely matched as they are, there is no second chance. With the lust draining away, he looks at her again, as if for the first time. He sees a mouth like a bloody open wound, breasts slack with their own weight, the spreading flesh of abdomen and upper legs, stretched and sagging—the impact of decades of motherhood. The streak of dried blood staining her inner thighs matches a knot of bulging veins that run down the side of one leg deep into her calf. She might pamper herself with all manner of bleaches and ointments, but there is nothing to heal the ravages of multiple pregnancies and births on a woman's flesh.

"Sweet Jesus," he says. "Look at you. You have the body of a sow. No wonder you don't lift up your skirts in public anymore."

She laughs, eager to show how much she is immune to him, but it comes out more like a cry. The injury is deeper than anything his prick could have inflicted. She launches herself at him, but he is ready and will have none of it. He meets her halfway, slamming her back across the room, and she loses her balance, falling heavily.

"What witch potions did you give your husbands that they could stay hard for you?" he says, spitting on the floor next to her as if to get any taste of her out of him.

It is her misfortune that this moment should trigger such a black memory in him. A certain prostitute during a night of whoring and drinking in Naples. It had become a contest of stamina: him, Alfonso and other nobles showing the papal legate a good time. The Borgias like to fuck. That's what they had been told. They also like to win. Maybe they had been told that too. The last one had been his. The last and the best, they had promised. A legend in the city. The sweetest snatch, just don't look in her eyes. The devil is in there. She had been propped against a wall, on cushions in the darkness, cooing to him in Spanish, the voice siren-sweet. He was so drunk that he almost couldn't get it in. When he did he found himself inside a marshland, big as a flooded tomb. As he pulled himself off her in disgust he reached for the lamp. She was a hag: a million years old with skin like a cow's hide, and when she grinned she had no teeth. It had given him such a fright. He, who was never frightened. Outside in the street, the others were falling over themselves laughing.

"Did she smile at you? She is a sibyl as well as a whore. If she smiled you are Fate's favorite. A man to whom everything will be given. She does not often smile, my lord legate."

He had laughed it off. God knows, he had done worse to friends. Next morning they all had sore heads and little memory. But Alfonso had gone out of his way to make sure he was all right. Weeks later, when the pain and the boils had started, though it could have been one of dozens of women, he had known it was her. God damn the House of Aragon. How many reasons does he have to hate his brother-in-law?

"Five thousand ducats, for a sack of skin and a worn-out snatch," he says flatly. He thinks of the bodies disemboweled, the eighty-year-old man's head splitting open as it bounced off the cobbles, two husbands chopped up into bits and dumped like trash. For what? This overripe flesh? It doesn't even warrant kicking.

"If you still want it so much, maybe the jailers in Castel Sant' Angelo will help you out." He moves toward the door, picking up his cloak. He has got what he came for. "As long as they blow out the light first."

"You think you can do it any better than me?" she screams after him. "You won't last a season here. They are traitors to their fingertips, all of them, and they will hate you faster than they hated me."

He does not answer. Her fury follows him down the stairs.

But when he wakes, two days later, one of his first acts is to call together the leading families of the city and announce a freeing of all political prisoners, a reduction in taxes and subsidies from the papal coffers to finance the rebuilding of the fortress and the damaged town. Defeating one's enemy: it can be done in all manner of ways.

Chapter 48

THE VICTORY PARADE THAT BRINGS DUKE VALENTINO AND HIS army into Rome takes place in the last week of February. Carefully picked by the Pope, it is a wondrous piece of timing: jubilee fever combined with Carnival to provide a captive audience of thousands of pilgrims and revellers, plus a flood of villagers who have swelled the ranks of the army as it approaches the northern gate, eager to join in the largesse that accompanies victory. The last time a Borgia son had come back from war, there had been food and wine free for the taking. And he, the Duke of Gandia—that was his name, yes? Already people can barely remember—he hadn't even won a battle.

But Cesare Borgia—oh, Cesare Borgia has proved himself a great warrior. The city is in an agony of anticipation. Beyond the gates the army stretches out half a mile, almost every man in new cloth or polished armor. Alongside the papal insignia and the colors of Valentinois, his men carry the banners of Imola and Forlì. Those same banners, copied and enlarged, are emblazoned across newly constructed towers in front of Castel Sant' Angelo: two great cities of the Romagna returned to the papacy. Everyone knows that, by rights, there should be a third banner flying there—the state of Pesaro, a gem waiting to fall into the duke's lap. But that is not what happened.

No one had felt more thwarted than Cesare himself.

"My lord, wake up. You are needed."

Early morning, barely a week after the taking of Forlì, and he is sleeping the sleep of a man who has only just gone to bed.

"God's wounds, Michelotto," he groans, rolling over. "Your face is a foul sight to open one's eyes to. This had better be important."

"It is. You are about to lose half the army. Ludovico Sforza is on the march to retake Milan."

Who would have believed the old tyrant had it in him? After the humiliation of his flight he had been consigned to the dungheap of history. But the poison he had been pouring into the ear of the German Emperor, Maximilian, has apparently borne fruit. To have Italy overrun by France and supported by the papacy with the Pope's own son leading the way: such an outcome would skew the whole balance of power in Europe. If Spain did not have the stomach to resist, then Germany must.

"Where are they?" Cesare is already up and dressed.

"Heading toward Lake Como."

"Then we still have time. If we break camp now we can reach Pesaro in a week."

The French, however, have other ideas. "It is just too difficult," Yves d'Alegre says, throwing up his hands in defeat. "To move a whole army out so fast, and in such . . . well, inclement weather."

"Nevertheless, it can be done." Cesare has brought his own artillery expert with him. "Vitelli?"

"I would say two, maybe three days to clean and move the guns. Less if everyone pitches in."

Behind d'Alegre, the Bailly de Dijon is busy making faces. Money, thinks Cesare. That is the only thing that enlivens those flabby features.

"Ah—here, you see, we encounter a little problem. The Swiss and Gascon infantry, they are most tired after their magnificent work taking the fortress."

"Tired?"

D'Alegre shrugs, as if to say, What can I do? Such a talent for war brings temperament with it. "And then, when the call comes for us to march to Milan, as it must, they will be . . ."

"Even more tired," Cesare says lightly. It has proved one of the hardest lessons of war, learning to keep his temper at bay. "What do they want?"

The Frenchman studies his cuffs. They are frayed; such a long time on the road. He could do with a return to court to contact his tailor. "When things go well, it is customary for elite troops to be rewarded with . . . how do you say? . . . A rise of pay." He sighs extravagantly. "Ah! I tell you, this business of making war is so expensive. Sometimes more when one is on the winning side."

Cesare snorts. "So why don't you share out your ransom money from your 'protected prisoner'? Or maybe I could rent her out for a couple of nights, raise a few hundred ducats that way. I'm sure we would get enough takers."

D'Alegre laughs. "Oh, Duke, you are a man of sublime wit. It is no surprise that our king is so very fond of you. But, of course, you will remember that you 'ave not paid us for the lady yet."

". . . manners of pigs and the morals of money lenders. French scum, all of them!" The plates and goblets at the dinner table chatter under the weight of Alexander's fist. "Your brother is risking his life to bring glory to the Mother Church and what do they do? Sit in their tents scratching their balls, demanding more money. If they had moved faster, we could have taken Pesaro by now."

Four years on and Pinturicchio's own brushstrokes in the Room of the Mysteries still shine off the walls. Inside the stone fireplace a roaring blaze lights up the gaudy-colored painted curtains and gilded tassels that drape and fall around the bottom half of the room. In comparison, the papal table in the center offers a poor man's feast. The taking of the cities in Romagna may be costing the Church a small fortune, but the Pope, as ever, is frugal: a jug of average Corsican wine and a couple of dishes of pasta and fried sardines to mark the Friday fast day. Whatever spices may be lacking are added by his spirit; sweet or sour dependent on the daily dispatches from the battlefield.

"Dear Papà, it is not such a disaster. The campaign is already a triumph. Everywhere you go in Rome, people talk only of Cesare's victories." Lucrezia's face, though it may have lost its plump prettiness, gives off a different glow these days. Perhaps it is as simple as happiness. It is also infectious. In the weeks since the birth of Rodrigo, the Pope cannot get enough of her. With his eldest son at war, he feels the need of his family around him.

"No, no, Father's right! They are scum," Jofré, well oiled as usual, jumps in gleefully. Barely two weeks before, the French army had been the glorious toast of the table. It had not been an easy mouthful for a family full of Aragonese in-laws to swallow. "Cesare should have shoved their pay rise up their asses. That's what I would have done."

"Then we must thank God you are nowhere near any army that bears our name," Alexander thunders. Jofré's sojourn in Castel Sant' Angelo has done little to improve his relations with his father, though it seems he is the only one not to notice it.

"Oh, he does not mean it, Father," Sancia intervenes gaily, sliding the wine jug out of her husband's reach. "It is only his humor."

Under the table Lucrezia reaches out for her own husband's hand.

"It's not the French but the Sforzas who are to blame. They are the reason Cesare lost half his army," Alfonso says quietly.

She knows there is part of him that is cheering Ludovico on: an army recalled to Milan cannot also be an army invading Naples. He is more of a politician these days, her fun-loving husband.

"Awh, I know all that well enough." Jofré is already in search of the wine jug. "The Sforzas! They are worse than scum. The Sforzas are . . . they are lice!" And his petulance is as funny as it is stupid, allowing everyone, even his father, to laugh at him.

"Lice! Yes. Very good. The Sforzas are a family of lice." Alexander thumps the table again, this time with more theater than anger. "Every time you think you have them between your fingertips, they scuttle off before you can crush them. But not now. Now we have the Virago behind bars and the French will grind Ludovico into dust soon enough. Which only leaves the puniest of all of them—Giovanni Louse."

Lucrezia's smile flickers for a second. She sees the salon of the ducal palace, its windows opened onto the sea breeze and a bustling little piazza beneath, pretty enough in its provincial way. Poor Giovanni Louse. He had always been more nuisance than evil, his only real sin not being powerful enough to choose his own marriage. For who in their right mind would take a Borgia daughter for his wife? She holds Alfonso's hand tighter under the table.

"Ah, look at that face, my sweet child." Alexander laughs delightedly. "My own daughter has compassion even for lice. Don't bother your head with him, *carissima,* you have a better man by your side now."

"Oh, indeed I know. And I thank God—and you—in my prayers every day."

"Hmm, yes. So, how is my favorite grandson? Ready to hold a sword yet?"

"You cannot imagine how fast he grows. From one day to the next, isn't that right, Alfonso? He has drunk two wet-nurses dry already."

"See! I told you. A warrior from birth. We will have his name in history soon enough. A second Rodrigo Borgia, no less. Go on. Give your sweet wife a kiss, Alfonso. A man whose right shoulder is pulled so low is surely playing palms under the table. You think I am too old to remember such games? Well, you are wrong." And he beams.

Lucrezia drops her eyes as her husband leans over and kisses her chastely on the cheek.

The Pope roars his satisfaction and the candles dance in his breath. Once Ludovico has been defeated, Cesare will get his army back and Pesaro, Rimini and Faenza will fall soon enough. Two months into the jubilee year of Our Lord and the Borgias are riding higher than ever before. His daughter-in-law, the lovely Charlotte of Navarre, is within weeks of delivering him a further grandchild, the papal lawyers are working on the bull which will recognize Giulia Farnese's young son as his own, and though the politics behind their union may be fragile, these lovebirds at the table will surely make another boy soon enough. A new generation of Borgias. There will be titles for all of them. He has already stripped the Gaetani family of their castles to the south of Rome, on the excuse of their support for Naples, selling the lands to Lucrezia at a knock-down price so that she in turn can pass them on to her son. The Colonna with their flip-flop loyalty will be next, and then, when he is no longer in need of their soldiers, the Orsini themselves.

With France behind Cesare's conquests, all who dare oppose them will go the same way. It is the moment he has worked toward his whole life.

Ah yes, this new grandfather with a warrior hero for a son is the happiest of men. Across the table Lucrezia smiles back at him. Please God let him stay that way.

Chapter 49

"IMOLA! FORLÌ! IMOLA! FORLÌ!"

As the procession moves toward the river, the crowds get bigger, yelling and pushing like a human battering ram against the makeshift barriers as the first wave of horses arrives, their snorting breaths making feather plumes of smoke in the winter air.

The Borgia spectacle has, as ever, been Johannes Burchard's nightmare. So much so that there have been times when, faced with another outrageous demand, Burchard has looked back to his life as a young priest in Alsace with uncharacteristic nostalgia. How God had cared for him then, endowing him with a prodigious memory and thus a place in the great cathedral school of Niederhaslach, far above any family expectations. A year after being sent to Rome he had found the job he was born to do. What he didn't know about Church ceremony he could learn faster than anyone else. But it was more than memory and pedantry: he also had a talent for organizing spectacle. Johannes was the right man at the right time. The papacy was growing richer, a consumer and patron of the new arts. The line between private and public was also changing, so that things once hidden were now more on display. How to bring the two together? How to celebrate weddings, baptisms and funerals for a papal family that ought not, by canon law, even to exist? Leave it to Burchard. How to negotiate the conflicting vanities of bishops, cardinals, papal legates, diplomats and foreign ambassadors? The Master of Ceremonies would find a way. No pope could do without him. What did he care if people made fun of him behind his back?

But what he could not bear was sloppiness, disorder, the cutting of corners, the patching-over of cracks. And in the Pope's determination to take advantage of the timing of Carnival, what should have been weeks of organization have been collapsed into days.

In the rising chaos had come increased squabbling. There were times when Cesare and his condottieri commanders treated him more like a messenger boy, with demands for scores of new uniforms and banners to be made in tailors' shops all over the city, collected and transported in time for the parade. Then, with barely hours to go, a small company of Gascon mercenaries had kicked up an almighty fuss about the order of entry. As foreigners in the army, protocol demanded they enter last. Yet they flatly refused, insisting on marching close to the duke. To have his authority so flouted by men of no rank with un-combed hair and filthy fingernails was insupportable. In the end he had gone to Cesare himself.

"I would have you tell them, Duke Valentinois"—not for him the diminutive Valentino—"that I am the Master of Papal Ceremonies."

"I am conqueror of half of Romagna," Cesare had added with un-characteristic good humor. "And I can't do anything with them either. Relax, Burchard. It's not worth it. Draw comfort from the fact that we are making history here."

But that is exactly what he is worried about it. Not least because of Cesare himself, who has adapted his name to become exactly that of the first conqueror of Romagna, has had the word "CAESAR" embroidered—silver thread on black velvet—on the chests of a hundred young grooms and mace bearers. And in case anyone should miss the message, the celebrations are to be continued next day with a series of tableaux in which Julius Caesar's own crossing of the Rubicon is to be re-created, the great Roman soldier in battle dress and crowned in laurel leaves riding in a chariot behind. In a last-minute act of humility, the duke has decided to give the role to someone else.

What can he, Johannes Burchard, possibly do against such flagrant arrogance? Except sit at his desk each night and note down every detail, so that those who come after will understand that this family was not his doing.

"Imola! Forlì! Imola! Forlì!"

From the windows in the upper story of her white house near the Tiber, the courtesan Fiammetta de Michelis looks down as the first carts and banners roll into sight, moving from the Piazza del Popolo to Ponte Sant' Angelo on their way to the Vatican. Hers is a prime view and she could have shared it with others—she has had enough offers—but she is sitting alone, save for a handsome gray bird perched upon her shoulder, its head cocked close to her ear, its long cherry-red tail perfectly complementing the gold and black of her dress.

"Fiiimetta. Fiiimetta," it cackles into her ear, rocking to and fro as it settles its claws more firmly into the padded material of her shoulders. She laughs, putting a nut between her rosebud lips and offering it up as a treat. The bird pecks it neatly, expertly, tossing it down its throat then cocking its head again to nibble at her ear like some eager young lover.

"It comes from the shores of Africa," he had said when he had delivered it a few days before his leaving for France. "Its eyes will turn yellow as it grows. But the tail will remain the same: an African parrot with the colors of Valentinois on its backside—just in case you should be tempted to forget me."

"But when you come back you will be a married man," she had teased him.

"And what difference will that make? Just don't keep it in your bedroom. If it hears names being moaned too often it will moan them back to the next man."

"Fro Valteeenwaw, Valteenwaw," it had squawked excitedly as soon as Cesare had removed the cap from its head. And she had clapped her hands in delight. She, who had grown used to expecting nothing from him, had been most pleased.

Fifteen months on, its feathers are a deeper gray and its eyes glint like wheat in the sun, but as promised the red tail remains shining fast. Its vocabulary has grown along with its plumage. It can now say the name of the Pope and the King of France and even mutter a few Latin words to welcome the odd cardinal client, drawn to the house by tales of her proficiency.

But in the last few weeks Fiammetta has been working hard to teach it two important new words.

"Imolaa, Forlìììi, Imolaa, Forlìììi," it cackles now, the last syllable rising in a cheeky shriek to join in the roar from the streets below.

Not far from the white house, the tavern at the southern end of Ponte Sant' Angelo boasts an even more impressive vista: across the bridge to Castel Sant' Angelo. Behind the banners, on the upper turrets, guards wait by the guns, ready to dispatch furious salvos as the parade arrives on the spanking new Via Alessandrina, the Pope's own jubilee gift to Rome, which joins the castle to the Basilica of St. Peter.

The owner of the tavern stands looking out over the bridge, empty for the first time in months in readiness for the parade. Behind her, servants scuttle around carrying food and wine to a crowd of guests. Vannozza dei Cataneis may be the mother of the conquering hero, but she is also a successful businesswoman and today is an opportunity for profit, with each inch of viewing space already rented out to those who have the purse to pay for it.

Whatever pain Vannozza experienced over Juan's death, it had been eclipsed by the theatrical suffering of his father and the political crises that followed. Excluded from public grief, she had withdrawn into herself and in the dark days that followed had turned to God and work as solace. The running of her vineyard and the tavern, always a pleasure, now gave her a continued sense of purpose. A year later, as she kissed goodbye to Cesare, she had invested in two new buildings in the reconstructed area of the city in anticipation of the jubilee, with loans guaranteed against her existing properties. The risk had been the challenge she needed. With her own estate supplying most of the food and wine, and her past an open secret to the kind of pilgrims who enjoy, and can afford, status in devotion, her new hostels have been full since long before the year began, so that she has already paid back half the loan. It may be a small achievement next to the glories of her elder son, but it brings her immense satisfaction.

She could be watching today's festivities from a room in the castle: the Pope, though absentminded about her, especially when things are going his way, has been kind enough to issue an invitation. But she is happier in the world she has built around herself. She has always been her own woman, and for all that Alexander might see his children as Borgias, he would, if asked, surely concede that something of her determination and self-sufficiency has made its way into them too.

The roads leading up to the bridge are seething, the crowd hemmed in by troops, their great staves plaited together to make the barrier. Half the religious movements of Europe are represented here: brown Franciscans, white Cistercians, black Dominicans, old and young, many with their cowls up against the winter wind. She watches as a young man—Jofré's age, maybe—with blunt features takes issue with the soldiers' roughness, yelling something in German as they push a woman to the floor. He helps her up then disappears into the crowd, muttering furiously. So many people, she thinks, each one with their own story, each following their own singular line of fate. The sound of trumpets rises up in the distance. It is time to open the best wine, which she has had brought over from her private cellar. There will be no better moment to drink it. Her son has come home.

PART IX

A Family Sacrifice

In the palace there is such envy and so many hatreds, old and new, that such scandal must needs occur.

Francesco Cappello, Florentine ambassador, Rome, August 1500

Chapter 50

I~N HIS ROOMS ABOVE THE BORGIA APARTMENTS, CESARE THE SOL-~dier is missing camp life. His temper frays easily and his moods shift like the weather. He cannot sleep: either his chamber is too hot or the bed is too soft. He douses the fire, wraps himself in his battle cloak and has the mattress transferred to the floor. He lives for the writing and reading of dispatches; detailed daily reports from Imola and Forlì left in the care of one of his Spanish captains, Ramiro de Lorqua—fashioning a new government is a full-time job—or the latest news from the French army, currently cutting a violent swath in forced march into Lombardy and on to Milan. Ludovico Sforza is poised to retake his old city. Cesare and Michelotto stay up long into the night discussing strategies, imagining the confrontation to come.

Meanwhile, the queue of servants bearing invitations is growing embarrassingly long. If the duke could see fit to find the time . . .

"Venice and Ferrara I'll see. The rest can wait."

"There is a further invitation from your sister, the Duchess of Bisceglie."

"Lucrezia, or her husband as well?"

Michelotto shrugs. "I don't see how you can avoid him forever."

"Why not?" he growls. "I have shaken his hand. What more does he want?"

On the morning of the parade, Alfonso had dressed and left their palazzo before dawn.

"Why, Duke Bisceglie, I do believe you are the most handsome man in all of Rome." Lucrezia, shivering in her nightrobes, had insisted on getting up with him.

"Not more handsome than your brother, I hope? Nobody must outshine him today. You had better rub some ash into my robes, or break a few of my cap feathers."

"It would do no good. It is your face that gives you away."

"Then I'll wear an eyepatch." They had laughed as he embraced her. "I have to go," he said after a while. "It would not do to be late." But she won't release him. "It is just a parade, Lucrezia. I will be back."

"I know, I know." She had made her voice gay. "What will you say to him?"

"I shall congratulate him on his brilliance as a soldier and a leader. And he will thank me. Because he will know that I am being sincere."

And so it had been. The two men had met in hazy first light as the horses were saddled and the grooms and mace bearers gathered, smoothing down their doublets and sticking out their chests so the name of Caesar could be read more easily. There had been a firm handshake, a few words and a fast embrace, as if both feared they might catch something from the other. They were saved from further intimacy by the arrival of Jofré, like an overexcited puppy whose master has just come home.

". . . Ah, the way you took the fortress of Imola . . . and the bombard of Forlì—so clever, just the right number of guns. And the right strategy . . ." He blathered on for a while. "Those poxy French. But you'll have Pesaro soon enough. And Rimini. I shall help you this time. We just need to persuade Father. I could be your second-in-command. I have decided every battle move ahead with you. Sancia will tell you. What was she like? Tell me."

"Who?" Cesare had allowed himself to be amused.

"The Virago Sforza, of course. Did you bed her? Yes, yes, of course you did. How many times? Did she fight you very hard?"

To shut him up, Cesare had shot out a hand and grabbed him around the neck, pulling him into a headlock the way he used to when they wrestled together.

"This is what I did to her," he said as the young man yelped indignantly. "And then I did this." He used his other hand to grab at Jofré's codpiece under his doublet. "And guess what I discovered, brother? Her balls were bigger than yours. Ah, my baby brother, the warrior!" he had yelled, releasing him and lifting up his hand high for all to see. "Now get on your horse. And don't fall off. If you are very good I'll arrange for you to visit her yourself."

But in fact it had been Caterina Sforza who had had the last word.

This splendid horsewoman, who had dispatched her best animals to Mantua rather than have them fall into the hands of her enemy, had suffered the indignity of crossing the Apennines in a supply cart. Yet she had still found ways to look her best when, as his prisoner, she had followed Cesare into the frescoed Room of the Consistories, where the Pope sat enthroned ready to receive them.

The Holy Father of all Christendom. But also a ridiculously proud father.

Cesare had barely brought his lips to the Pope's feet before Alexander was leaping up, gathering him to his chest, laughing and chattering in effusive Catalán. On this, one of the most triumphant days of his life, how could he not show beneficence to such a fine-looking woman whose defeat had been their glory?

"I give myself into your hands, Holy Father," she had said, her voice low and thrilling. "Duke Valentino is a warrior with the power of the ancients. I have met no man like him."

In that moment, dead soldiers, broken promises, threats and poisoned shrouds were all lost in the pleasure of watching a lovely woman, with milk white breasts propelled upward from a tight bodice, sinking into a deep curtsy at his feet.

"You are right. And only such a man could defeat a warrior like yourself. Welcome to Rome, Caterina Sforza."

Behind him, Cesare growled softly.

"You are our guest as well as our prisoner and you shall stay in the Belvedere Palace in my own gardens. There will be rooms made ready for you."

As the guards stepped forward to accompany her, she moved past Cesare, a quiet but unmistakable smile on her face.

"Not everyone approves of the idea of war against a woman. We will win more support with magnanimity than revenge now."

"Except it's not finished. She must renounce her claim on behalf of her children, and living in luxury gives her no incentive to do it."

Amid the madness of celebrations, it is days before father and son find themselves properly alone together.

"So, we will use the threat of the dungeons to persuade her. By then she will be forgotten anyway. Come, let us not argue over details. You have made me the happiest man in Christendom. Tell me, what can this loving father give you in return, O Duke of half of Romagna?"

"The means to take the other half."

"Ah, you are on fire still." Alexander beams with delight. "And you shall have it. You will be Gonfaloniere and Captain-General of the Church within the month. Burchard is already drawing up the papers."

"And the army to go with it? We need to raise more soldiers and artillery."

"I know. But we have time." This warrior son of his is so impatient. "Nothing can be done until Milan is settled."

"No. That is the whole problem, Father. As long as we depend on the French, we are not in command of our own destiny. I know that now. I tell you, for this to work we need our own army made up of our own mercenaries. Spanish if possible, so their loyalty is set. The rest we can draw from inside the Romagna."

"What about Vitelli, the Orsini and the others? They fought well for you."

"Well enough. But at root they are like everyone else. Their first loyalty is to themselves. And if we are successful in the taking of the cities—and we will be—eventually we will be looking at theirs too. The Orsini won't know what's hit them."

"Ah—listen to the ambition!" He has been waiting for this moment for months; to taste the victory and make it his own. "I believe war has changed you. Even your face is more soldier than courtier. You know, when I was young, I used to look a little like you. Gladiator chest and shoulders. Ah, how women love a warrior. Sweet Mother of God, we are a family to be proud of, with such triumph to celebrate."

"So when do we start?"

"Start what?"

"Recruiting. It is the perfect time." Cesare gestures to the window and the city outside. "Half of Europe is pouring tribute into the Church this year."

"What? You are Pope as well as captain-general now?" He laughs. "I should remind you there are a few other . . . meager demands on the papacy. Venice is calling for a crusade: pirate infidels are plundering her ships halfway to the Indies."

"Then we can use the demand to make her give us something in return."

"You think I am not working on it already? By the time you are back on the road she will have withdrawn all support from the cities of the Romagna. Aaah! You young pups think it is all done with clashing steel and bom-bard cannonballs. The battles I fight here demand at least as much strategy. Now do me the favor to stop pacing like a wolf in the forest and relax for a moment. Sit, will you!"

Cesare does as he is told, finding his old chair and throwing his body into it, his feet sprawled halfway across the arms.

"I hear that there is a most lovely courtesan in Rome who has a parrot that swears in Latin. And that the same bird squawks *your* name while its mistress is busy murmuring other men's. I wonder who gave her that?"

"Father, we are talking of armies, not women."

"No. We are talking of life." The Pope sighs, as if giving up on him. "Or have you given up everything for war? Maybe it is the Virago who changed you. Wore you out, perhaps. My—you have no idea what stories reached us here."

"Gossip is not truth," Cesare says baldly. He has felt a recurring disgust at the memory of the encounter, not all of it directed toward her. Yes, it is true that he had caught a glimpse of Fiammetta at her window as they paraded past. But by the time he crossed the bridge he had forgotten her again. If he dwelt on it, he too might find it strange, how inside all this driving energy of victory there has been little obvious sexual desire. At times he has found his thoughts turning more to his modest, pliant wife, now fat with child. Her expressed delight at the Venetian silks and glass that he has sent to her speaks of different affection; a fondness born of admiration rather than lust. It is a long time since he has felt such female warmth inside his blood family.

"What about my sister?" he says sharply. "Is she still besotted with Naples?"

"She is happy, yes, and in great excitement at your return." Alexander, as always, lies with admirable gusto.

"And our traitor in-laws, the Aragonese? How are they?"

"Ah, my son, don't be so harsh. Their name is as much a burden to them as it is to us."

"Nevertheless, we—"

"And before you say more." He talks over him now, his voice more forceful. "Until Milan is taken and there is an army heading for Naples that matter will not be spoken of between us. We shall enjoy a little harmony alongside the fruits of victory. Is that understood?"

Cesare bows his head in obedience.

"Good. Since you are more interested in work than diversion, let us talk cardinals. Four deaths mean four vacancies in the College, but since there are at least two dozen contenders with open purses, perhaps we might appoint more. A few fellow Spaniards will work well for our future. You can start to pay for your army from there. I shall send you a list. And now we shall drink wine and play at war, you and I. You will show me how you took Forlì. I have had them put extra condiments on the table and a set of new silver French forks so we will have enough to designate each part of the army. See . . . just like it was all those years ago in the Palazzo Borgia. Ah, what a journey it has been."

And as he says it two fat tears of joy start their way up and over the flesh foothills of his craggy cheeks. What depth of fatherly love. Impossible to resist. As the two men settle over the mustard pots, forks and pasta spoons, with the south wall of the fortress of Forlì a thick napkin propped against a goblet, a spike of pain shoots up through Cesare's leg, deep into his groin. It is the second time in a week that he has felt it. God's wounds, he thinks. Not again. Not now.

Chapter 51

"How it is possible for something that does not kill to hurt so much, Torella? I've had bull-horn injuries that have been easier to bear."

"My lord, it is one of the mysteries of the disease. How it seems to enter into the bone itself."

"And to come so suddenly? One day I am in perfect health, then—and don't dare to tell me it is a mystery. You are a man of medicine. If I wanted to hear about mysteries I would employ a magus."

"If I may speak, my lord?"

"Haaaa!" Cesare is on the bed, his legs stretched out at strange angles as if bent iron bars are running through them. The agony is almost continuous, as it has been for the last two days, and his face is gray with pain.

"I would say that its arrival is not so sudden. Since our return to Rome you have suffered certain"—he feels for the right words—"certain changes of mood." He glances toward Michelotto, who sits assiduously studying the floor tiles. When the news of Ludovico's retaking of Milan had come through a week ago, Cesare's tantrum had broken two chairs, one of them narrowly missing the messenger's head. It had been then that Michelotto had noticed the blotches starting to rise on his master's face and called for the doctor.

"What—my temper is also the disease now!"

"It seems there may be some relation between the two, yes."

On Torella's desk sit letters from the city of Ferrara, where it appears half the court is infected: descriptions of smitten men chased by the dogs of depression or in thrall to such moods and furies that at times they have had to be restrained. Like the blotches and the pains, the devil comes and goes.

"So do something. What about the ointment that the doctor gave that old cardinal?"

"My lord, the man was a Portuguese quack! Cardinal Bertomeu died of it! And for every moment of relief, he suffered tenfold as it wore off. I stake my reputation that is not the way to treat it."

"Then what is?"

Torella sighs. "I do believe . . ."

"All right, all right. I will try your damn steam barrel. But it had better work, Torella. I am a man with wars to fight and I cannot—aaaghh!" He breaks off as the next spasm thrusts a sword through his body.

It is Torella's great experiment and he is set to make a small fortune on it. He had perfected the design during the stay in France and had the whole thing built, then dismantled and carried home in the baggage carts. It is housed inside an old oak wine barrel, with a door for the patient to enter and leave, a bench seat and a small fire grate where the coals are kept red-hot, liberally doused with drops of his special compound: quicksilver, myrrh and secret herbs mixed in secret quantities. The naked patient sits inside for two to three hours, working up a ferocious sweat, which allows the worst of the humors to be expelled at the same time as the infused steam enters through the pores and the airways. In this way the bad humors of the disease are chased out and the remedy flows in. As long as the patient can stand the heat, after three or four sessions the skewering within the bones subsides and the blotches start to fade.

Cesare, who must always be the best at everything, even suffering, emerges parboiled after a second gruellingly long session and, with Torella's help, sits gasping in a chair, nodding grimly.

"The stabbing is less. Definitely. It is a good cure, Torella."

From outside the door there are raised voices; a man's followed by another lighter tone, plus the sound of screeching.

"Well?" Cesare says as Michelotto puts his head around the door. "What? What are you staring at?"

"Nothing. Except that it is a wonder to see you upright again."

But that is not what Michelotto is thinking. He is thinking, Beetroot: the doctor has boiled the duke to the color of beetroot.

"Who is it? I said I would see no one."

"It is . . . it is the Duchess of Bisceglie. She has been here for some time."

Cesare looks at Torella. The doctor shrugs. "If you have the energy."

"How do I look?"

"Like a man who is no longer in pain," the doctor says mildly, judging this rebirth of vanity as a healthy sign in itself.

Cesare lifts himself a little higher in the chair. "Get me a towel."

In the antechamber, Lucrezia keeps her distance from Michelotto. Over the years nothing has happened to make his face any more attractive to her, but there is no doubt that he, like her, cares greatly for her brother.

"The duke will be pleased to see you now."

She nods at him haughtily as she passes.

"Duchess Bisceglie, if I may . . . ?" She stops, but still does not look at him directly. "If he asks you how he looks . . . don't tell him."

At least she is prepared. "Oh, my sweet brother!" It is hard to know what is strangest—the flayed color of his body or the wooden contraption that sits in the middle of the room, steaming gently.

"It is Torella's health machine. Men go in ill and come out well. Though they roast a little on the way."

She comes straight up to him, sitting close and laying a hand on his forehead. "You are so hot, but—"

"It is the fire, not the fever."

She glances at Torella, who looks on appreciatively as this pretty young woman becomes the instant nurse, soaking a sponge in the bowl of water and using it to dab and soothe the patient's face.

"You can leave us now, Torella," Cesare mutters.

"Indeed. And if I may, madam? He must also drink."

"Yes, yes." Lucrezia lifts up the glass of water and helps hold it to his lips. "Come," she says sternly as the door closes behind her. "Do not make that face. You must do as you are told for once."

Cesare, a stranger to being weak in female hands, sits back, unexpectedly calm. "How did you know I was ill?"

"Ah, there are no secrets in this palace. You should know that. Thank the Lord you are safe now."

As the high color in his skin begins to fade his semi-nakedness becomes more powerful: there is an old duelling scar, a pale ridge running halfway across his chest, and his upper arms are knotted with muscles.

"I was never in any danger," he says gruffly. "What? Are those tears? You are not crying for me. I am strong as a bull."

"But . . . but you might not have been. There has been so much fighting, Cesare. What if you had been wounded? Or even killed."

"How sad would you have been then?"

"How can you ask that?" she says angrily. "You are my brother."

"How can I ask it? Perhaps because it has been a while since I have seen you show any love for me."

"And whose fault is that?" she shoots back, almost too fast. The fact is that, though she is crying for him, she is also crying for other things. "I have missed you sorely and sent invitations by the barrelful for you to join us since your return. But you have ignored them."

"Us," he repeats. "To join 'us.'"

"Yes, us. Because though it seems to cause you nothing but anger these days, as well as your sister I am also a married woman."

When she set out from the palace hours ago she had not felt so brave. What had she come for? In fear of his health? Or to try and placate his aggression against the House of Aragon? The news from Milan has the French army and Ludovico Sforza ready to meet in battle, each side rich with Swiss troops, men who, it seems, will kill even their own brothers if someone pays them enough. What a foul thing is war. Whoever wins, someone loses. And in this battle she, Lucrezia, who does not fight anyone, stands to lose more than most.

"Cesare, I am your loving sister and I would ask you to listen to me." She lifts up the sponge to mop his face again so that he cannot but look at her. "We both know this marriage to Naples was not of my choosing. The decision was yours and Papà's. I did as I was told. Just as when I married Giovanni Sforza. Then, when it was Papà's wish, for the good of the family, I allowed—no, no, I helped—to have him put aside. But Giovanni was a traitor. You said so yourself. He betrayed us. Alfonso is not like him. He is a man of honor and the father of my son, a Borgia child."

"He is from the House of Aragon and they are our enemy," he says flatly.

"Only because you have made it so. If Federico had given you his daughter as you wished—"

"It has nothing to do with his hideous daughter," Cesare yells: even more than his father, he does not like to be reminded of failures.

"I agree." She realizes her mistake fast. "Oh, I agree. You have a much better wife now and another alliance to bring the family even more greatness. You are Duke of half of the Romagna already and will surely take the rest. Naples is not important."

"Is this what you are come for?" he says sourly, pulling away from her ministrations. "To plead for your husband?"

"No." And she is surprised by her own firmness. "No, I am not here to plead."

Because why should she? She has done nothing wrong. In all her life she has done nothing but love and obey her family. Except perhaps for once . . . but she does not like to think of Pedro Calderón; there is too much guilt woven in with the suffering. Is that what she is paying for now? If so, then surely it is God's business to punish her, not anyone else's. "I am come to see my brother. But as his sister, not a supplicant. I am a Borgia too, married, before God, to a man who has done us no wrong. And I ask you to respect that."

"Bravo, sister." The battle between displeasure and admiration is over too fast for it to be read in his features. "Such spirit suits you very well." He leans over and takes her face between his hands, staring at her, studying her approvingly. Ah, but she is lovely indeed. "I have missed you too. I did not realize how much until this moment."

For a second she thinks that he might try to kiss her and she stiffens involuntarily. But instead he releases her, a broad smile on his face. As he does so there is a great commotion next door, a squawking and then a swearing.

"God's blood. Michelotto? What is that racket?"

The door opens. "My lord. Do you need Torella?"

"No! My sister has cured me. But I don't need bloody murder going on outside my door."

Michelotto throws up his hands. "Once its hood is off you can't stop it."

"Stop what?"

"The damn bird! The note that came with it called it a messenger with a cherry-red tail."

"Ah yes! And what does it say?"

"Valentwah." Through the open door the screech is audible to all. "Forliiii. Forlii. Valentwah."

Cesare laughs. "I will answer it later."

But when he turns back to her, Lucrezia is still looking at him, waiting for some kind of response.

He takes her hand and kisses it. "My beautiful Borgia sister, hurting you would be like hurting myself. What more can I say?"

Chapter 52

THE POWER OF FAMILY. SFORZA IN MILAN. ARAGON IN NAPLES.
For near on half a century their mutual ambitions have affected the balance between north and south, their dynastic webs spun together with threads of blood through marriage and offspring. Perhaps it is fitting, then, that when one falls the other should be taken down with it.

On the battlefield outside Milan the French army decisively crush the Sforza force. Victory is made sweeter a day later with the capture of a swarthy Swiss soldier, a man with such execrable German and soft, manicured hands that it takes no time for him to be unmasked. Ludovico Sforza, once the scourge of Italy, is put into chains and loaded onto a cart bound for France, where King Louis himself is waiting to welcome him to a royal castle where he will reign undisturbed over a water-soaked dungeon with a court of rats for company.

With one brother taken, the next follows swiftly. Vice-Chancellor Ascanio Sforza, excommunicated as a traitor, is also imprisoned, his palace and his cardinal's assets forfeited to the Church. Sforza. Who would have that name now? In Pesaro, Giovanni spends his life in the privy, his bowels turned to water in panic, while in Rome, Caterina is escorted by soldiers from the Belvedere Palace to less salubrious rooms in Castel Sant' Angelo that might concentrate her mind better on the signing away of her birthright.

Cesare, his temper much improved by the news, takes to the bullring with public displays of strength, dispatching seven bulls in a series of bloody fights. Rome falls in love with him all over again.

It is not long before the French ambassadors arrive, smiles on their faces and the word "Naples" on their lips. A few days later a Spanish contingent joins them. In the Pope's receiving room old enemies now shake hands and exchange compliments. The conquest of southern Italy is such a great undertaking; surely it would be better for the balance of Europe if it could be shared rather than opposed?

Of course, nothing can be done without the blessing of the Pope. The crown of Naples sits in his hands and his own warrior son will be part of the conquering force. Not quite yet though. First Cesare has his own war to finish, for which the French king will gladly furnish part of his own army to knock down any walls that withstand him.

Political stitch-ups do not come much tidier or more cynical than this.

Amid such satisfying developments, the news from France that the lovely Charlotte d'Albret Borgia has safely given birth is diplomatically underwhelming. The opening words say it all. A baby girl. Alexander dispatches best wishes and presents. Cesare, in contrast, finds himself unexpectedly touched, but nothing either of them can do will shift the fact that his wife is rooted in France, where King Louis seems determined to keep her.

Alas, even a pope as creative as Alexander cannot find a way to put asunder this marriage. It is unfortunate, because Cesare would be a great catch on the Italian marriage market now. And as he keeps telling his father, the new state they are building will need a key Borgia alliance to protect it.

"Naples will not fall for at least a year. The sooner Lucrezia is free the better, Father. You have always said yourself that Fate favors those who act without waiting for tomorrow. You are almost seventy, and—"

"Sweet Mother of God, not this again. Look at me! Do you see a man who is about to die? I have never felt better, as everyone but you is telling me."

It is true: Alexander does have more energy these days. A few months before, when the world was filled with business and strife, he had given Giulia permission to visit her husband in the country, but now success has increased his appetite in many things, so that recently his eye has started wandering over one or two of Lucrezia's prettier ladies-in-waiting. "We will come to it when the time is right, Cesare. Let us at least enjoy a little sunshine before negotiating another storm."

Cesare, whose faith in Fate grows greater with each passing year, will remember the choice of words for some time to come.

June 29, late afternoon of a blazing hot day. Rome is bursting with pilgrims and the Pope is seated on his throne in the great Sala dei Papi, with his personal chamberlain in conference with a Spanish cardinal, the windows thrown open wide to let in a welcome breeze from across the river.

It is a common enough marvel, the way a summer storm in Rome can arrive out of nowhere: a sudden rising wind shunting in fat-bellied clouds and letting loose such sheets of rain that within the half-hour it might last there can be flash floods in the streets or rivers gushing down chimneys.

Today, the force is furious. First comes rain, then hailstones, big as nails, driven sideways by the gale. The cardinal and the chamberlain rush to the windows, struggling to secure them as the thick circles of glass rattle in their metal frames. As lightning tears a jagged hole in the sky, a thunderclap arrives at exactly the same moment, exploding directly overhead. It is so loud the cardinal cries out at the sound. On the roof, the bolt scores a direct hit on the chimney breast, bringing down the whole stone fireplace in the room above and smashing through the floorboards into the salon below.

As the two men turn from the window, the room is a dust storm. Most of the ceiling has gone. So has the Pope: man and throne engulfed by an avalanche of wood and plaster.

"Holy Father!" the chamberlain calls out hoarsely. "Holy Father?"

There is no sound. Nothing. No living soul could have withstood such a weight of masonry.

"The Pope!" both men scream as the doors open. "Help! Help! The Pope is dead."

The dreaded words fly down the Vatican corridors, even as the papal guards rush in, throwing themselves onto the pile, tearing at the rubble with their bare hands, causing more debris to dislodge and fall, until the captain arrives and shouts for them to halt. "Slowly! One piece at a time. More men. Get more men."

In the open doorway Burchard stands, his thin sculpted face without expression. He turns to a servant behind him and nods, the man disappearing like a rabbit down a hole.

"The Pope is dead!"

In Santa Maria in Portico next door, Sancia is visiting Lucrezia; they, their women and baby Rodrigo are now gathered in the main salon, driven from the garden by the storm. They hear the shouting but not the words, but it is enough to send them, skirts flying, through the secret corridors into the palace beyond.

"The Pope is dead!"

Cardinal della Rovere is halfway through a dispatch to France when the messenger arrives. He drops the pen and is out of the door. He will find the inkblot spreading when he returns.

By the time Cesare gets there (how Fate adores this young man: it is one of his rooms, which he had left barely an hour before, that has taken the brunt of the damage) the chamber is filled with soldiers, cardinals and doctors. In the center, edges of the throne are now visible while men work methodically, lifting chunks of masonry and wood, some of it decorated with the Borgia coat of arms. How could God be so cruel? To kill a pope using the weapon of his own name. And every few minutes the captain of the guards shouts for silence, then calls: "Holy Father. Your Holiness, can you hear us?"

It is at the tenth time of asking, with a sense of theater that Burchard himself could not match, that a wavering voice replies.

The whole room erupts in a cheer, and the guards go at it even faster, clearing the surrounding debris until at last the Pope is revealed, bolt-upright in his seat, his right arm caught under a lump of wood, head covered in plaster dust and a slice of blood across one cheek, but palpably alive: a fortuitous collision of two beams meeting over his head and taking the weight of what should have crushed the life out of him.

"Holy Father. You are saved!"

"Yes," he says, as he takes in the waiting, stunned crowd. "Yes. I am." And that famed Borgia smile cracks from ear to ear.

Cesare backs out of the door to find Burchard standing outside and, coming swiftly toward them down the corridor that links the public rooms to the papal apartments, the tall, gangling figure of Giuliano della Rovere, his cardinal's robes like lapping waves around him. Vultures, Cesare thinks. In Rome it is the ear rather than any sense of smell that has them gathering.

He moves to block his path. During their months of enforced cohabitation at the French court the two of them have perfected a tone of sincere insincerity. But since their arrival in Rome they have studiously avoided each other.

"My lord duke." Della Rovere is breathless. "I came as soon as I heard. I—"

"Yes, yes," Cesare interrupts loudly. "The most terrible accident. The ceiling of the room above has fallen directly on to the throne where he was seated."

"Oh, may Jesus Christ Our Lord have mercy on us all. Our beloved Holy Father? He is badly hurt?"

Cesare makes a stiff little gesture, as if he cannot speak.

"No, oh—no—he is not dead?"

Cesare tastes the honey in the timing. "No, he isn't. That is the wonder of it. He is very much alive."

Della Rovere, for a second unsure how to proceed, crosses himself and pulls his hands together in prayer. "Praise be to all the saints."

"And how good of you to come to his aid so fast, Cardinal. You must have men of great prescience around you."

Della Rovere's smile barely flickers. Behind them, Burchard is already moving back to the Pope's chamber. Cesare's voice reaches after him.

"Is there anyone else we should disinform?"

Alexander, his right arm badly bruised and with various cuts and scratches to his head and face, is carried gently to his bedchamber. The word "miracle" is already starting to whisper its way around the Vatican palace as Cesare walks out into the gardens that adjoin the Borgia apartments. The torrential rain has stopped as fast as it arrived and the sky is already clearing. The gravel and the flowerbeds are soaked and as the sun comes out it picks out trembling diamond drops of water on the leaves of the Seville orange trees that the Pope loves so much because they remind him of the Spanish home that he no longer quite remembers from his childhood. The hailstones have knocked some of the riper oranges to the ground: an early harvest for the Vatican kitchens, their pulp strong, slightly bitter to the taste. Borgia fruit. Della Rovere would no doubt have them all dug up and replanted. How fast it could all come apart, Cesare thinks: coats of arms covered up or chipped away, new apartments fashioned for a new papacy. He pushes the nightmare further: what future would there be then for a Borgia son with no army and just a few cities, still half owned by the papacy, in his grasp? No, if the Borgias are to survive, then the rest of Romagna must be secured and buffered by states in order to give it muscle against the belligerence of any new pope. And it must happen fast. Another campaign will take the cities he needs, and the fall of Naples to the French will cushion him in the south. To the north one state has long been the obvious choice. Ferrara. But to persuade the proud house of Este that they need an alliance with the new Duke of the Romagna will take the combined weight of a French king, a Borgia pope and a high-level marriage to formalize the good will.

Once again Fate, this time in the form of a summer storm and a fallen chimney breast, is his mentor.

Chapter 53

In his chamber, Alexander is soon enjoying the status of a man cradled in the hand of God. He holds court in bed, a doctor for each wound, offering salves and potions until he shoos them away in favor of another kind of healing. The door opens in a rush of perfumed silk on a flock of colorful birds: Lucrezia and Sancia with all of their ladies, bearing fruits and flowers and twittering welcome. He sits, his great tonsured head bandaged and his florid face bathed in smiles, as they arrange themselves around the bed. They stay from morning till night, feeding and amusing him with chatter and word games. The infidel Turkish potentate, it is said, keeps a whole house of women just for himself. Well, they cannot be prettier or more solicitous than these dear things. Ah, to be so loved! Someone had better tell Vannozza and Giulia. They will surely be beside themselves with worry and want to visit too. It is almost worth injury to gain such love and attention.

Two weeks later. Midsummer's twilight, the kind of sky that has Pinturicchio crying into his palette with envy: a blood-orange sun dipping behind banks of cloud washed with such riotous, rapturous shades of color that one almost expects Our Lady and all the angels to rise out of them into the heavens above.

Below are the steps of the Basilica of St. Peter, old majesty crumbling under the weight of history, a place which has given sustenance to persecuted Christians over the centuries, but whose portico now offers something more humble, a stone bed for those pilgrims who cannot afford the price of a room.

A group of them lie huddled near one of the pillars, not far from the gates of the Vatican. Given the clemency of the weather one might have expected more people to take advantage of the spot. Certainly the night watchman who passed by a few moments earlier had been surprised to find the steps so empty. If he had looked closer he would also have noticed that these men were far from destitute: their boots are of good leather, their cloaks have a rich weave. Not that that in itself is so strange. For every ten pilgrims who sleep on stone out of necessity there will be a few who do so out of choice: a deliberate espousal of austerity in their journey to get closer to God. These fellows here are possibly a fraternity of cloth or leather merchants traveling together on a vow of poverty. They must be very tired now, for they have wrapped their cloaks around their heads as well as their bodies to keep out the glorious sunset. Ah well, waking to dawn on the steps of St. Peter's will be its own reward.

As the light dies the gates to the Vatican, to the right-hand side of the portico, unbolt and open just enough to let out three men, hats pulled down over their eyes and well dressed, though one of them more so, with pleats of gold edging to his velvet doublet. They all have swords swinging by their sides.

They take in the view around them, noting the sleeping pilgrims and the empty piazza, then move quickly down the stairs and across their side of the square toward the building next door, where there is a side entrance hidden in the shadow. They could have used the back way inside the two palaces, but that would have involved a trek through corridors and secret doors. It is a fine enough route in rain or cold, but in summer the passages are stuffy and with such a gorgeous sunset who would not want to step outside and see the sky, even if only for a few moments?

They must be halfway to home when, from the steps of the church behind them, the cloaked huddle rises up like a dark wraith, then separates out to become six—no, seven—figures, flinging off their cloaks and unsheathing their swords. Within seconds, they have the three men surrounded, cutting them off from both palaces and flinging themselves upon them.

Alfonso of Aragon, his sword already out of its scabbard, turns to meet his attackers. How long has he been waiting for this moment? There had been a time, after Rodrigo was born, when he had hoped that the Pope's good will toward them all would save him. But since his brother-in-law's return, he has known that even the fortress of love that Lucrezia has thrown up around them is not strong enough to protect him from Cesare's murderous rage.

This good-natured young man, unspoiled by ambition or too much intelligence, has little of the hero about him; yet he has walked toward his fate with his eyes open. Of course he has done what he can: he has given up hunting, because the world is full of stories of hunters who mistake a man's coat for an animal's flank; and these days he only leaves the confines of the palaces with bodyguards. But there has been nothing about this evening to arouse suspicion. He had joined his wife in the late afternoon, where she, the Pope, Sancia and Jofré were enjoying a tournament of checkers around the table in Alexander's bedroom (how well the old man is doing!) and then he had stayed for an early supper. Lucrezia could well have accompanied him home—as she does sometimes—and it would take an insider's knowledge to know that to-night she does not.

Well, so be it. God's portico echoes with a chorus of clashing steel. He dispatches his first opponent fast, forcing the man's blade high into the air then ramming him backward with such ferocity that he loses his footing. It is not just for sport that he and his gentleman, Albanese, have returned to practicing swordplay. If he is going to perish here then he will take a few with him. He catches Albanese's eye and they both let out a howl at the same time: the exhilaration of dying. When they bring the news to King Federico, Naples will have reason to be proud of them both.

"Murder! Murder!" Behind them, his groom is yelling at the top of his lungs as his sword flails around him. "The Duke of Bisceglie is attacked! Open the doors. Let us in."

It is not long before Alfonso takes the first wound to his arm. Left arm though. Fine, he doesn't need it. He feels the stab of pain, then nothing. He turns to the sword that delivers it and as he does so he notices a group of horses in the shadows at the bottom of the steps. By God, he thinks, they mean to take us somewhere else if they cannot dispatch us here. He has a flash of the Tiber, stinking weeds in his hair. Knowing there is no safety to be had in trying to reach the entrance, the three of them are falling back toward the Vatican gates, their shouts and ringing steel a terrible percussion in the night. "Murder. Bloody murder!" Dear God, are the guards all deaf?

The next blow is to his head. It stuns him and he stands for a second undefended and would go down if Albanese doesn't step in to save him. They cannot keep this up much longer; there are too many of them. Then a shaft of steel enters his thigh, high up, where the blood runs in rope-thick veins which if punctured can spurt out a life in minutes. He lifts his weapon to take out the man who did it, but he is falling already. On the ground someone is groaning—himself?—then a hand is grabbing his cloak and collar. "My lord, my lord!" and he hears his groom's voice, frantic, as he is dragged backward up the stairs to the gates.

He feels the darkness upon him. I love my wife, he thinks. My wife, my sister, my son. I would die for them if I could. Is that what I am doing? He remembers nothing more.

Finally, the great Vatican gate clanks open. Albanese is still fighting like a man possessed, but they are already saved. At the first sign of help the attackers take to their heels, scattering across the piazza to the waiting horses. By the time the guards are out and following, they are gone, kicking up dust into the near-darkness.

In the Pope's bedroom, Sancia is squeaking at the audacity of some move that her father-in-law has made on the board when the commotion reaches them.

Without ceremony, the door is flung open by the captain of the guards, and four men stagger in, carrying Alfonso, his head and his leg a mass of red, blood everywhere.

Sancia screams, the Pope yells and Lucrezia, on her feet immediately, looks at her husband's body and faints to the floor. It is only later, when she is revived, that she hears the words, "He is breathing still. They have not killed him."

———

"God's blood, how is it possible? Seven men against two fighters and a page? They were paid half a king's ransom."

"Assassins are keen to stay alive to enjoy the money. I said you should have let me do it."

"You'd need to be blind and crippled to fail with those odds." Cesare, disturbed by Michelotto in Fiammetta's house, is exhibiting the fury of a thwarted child. "If you had done it, someone would have known and my name would be on everyone's lips."

"You think it won't be anyway? Who else would pay a gang of Orsini louts to attack the Pope's son-in-law?"

"I'm not the only one who wants him dead," he snarls. "The Pope has given him land from Rome's best families, and anyone who supports the French hates Naples."

"Not as much as you hate Alfonso. We could be lucky yet, my lord. He may die of his wounds."

But Fate, usually so generous to Cesare, in this case is not to be relied upon. Alexander, shocked by the insolence of the attack, has Alfonso put to bed in a room in his private apartments in the Borgia tower. Half hospital, half fortress, sixteen men from the Vatican guard are stationed outside, while the Pope's own doctors tend him, every move watched by his wife and sister, who never leave his side. He survives the night. Two days later the King of Naples's own surgeon arrives to take over. The duke's wounds, it seems, are not mortal—"unless," as one of the papal secretaries writes to his old employer, the Duchess of Urbino, "some new accident intervenes."

He, like every other commentator in town, knows who is behind the attack, though many are too nervous to commit the name to paper for fear of reprisals. Such is the Pope's son's growing power. Cesare for his part bluffs it out, visiting the duke soon after, while he is still half conscious. At their places by the bed, neither woman will look at him.

"You are a most fortunate man to be so cared for," he says, staring down at the swollen face.

Alfonso's eyelids flicker open, then close again.

"My dear sister," Cesare says, directly to Lucrezia. She lifts her eyes but they are blank, cold. Behind her, Sancia hisses like a cornered cat.

"We will find out who did this," he says sternly. "The duke is a man with many enemies."

To the Pope he is more forthright. "Neither I nor any of my men laid a finger on the Duke de Bisceglie. But I tell you that I am not sorry for what happened. The man is a liability to our cause and as long as he remains alive in the palace it will lead to more conspiracy and discord."

Alexander, harried on all sides, is vacillating between outrage and strategy. "The King of Naples is demanding that we send him home as soon as he is fit. It may be for the best."

"Just so long as she doesn't go with him."

But that is exactly what they are planning. Lucrezia and Sancia have taken up residence in the patient's chamber. They sleep on pallets at the end of the bed, dressed in simple gowns, their hair pulled back in white cloth like working girls. They are tireless in his care, bathing, feeding, dressing his wounds and overseeing the preparation of every meal in case of malevolent intent. They play their roles with a sweet intensity: ladies of leisure are not often given such a profound sense of purpose.

When he is strong enough to speak, at first he and Lucrezia talk only of mundane things: the warmth of the day, which meat he would like to taste, how the bolster pillow must be laid so that it does not touch his head wound. The world they have created inside this room, regulated by the progress of the sun and the humble repetition of domestic chores, feels unmarked by malice.

It is not until the first week has passed and Sancia is called out by a message from Jofré that the two of them are alone.

"She has been like a wild animal in your defense, you know," Lucrezia jokes. "Even the royal surgeon from Naples is frightened of her. He marvels at your recovery. Says he has never seen such a thing and that you will be dancing again soon."

"Not in this palace. No, Lucrezia," he says firmly as she tries to interrupt. "It must be talked of. We cannot live in this room forever. Sooner or later your brother will kill me, or have me killed. Unless I kill him first—"

"No! No. We will protect you."

"What? A man hiding behind his wife and his sister's skirts? What kind of image will that give to our son of his father?"

"Then you will go to Naples. As soon as you are well enough to travel. The Pope has promised your uncle—"

"Not without you."

"I will follow when I can."

There is silence. There is no point in saying the words.

"They will not stop me," she says fiercely. "I am not a child anymore. We will be together in Naples."

"And when the French attack us there?"

"Then we will go to Bisceglie. Or somewhere else. Anywhere. Anywhere that is not here."

"Don't cry. You are right. We will find a way." And he uses his good hand to pull her head on to his chest.

"Look at you—two lovebirds." Sancia comes in, carrying a tray of oven-fresh biscuits. "See what a good job we have done. Angels of mercy, that is what we are."

"Indeed you are," he says.

But when he lies back in the bed the gold-embossed Borgia coat of arms glowers down from the ceiling and in his dreams he fights with the hooded skeletons of death.

After two weeks, his youthful strength and their nursing begin to have an effect: with help, the leg wound is healed enough for him to leave his bed. When the women are sleeping one afternoon, he manages to get himself up as far as the window, with its view of the Borgia gardens beneath.

Cesare, whose day is just beginning at this hour, has taken to walking amid the orange trees in the garden to clear his head. The two men register each other's presence at the same moment. Alfonso feels a hot knot of fear rise in his gut, but he makes himself tall on his good leg, lifting the catch to pull the window open.

Below, Cesare, unarmed, stands immobile, staring up at him.

What a target he would make from here, Alfonso thinks. If I had a weapon now I could do it. I swear I could.

Then, as if the thought has traveled from one to other, Cesare opens his arms out wide to expose his chest to the world and smiles. Alfonso's head throbs, excitement and pain colliding. As he turns clumsily back from the window, Sancia is waking.

"What are you doing? Get back to bed!"

He lets her help him, but as she settles the covers he grabs her hand. "I need you to do something for me."

"What? Anything."

"Get me my crossbow from the palace and bring it here."

"Your crossbow? But you have no—"

"Just do it, Sancia. Please."

By the time she gets back, Cesare is long gone from the garden.

The bow sits propped by the window. "No reason—I just feel better with it here," he explains when Lucrezia questions him.

Over the next week he waits and waits for another time, but either he is never awake when his carers sleep or, if he is, the garden is empty. He would probably not have had the strength anyway. A few days later Jofré visits for a few hours, sitting uncomfortably by the bed as he flounders for things to talk about. This split in the palace has made his life miserable. His natural allegiance is all to his brother, whom he adores, but he misses his wife badly and resents the way her attention is lavished on someone else.

When Cesare hears of the visit he takes his brother to one side.

"I only went because of Sancia," Jofré mutters, fearing he has been disloyal. "I never see her otherwise."

"I understand. You have been abandoned. I would feel the same if she was my wife. How was it in there?"

"Ugh, it smells of death."

"What does he do all day? Just sit, smothered by women's talk?"

"More or less. Though he has a weapon with him now."

"Really." From the tone of his voice, Cesare could not be less interested. "What kind?"

"A crossbow. It sits by the window."

"Fine weapon. If he had the strength to use it," he says carelessly. "Why don't you and I get out of this hothouse, little brother? Go out into town. Fiammetta can bring in some other ladies. Would you like that?"

Chapter 54

IF ALFONSO HAD BEEN KILLED ON THE STEPS OF THE BASILICA THAT night it would have been so much simpler: less scandal, less fury, less suffering. For everyone. A calculated sword-thrust up and under the ribs to the heart would have done it in a matter of minutes. He might have died cradled in the arms of his Neapolitan comrade, for the order was to murder him, not all of them. Only him. Alfonso de Aragona: young, brave and honorable. A manly death, followed by suitable, traditional womanly grief: intense, certainly; spiced with outrage, no doubt, but clean and eventually over.

But weeks of high drama, of swooning, tension, coddling and pampering, the intimacies of wounded flesh and the gushing of women's bleeding hearts as they pull a man back from the brink, a rope of salvation plaited thick with love and tears . . . all this means that the real death—which must follow—can only be a messier, more humiliating affair, and the grief that it triggers will carry long-term infection.

The afternoon of August 18, 1500. The door to the room where Alfonso lies is smashed open and a squad of Cesare's own men, led by Michelotto, throw themselves in, shouting about a bloody plot against the Borgias. They seize everyone, guards, servants and the Neapolitan doctors who are in the middle of their daily examination of the wounded body of their patient.

Lucrezia and Sancia rise up like harpies, screaming and protesting, throwing themselves at Michelotto. He steps back, defending himself as best he can, his face in ugly anguish.

"But I am ordered, Your Ladyships, I am ordered." And his voice is filled with such patent distress that for a second they are caught off guard. "There is a plot to kill my lord Duke Valentino and I am ordered—"

"By whom? Ordered by whom?" the women scream back. "Not by the Pope."

"I—I do not know. I thought . . . but if this is wrong then . . . then the Holy Father is only doors away . . ." And he glances anxiously toward the soldiers holding the prisoners, as if to stop them from going any further. "I am ordered," he repeats plaintively.

"No!" Lucrezia is already out of the room, hurling herself down the long corridor that connects the apartments, shouting, shouting for her father, Sancia fast on her heels.

Three doors down in the newly repaired papal salon, Burchard steps back as the women rush in toward the Pope, who is already rising from his chair. "What? What is happening?" he says, taking in the panic of these madwomen.

"Did you order the arrest of Alfonso's doctors and guards?" Sancia is close to hysteria.

But Lucrezia doesn't wait for an answer. Everything she needs to know is in her father's face. She lets out another howl and turns on her heel, careering back along the corridor.

She has been gone—what? Four, maybe five minutes? You could measure the time in heartbeats.

The door to the room is shut, two of Cesare's guards in front of it. They have orders too, oh yes. But even they are not going to physically manhandle the Pope's own daughter. They stand shamefaced as she screams, then step aside as she moves toward them. One of them has been holding the handle on the smashed bolt so that the door now swings open easily.

The room is empty of guards and prisoners. Michelotto stands by the head of the carved bed. At his feet lies the crumpled body of Alfonso, his head caught at a strange angle and his face, open-mouthed, in a rictus of terror.

"I am so sorry, Duchess Bisceglie." Michelotto's voice, in contrast, is now quite calm. "He was trying to get up out of bed. I think the shock of our intrusion must have started some internal bleeding and in his— weak state, well . . . he has hemorrhaged to death."

And as he says this he brings up both his hands as if to make it clear that at no point during the last five minutes have they been around Alfonso's throat.

The wailing is everywhere. Down the corridors, out of the windows, across the garden. The peace of the palace has not been so shattered since that terrible night when the Pope lost his son. And not just in the Vatican; in Santa Maria in Portico Lucrezia's ladies take up the crying: high-pitched, like animals being gutted alive. Women's grief: nothing rends the air quite like it.

They have to use measured force to recover the body. Michelotto, who does not try to defend himself, leaves the room with the mark of Sancia's nails as further decoration on his face. By the time the Pope and the papal guards arrive the room is in chaos, Sancia's rage unstoppable: chairs upturned, covers thrown off the bed, pillows ripped open spewing hair and feathers everywhere, so that the garden on this hot August day sees a gentle snowstorm falling onto the orange trees. Lucrezia meanwhile sits on the floor by the bed, cradling her husband's body in her lap like the dead Christ, sobbing, sobbing, sobbing. When they try to take him from her, she throws her own body over his, and no one, not even the Pope, knows what to do. It takes her women, a wailing Greek chorus descending and enveloping, touching, fussing, stroking, to gradually release her grasp on him, so that he can be lifted up and carried away to be made ready for burial.

Not for Alfonso the skilled hands of the beauticians of death, no bier surrounded by flowers carried by noblemen, no obligatory parade of mourners. For him burial is a mean affair. Neither wife nor sister is allowed to attend. By nightfall it is all over; his body, accompanied by a small band of friars, entombed in a tiny church so close to St. Peter's that there is no room for any public display at all.

But it is not over for the women. On the contrary, the violence of their grief keeps the palace awake all night. By next morning a small crowd is gathered outside the gates of the Vatican just to hear the noise, and the Pope's waiting room is packed with dignitaries and ambassadors desperate to pay their respects and hone their stories. It is, everyone agrees, the most scandalous thing ever to have taken place in the history of an already scandalous papacy. How delicious.

Cesare faces Alexander while the body is still being laid out and Burchard is waiting on instructions for the burial. The women's ululation is a backdrop to the encounter.

"It is insupportable!" The Pope's fury is almost as great as his daughter's. "To kill a man inside the Vatican palace when he was under my protection. What? Have you gone mad? It makes a mockery of my authority."

"Worse than mad. I am very sane indeed. Tell me, Father, what else would you have had me do? If I had come to you and told you that he had tried to kill me, would you have given me permission to do this? No—how could you? I had no option but to do it without you."

"What do you mean, tried to kill you?" These last weeks have tested Alexander's patience sorely: though he knows that Naples is the price he must pay for his ambitions, such gross public violence is a challenge to his style of politics. "The man was half dead."

"Well, I tell you this: he was not so dead that he could not pick up a crossbow and aim it out of a window. He had enough strength for that."

"When? How? What happened?" he pushes, as Cesare falls silent as if reluctant to repeat the tale. "Tell me!"

"I was in the garden five days ago—you know I walk there sometimes when I wake. I was unarmed, no chain mail, simply a shirt and open doublet in the summer heat. I happened to look up toward the tower. And there he was, at the window with a weapon drawn. He must have had it brought to him. Indeed it must still be there, somewhere in the room—others must have seen it. And then he shot at me; though I daresay it caused him pain to pull back the bow, it nearly caused me a great deal more. If I had not turned at that second it would have gone through my neck. As it is, it only grazed my cheek."

And he tilts his face up so that it is possible now to see a line of newly broken flesh moving into his hairline.

"Should you need more than my word, here is the arrow itself," he says, pulling it from his belt and handing it to the Pope. "You can see the mark of the duke on its head. I am sure if your men were to check the quiver in the room they would find that one is missing."

Alexander is aghast. Though the story may be bizarre, the passion with which Cesare tells it and the evidence he brings give it conviction. Later, he will call the guards and they will find Alfonso's crossbow leaning beside the window. They will ask the doctors and the servants how long it has been there and when they examine the quiver there will indeed be an arrow missing, though at what point that happened, how can anyone know?

"The man may have had good reason to hate me, Father. I do not deny that. I hated him too. But it was my life against his. The House of Aragon would be only too happy to see me dead. As a soldier I have the right to defend myself when threatened." He drops to his knees before the Pope. "If you had known—had been a party to it—that would have made you guilty too. As it is, I carry his death on my shoulders. If what I did abused your authority, then I ask your forgiveness."

Alexander puts a hand on this handsome head of hair. What is it that he feels? Does he doubt his son's word? Surely he must. But if so, it is a fleeting thought. The madness of hot blood, vendettas, the super-human strength of a wounded but athletic young man driven by fear and the need for revenge; if one wants to believe, it is surely credible enough. For death to have come so close to his beloved son, this mar-velous young man who is poised to take the family from greatness of present into greatness of future. To have lost him! Sweet Mary, Mother of God, what is the death of Alfonso, half traitor by his allegiance to Naples, compared to that? From beyond the door, they both hear the muffled wails inside the palace. The Pope lifts him up.

"Come, embrace me. It was a brutal act, but you have made confes-sion. And you will do so again to God. I give you my forgiveness. But you must make it right with your sister. For she is the one who has lost most."

It is possible that if Cesare could have repeated his side of events to others with the same fire in his eyes, he might have found more people willing to swallow it. But with his father convinced, there is too much work to be done on his future to dwell on the past. As he goes about his business raising the next army, the details of his story—the crossbow at the window, the garden, the attempted murder—all leak out, as they must. But rather than offering a defense, they simply show the lengths to which the Duke Valentino will go to get what he wants. People begin to remember that earlier death within the family: another young man cruelly cut down in his prime, and how much Cesare Borgia had gained from that also. What had once been unsubstantiated gossip now becomes fact. His reputation slips from dark to black, condemnation colliding with fear. It is not something that will keep him awake at night.

But Lucrezia. Lucrezia is another matter.

He visits her the day after the murder. The Vatican and Santa Maria in Portico are still in an uproar and he arrives—as he goes everywhere in the days following—surrounded by armed guards, players in his manufactured scenario of the plot against himself.

He and his guards are admitted to the receiving room, where they stand awkwardly, grown men listening to the wailing of women, a wailing that has not stopped since the duke's death more than twenty-four hours ago. It is even possible to make out the angry sound of baby Rodrigo, whose pampered life has been torn apart by a house of mayhem.

The crying—his and theirs—grows louder until the door opens and Lucrezia enters flanked by her women, seven, maybe eight of them, every one disheveled and weeping. In her arms she holds the wriggling, bawling baby. The level of noise is quite remarkable. The soldiers, who have withstood cannon fire in their time, fidget awkwardly.

"Hush, hush, sweet one." Lucrezia, busy with the child, does not even look at her brother. "Hush, such pain cannot be cried away."

But it is clear Rodrigo will not be soothed. She turns and hands him to a nurse, who wraps him tighter and takes him out. Now at last she turns to face Cesare. She is still wearing yesterday's bloodstained clothes and her face is flushed, eyes raw and swollen with tears.

"My dearest sister. I am come . . . I am come"—and his voice struggles to rise above the women, who are the filling the air with a keening dirge. Surely the great Duke Valentino is not intimidated by the emotions of women—"to offer my condolences for the loss of your husband."

"Do you think you have enough soldiers to protect you?"

"The House of Borgia has been threatened by gross conspiracy," he plows on. "The worst is thwarted, thank God. But we shall leave no stone unturned until we find who was behind it."

"Shall we indeed?" Her sarcasm is icy. It would seem she can stop crying when she chooses, though she is trembling as she speaks. "And what will you find hidden beneath them?"

They stand, brother and sister, their respective armies behind them and a bloody death in between. The encounter, so painfully absurd, must be played out to its end.

"This is not the time for us to talk in depth, sister. There are still issues of security to address—but if you would like—"

"Oh no. I would not like," she says abruptly. "Are you come for anything else?"

"Only to make sure that you are safe here."

"Safe! Here?" And having done so well, she is struggling now to keep the ice from breaking up. "After what has happened I will never be safe in Rome again."

Behind her one of the women lets out a harsh, strangled cry, and now the others join in, like a chorus that has been practicing. "If you will excuse us, brother. We have a house to put into mourning."

And they sweep out, the rising wails leaving Cesare and his men, armed to the teeth yet strangely vulnerable.

Chapter 55

WHEN DOES HER SORROW BECOME STRATEGY? NOT FOR A WHILE.
No. For those first endless days and nights she envelops herself in suffering as a means of survival. As long as she is crying it is not over. The
rest of the world may walk around as if his death has not changed anything, but she will never let that happen; as she weeps, her body in
spasm, her head glue-sticky with tears, he is still alive inside her.

For the first few days she returns to the room itself, sitting where
she sat with his body, Sancia and a few women with her. The Pope,
never at his best with women's tears, allows it, hoping it will provide a
catharsis. But it soon becomes apparent that, far from abating, the emotional storm is growing in power.

"Is she still crying?" he says one morning, though the question is
surely rhetorical.

"Either the duchess or some of her ladies." His chamberlain is anxious. He has seen the Pope buried under a ton of rubble, but never have
his master's nerves been quite so frayed. A house of men besieged by
women's tears: it is a novel form of warfare.

"Don't they ever sleep?"

"I think not all at the same time, Your Holiness."

What is a man to do? One cannot gag two duchesses. Alexander
tries to be kind. When he visits her she rises and throws herself into his
arms, sobbing. He dismisses the women and sits with her on the bed,
stroking her hair, murmuring. "Yes, yes, it is dreadful. I pray constantly
to Our Lady, who understands better than all of us the death of a beloved, to intercede to bring you rest. Like her, you must find peace in

God's greater plan. You are young; you will find another life, this will not be your only love."

But she does not want peace, or another life. Most of all she does not want another love.

"What? You will marry me again and I will kill someone else. Because I will. I am like that—that spider of death, which once it has mated destroys its own husband."

The Pope is quite struck by the image. He himself has little time for poetry, but it is known that Lucrezia likes to gather men of culture around her. Do they encourage such fancy hyperbole? Too much romance can be unhealthy for febrile female minds.

When sympathy does not work he tries other strategies.

"It is painful, yes, but we are surrounded by enemies. This plot that your brother uncovered—what would have happened if he himself had been killed?"

"Oh! How can you believe such nonsense! Alfonso was weak as a baby. He could barely pick up a spoon to feed himself."

"You would be surprised by the strength of a desperate man."

But he, in turn, is surprised by the naked contempt in her eyes. How could you be so fooled? it says.

No. It is clear enough that his daughter does not want to be comforted.

He has the room sealed off with guards outside. "It is not good for you to be so reminded."

They transfer their grief next door. With all the Vatican doors and windows closed it might be possible to block it off, but it is summer and the rooms are unbearable without a breeze. The ululating continues, poisoning the very air, so that all who hear it feel out of sorts.

The Pope grows fractious. Not only does it personally upset him, but this excess of grief is fast becoming public gossip. While he is talking treaties and crusades, the diplomats are hearing it too. "Such remarkable sorrow, Your Holiness." "It must be hard to bear." "A dreadful tragedy, to be sure," they say, thus drawing further attention to a scandal that it would be best for everyone to pass on from.

How can I run Christendom when I cannot even hear myself think?

Alexander says to himself after a while. Sorrow is one thing. Madness is another. No one sees fit to remind him of those days when he too could barely breathe from the stranglehold of grief.

"Enough now, daughter."

It is twelve days since the murder and when he visits he orders her women upstairs to a room where they must close the door. "I want this to stop. It can only be of harm to you now. What about the care of your son?"

"My son is left fatherless," she says in a dead voice.

He sighs. The fact is, he is growing less fond of this stricken young woman with eyes that are either cold or overflowing. She must have stopped eating, for her face is gaunt, her skin blotchy and tired. His pretty, charming daughter is turning into a harrowed widow in front of his eyes. And worse, this death is splitting the family. It cannot be allowed to continue. Not when they are close to such spectacular success.

"I order you to stop this mad grief, Lucrezia. If not—if not, I shall send you away! Such madness can only harm us all."

"How can I stop? It is a wife's duty to mourn her husband."

"And it is a daughter's duty to obey her father," he says, raising his voice in just the way he promised himself he would not do. "I will not have it. Do you hear?"

She stares at him. Then, after an exquisitely timed pause, her eyes fill up and the wailing starts again.

"Aaah." He leaves in frustration.

Lucrezia, though she would probably deny it if it was suggested to her, is discovering disobedience. She, who has been brought up to honor her family and to do everything she is told. She, who has asked only for two things directly in her life: that the two men for whom she felt affection should be spared, only to see both of them slaughtered. She, who has been so good for so long, is being good no longer. And though her rebellion will not bring back her husband, it is keeping the blood flowing in her veins.

A few days after their encounter, she asks for an audience with her father.

"I seek your permission to leave Rome, Father," she says, head high, eyes temporarily dry.

"Leave? To go where?"

"To my fortress in Nepi."

"I would prefer you here. People will think that—"

"Very well." She begins to cry.

"Ah—wait. Why Nepi?"

"Because it is not far. But it is not here," she says in a small but determined voice. "I believe at Nepi I might stop crying."

"Well, God be praised for that." He fiddles with his fisherman ring. In the last few years it has started to embed itself into his flesh. "It has been a difficult summer for all of us. You have my permission. When will you leave?"

"Tomorrow. And if you allow, I will take Sancia with me."

When the news of her departure leaks out, rumors fly.

"Donna Lucrezia used to be in the Pope's good graces," writes the Venetian ambassador, who is an inveterate gossip but has the Pope's ear these days, for Alexander needs Venice's good will in Cesare's campaigns. *"But now it seems he does not love her so much."*

Or perhaps it is the other way around.

Chapter 56

A STURDY LITTLE TOWN, NEPI: OLDER EVEN THAN ROME AND QUI-
etly proud of itself. It had been in the Borgia family for decades when
Alexander handed it to Ascanio Sforza as reward for his support in the
conclave of 1492. But as the French army had approached Milan and the
Sforza cardinal had fled Rome, he had taken it back and given it instead
to his beloved daughter.

She has been there only once, barely a year ago, when she came to
receive the keys of the city. She had been heavily pregnant—the peasant
midwife had already seen the baby boy swimming in her womb—and
Alfonso had been with her. They had stayed a few days, and the visit
had been full of sunshine. She remembers a waterfall gushing over a
rockface, soothing and playful at the same time, and how the old fortress housed a handsome palace within, its rooms heady with the smell
of herb sack: rosemary, lavender and cloves sewn on to the back of the
tapestries to stop the moths, which over years of packing and repacking
had become more plentiful than visitors.

They arrive on the last day of August, when the worst of the summer heat has passed. She keeps the chamber where they once slept together locked, but opens up other rooms for daily living. After two days
in the saddle she is too tired to cry. That first night she sleeps so deeply
that when she wakes, to a glow around an unfamiliar shuttered window, she is confused for a moment as to where she is. Then the grief
pours back in, blackening the air and weighing on her chest like a squat-
ting incubus until she cannot breathe properly.

How can I live without you? she thinks. It is too painful.

In the weeks since the attack she has been sustained by the giddy energy of drama, but now, lying here, there is no reason to fight anymore. Her husband is murdered, her brother has blood on his hands and her father does not care. Even if she could stop crying, what future could there be for a woman so wronged? "I cannot do it. It would be better to be dead."

She traces the shining rectangle of sun around the shutter. How would it be to leave this darkness and open one's soul to the greater light on the other side? "I will stay and die here. Here in this fortress, here in this room, in this bed." The thought makes her heart beat faster. "God will surely understand. He will take me to Him and reunite me with Alfonso."

She lies still, closes her eyes and waits.

It is not that she doesn't have the will; women with less strength than her have died of sorrow. No, it is simply that there is so much to be done first. Even as she lies there, searching for the right words of prayer, she is disturbed by the stomp and clatter of feet and whispered voices outside the door.

"We beg forgiveness, Duchess." Her bedchamber ladies flutter and chirrup when she bids them enter. "But the chest filled with your mourning day dresses; it seems it has been left behind in Rome. We can send for it but it will take days there and back and until then we don't know . . ."

It is a story repeated throughout the fortress. Uprooting and moving two duchesses and a ten-month baby is no small work and they had fled Rome in such a dreadful rush—a hundred or more chests packed and loaded and heaved on to carts before proper inventories could be made of their contents—that, of course, much has been forgotten. Medicines, clothing, all manner of supplies . . . She may be disembowelled with grief, but she is still the head of a great household and she cannot ignore her responsibilities.

Tomorrow then, she thinks. I will do what has to be done today and set about the business of dying tomorrow. Or the day after.

Things are no easier for Sancia. So fierce and furious in her defense of her brother, the exhaustion hits her even harder and she develops a fever. When Lucrezia visits her, she is propped in bed, her jet-black hair streaked with sweat, and those bright blue eyes shining like wet jewels in the paleness of her face. Sancia, who has always been so ready to fight, is now in need of someone to fight for her.

"If I die, I want to be buried next to him. You will do that for me, won't you? They will listen to you." She grabs her sister-in-law's hand, squeezing it hard. Such passion, even in illness.

"Sancia, you are not going to die."

"Why not? I have no one in the world to care for me now."

"That is not true. You have Jofré." She hesitates. Perhaps she must put off her own death a little longer. "And you have me."

"Jofré!" She shrugs. "I swear God does not give me children because he knows I am married to one. And you—oh, you will not be here long."

"What do you mean?" Does her yearning for God show in her eyes?

"You are too valuable. You'll be back in Rome and married off soon enough."

"No!" It is Lucrezia's turn to be fierce. "No, I will not!"

"No, I will not." She says it again that night as she curls herself around the bolster pillow, imagining it to be Alfonso's body. "I will never have another husband."

Then there is Rodrigo. How can she make him an orphan? He needs her even more now, this poor unfortunate child. Except he doesn't know that. Though he can cry as loudly as any baby, he is of a naturally sunny disposition, like his father, more himself when laughing than cross or sad. He is also at that tender age where every second day brings a new accomplishment. All manner of sounds are pouring out of his mouth: babas and chuurs and rrrrlls, as if he might at any moment break into an entirely new language. One of his Spanish nursemaids delights in swapping guttural with him, trying to get him to say the word "Borja" with its harsh ring, but he is more interested in experimentation than learning.

Nevertheless words are forming. "Mamamama," he now says as she comes toward him, throwing up his arms toward her. In Rome be-

fore Alfonso's death she was always so occupied that he would lift his
arms to his nurse more eagerly than to her. But here, now, there is time
to play. She comes out to the garden in the early evening as the heat
subsides and slips down next to him onto the blanket under the bay
tree.

He is a large baby, and his placid nature has meant that he has felt
little compulsion to be mobile: or maybe he is spoiled—in the weeks
since his father's death even the smallest fuss gets him everything he
needs. But now, settled on a blanket with insects and birds all around to
catch his attention, he gets the urge to move, so that suddenly Lucrezia
finds herself laughing with joy as he pulls himself up on to one fat knee
and starts to crawl laboriously across the grass.

"Look! Look! He is moving!" As if it was God's greatest miracle, all
the ladies laugh and clap until suddenly he plops back down on to his
bottom and grins up at them, four teeth shining like little pearls in his
mouth. Was a baby ever so clever or so much loved? Even Sancia, who
with sleep and good nursing is recovered enough to join them, is
warmed by the sight. In the golden light, this raven-haired beauty looks
even lovelier, as if grief has given her a new luminescence. Lucrezia,
who has turned her mirror to the wall in readiness for death, begins to
wonder if something similar might be happening to her own face.
There is the time for such thoughts now. The late-summer days are
long, and with the first frantic organization passed, the household falls
into a gentle rhythm. The two women sleep in the afternoon and then,
as the day ends, sit in the garden or find a spot close to the waterfall
which plunges from the edge of the fortress down into a chasm below,
its tumbling music mixing with the twilight chorus of starlings. Sometimes darkness falls and they bring out citronella lamps to perfume the
night air and keep the mosquitoes at bay. Why not? There are no visitors to entertain, no appearances to keep up. For once, she and Sancia
are mistresses of their own lives and despite themselves they start to
squeeze a little pleasure from it.

Behind the scenes the ladies say to each other, "Thank the good
Lord for the baby. He will save the duchess's life." But after a while, one
or other of them voices the thought that others cannot bear to. "What

about the next husband? Whoever he is, he will not want to take charge of another man's child."

As the pull toward death subsides, so Lucrezia too must start to think about her future. Which means thinking about her past. Born into the close weave of such a family, she has never had the space—or perhaps the courage—to look at it from the outside. But if she is to survive, she must do so now. Even in the peace of Nepi, the maneuverings of Borgia power are obvious. This fortress, all her other estates and towns, everything she owns, has been wrenched from someone else, and the gossip leaks through despite the fact that she is not always listening: like the story of Giacomo Gaetani, dying in sudden agony in the dungeons of Castel Sant' Angelo barely a few months after he had "forfeited" his lands because his was suddenly the wrong family name. Over the years, how many bodies have been scooped up from the Tiber with debris in their hair and hands tied behind their backs? When she was younger or busy in love, it had been easier not to dwell on these things, but you would need to be deaf, dumb and blind not to notice how so many of the corpses these days are their enemies'.

And then there are the friends who are friends no longer. Juan Cervillion, the Neapolitan soldier who negotiated Alfonso's return to Rome and held baby Rodrigo over the font at his baptism, was murdered in the back streets as soon as he left the Vatican to return to his family in Naples. She had been raw still with the wonder of birth, and had cried for hours when they brought her the news.

"Oh, Rome! Its streets are full of men who like to use their swords rather than their tongues," her father had said extravagantly when she had asked.

Only she knows that is not true. Tongues *are* swords in Rome. She remembers the guest at the Sforza palace whose casual insult to Juan led to summary execution. Not only insults. There is no safety in love. What had Pedro Calderón ever done but feel affection for her? And Alfonso . . . Even in her father's house Alfonso had not been safe. Rome. When she thinks of it now, it makes her shiver: the corridors between Santa Maria in Portico and the Vatican dank with intrigue, the fake bonhomie of courtiers and diplomats, the sneers beneath the smiles. It is everything she mistrusts and fears. There will be a feeding frenzy when she returns. She can already smell the perfumed sweat of her father's robes, hear the ripples of shocked laughter through closed doors.

I won't go back, she thinks. I will stay and make my life here, a widow caring for my son.

But of course it will never be allowed. So, if it is not to be death or marriage, then it must be the convent.

"The unhappiest of duchesses" she signs herself in her letters to her father. To Cesare, she does not write at all. It is the first time in her life that she has not been in contact with him.

At the end of October, Duke Valentino, on the way to war, travels north to Nepi with an army behind him, though this time he is careful to leave most of it camped elsewhere.

If Cesare's conscience has been giving him any trouble, there has been no time to listen to it. Alfonso had still been nursing his wounds when Cesare had ridden incognito out of Rome to meet the French ambassador and hammer vague promises into hard numbers. King Louis would give him three hundred lancers and two thousand cavalry for this, his new campaign. He renews his contacts with the condottieri and on the streets of Rome there is a sudden influx of Spaniards, tough, brawny men who have heard there is money to be made for the price of their fingerprint on a contract.

Their loyalty and their fighting qualities are undisputed. All he needs is the wherewithal to pay them. That September sees twelve successful candidates for the Sacred College of Cardinals. Twelve! And while they are not unworthy—Cesare has too much experience of the Church to be so crass—they are only too happy to pay for entry into such an exclusive club. The night after their election they all dine together in his apartments (the Pope has business elsewhere). It is a grand, raucous affair. Their host is 120,000 ducats richer, which according to his administrators—including his old tutor, also a new cardinal—will be enough to finance an army on the road for four or five months. "War," as d'Alegre had put it so succinctly, "is such an expensive business."

By the time the army marches out of Rome, Cesare has already made one conquest. The thriving little town of Cesena, neighbor to Faenza and Forlì, has offered itself into his hands. It is the wisdom of pragmatism: Venice, having gained a promise of help against the Turks, has withdrawn her support from the bigger cities of the Romagna and the Pope has excommunicated their leaders. The citizens of Cesena know that it is better to give in early peacefully rather than violently late.

Lucrezia receives only a few days' notice of her brother's coming. There is no way she can refuse him. Her ladies, who keep their expressions guarded, are excited. Eight weeks in the country have been pleasant enough and it has been wonderful to see their mistress laugh again, but they are court animals, bred for fashion and flirtation, and it has been a long time since they have enjoyed either.

Cesare brings a few of his most lively captains with him (Michelotto is not one of them). Young men with feathered hats, and velvet slashes over flashing steel, they cause a flutter of hearts as they ride in. They are off to war and there is nothing they would enjoy more than the admiration of pretty women to help them on their way.

Even Sancia, who vows that she will never be in the same room as her brother's murderer, relents. At dinner she finds herself placed between two Spanish captains, who compete tirelessly for her attention. Her notoriety, her beauty and her new radiance take no prisoners, and as she turns from one to the other she begins to remember what it is like not to be in tears. Who can blame her?

In contrast, Cesare and Lucrezia are like strangers. They greet each other with a polite embrace and he feels her body tight, unyielding against his. She makes sure that they are seated at different parts of the table, and while he looks at her often, she never returns the gaze, though of course she is aware of it. So is everyone else. It is hard not to be aware of Cesare Borgia. Dressed in black—style rather than any statement of mourning—he both exudes and attracts energy, like iron to a lodestone. He appears exuberantly well; the only sign of purple flowers now a few clusters of pit marks in his skin. Invincibility is so much his natural state that when the disease is dormant it is impossible for him—or anyone else—to imagine the agonies of it. Nevertheless, when the rest of the party retire to their rooms and the two of them are left alone, it is he who is the more uncomfortable.

"You look well, Lucrezia," he says. It is not his intention to begin with a lie, but her self-possession unnerves him: the loving little sister who used to run into his arms, admiration shining out of her eyes, has gone. In her place sits a calm but distant woman who seems to be standing behind herself, watching how she behaves.

"Thank you," she says evenly. "I am . . . quieter."

"Yes. It is exceedingly quiet here." He looks toward the window. "I am more used to being on the outside of fortresses with the sound of cannon fire in my ears."

"And if you were outside this fortress," she says, because it seems they must talk of something, "how long would it take for you to break down its walls?"

"Three . . . four days. Maybe longer." Because of course he has thought about it. "Da Sangallo did a good job when he rebuilt them, but that was twenty years ago. Our new guns have better range and the north front is vulnerable."

"And for those inside? What is it like to be under siege?"

"People say it is like being in a thunderstorm that rains death and never stops. That you cannot hear yourself speak. Or think. It drives men mad." He shrugs. "Almost as bad as your crying," he says lightly.

She does not smile.

"Well." He shrugs again. "Perhaps bombardment would be worse."

From somewhere in the garden comes the sound of fluttering laughter. No doubt one of her ladies is showing a captain the delights of a country moon; so carefree, the music of courtship. I will never feel that again, she thinks. Then catches herself. Self-pity will get her nowhere. The silence returns. By rights she should be asking about their father: his health, his happiness. There is a rumor that Giulia Farnese is returned to Rome, a widow herself after the roof fell in on her husband in their house in the country. How much crying has she done? she wonders.

BLOOD & BEAUTY   465

"I see I am not yet forgiven."

She frowns, as if the question makes no sense. "Forgiveness is more God's business than mine."

"I don't care about God," he replies swiftly. "I only care about you."

"You must not say things like that, Cesare. It is not right."

"I can't help it. I can't help it. It's how I feel. I might wish I didn't, but it would be like asking the sun not to rise." He, who spends his life feeling one thing but showing another, is suddenly openly angry. "You think I don't understand what I did to you? You think I don't know? Ha! But there was no other way. Do you hear me? No. Other. Way. We are too far down the road to turn back. Our future is in the north. Naples is doomed. We must find allies elsewhere or we will be crushed along with it. Your marriage could not have continued. And divorce was impossible. There was no other way." He stops, as if it is only now he realizes how close to being out of control he is.

"I don't believe that," she says, quietly, because having looked back unblinking she has seen many things that she might have chosen not to see before. "What about Jofré? He is a Borgia too. His union with Sancia is not a happy one and there are no children after many years. Why didn't Father dissolve that marriage and use Jofré as your tool of alliance?"

"Because it would have taken too long and because Jofré is an impotent fool and no one of any importance would have him."

How like Father you sound, she thinks. "What? And they would have me instead? Me—the illegitimate daughter of a pope, known throughout the land as a whore and now the widow of a man butchered by my own brother?" Careful, Lucrezia, she thinks. Careful. Do not cry. If you cry now all will be lost.

"You don't need to worry about that. Believe me, sister, there is not a man in Italy now who wouldn't want to be your husband."

"And what if I do not want to be anyone's wife?" she says coolly. "What if I would prefer to be married to God?"

He smiles. "We both know you were not made for a convent."

"How do you know that?" To her consternation her voice is trembling. "How do you know anything about me, Cesare? You say you love me, but you know nothing about who I am or what I might want. For you, in the end, I am just a piece on a chessboard to be moved or taken when and where it suits your ambitions."

"That is not true. You are my sister and this is no game: it is our future."

She shakes her head sadly.

"If Father was to die, how long would you have lasted with Alfonso then?" he presses on. "The French would have chewed and spat out Naples. And you two with it. And when you say I don't know you, you are wrong. I know you very well. Maybe better than you know yourself. I know you have a sweet soul and find comfort in God, but I also know that you are too hungry for life for that to be enough for you. You are too clever to be thrown away on another . . . inconsequential union. I know how much you yearn to build a court of your own, poets and musicians around you. But I tell you, as long as Father keeps you with him in Rome that will never happen. Because in Rome you will indeed always be on the chessboard. Regardless of whom you marry, if your next husband is not powerful enough to take you away, you will always be a Borgia first and someone's wife second."

She sits stock-still, her gaze concentrated on her hands entwined in her lap. Everything he says is true. She has known it even when she couldn't bear to think about it.

"No, to get what you want—what you deserve—the next marriage must be another kind of union; a legitimate ruler with real power, from a family with roots deep enough to withstand the gales of history. That is the only way forward. And it will give you more life than burying yourself in a convent cell. So tell me now that I don't know my beloved sister or have her best interests close to my heart."

She closes her eyes. Alfonso is cold in the ground barely six weeks, yet if she is to have any say in her future, she must leave him behind and move on.

"You have come to make me an offer," she says quietly. "Very well, brother. I am listening."

He stares at her for a moment. Perhaps he is hoping for something more; some kind of conciliation, a hint of forgiveness. It does not come.

It would seem that whatever sweetness there is in her, she is more a Borgia than she might choose to be.

"By the end of the winter, I will have all the main cities of the Romagna in my power. And after I help France take Naples, King Louis will look favorably when we expand further. Perugia, Bologna, maybe even Florence. They are all weakened and vulnerable. Within two years and with a fair wind, we will have a Borgia state in the middle of Italy to rival almost anything around it."

"What about Venice?" she says, because even in her grief she remembers how her first husband was always looking over his shoulder to the north. "Venice will surely try and stop you."

"Of course she will. Which is why we need an ally to stand between her territories and our own. A state with its own history and confidence to stand firm between us. We need Ferrara."

"Ferrara?" Her voice shows her amazement. "You want to marry me into Ferrara!"

"And why not? Duke Ercole d'Este is an old man and his heir, Alfonso, is a widower with no legitimate children. He needs a wife who can give sons to the Este family. A wife who will go on to become duchess of the state, to preside over a great court and a greater city."

"Ferrara." She says it again and laughs, though it is hard to tell whether from excitement or disbelief. "You'll never do it. Este is one of the oldest houses in Italy. They could have anyone they wanted. They will never take me."

"Oh yes they will, Lucrezia. That I promise you."

PART X

Leaving the Family

Speak clearly to His Majesty: we will never consent to giving Madonna Lucrezia to Don Alfonso, nor will Don Alfonso ever be induced to take her.

Duke Ercole d'Este, in a letter to the Ferrarese ambassador at the court of Louis XII, February 1501

Chapter 57

As winter closes in, the household at Nepi packs up its one hundred chests and heads back to Rome. The Pope has forgiven his daughter and is in love with her all over again. He is also busy negotiating offers for her hand. He has already welcomed a cousin of the French king, as well as an Orsini duke and a Spanish count. Cesare was right: she may be notorious, but with the power of the papacy and an armed brother behind her, Lucrezia Borgia is still an attractive prospect on the marriage market.

Alexander has no real interest in any of the suitors, but the more who are seen to ask and be refused, the more likely Duke Ercole d'Este will realize how desired the Pope's daughter is. In such things Alexander plays his hand like the political veteran he is: charming to those who must be charmed and quietly ruthless when they are no longer needed. In November, when the Spanish and the French sign their "secret" treaty divvying up the spoils of Naples in advance of its fall, he makes his wishes known to the French ambassador.

The response is perfect. "I am sure that King Louis will be only too pleased to give any assistance that he can."

When the first overtures reach Duke Ercole in Ferrara he does not bother to hide his disdain. The d'Este family was ruling Ferrara when the Borgias were still scraping the earth in Valencia, and nothing the Spanish interlopers have done since then has made them worthy of anything more than contempt. It had been Ercole's diplomats who brought back the rumor of a baby born to Lucrezia nine months after her stay in the convent, a baby whose father might even have been the Pope himself! No, this offered bride is an insult: damaged goods from a parvenu family. Ercole huffs and puffs diplomatic excuses, while sending secret letters to the King of France begging that he find another more suitable bride for his son to save the family from the embarrassment of direct refusal.

King Louis himself, whose natural expression these days is two-faced, is torn. He would actually quite enjoy shoving the knife into the Este family—it would pay them back for their support of Ludovico Sforza in Milan, and he knows that without the Pope's blessing he will never have the crown of Naples. On the other hand, he is not bringing down the houses of Aragon and Sforza only to replace them with Borgia. He tells both sides what they want to hear and waits to see how the wind blows.

In Rome, Lucrezia's homecoming has not been easy. In the wake of Cesare's visit, Nepi's silence no longer offered balm to the soul, and as the weather grew more inhospitable her return became inevitable. But once back in her palace, there was nothing to cushion her against the pain of memory and the list of lackluster suitors makes her sick to the stomach. While Alexander accepts her spirited refusals with good grace (such sentiments perfectly echo his own), it is clear that even if she could imagine herself in a convent—and the cells at San Sisto had been chilly even when the weather was hot—he would never, ever countenance such a thing. Once again Cesare is right. Marriage is the only way out.

"It is not your color, black," the Pope says as the city moves into Carnival season. "Why don't you add some gold or greens to your wardrobe now?"

"I am still in mourning, Father."

She has come home to a court full of new fabrics and fashions. Sancia has taken to wearing a silvered voile headdress that brings out the drama of her coloring. "I do not think Alfonso would mind," she says defensively, before Lucrezia asks. "He loved clothes and loved to see women well dressed. We can remember him without having to look like nuns."

How would such a fashion suit her own hair? Lucrezia wonders. Is that such a terrible thing to be thinking? Nothing she can do will bring him back, and for a young woman of nineteen, six months is a long time to be buried in the past, however tender the pain.

"Six months." Her father seems to read her thoughts. "It is long enough. You are a beautiful woman and when the Ferrarese ambassadors come to meet you, it would be good for you to look your best."

"The ambassadors? When will that be?" she asks, for though she does not know it yet herself, the idea of Ferrara, with its poets and music and glittering court, is already germinating inside her.

"When? Oh, when the duke has had a chance to think about it. I would not have it happen too soon, for then you would be gone from me and how could I bear that?"

She remembers Cesare's words and her two worst fears now collide: that she should abandon her love for Alfonso, and that deep down her father would prefer an alliance that will keep her in Rome forever.

"I know how important this union is to the family, Father," she says firmly. "And I will do whatever I can to bring it to pass."

"Ah! What joy it is to have my Lucrezia back again. Ercole's son will be the most fortunate man in Italy. You met him once, you know. Years ago when he came to Rome to plead for a cardinal's hat for his brother."

"I . . . I do not remember him at all."

"Well, you were very young. But I am sure you will like him well enough now. Everyone says he is a—a sturdy fellow."

She smiles gamely, but she does not allow herself to think of the man; only the distance between their two cities.

Alexander, overjoyed at her renewed obedience, wraps her in his arms, so that the old smell of family is once again deep in her nostrils.

Forgive me, Alfonso, she thinks, extracting herself gently from his grip, but if I am to get out of here there is no other way.

As winter progresses, diplomacy stalls. What is required is someone to push King Louis's hand. Cesare, whose soldiers he will need if he is to take Naples, would happily oblige, only right at this moment Cesare has problems of his own: a set of city walls that will not fall down.

———

It had all been going so well. Giovanni Sforza had fled long before Cesare had marched his army into Pesaro and no sooner had he taken up residence in the palace than the nearby city of Rimini offered itself up in his hands. Instead it had fallen to the little town of Faenza to take on this new Goliath, and its defiance teaches Cesare a valuable lesson in statecraft.

Barely a few miles down the road from Forlì, where the Virago has been unseated as much by her own people as an invading army, Faenza is ruled by a sixteen-year-old boy in conjunction with the city council, and a fairer government you could not want for. So fair in fact that its young lord offers to surrender himself to save his city from destruction. But his citizens will not hear of it. As the artillery rolls up, the citizens tighten their belts and stuff bits of wax into their ears to keep out the thunder of the cannons.

The weather backs up their bravery. Weeks of torrential rains mean that the powder in the cannons doesn't light, and then winter roars in, frost hardening the earth and making skating rinks of the mud paths in the camp. The soldiers fall if they move and freeze if they don't. Cesare, sharing the vicissitudes of his men, and well aware that a successful army is one that is well taken care of, cuts his losses and calls off the siege, leaving a small force to block the supply route into the town.

Though it is a setback, he is determined not to be set back by it. In his palace in Cesena he uses the winter months to bring in administrators, assess taxes and regulate new courts. Cannons can break down walls, but he needs to build bridges now. He throws a lavish Christmas dinner for the town councillors, and opens his home so that anyone and everyone might see how their new duke lives. He hosts jousts and games of strength in the piazza, and the word goes out around the villages near Cesena that Duke Valentino will take on anyone who thinks he might run faster or be able to wrestle him to the ground. To get one's hands on one's own lord, to feel the muscles of the state through grappling with his very body, is indeed a wonder. In every contest, he wins and they lose (however hard they try not to), but it is done with equal grace on both sides and an excellent time is had by all.

"Is it to become an annual event?" Ramirez de Lorqua, his Spanish captain who is now the city's governor, inquires as they sit down together when it is all over.

"Perhaps. Why not?"

"I . . . I think they will begin to take liberties. You are known as a great soldier. They expect you to keep your distance."

"I think it is better that I am known for doing what is not expected," Cesare says carefully. Lorqua has a reputation for severity, not always connected with justice. Among the many things he is doing with this enforced rest is to observe those who are ruling in his absence. How his father would approve. There are times when this brash young man has a surprisingly old head on his shoulders.

When his guns begin firing on Faenza again in early spring, everyone—the French and the Ferrarese in particular—is watching intently.

"My God, with troops like these I could take the whole of Italy," Cesare declares as he sees women standing side by side with men on the barricades, and the news comes that inside the city the rich have opened their cellars to feed the poor. But it is not enough to halt the inevitable. Final victory comes through betrayal when a local merchant escapes the city and shows them a vulnerable place in the defenses. Before he moves his cannons into place, Cesare has the man strung up as a traitor for all the town to see.

With the walls breached, the young Manfredi and his even younger brothers surrender. Cesare sends food and supplies and a strict no-plunder order goes out to the troops. That night Manfredi joins him at his table and accepts his generous offer of a place in his army. If there is any other thought in the duke's mind, he keeps it well hidden.

With the fall of Faenza, Duke Valentino is lord of the whole of the Romagna, just as he said he would be that night in Nepi when he had convinced Lucrezia that her destiny lay in marriage to Ferrara. Now he needs to make good his promise that he can achieve it. The great military wheel starts to roll again. Within days the Borgia army is back on the road, but this time marching in the opposite direction. In thirty-six hours they are on the outskirts of Bologna. Thirty-six hours! Bologna, no less! A direct attack is bought off by the offer of another fortress in the Romagna, and the army swerves south—into the territory of Florence this time.

With the wolf in the sheep pen there is instant panic. Both cities are under the formal protection of France. In Rome, the Pope publicly disowns his son and orders him to return home, while privately delighting at the chaos he is causing: it is a strategy between them that is fast becoming an art. Cesare's army gets to within six miles of the walls of Florence before the struggling government agrees to pay a hefty sum to have the duke as its ally rather than its enemy.

For King Louis, whose own attack on Naples is scheduled to begin in a few months' time, the point is well made: if the Pope doesn't get what he wants, his son will get it for him. He remembers that hunter alone in the royal forest, his hands thick with boar's blood, and the marriage night with so many broken lances. Who would not want to have such a man on one's side? His daring and his skill make the rest of Italy feel like a bunch of sniveling virgins.

Louis takes up his royal pen and uses it as a knife to cut the rope by which he has had the Duke of Ferrara dangling. If Ercole d'Este really cannot bear the thought of such a match, then when they start negotiations, he should try making his demands too outrageous to be accepted. The king even offers a few suggestions as to what he might ask for.

But as for French brides—alas, there are none available at present.

Ercole d'Este receives the news having come from visiting one of his favorite women—saintly Sister Lucia (he collects visionaries with as much passion as he collects composers and architects, though he tries to get them all equally cheaply).

"It seems you will have to marry this Borgia whore after all," he says to his son, who has had to be extracted from a nearby basement where he runs his own weapons forge. "It is the victory of the practical over the honorable."

"I don't really mind that much," Alfonso replies, wiping a black hand over an even blacker face. "As long as she isn't ugly and doesn't need coddling."

The duke shakes his head. He is the ruler of one of the most sophisticated courts in Europe—and his first-born son only wants to play with guns. Well, he will have the money to build whatever defenses he likes when they have bled the Borgias dry.

Ercole starts to compose his wish list.

Chapter 58

Lucrezia and Alfonso. It is unfortunate that her prospective new husband shares the name of her old one. It is even more unfortunate when one considers what he looks like. His portrait arrives as the dowry negotiations begin in earnest. Surely she has never met this man before? Even a young girl would remember such ugliness. It is a wonder the court artist still has his job. At twenty-five, Alfonso d'Este has the face and build of a street fighter: square jaw, thick nose, thick eyebrows and cheeks flushed by the freezing winter fogs that roll off the River Po. The gossip—which flows both ways—says that the only thing he loves more than his cannons are women who are not his wife. His first marriage to Anna Sforza had ended when she died soon after her stillborn child. They had been together since she was fifteen and some say he had made her cry so much that death was an easy way out.

She studies the portrait again. A child of her time, Lucrezia knows that while female beauty is a mirror to the inner sweetness of the soul, men are less constricted by the niceties of Platonic theory. If Cesare's face fools no one anymore, then surely boorish features do not necessarily mean a boorish soul? Alexander's own commentators do their best. The bridegroom, they assure her, is an honest, manly man, plain-spoken with none of the flounces or counterfeit emotions of the wily courtier. He is a talented soldier who takes the well-being of his state seriously—hence his passion for the techniques of new warfare. But he can dance until the sun comes up and those same blunt hands that weld metal over a blacksmith's fire also play the viol with the delicacy of an angel.

Vulcan with a streak of celestial music. How . . . how charming, she thinks.

"And what will he think of me?" she asks coyly.

"Oh, he will worship you," they say with all the counterfeit conviction of wily courtiers.

There is one man in Rome who might be able to give her a more honest answer. When Gaspare Torella is not overseeing treatments in his steam bath he spends hours in communication with university doctors in Ferrara, and his notebooks are filled with descriptions taken from their noble clientele, a number of whom are from the Este family. Given Alfonso's appetite for prostitutes, it is not surprising that the heir apparent is on the list. The truth is (and it is the truth, for men of science pride themselves on avoiding gossip) that the man has been so ill with the French pox that he was forced to miss his own wife's funeral.

But what good would it do for Lucrezia or indeed anyone else to know such things? This is not a union of love. Not even of affection. It is a brutally imposed political treaty. Ferrara will gain an ally against Venice, immunity from Cesare's vaulting ambition and an eye-watering dowry, while the Borgias will secure a northern border for their emerging state and a legitimate branch for their family tree, grafted onto one of Italy's most distinguished dynasties. Who is to say which one will be the final winner and which the loser?

"The man bargains like a common tradesman," Alexander explodes as the negotiators leave the room. "How much is it now?"

Burchard and the secretaries pore over the figures. "With the castles of Pavia and Pieve and the benefices to Alfonso's brother, Cardinal Ippolito, as well as the jewels and the cash dowry, it is . . . it is close to four hundred thousand ducats."

"Bloodsuckers! You are an expert at parsimony, Burchard. Can't we beat them down?"

"Not if Your Holiness wants the marriage to take place while the Lady Lucrezia is still of childbearing age," says Burchard in a rare flash of humor, though the smile is so thin that his lips look glued together.

"Ha! The older the family, the deeper the greed, eh? Still, I daresay it will not seem so much when my grandsons are ruling Ferrara." And he grins. He has celebrated his seventieth birthday a few weeks before and his energy, far from waning, seems to be keeping pace with his circumference.

Burchard returns to his figures. With Vice-Chancellor Sforza still in prison, more of the financial work has fallen onto his shoulders, which gives him ample scope for the pleasures of disapproval. These are most expensive days for the papacy. Besides Cesare's war chest, half a French army is currently camped on the outskirts of Rome, en route to the great assault on Naples. With memories of the last French invasion still raw in people's minds, Alexander is determined to keep them outside the walls, but to do so he must supply them with everything they need so they don't take it from the land. Burchard's diaries are full of loaves and fishes, with little sign of a miracle to keep the costs down.

Nevertheless the French manage to make their presence felt. Their commanders have not forgotten their chivalrous commitment to Caterina Sforza, and from France, King Louis presses for her to be set free to go into exile in Florence.

"The woman can go wherever she likes, as long as she and her children sign away their rights to the Romagna," the Pope says airily.

Caterina, whose hair has turned gray without her special dyes and potions, signs and is released from her dungeon apartments in Castel Sant' Angelo. She has gambled hard all her life and has always known that to survive one must know how to lose as well as how to win.

No sooner is she freed than the two Manfredi brothers of Faenza, who have been "traveling" with Cesare's army over the last months, are imprisoned in her place. The young lord's only sin is to be exceedingly well loved by his people and therefore too dangerous to be left roaming free. It is a bold-faced betrayal of the promises Cesare made him, but it surprises almost nobody. Covering one's back is an age-old political strategy and it is not as if the Borgias are unique in their flouting of morality. Only a few months before, in the city of Perugia, one half of the ruling Baglioni family had massacred the other half in their beds, using a wedding reception as a smokescreen for the violence. Of course there had been flurries of diplomatic outrage, but behind closed doors there had been an equal admiration for the sheer audacity of the move. Compared with that, the Manfredi brothers are lucky still to be alive. Though few would take bets on how long such a state will continue. One enemy at a time.

Cesare, as usual, is too busy for matters of conscience. He must pay his debt to the French king and having frozen in winter he must now look forward to roasting in summer. It is mid-July when he and his crack troops, sweat pouring from under their monstrous armor, join the forces of France to advance on Naples. Within a few weeks it is all over. The House of Aragon is finished and the doomed King Federico goes into exile in France, where at least he will be in the company of his graceless daughter, Carlotta. How different all of their lives might have been if Federico had made her take Cesare Borgia for her husband.

Duke Ercole d'Este, surely not the only one to muse on the power of marriage, takes comfort in the number of noughts negotiated into the dowry and writes to the Pope and then Cesare separately, declaring his deep delight at the union.

Lucrezia's household packs away the earthenware dishes and brings out the silver plate. Though the year is not yet up, her mourning is over. Bedecked again in bright colors and jewels, she makes the acquaintance of a new young woman in the mirror. The hollowed-out sadness has gone. In its place has come a quiet, clear-eyed determination. Radiance seems to have passed her by.

With a settlement more or less hammered out, Ercole sends two special envoys to make the further acquaintance of the bride-to-be. For a while it is all the two men can do to keep up with the pace of celebrations that follow the public announcement of the betrothal. Cesare throws off his surliness and joins the Borgia charm offensive. The Pope, growing sprightlier with each triumph, stays up to greet the dawn, and because it has always been his greatest pleasure to watch his children dancing together, everyone must stay up with him to watch too.

"I think you will agree—your future duchess is not lame," he quips proudly as the two envoys prop their eyes open.

It is a sight worth missing sleep for. The room is lit with torches and standing candelabra and the brightly colored tiled floor glows beneath their feet. Lucrezia is renowned for the vibrancy of her dancing and Cesare has always been the only man at court to match her. The drum and pipes offer up a bright beat, so that there are moments when the music seems to have them dancing on air. Then there are other passages, laid on a bed of plucked lute strings, where they slide and prowl around each other and, like candle flares, there are flashes of tension, aggression almost, inside their grace that communicate immediately to the audience. Everyone in the room is aware of the wound between this beautiful brother and sister. How long is it since they last danced together? But of course everyone knows. In the intervening months since Alfonso's death they have led almost separate lives, busy with war and marriage. It is as if their bodies now are saying things that their tongues could never dare to.

"The duke and his sister are both in love and in hate." The idea slips its way into the watching crowd while the Pope, oblivious, beams his approval. The ambassadors, scorched by the heat, sit wondering what words they can find to convey the complexity of this family that will soon be joined with theirs.

In private audience with the duchess there can, of course, be no mention of such things. Instead, she appears light, almost sunny with excitement of the future.

"Oh, Madonna Lucrezia, you will be amazed by the city."

"Yes, yes, I am sure I will. It is true that Duke Ercole has knocked down half the town in order to build it anew?"

"My lady, it is the most ambitious plan that any city in Italy has seen. The roads are wide enough for chariot races and every house built is of the new style, with its own courtyard and garden. There is one palace which, when finished, will have jewels for its outside walls."

"Jewels?"

"Well, stone diamonds anyway. It is a new kind of rustication that the duke's architect has dreamed up. Then there is the castle, and near to the river the great palace of Schifanoia, built to banish boredom. Yes! That is how it is named! The frescoes are unequaled in their brilliance, and the concerts—oh, the concerts they put on there! Well, the duke is renowned for his love of music. You will see for yourself soon enough."

"And poets? You have poets and writers too?"

"Oh, poets help run the state." Lawyers by training and career diplomats by trade, Ercole's men are a well-honed double act when it comes to painting glorious pictures of their home. "Matteo Boiardo was Governor of Reggio and Modena and his words flowed like liquid gold. You are fond of poets, yes?"

"Yes, very," she says. "I have some men about me who in the past—well, when my husband was alive . . ." She trails off.

Their smiles stay fixed as she makes a gay little gesture with her hand. My husband: one might think she had never had a second marriage, his presence is so absent in Rome these days. For a moment she is thrown off her stride; her mind filled with an image of a sculpture she has seen in St. Peter's Basilica: white marble, a woman serene, resigned, holding the body of a beautiful dead man in her lap. Not now, she thinks. There will be time later. Do not think of it now.

"Yes," she says again quietly. "I am fond of poetry."

"In which case you will know of Petro Bembo. A scholar of the highest order who visits Ferrara often. They say he is writing the greatest poem on love since Petrarch dipped his pen in the ink for his sonnets."

"Petro Bembo? I think I have heard of him. But perhaps not." She shakes her head, still disturbed by the sad beauty of marble. "It seems I have much to learn, sirs. I will trust in God to help me find my way in such a wondrous journey."

And they smile. It is one of many endearing things about the woman who will be their new duchess that she does not pretend to know that which she doesn't. Indeed, the more time they spend with her the more they find to admire.

"Your Highness and Lord Alfonso will be well satisfied." They sit with their reports late into the night. "The Lady Lucrezia is most intelligent and most lovely, and her manners add to her charm. She is a devout and God-fearing Christian, modest and affable in every way. In short her character is such that we cannot suspect her of any . . . unseemly behavior."

As if there could remain any doubt about her worth, when the Pope and his son leave for a tour of inspection of their latest batch of seized castles north of Rome, it is Lucrezia who is left in charge of Vatican business while they are away. A woman sitting in the papal apartments opening correspondence and offering opinions. Perhaps the only thing more shocking is that the cardinals who advise and watch over her do not seem to find it shocking at all. She is diligent and careful certainly. But it is not all so dour. Cardinal Costa, at eighty-five years old a veteran of the Borgia administration, can often be heard laughing with her as they work side by side. Lucrezia has a natural aptitude in such relationships. While Alexander's love for his daughter may appear almost unhealthy at times, it has given her advantages in the world when it comes to dealing with powerful old men. It is as if she expects them to like her, and so, of course, they do.

From the sidelines, the Ferrarese envoys watch with particular interest. Their lord and master Duke Ercole is a very powerful old man, used to getting his own way. Privately they take a wager on how he will get on with his daughter-in-law; how far she will charm him and how long it will take for him to expose his steel.

Given the importance of their dispatches home, it is just as well that they are busy elsewhere when Cesare hosts a certain informal dinner party in his apartments in the Vatican in late October. The guest list is exclusive—family and close family friends, though Cesare makes a point of informing Burchard so that he is on hand should anything be called for. The table, however, is laid for a much larger gathering. Just before the food is served the doors are flung open and a group of lovely, laughing ladies arrive, as fragrant and fashionable as any courtiers, but with an infectious informality to their manner. Perched on the back of one of their chairs as they sit to eat, a red and yellow parrot bobs up and down, squawking the name of his host to the approval of the whole gathering.

After dinner the women's work begins. It is proposed that they play a game of chestnuts: the men will scatter them to the floor and the women will pick them up in their teeth. If, that is, their clothes don't get in the way. And if they want to win, then of course . . .

Lucrezia chooses the moment to slip away. That such—things— take place in her brother's house does not surprise her, but she has not worked this hard to woo the Ferrarese for it to be so easily squandered. As she goes she catches sight of Burchard, his mask of bureaucratic non-chalance slipping for a moment.

Oh, how this man hates us, she thinks. Perhaps if I were him, I would feel the same way too.

She is still in the antechamber when Cesare's voice calls her back.

"Leaving so soon, sister?"

"Why did you invite me here, Cesare?" She turns to him, face flushed. "This is not a fit evening for me to attend."

"Why not? What is wrong with my guests? They are honest women." His insolence has its own anger. "More honest than most of the whores who ply their trade in a court."

"That's as may be, but I would not be seen as honest if I spent time with them."

"Well, at least I have some reaction from you. It is better than being ignored."

"I am not ignoring you," she says quietly. "You have been away for months campaigning and I have been consumed by this work of marriage. There is a great deal to do before—"

"Before you become Duchess of Ferrara. Yes, I know. Duchess of Ferrara. I have kept my promise to you, sister. Remember? You are out of Rome. Whatever happens here, you will prosper."

"I hope so."

"And?" He waits.

"And I thank you for it."

"So. I am forgiven now?"

"Valentwaah. Valentwaaah." The parrot's voice rises above raucous female laughter.

"Why is Johannes Burchard here?" she says, sliding away from the question. "Have you seen his face? He is in a fury of disgust."

"Burchard? I thought Fiammetta might melt his ice." He laughs. "I like to see him shocked. He writes it all down, you know. Every disapproving detail."

"Oh! Then we must hope that no one ever reads it. We will be damned by his outrage."

"On the contrary, sweet sister. The more outrage the better. This way people will fear us while we are alive and never—ever—forget us when we are dead."

But Lucrezia has her own fears about being forgotten. In the months since their return from Nepi, Rodrigo has grown from a baby into a vigorous, noisy little boy. Now when she visits, rather than running into her arms he runs away from her, because he likes nothing better than to be chased around the room, squealing with joy until he is caught and tickled as he rolls on the floor. The noise of his helpless giggles brings back memories of her own childhood in Aunt Adriana Mila's house: the sounds of Juan and Jofré cavorting and spatting together. She, however, will not see Rodrigo grow to be either of their ages.

"Of course, my son will not accompany me to Ferrara," she tells one of the envoys as she shows him around the Vatican one afternoon, the golden-haired child pulling and playing at her skirts as they go. "He is to be given into the guardianship of my father's nephew, Cardinal Costenza."

"The duke will be most content to hear that. And I am sure your son will be excellently looked after." It is a relief to have the conversation out of the way; the instructions from Ferrara have been explicit on the matter.

"Most certainly he will," she says, her eyes bright with the tears she refuses to shed as she ruffles the child's hair.

Some would call it fortune. Instead of a mother and father this two-year-old boy has a title—the Duke of Sermoneta—a private income of fifteen thousand ducats and all manner of lands; a few that the Pope has only just prised out of the hands of the Colonna family, as punishment for their support of Naples. The Borgias are settling old scores fast these days.

As the wedding draws closer she must say goodbye to him herself. The house is already being packed up and it is better if he leaves before she does.

"Mamma! Mamma!" In the nursery the ritual of the running and the catching takes place, the little body wriggling on the floor in breathless squeals.

"You must be a good boy, Rodrigo," she says when the fit is passed and she has pulled him to her. "Do everything your uncle and your teachers tell you. I will write to you every day, and as soon as you can write, you will reply, yes?"

Near them, one of his nursemaids is crying silently.

When he asks where she is going, Lucrezia says lightly, "Oh—just to another city for a while."

The reply seems to satisfy him, so that when she hugs him, tighter this time, he struggles to get free and starts careering around the room once more.

"Again. Mamma. Catch again!" he shouts to her.

For the first time in many years, she thinks about her own mother, Vannozza, and wonders how she had felt the day when she had kissed her children goodbye. But still she does not cry.

Chapter 59

Leaving Sancia brings another kind of pain. The world has not been kind to her sister-in-law. Not only does she no longer have a brother, but also her beloved Naples is gone forever. Unable to hide her feelings, she has annoyed the Pope so much that he has banished her from court. Lucrezia now begs that he reinstate her, and because he can deny his perfect daughter nothing, he complies.

"It is not his nature to be cruel. You'll be back in his affections soon enough if you grant him a smile now and then."

"People do not smile when they are in hell," she says sullenly. "It is easy for you. He adores you and now you are free to go. But that will never happen to me. I hate it here. I hate everything about it."

"Nevertheless it is where you live and you must bear it."

"I wish they were all dead. I know they are your family. But that is what I feel. I am not the only one who hates them. You have read the letter?"

"What letter?" With the wedding almost upon them she has been too busy for gossip. Or maybe she has chosen not to listen again.

"Oh—it is all over Rome. It's addressed to a member of the Savelli family who lost his lands last year. Jofré says it is a fraud, made up in Venice as propaganda against the papacy, but I think it is real."

"What does it say?"

"That your father and your brother share the perversion of the Turks, that the Vatican is full of prostitutes who dance naked and play games. And that Cesare Borgia murders anyone who disagrees with him."

"I don't see how men who favor Turkish manners can keep a palace of prostitutes," she says mildly, but of course she is thinking about Burchard's diary. "Jofré is right. It sounds like slander to me."

"Slander is when something isn't true. It's true enough about Cesare. The letter compares him to Caligula and Nero in his cruelty. Maybe you haven't heard what he did to the man from Naples."

"Which man?"

"Oh, just someone who was repeating stories from the letter about town. Cesare had him arrested and his hand and his tongue cut out and stuck outside the prison window for all to see. And do not tell me he wouldn't do such a thing. You know as well as I do that he is a monster."

Outrage. This way people will fear us when we are alive and never—ever—forget us when we are dead.

"Oh, Sancia," she says softly. "Whatever I think of him, he is still my brother. Please. Let it not come between us. I want us to part as friends."

Sancia, whose passion always hurts herself most of all, bursts into tears. "I can't bear it. What will I do without you?"

"You will be fine. You are more beautiful than ever and you will find someone to love you, I promise." And if it is not Jofré, so be it, she thinks. Because she knows now that it is only fools who look for love within marriage. "I will pray for you every day."

"I wouldn't bother. God does not care about the House of Aragon anymore."

If outrage is the intention, then there are ways other than sexual games or violence to achieve it; the flaunting of wealth is the most colorful one. First there had been Juan's departure for Spain. Then Cesare's leaving for France. But all this is as nothing when compared to Lucrezia's marriage to Ferrara.

Some of it is one-upmanship: if the d'Este think themselves superior to the Borgias, then it is time they saw what real power looks like.

Some of it is love: who would not want to deck his only daughter in the most beautiful fabrics—gold, damasks, brocades—with diamonds, rubies and sapphires sewn into every sleeve, every bodice, every veil and net over the sunshine of her hair?

Some of it is tradition: it is a bride's role to dazzle all who see her, and with so many ceremonies and parties there must always be another costume, more lovely than the last. What young woman could not take a little pleasure in such a thing? Rich cloth and jewels are not inherently immoral. They speak of man's ability to value and create beauty. A young bride walking toward her future husband in a cascade of white silk would do the world a disservice if she didn't hold her head high, making those who watch catch their breath in wonder as she goes.

And some of it is not the Borgias' fault.

A daughter always costs more to marry than a son because of the dowry she must bring. And this particular dowry—its details fought over as hard as any war—nudges outrage toward obscenity. After all the clothing, the jewels, the household wealth, the reduction of papal taxes from Ferrara, the benefices and the transfer of lands and castles, there remains still the sum of one hundred thousand ducats in hard cash.

January 1, 1502. A room is set out in the Vatican palace for the business to take place. On one side sit full Borgia chests, on the other empty Ferrarese ones, and in the middle a table with counters and witnesses. The ducats must be considered one by one, and none of the "chamber" sort—where the gold content is less—will be accepted. When this final stipulation is put to Alexander the day before they are due to begin, he goes puce with fury.

"I think he will pay with whatever kind of ducats he wants," the Ferrarese ambassador reports back as diplomatically as he can. One can push a pope too far.

Two, five, ten, one hundred, five hundred, one thousand . . . whatever the insult, they cannot stop now. As of twenty-four hours ago, Lucrezia and Alfonso are man and wife, at least by proxy. The Ferrarese wedding party arrived ten days before, and barely had time to unpack their wardrobe chests before the festivities began. In place of the bridegroom (Alfonso and his father do not budge from Ferrara), Lucrezia says her vows and receives the ring from his younger brother, Don Ferrante Siena—more personable in all manner of ways—while the other brothers, Sigismundo and the flamboyant Cardinal Ippolito, bear witness.

One thousand five hundred, two thousand, three, four, five . . . the air grows warm with the clink and shuffle. The counters take their meals at the table and the wine, though good, is rationed. Clear heads are essential.

That night, the wedding parties listen to orations to the bride and groom and their prestigious families, and then a comedy is performed—or rather half performed, as the Pope pronounces it "Boring!" halfway through and the floor is cleared for the dancing to begin. Lucrezia, sitting on a silken cushion at her place of honor at her father's feet, is somewhat hampered by the weight of family jewelery she is wearing.

By the middle of the next day twenty thousand ducats have moved across the table. The work goes so well that they overfill the first chest. Too heavy to be carried, its iron bindings scratch tracks into the tiles on the floor. Twenty-five, twenty-seven, thirty thousand.

Outside, in the piazza in front of the basilica, there is a staged bullfight; Cesare renounces black in favor of gold, so that he contrasts better with the animals. Everyone has heard of his feats of strength and now they madly cheer him on as he skewers two bulls from his horse, then finishes them off on foot. His new brothers-in-law are most impressed. Whatever the gossip, these Borgias are to be taken notice of. Don Ferrante, who having stood in for his brother at the wedding is already half in love, turns to Lucrezia. "Such blood and beauty in one family," he says, and he waves his feathered cap like a perfect courtier. She smiles happily. He is a professional charmer, of course. They all are. And not only to her. Cardinal Ippolito, who has grown up a great deal since Alexander gave him his scarlet hat at the age of fifteen, has been paying unexpected attention to Sancia, whose eyes flash a little fire now she is brought back into the fold. She waves to Lucrezia across the crowd. It is impossible not to wish her well.

Forty-five thousand . . . They are almost halfway there. Ah—but now they are finding a few worn ones. Even—God forbid—some counterfeits. They slacken the pace, stopping as soon as daylight fades, since the flicker of torches makes it hard to study the coins. If any of them are tempted to slip a few up their sleeves or inside their jerkins, they are put off by the search that takes place each time the shift changes. Wealth sticks to wealth. Fifty thousand ducats. Sixty. Still counting.

The next day, another play and more dancing. Is it possible to have too much pleasure? The day after, everyone rests. The coins however continue their restless march across the table.

On the afternoon of January 5 the Ferrarese envoy and Ferrante, the proxy bridegroom, are called into the room to survey the chests. One hundred thousand ducats. Don Ferrante then visits the Pope. The two men embrace each other and flowery words are shared. It is done. The dowry is exchanged. The bride can leave.

Lucrezia is ready. In her palace next door, her leaving costume is laid out waiting and in the courtyard the carts are loaded and mules and horses rounded up. In among them sits a litter, a present from her father: a wooden room lined with gold and padded upholstery. The road to Ferrara will take her north into Umbria, then over the Apennines through Urbino into the Romagna, and not all the roads will be as straight and well kept as the Via Emilia. The route is carefully designed to take in a dozen or more important cities, where she and her court will be fêted and entertained. She will be on show constantly, for this is as much a victory parade for the Borgias as it is the arrival of a bride. It will demand stamina as well as buckets of grace and charm. She will be smiling for weeks.

But this final night in Rome she is her own mistress. Of course she cannot sleep and there is a last thing that she must do. She calls for her maidservant and puts on an ordinary overcloak and walking shoes.

"I should call for the guards, my lady."

"No, we will go alone."

The girl's face shows her uncertainty. "But it is dark and—"

"It is barely a few paces from here, as you know, and we will not be gone long. I have arranged it already."

Outside, it is much colder that she expects, freezing almost. Perhaps it is because she is tired. She pulls her cloak around her and moves faster. It takes them no time to cross from the back door of the palazzo to the steps of the Basilica of St. Peter. In the great piazza at the bottom of the stairs, Cesare had been killing bulls two days ago. But this walk has another kind of violence attached to it. The bloodstains from her husband's body are no longer there—she looked once in the daylight—but in a city of increasing violence there will be other swords drawn here soon enough.

The side door to the church pushes open and they walk inside. A watchman is sitting on a small stool with a candle by his side.

"It is the Pope's daughter," she says, slipping off the hood of her cloak. "You know me, sir, I think, from times before."

He bows his head and she slips a coin into his hand. His fingers close over it and he is murmuring prayers even before she moves on.

St. Peter's. Old, cold and cavernous, its flagstones worn smooth by a million feet. Inside it feels too big for itself: empty even when it is full. She and her maid move swiftly through the nave, their lamp held high. To either side there are chapels hidden in the shadows, many of them dating from centuries before. The most recent, that of Sixtus IV, stands out because it is grander than the rest and there are candles kept burning throughout the night.

In the course of Vatican business, she has heard many people talk about the basilica; how in modern Rome, with so many new palaces and churches, this great barn is no longer a fitting monument for the center of Christendom. What a triumph it would be if another, greater St. Peter's could be built on this same spot, a church designed with the eyes of our new understanding of the ancients, a building like the Duomo in Florence that is rightly famous throughout the world. A pope who cared for the Church as much as for his family might be thinking of that, she once heard the Spanish ambassador say when he did not know she was within earshot. He dropped his eyes quickly enough when he saw her.

The chapel she is looking for is that of Santa Petronilla, the daughter of St. Peter, in the left transept. It too has been rebuilt, the last time barely two years ago. Now it houses the tomb of the French Cardinal Bilhères. His funeral statue had been finished, but not yet in place, when he died of summer fever. The monument had been the talk of Rome for a while: how this brilliant young sculptor from Florence—

barely twenty when he arrived—had done something most unusual, taking an image that was more common in the north of Europe and using it to express his own representation of the dead Christ with his mother.

She had visited it first soon after she got back from Nepi, when her own grief was still huge and undigested inside her, and whenever she has felt overwhelmed by life since then, she has returned. There is a comfort here that is sorely lacking in the church where the body of Alfonso is interred. It had been such a mean, hurried burial and the marble slab with its bland lettering is only a reminder of the pain: her husband lies neglected in a neglected place; such was the insult of his death.

But this monument is extraordinary. She has seen paintings of the Virgin, with the dead Christ being taken down from the cross, but they have always been crowded affairs: disciples and ladies all helping her to bear His weight, because Mary's aging body, destroyed by grief, is as stricken as His. But this is an altogether new way of seeing that moment. Because in this sculpture the Virgin is alone with Him. Here, she is neither stricken nor aging. Instead she is a sublimely graceful young woman, sitting firm, her head slightly bowed, her legs parted under voluminous robes the better to support the unbearable weight of her dead son. But though the moment it represents is filled with pain, there is nothing painful about it. On the contrary. Her face is free from suffering. There is sadness, oh yes, but also serenity. Whatever sorrow has been given to her, she has accepted it, has known it somehow from the moment when the angel first appeared to her. Mary, Mother of God, full of grace.

In the night, the lamp throwing its glow up into her face shows all this clearly. In daylight it is there too, but the arrangement of light falls differently then, slicing in from a window above, so that it moves past her face and draws attention to the precious cargo in her lap: the body of her son. And He—well, He is just so beautiful. The ravages of the cross are muted here. There are no gory holes in hands and feet, no leaking wound in His side and His head is not battered and bloodied after the crown of thorns. There is nothing, in fact, to take away from the appreciation of God's greatest work: His only son made perfect human flesh. That flesh brought alive again in marble by the hand of man. The circle is complete.

They had not let Lucrezia hold Alfonso's body long. The room had been a madhouse of screaming and shouting, with no time for contemplation, no proper grief. But here, in front of Christ's cradled body, she has drunk deep of sorrow and managed to find some peace. Here she can pray and feel that she is heard. Here she has been able to let go of the past in the knowledge that God gives and God takes away and that whatever it is, it must be accepted.

She stands for a while longer, trying to memorize each fold of the marble drapery, every line of that dear, dear body. It cannot be done, but it doesn't matter; when she closes her eyes, enough remains. She nods to her servant and they move out as quickly as they can through the darkness of the nave to the door, bracing themselves for an even greater darkness outside.

It is not there. When they come out into the night, it is light. The sky is filled with thick white specks. It is snow! Snow is falling. Snow! In all her life in Rome she has never seen such a thing.

The two women stand, entranced. Her servant puts up her hands in spontaneous wonder and Lucrezia joins her. They smile at each other, laugh even, like children, before wrapping their cloaks tighter and running across to the door, their footsteps leaving wet marks in the thin carpet of white. Snow. What a way to leave!

The palace is already awake. In the courtyard, the servants are securing the last bundles onto the mules, their shoulders already caped in white, heads down to keep the sticky flakes out of their eyes. Her wardrobe mistress is moving among them, in search of the right chest that she needs now to unpack. The chosen outfit will not be warm enough. They must find the furs and overcoats put away ready for the road across the Apennines. She catches sight of her mistress on the stairs. "My lady, go back to bed. You will freeze here."

"How can I sleep? We are leaving," she says, looking up into the silent poetry of a white night sky. "Look! It is wonderful."

But not for those working through it. They blow on their raw fingers and stamp their feet; their future will be chilblains and mottled skin. She orders hot wine to be served to them. It will be her last act as head of her Roman household.

"Anything, my daughter, anything you want. Just tell me."

An hour later she takes her leave of the Pope. He sits propped in his chair, where he spends much of his life these days, she on the silken cushion at his feet, their hands clasped together. She is leaving but it is her job to comfort him. His tears splash on to their joined hands. Once he has started crying, everyone knows the Pope finds it hard to stop.

"You will write to me every day, in your own hand. Do you hear? The horses will fly between us, so that it will feel as if we are talking to each other over the land. Your new father-in-law has a reputation for— well, for miserliness. Don't let him short-change you on your dowry. Anything you need you tell me, you understand. Oh, how can I let you go?"

And he pulls her up from the cushion and crushes her to him.

"I will be fine, Father. We have borne separation before and we will bear this one." She extricates herself gently. "It is almost dawn. I must go soon."

"You must make sure that your husband comes to you every night. They will want an heir fast. So—every night . . ." He speaks with sudden passion, as if he has just remembered a mass of vital things he must tell her. "Open your arms to him. Make him welcome, but never complain when he leaves you . . . Men—well, men are often like that. You are a Borgia and deserve to be worshipped, but you may have to put up with a—"

"Papà, it is fine. I have been married twice before. I know what my duties are. But . . . now . . . the weather is most inclement. If we don't leave soon . . ."

He looks up toward the window and its ghostly light. "No, oh no— look at it . . . it is dreadful out there."

She starts to rise as the door opens: Cesare, sleek and black as a panther, a man halfway through his day, pulsating with energy.

"Ah, Cesare! Tell your sister she must not leave. Look at the sky. Tell her she must stay another day."

"I am afraid it cannot be done." He moves to the throne and gives her his hand to help her rise, as if he were inviting her to dance. "It is a long journey and the whole of Ferrara is waiting to see its new duchess. Isn't that right, sister?"

"Yes," she says smiling, because nothing can dampen the excitement. These final days have been mad with public celebration and with no time for intimacy brother and sister have moved around rather than toward each other. So here it is: the last goodbye. "Yes, that is right."

"Have you told her, Papà?" He keeps her hand tight inside his own.

"Told me what?"

"About what is to come."

"You mean my husband and my father-in-law? You need not worry on that score. I have had some experience of living with difficult men."

"Ha! Well said!" The Pope laughs. "My God, I would like to see the old miser's face when he meets you. The rest she doesn't need to know, Cesare."

"What rest?" she says, glancing at them both.

Alexander waves an arm. "Just plans. Plans!"

"I still say it is better if she is prepared." And his voice is curt: more like father to son than the other way around. Alexander makes a small, dismissive gesture as if it is not worth the argument. As Cesare's star rises ever higher, the Pope seems to be growing almost afraid of his own son.

"In the year to come great things will happen for us, Lucrezia: events that will change the face of Italy. But it will also make us more enemies."

"In which case, Papà is surely right," Lucrezia says, uneasily. "It is better if I do not know."

"Nevertheless, it will affect you. This is family business and as a Borgia they will see you as part of it."

Family business. She stares at him. "But you forget, Cesare, you have married me to Ferrara. I am only half Borgia now. The other half of me is Este." And she smiles brightly, as if it is, after all, simply a joke. She glances to the window, where the snow is falling relentlessly now. "I must go."

"Yes, if you must, you must. Oh, come, come, kiss me again." The Pope opens his arms wide and she feels for a last time that bear hug of love. "How will I live without you?" She hears his voice catching as the tears come again and now it is all she can do not to join in.

On the other side of the room, Cesare watches, dry-eyed.

She smoothes down her skirts and lifts her head high as she walks toward him. Such a handsome man, Cesare Borgia, so full of ice and fire. Except recently, close to, she has noticed that his complexion is sometimes a little flushed, with blemishes here and there where the purple flowers have left pitted stains. No longer flawless then.

"Goodbye, my dear, dear Duke Valentino," she says as she embraces him. "Promise me you will take good care of yourself as you fight all those battles."

"And you also take care." He lets her go, but only enough to hold her at arm's length. "So?" He lowers his voice until it is a whisper. "So, my beloved sister, do I hear it now?"

"Hear what?" she says, the smile still hovering on her lips.

"The words that say you love me and that I am forgiven."

"Oh, Cesare, I . . . of course I love you. You are my brother."

But he is still waiting.

"You are my brother," she repeats, and the catch is in her own voice now as she slips her hands away from his.

Outside the Sala dei Papi, Johannes Burchard stands so close to the door that it seems inconceivable that his ear was not bent to the keyhole. After all these years, he has still not mastered the rapid flow of Catalán, but the emotion behind the words he knows only too well.

"Madam," he says, stiffening up immediately. "I . . . They—they are asking for you in your courtyard."

"Yes, yes, I am coming now," she says as she collects herself.

"I wish you a most safe journey." He bows. "And I pray that the city of Ferrara will look after you as well as you deserve."

"Goodbye." She takes his hand. "And thank you, thank you for your good wishes."

There is an awkward little silence, then impetuously she adds, "Johannes, I know . . . I know that sometimes we are . . . well, as a family we have many enemies. But my father needs you so much. And I know that you do care for him. For which I thank you," she says again and leans over and kisses him on the cheek.

His look of astonishment will stay with her for miles down the road.

In her own palace, her ladies fuss around her, wrapping her further in woollen capes, fur hats and gloves. Surely she should use the litter. That would keep her dry. But she is too eager to be seeing it all. She climbs onto her mule, with its special saddle to hold her better in place, and the cavalcade begins its journey, out of the courtyard and across the front of the Vatican toward the Via Alessandrina, the snow dense now, the flakes whirling like confused dancers as they fall.

She looks up to the first-floor windows because she knows she will see him there, his large face pressed against the thick glass, his hands in the air, waving, waving. She waves back, then turns her attention to her mule, which, left to its own devices, would be going nowhere in such weather. As she moves, so does he, to the next window in the room. Then the next. And the next. He will be changing rooms now, puffing his way down the long Vatican corridor to keep pace with her, desperate for a last glimpse before, finally, she turns the corner and so slips out of his sight.

The procession crosses Ponte Sant' Angelo, then makes its way slowly toward the Piazza del Popolo. The eerie silence of snow is everywhere, the flakes so dense that it feels as if a wet fog is wrapping itself around them. Fog. She is going to a city of fog. It rolls off the river unfolding like a blanket, so that sometimes they say you cannot see your hand in front of your face. She holds up her glove. She can just make out the embroidered leather, but nothing beyond.

Rome has already disappeared and Ferrara is calling to her. She pushes her heels into the mule's flanks. There can be no going back now.

"Your Holiness?" Burchard is calling to him. "Are you all right?"

Alexander is standing crumpled against the wall near the last window, his face convulsed with sobs. "She is gone. She is gone, Burchard. I will never see her sweet smiling face again."

"Of course you will, Holy Father. There is a clause inserted in the marriage contract, you remember? You will lead a gathering of cardinals to Ferrara to visit her next year."

He shakes his head. "It will never happen. I know it. I feel it. Feel it: here, like a pain," he adds, dramatically clutching his heart.

"Would you like me to call the doctors?"

"Ha! Doctors! They can do nothing for such things. It is not illness, it is a premonition. A father's premonition."

Burchard stares at him. In all his life he has never met a man who feels so much so constantly. They have worked for almost ten years together yoked in an unlikely partnership. And for all that he disapproves . . . "The Pope ran from window to window to see her. Because he misses his daughter so." That is what those who saw it will say about this moment, he thinks, and without realizing it he brushes his cheek where Lucrezia's lips have been.

"We shall take you to your bed, Holy Father." He gestures to the Pope's chamberlain, hovering, as ever, in the background.

"No. No, not to bed." Alexander is rallying now. "Bed will do me no good. Not now. The day has begun."

He turns. At the end of the open doors through which he has come, the figure of Cesare stands waiting, black against the ghostly white light of the snowy morning.

"I will take some hot wine and a little soup," he calls back as he starts padding his way back along the long corridor, the papal robes like rising silk waters around the great bulk of the man. "The duke and I have work to do."

HISTORICAL EPILOGUE

More than many in history, the Borgias have suffered from an excess of bad press. While their behavior—personal and political—was often brutal and corrupt, they lived in brutal and corrupt times; and the thirst for diplomatic gossip and scandal, along with undoubted prejudice against their Spanish nationality, played its part in embellishing what was already a colorful story. Once the slander was abroad, much of it was incorporated into the historical record without being challenged. Spin, it seems, was a political art long before the modern word was introduced.

While *Blood & Beauty* is unapologetically an act of the imagination, the novel draws heavily on the work of modern historians whose judgment on the Borgias is more scrupulous and discriminating than many in the past. I have listened to their views and where there is contemporary evidence (be it true or false), through letters, reports, speeches, or diaries, I have incorporated it into the text. My one liberty has to do with the career of Pedro Calderón who, while he was a chamberlain in the Pope's household, never, to my knowledge, worked exclusively for Cesare Borgia.

Apart from that, there remain certain contested incidents within this tangled story.

In particular there is the question of who killed Juan Borgia. While many historians now believe the assassination was the work of the Orsini family, there are still those who think it was Cesare himself (though there is no contemporary suggestion that he is a suspect until almost a year after Juan's death). Equally, there are a few who speculate that in the early months of 1498, after a liaison with Pedro Calderón, Lucrezia gave birth to a child. Others are of the opinion that the baby was that of the Pope and his mistress, Giulia Farnese (Alexander acknowledged the child as his own later); others still, that it was Cesare's. In these and similar areas where historians have disagreed among themselves (did Caterina Sforza try to kill the Pope or did the Borgias manufacture the plot to justify their aggression? Did Cesare Borgia host an evening of courtesans in the Vatican palace or was this slander becoming fact?) I have taken the liberty of writing what feels to me to be the psychological truth of the personalities as they have emerged from the research. In this I am no more right—or possibly no more wrong—than anyone else. It is one of the most compelling things about history, and this family in particular, that sometimes we simply do not know. Which is, of course, where the pleasure and challenge of fiction comes in.

Should you wish to make up your own mind on such things, and on the Borgias themselves, the reading list on pages 505–506 will be a good place to start. I could not have written *Blood & Beauty* without these books, and I am much indebted to their authors, alive and dead.

Fate—a capricious goddess, as we know—permitting, there will be a concluding novel in a few years' time. It may not surprise you to learn that the story of the Borgias does not get any less exciting.

Sarah Dunant

Florence

BIBLIOGRAPHY

Arrizabalaga, Jon, Henderson, John and French, Roger, *The Great Pox: The French Disease in Renaissance Europe* (Yale University Press, 1997).

Bellonci, Maria, *Lucrezia Borgia* (Phoenix Press, 2003).

Bradford, Sarah, *Cesare Borgia: His Life and Times* (Weidenfeld & Nicolson, 1976).

————, *Lucrezia Borgia: Life, Love, and Death in Renaissance Italy* (Viking Press, 2004).

Brown, Kevin, *The Pox: The Life and Near Death of a Very Social Disease* (Sutton Publishing, 2006).

Burchard, Johann (ed. and trans. Geoffrey Parker), *At the Court of the Borgia* (Folio Society, 1963).

Castiglione, Baldassare (trans. George Bull), *The Book of the Courtier* (Penguin, 1967).

Chamberlin, E. R., *The Fall of the House of Borgia* (Temple Smith, 1974).

Chambers, David, "Papal conclaves and prophetic mystery in the Sistine Chapel" (*Journal of the Warburg and Courtauld Institutes*, 1978).

Cummins, J. S., "Pox and paranoia in Renaissance Europe" (*History Today*, 1988).

Gregorovius, Ferdinand (trans. J. L. Garner), *Lucretia Borgia* (John Murray, 1908).

Grendler, Paul F., *Schooling in Renaissance Italy: Literacy and Learning, 1300–1600* (Johns Hopkins University Press, 1989).

————, *The Universities of the Italian Renaissance* (Johns Hopkins University Press, 2002).

Lev, Elizabeth, *The Tigress of Forlì: Renaissance Italy's Most Courageous and Notorious Countess, Caterina Riario Sforza de' Medici* (Houghton Mifflin Harcourt, 2011).

Machiavelli, Niccolò, *The Art of War* (Dover Publications, 2006).

————, *The Prince* (University of Chicago Press, 1998).

Majanlahti, Anthony, *The Families Who Made Rome: A History and a Guide* (Chatto & Windus, 2005).

Mallett, Michael, *The Borgias: The Rise and Fall of a Renaissance Dynasty* (Academy Chicago, 1987).

Partner, Peter, "Papal financial policy in the Renaissance and Counter-Reformation" (*Past and Present*, 1980).

Pastor, Ludwig, *The History of the Popes from the Close of the Middle Ages* (Kegan Paul, Trench, Trubner and Co., 1899–1908).

Rolfe, Frederick (Baron Corvo), *A History of the Borgias* (Modern Library, 1931).

Roo, Peter de, *Material for a History of Pope Alexander VI: His Relatives and His Time* (Desclée, De Brouwer, 1924).

Rowland, Ingrid D., *The Culture of the High Renaissance: Ancients and Moderns in Sixteenth-Century Rome* (Cambridge University Press, 1998).

Sabatini, Rafael, *The Life of Cesare Borgia: A History and Some Criticisms* (S. Paul, 1926).

Setton, Kenneth M., *The Papacy and the Levant, 1204–1571* (American Philosophical Society, 1976).

Shaw, Christine, *Julius II: The Warrior Pope* (Blackwell, 1993).

Stinger, Charles L., *The Renaissance in Rome* (Indiana University Press, 1998).

Taylor, F. L., *The Art of War in Italy, 1494–1529* (Cambridge University Press, 1921).

ACKNOWLEDGMENTS

In the writing of *Blood & Beauty* I am indebted to a number of places and people.

In London, the British Library and the Warburg at the University of London were invaluable for research. For early helpful readings, I must thank Clare Alexander, Hannah Charlton, and Ian Grojnowski, and for later ones William Wallace and Tim Demetris, who, in particular, saved me from my own mistakes many times.

In Italy, the cities of Forlì, Imola, Faenza, Cesena, and Nepi offered tantalizing glimpses into their bellicose past while in Rome at the Vatican Museum, Carlos Maldonado gave me special help and access when visiting the Borgia apartments.

London
www.sarahdunant.com

ABOUT THE AUTHOR

Sarah Dunant is the author of the international bestsellers *The Birth of Venus, In the Company of the Courtesan,* and *Sacred Hearts,* which have received major acclaim on both sides of the Atlantic. Her earlier novels include three Hannah Wolfe crime thrillers, as well as *Snowstorms in a Hot Climate, Transgressions,* and *Mapping the Edge,* all three of which are available as Random House Trade Paperbacks. She has two daughters and lives in London and Florence.

ABOUT THE TYPE

This book was set in Monotype Dante, a typeface designed by Giovanni Mardersteig (1892–1977). Conceived as a private type for the Officina Bodoni in Verona, Italy, Dante was originally cut only for hand composition by Charles Malin, the famous Parisian punch cutter, between 1946 and 1952. Its first use was in an edition of Boccaccio's *Trattatello in laude di Dante* that appeared in 1954. The Monotype Corporation's version of Dante followed in 1957. Though modeled on the Aldine type used for Pietro Cardinal Bembo's treatise. *De Aetna* in 1495, Dante is a thoroughly modern interpretation of that venerable face.